Born in the London borough of Islington, Victor Pemberton is a successful playwright and TV producer, as well as being the author of eight highly popular London sagas, all of which are published by Headline. His first novel, OUR FAMILY, was based on his highly successful trilogy of radio plays of the same name. Victor has worked with some of the great names of entertainment, including Benny Hill and Dodie Smith, had a longstanding correspondence with Stan Laurel, and scripted and produced many of the BBC's 'Dr Who' series. In recent years he has worked as a producer for Jim Henson and set up his own production company, Saffron, whose first TV documentary won an Emmy Award. He lives in Essex.

Leo's Girl

Victor Pemberton

HEADLINE

First published in 2001
by HEADLINE BOOK PUBLISHING

First published in paperback in 2001
by HEADLINE BOOK PUBLISHING

10 9 8 7 6 5 4 3 2 1

ISBN 0 7472 6652 2

Typeset by Avon Dataset Ltd, Bidford-on-Avon, Warks

Printed and bound in Great Britain by
Mackays of Chatham plc, Chatham, Kent

HEADLINE BOOK PUBLISHING
A division of Hodder Headline
338 Euston Road
London NW1 3BH

www.headline.co.uk
www.hodderheadline.com

For Stan and Audrey
with fond love and thanks

And dedicated to
the clippies of World War II
whose heroic determination
helped to keep London on the move

Chapter 1

It was still partially dark when Peggy Thornton and her mother, Catherine, emerged from the Morrison air-raid shelter in the dining room of number 49A Highgate Hill. Although the All Clear had come soon after six o'clock on that grey November morning, it was some time before they felt safe enough to raise the wire mesh on the side of the shelter, and when they finally did, they had no idea what they might find. After almost a year of what had become known as the 'phoney war', the relentless German air raids on London were turning the final months of 1940 into a nightmare, and being cooped up beneath a steel table in the middle of the once elegant dining room was proving to be an unpalatable experience for both Peggy and her mother. The most unnerving part was having to lie there in the dark night after night, listening to the terrifying cacophony of enemy bombs as they came screeching down on to the heavily populated streets, the sound of bricks and masonry crumbling beneath the force of ferocious aerial onslaughts, of which innocent people were the victims. This particular night had been especially alarming, for during the few moments when Peggy and her mother had finally managed to get some sleep, the whole house had been rocked by the blast from a devastating explosion from somewhere down the hill, in the direction of the Nag's Head in Lower Holloway.

'The power's off,' called Peggy, trying the electric light switch by the door on the other side of the room. 'Stay where you are till I get the torch. There's glass on the floor.'

Catherine had no intention of moving. She squatted on the mattress in the dark, pulled her fleece-lined dressing gown snugly around her shoulders, and waited. When the torch beam finally shot across the room at her, she shielded her eyes with one hand.

'I can feel a draught,' she said nervously. 'Have the windows gone?'

Peggy made her way to the bow window, gently easing broken glass to one side with her carpet slippers as she went. 'As far as I can tell, it's just the small one at the top. Thank God for the blackout curtains.'

It was still bedlam on the hill outside. Ambulances, fire engines and police cars were rushing off to 'incidents' up and down the main road, the sound from their emergency bells wiping out the dawn chorus, and sending the birds fluttering from the trees in a frenzy of panic. Peggy drew back the central blackout curtain, peered out, but could only just see the towering outline of St Joseph's school through the dirty grey mist on the opposite side of the road. The smell of smouldering fires immediately seeped through the one small shattered top window pane.

With a soulless dim light now flooding the room, Catherine finally felt confident enough to ease her feet into her carpet slippers, and raise herself up from the mattress beneath the steel-topped shelter. Her shoulders were stiff with cramp.

'This is so uncivilised,' she said, trying to massage one shoulder with her fingers. 'If someone had told me a few months ago that we were going to have to live like this, I'd never have believed them.'

Peggy switched off the torch. 'Well, at least we're still alive. That's something to be grateful for.'

Catherine had only moved a few steps when her slipper touched broken glass. She stooped down to find the

2

remains of a large, floral-patterned china vase. 'Oh no,' she sighed. 'Your father's wedding present to me.' She picked up one of the broken pieces, and held it in her fingers. 'It was so beautiful.'

Peggy went to her mother, and put a comforting arm around her waist. 'Beautiful things can be replaced, Mother,' she said.

A deep booming voice suddenly called from the hall outside: 'Are you all right in there?'

'Come in, Father!' called Peggy.

Robert Thornton entered the room, the beam from his torch searching for his wife and daughter. The moment it found Peggy, he switched off the torch. Thornton, still wearing his pyjamas and dressing gown, was tall, and towered over his wife and daughter. 'It's been one hell of a night,' he boomed. 'I've got an idea we've lost some slates from the roof. I shall have to get Jackson in to look it over.' As he spoke, the lights came on. 'Good God!' he gasped, suddenly noticing the broken pieces of glass and china scattered around the floor. 'What the devil's all this?'

'I don't know where that last explosion came from,' said Peggy, drawing back the blackout curtains at the side windows, 'but it looks as though we've had a lucky escape.'

'Oh, Robert,' said Catherine, flustering around aimlessly, 'I do wish you wouldn't insist on sleeping under the stairs each night. I do so worry about you.'

'This was one of my wedding presents to you,' returned Thornton, ignoring his wife's concerns, and inspecting a piece of the broken china vase.

'I know, my dear,' she said, going to him. 'I'm very distressed. It's so sad.'

'So negligent, you mean!' he snapped. 'Ever since the air raids started in September I told you to put away all breakable items. How many times do you have to be told, Catherine? How many times?'

Peggy immediately came to her mother's defence. 'It's my fault, Father,' she said, helping her mother into her dressing gown. 'Mother asked me to put everything away long ago. I just haven't had the time to get round to it.'

Thornton snorted, and ignored her.

'Perhaps we could glue the pieces back together again, dear?' suggested Catherine nervously.

'Don't be ridiculous!' Thornton dropped the piece of broken china to the floor, turned, and angrily left the room.

Peggy gave her mother a reassuring hug, and glared as her father slammed the door behind him. 'We could have been killed last night,' she said contemptuously, into her mother's ear. 'And all he cares about is an old china vase.'

'Your father's a good man, Peggy,' whispered Catherine defensively. 'He doesn't mean what he says. You mustn't blame him, dear.'

Peggy pulled away, and smiled stiffly at her as she gently used her fingers to ease away a curl of greying ginger hair that had strayed across one of her mother's eyes. 'I don't blame *him*,' she replied tersely. 'I blame *myself.*'

Despite the intensity of the night's raid, Mrs Bailey, the family retainer, arrived at her usual time, on the dot of eight o'clock, and by half-past, she had breakfast ready on the kitchen table. Ever since food rationing had been introduced during the first month of the year, the choice available for a cooked breakfast had become somewhat limited, which meant that fried or boiled eggs and bacon were luxuries reserved for Sundays only. However, the main beneficiary was always Major Thornton, for his wife and daughter could rarely face anything quite so substantial first thing in the morning.

4

'They've made a nasty mess of that pub down 'Olloway Road,' said Lil Bailey, as she brought in a pot of tea and placed it on the table beside Catherine. 'D'rect 'it, they say.'

'Oh, how terrible, Mrs B,' said Peggy, passing her father the toast rack. 'Were there many people killed?'

'No, fank Gord. Middle of the night. A few hours earlier, it would've bin packed out.'

Thornton peered up briefly from his copy of *The Times*. 'Thank you, Mrs Bailey,' he said. 'I think we can do without the details.'

Lil, who was fat and comfortable, and in her late sixties, sniffed indignantly. 'I wasn't goin' ter give yer none,' she snorted, going off to do her chores. 'If yer want any more tea, there's 'ot water in the kettle.'

'Intolerable woman,' said Thornton, briefly putting down his newspaper whilst he spread some of Lil's home-made strawberry jam on to a slice of toast. 'It's time we retired her.'

'I don't think that would be a good idea,' replied Catherine, pouring the tea. 'It's getting increasingly difficult to get staff now that the Government are calling up younger women.'

Thornton, a former army major, and now a magistrate at the local courts at Highbury, had an appearance which suggested that he had stepped out of another age, for there was a middle parting in his well-greased but severely cut black hair, and his rounded face and firm chin looked a little naked without a Victorian moustache. 'Women in the forces!' he spluttered, mouth full of toast. 'Put a rifle in their hands and they'd run a mile.'

Catherine knew that Peggy was watching her, but she averted her gaze. Catherine was a pasty-faced, frail-looking woman, whose emerald eyes beautifully set off her head of tight red curls. 'There's no alternative,' she said dangerously. 'The call-up is taking men away from all the vital services. Someone's got to take over from them.'

'Then put them in the factories,' snapped Thornton, 'not in the army!'

Peggy took a cup of tea from her mother, and placed it beside her father. For a twenty-year-old, she had the poise of someone several years more mature. Fortunately she had inherited her mother's features, small, oval green eyes, and her shining red hair was cut into a fashionable short bob with two curls draped around each ear.

'I wouldn't have thought that every woman will go into the army, Father,' she said, daring to correct him. 'Surely most of us will be used on the home front.'

'*Us?*' asked Thornton, easing off his reading spectacles. 'I hope you're not including yourself in all this nonsense, young lady?'

Peggy always hated to be addressed so formally by her father. It was so petty, so irritating. 'Believe it or not, I'm a woman too, Father,' she replied provocatively. 'Sooner or later I shall have to do my bit.'

For one brief moment, to Peggy the kitchen seemed smaller than it had ever been. It was bad enough that the family had to use the place at all for their meals, with the constant smell of cooking permeating from the top of the gas stove, but to be trapped in such a confined space between an opinionated father and a dithering mother was more than she could take.

Thornton calmly folded his newspaper and placed it on the table to one side. 'Doing your bit, young lady,' he replied quietly but determinedly, 'is earning your living in a good, respectable job, a job with prospects. That is why I spoke up for you at Parks and Stevens.'

Peggy stiffened. 'Father,' she countered fearlessly,

'working as a clerk in a solicitor's office is not doing my bit for the war effort.'

'Oh, really? And what is?'

Peggy ignored her mother, who was kicking her underneath the table. 'I don't know,' she replied defiantly. 'In a factory, an ambulance driver, a mechanic, the Women's Land Army. Anything, as long as I felt I was doing at least something to help bring this war to an end. In any case, there's conscription for women now. Sooner or later I shall have to register.'

'We've discussed this before,' said Thornton, irritably. 'You know very well I have connections. You have absolutely no need to register.'

'But you don't understand, Father,' said Peggy, pushing her plate to one side. 'I don't want you to use your connections. I *want* to register. I want to be just like any other woman in this war.'

Thornton dabbed his mouth with his cotton table napkin, took his watch out of his waistcoat pocket, and checked it. 'It's getting late,' he said, deliberately fending off any more discussion. 'I'm due in court at ten.' He rose from the table and, without another word, left the room. His wife also rose and, after exchanging a look of despair with Peggy, followed Thornton out.

For a moment or so, Peggy sat alone in silence, mulling over in her mind the times she had had just such a conversation with her father. Ever since she was a child, she had remembered him as a bully, someone who had to have his own way whatever the cost. It was such a pity, for Thornton was a clever man, highly respected by everyone in the legal profession who knew him. And yet it was odd that he should be known as such a fair-minded man to those who were brought before him in court, when it was the complete opposite in his dealings with his own family.

Her mother was no better, for she was weak, and even when she wished to stand up to her husband, she never even contemplated such a thing. It was at times like this that Peggy felt the strain of being an only child. If only she'd had a brother or a sister, she would at least have had an ally. If only . . .

She sighed, picked up her cup and saucer, and took it to the enamel sink by the window. She looked out on to the small sloping garden at the back of the house. Her father was right. Several slates had come down from the roof during the air raid. Even worse was that some of them had crashed down on to her father's greenhouse at the end of the garden. The greenhouse was always neat and well looked after, his pride and joy. When he found out, he would be furious. Peggy smiled wryly.

Archway Junction was in a real mess. The previous night's air raid had not only caused havoc and destruction, but also a major disruption to public transport. Several streets around had received direct hits from either high-explosive bombs, or from a cluster of incendiary bombs, nicknamed 'Molotov cocktails', which had set fires burning rapidly, and had been difficult to bring under control. The chaos meant that Peggy was unable to catch her usual trolley bus on the hill, and had to walk over half a mile, down past the maze of hose pipes and emergency service vehicles that had blocked the four main roads which fed into the busy junction itself. The amazing thing was that despite the pandemonium, the streets were filled with people determined to get to work, no matter how difficult. There were hastily scribbled notices on shop fronts everywhere proclaiming 'BUSINESS AS USUAL', ignoring the fact that their front windows had been shattered by bomb blast. Spirits were high, concealing the endless tragedies and grief induced by a night of hell.

It was now after nine in the morning and, as she picked her way past the junction and headed off down Holloway Road, Peggy was convinced that there was no way she was going to get to her office in Upper Street by nine thirty. But at least she had a good excuse, and, under the circumstances, she doubted very much whether her employer, Mr Stevens, was going to think any the worse of her, and if he did, she would casually remind him that she was after all the daughter of Highbury Magistrate Robert Thornton. Her only hope was to get as far as St John's Grove, and hope that she would be able to pick up a bus coming out from the bus garage in Pemberton Gardens. However, that idea soon proved to be a false hope, for by the time she reached the bus stop in Holloway Road, a queue nearly fifty yards long had formed, which meant that it would be a very long time before there would be enough buses or trams to cope with so many passengers. There was therefore only one alternative, and that was to walk on to the Nag's Head, where, with a bit of luck, there would be a chance of picking up some transport from alternative routes. Unfortunately, it started to rain.

A few minutes later, Peggy was heading off briskly past the small shops and houses along what was usually the busy Holloway Road. It was bucketing down, and if it hadn't been for the threadbare Chinese umbrella her father had given her mother when he had been serving in the army in India shortly after the First World War, she would have been soaked. On the way, she passed a mobile canteen, where weary firemen and ambulance drivers were being served well-earned cups of tea by two stalwart members of the Women's Voluntary Service. As she eased her way slowly through the crowd blocking the pavement, she felt guilty. Those women, she thought, must have been brewing tea all through the night, and yet here they were, still laughing and joking and exchanging cheeky banter with the men and women who had been in the thick of the previous night's terrible ordeal whilst she was resentful at having to be at work by nine thirty in the morning, with her duties ending at four thirty in the afternoon. Was it right that she should live the leisurely life of a lady, she asked herself, when women of all ages around her were roughing it for the war effort?

'Peggy, my dear!'

The voice behind her was unmistakable. 'Mrs Desmond!'

The tall, lanky woman in the grey-green tweed suit, red jumper, felt hat, and grey overcoat, would have looked every bit the cosy, middle-class WVS volunteer if it hadn't been for the fact that her face and metal-rimmed spectacles were covered in thick black dust. 'Don't tell me you're trying to get to work on a day like this?' she quipped, rubbing a huge smudge across her forehead with the back of her hand. 'The road's completely closed right down to the Nag's Head.'

Peggy looked dismayed. 'Why, what's happened?'

'Direct hit on a public house, I'm afraid. Nothing left but a pile of rubble.' Betty Desmond usually punctuated each sentence with a nervous laugh, but today her manner was subdued and weary. 'There was nobody in the bar at the time, but they think there were about a dozen people taking shelter in the cellar. We've all been helping to dig them out.' She slowly shook her head. 'It was a waste of time. Nobody survived.'

Peggy felt her stomach churning over. 'How terrible,' she sighed. 'You must be exhausted.'

'All in a night's work,' Betty said, with brave cheeriness. 'Thank God there were plenty of volunteers to help, especially amongst the women. I don't know what they'd do without us these days.'

Peggy lowered her eyes guiltily.

People were now swarming all around them, and they had to keep on the move to prevent blocking their path. The rain gradually became a drizzle, leaving everyone's topcoats and tin helmets glistening in a watery sun that was straining to peer from behind dark grey clouds.

'How's your mother?' Betty asked suddenly. 'Haven't seen her for quite a time, not since I stopped going to the bridge club on Tuesday evenings.'

Peggy shrugged as she struggled to keep her umbrella up over the two of them. 'Much the same, I suppose. The same as she'll ever be.'

Betty smiled. 'I've always had a soft spot for Catherine, you know,' she said affectionately. 'I mean, she's such a thoroughly *good* woman, isn't she? Even if she is a terrible snob.'

Peggy swung a sharp look at her.

'Oh, she is, Peggy, my dear.' Betty gave the younger woman's arm a gentle, reassuring squeeze. 'Ever since I first met your mother when you all moved on to the hill, I knew she was a snob. She always has something or someone to boast about. Especially when there are lower-class people around!'

Peggy didn't know what she was talking about. In fact, for some time now it had been a mystery to her why Betty Desmond and her mother had not been seeing each other, when at one time they seemed quite inseparable.

'When I first registered for wartime service,' continued Betty, 'I asked Catherine to join me. It seemed to me that people like us had a duty to give some support to our men in this war. I told her I was doing it for my Brian, and all the men like him who are doing their best to defend this country.' She turned, and smiled wryly. 'I'm afraid the idea of working alongside people from different stratas of society didn't quite appeal to her.'

Peggy thought she ought to take offence, to defend her mother by saying that she wasn't like that at all, that she was just the same as anyone else in the whole world. But the more she thought about it, the more she knew that what Betty Desmond was saying was true. But if her mother was a snob, then so was her father. Between them, they made life quite intolerable for a twenty-year-old only child living at home.

Once they had cleared the crowds around the mobile canteen, Betty brought them both to a halt. She was dead on her feet. 'I'm going home now, Peggy,' she said, looking fit to drop. 'I'm desperate for a soak in the bath and a stiff gin and tonic for my breakfast!' She leaned forward and kissed Peggy gently on the cheek. 'Cheerio for now, my dear,' she said a little guiltily. 'And I didn't mean a word of what I said about your mother. She *is* a good woman. It's just that none of us knows where this war is going. Until I started doing all this nonsense, I never realised that it takes all sorts to make a world.'

The lanky figure was quickly swallowed up by the crowd again. Within seconds, she was gone.

Peggy reached the offices of Parks and Stevens soon after ten a.m. The firm itself was situated on the top two floors above an undertakers' parlour in Upper Street, and could only be reached by a side door which led to a narrow staircase. Peggy hated the place, and always arrived and left as rapidly as she possibly could, especially as business downstairs was brisk at all times during these turbulent days of the Blitz. Parks and Stevens was quite small, and dealt mainly with housing disputes, wills, legal claims, and minor criminal charges such as street theft or break-ins. However, the partners had a good reputation in the area, gained mainly from their one big success involving a city banker named Jacob Horrocks, who had been accused of embezzlement. A year before, Jocelyn Parks had died, leaving his partner, Edwin Stevens, in sole charge. Peggy had worked at Parks and Stevens for two years; it had been her first and only job since leaving boarding school in Hampshire, and acquired through her father, who had convinced the partners how 'beneficial' it would be to have the daughter of a local magistrate working for them. Despite this, the job consisted of little more than stuffy clerical work, for Peggy was junior to Stevens' son Joe, who handled most of the firm's clientele.

As she climbed the narrow wooden staircase, Peggy could feel warmth seeping out from beneath the reception office door on the first-floor landing, which meant that either Joe, or Mr Stevens' middle-aged secretary, Irene, had lit the gas fire.

'Well, this is a surprise,' said Joe, looking up from his desk the moment Peggy came in. 'Didn't expect to see you in today. I hear Holloway Road's been closed off after that bomb on the pub.'

'I had to walk most of the way,' Peggy said, removing her hat pin and taking off her coat. 'There were queues everywhere. It must have been a bad night last night. There were fires all over the place.' She hung her coat and hat on a dark varnished coat-stand in the corner. 'Couldn't get on a tram until Highbury Corner.'

'Highbury Corner!' Irene was horrified. 'But that's miles from Highgate Hill,' she gasped, easing off her reading glasses. 'You must be worn out, you poor thing.'

'What else can you do?' said Peggy, briefly tidying her hair with one hand. 'It's nothing compared to what some people had to go through last night.'

Irene, who was more attractive than she allowed herself to be, shook her head in admiration.

Joe watched Peggy go to her tiny desk, which was tucked away in the corner by the window. He had taken a shine to her the first day she joined the firm, but so far the attraction had not proved to be mutual. 'Wouldn't get too comfortable if I was you,' he said, sipping from his cup of tea. 'Father wants a word with you.'

Peggy swung a puzzled look at Irene, who had always been her staunch support.

Irene, pouring tea from a well-used brown teapot, gave her a reassuring smile. 'Have a hot cup of tea first,' she said, taking the tea across to Peggy after putting a splash of made-up powdered milk into it. 'I'll go and tell him you're here.'

Joe waited for Irene to disappear before turning his swivel chair around towards Peggy. 'Nothing to worry about, Peggs,' he said reassuringly. 'In fact I reckon it's good news. For you that is, not me.'

Peggy looked across the small office at him. The place was full of shelves containing clients' files and ancient law books, and the dust covering them often gave her bouts of sneezing.

'What do you mean?' she asked.

Joe got up from his desk, and came across to her. In some ways, he looked like a carbon copy of his father – short, stocky build, a constantly flushed face, and the first signs of receding hair. 'I got my call-up papers this morning – registered for the navy. I have to report for training at Gosport on Monday week.'

Peggy was shocked. 'Joe!' she gasped, genuinely concerned. 'I had no idea . . .'

Joe smiled. 'Oh, it's no problem, Peggs,' he said, his

hopes raised by her interest. 'I've known about it for some time. In fact I took my initial exams and had my medical weeks ago. I'm going to try and get a commission.'

Peggy was still taken aback. 'But the war . . . it's getting so . . . dangerous.'

'I can't escape doing my bit, Peggs. I'm well over the age for conscription. Old Churchill was bound to catch up with me sooner or later.'

Peggy was horrified. Joe had always been very kind and considerate to her. 'Your parents must be very upset,' she said. 'Isn't there something your father can do?'

Joe smiled again. Peggy's luminous green eyes melted him. 'This is a war we all have to fight, Peggs,' he replied. 'If we don't, life will never be the same again.'

Peggy sighed, and looked down despondently at her desk.

'But it's a wonderful opportunity for you.'

Peggy looked up with a puzzled start.

Joe perched himself on the edge of her desk. 'Father's going to ask you to take over my job. At least, until the end of the war.'

Peggy froze. She was about to speak when Irene came back into the office.

'You can go up,' she said briskly. 'He's waiting for you.'

Edwin Stevens liked to refer to his office as his 'room'. It was easy to see why, for there were very few signs that the place had anything to do with a solicitor. This was due, in part, to the fact that most of his own clients' files were stored in filing cabinets in his secretary's office adjoining his own, and the only working books on view were those referring to current political and local council legislation. To make matters even more improbable, the place was festooned with exotic indoor plants of every description, which clearly owed something to the fact that in his spare time, Edwin Stevens was a keen gardener. The other excesses were framed photographs of his family, including his wife, Emma, and Joe and his elder sister, Louise, who now lived in Canada with her rich banker husband.

'Come in, my dear,' Mr Stevens called affably from behind his desk, as Peggy entered the room. 'Sit yourself down.'

Peggy sat in the black leather chair facing him, which was usually reserved for his clients.

'And how are your parents?' he asked. Without really waiting for a reply, he went on, 'Is Mr Thornton in court today?'

Peggy nodded. As always, whenever she was talking to Stevens, her eyes were drawn to his left eye, which, to her, looked definitely out of alignment with the other. 'Yes, sir,' she replied. 'Unless of course there was any bomb damage.'

'Yes, indeed. That was an appalling air raid last night.' He sighed, and sat back in his chair. 'I'm afraid it's going to get worse before it gets better.'

Peggy smiled weakly. During the fraction of a pause that followed, she was convinced that his eyes sneaked a look at her bosom. She knew it wouldn't be the first time. Yes, Edwin Stevens was a happily married family man, but, like his son, he had an eye for a good bosom, especially one as full as her own.

'So,' he said, leaning his elbows on the arms of his chair, and rolling both thumbs around each other as he talked, 'you will have heard about Joseph by now?'

Peggy sat straight up in her chair, and sighed. 'It's terrible, sir. I'm so sorry.'

'You mustn't be,' he said, fixing her with an attempt at a fatherly smile. 'As a matter of fact, his mother and I are immensely proud of the boy. He wants to go in the navy. Like his grandfather. He had command of his own ship, you know. In the last war. Joseph takes after him.'

Peggy hadn't the faintest idea what interest all this could possibly be to her, but she smiled back as admiringly as she could.

'However, Joseph's departure does leave our little firm with a problem.' Stevens took off his spectacles, which immediately revealed a rather large cyst on the side of his nose. 'I'm sure you've noticed that, despite the war, we're busier than we've ever been. Losing Joseph at a time like this is going to make life very difficult for us. I was hoping to retire in a few years. That's why Joseph has been taking over more and more of the minor cases for me. Ever since Mr Parks died, the workload has been piling up on me. However . . .' He leaned forward again, and put his spectacles down gently on the desk in front of him.

Peggy knew what he was going to say, and she dreaded it. To be fair, Stevens had quite a pleasant face, even if it was a bit pallid, like most solicitors she'd met, and his gently receding hair, now just showing signs of grey, convinced her that this was exactly how Joseph was going to look in a few years' time.

'I've been thinking hard and long about this for some while, Peggy, my dear,' Stevens continued, 'and I've come to the decision that you are now ready to take over from Joseph.'

Peggy tried to say something, but was prevented from doing so by Stevens raising the palm of his hand.

'Oh, I know what you're thinking,' he said. 'You're only a girl, and not qualified to take over from someone as experienced as Joseph.'

Peggy stiffened. She wasn't thinking any such thing. As far as she was concerned, she knew just as much, and perhaps even more than Joseph. In fact, for most of the time she had done a great deal of the dirty work for him, rummaging into files whenever he wanted anything, looking up obscure references in books that had been tucked away in places that everyone had forgotten about. It made her feel quite cross that gender should play any part in what the old boy was saying.

'But let me assure you, my dear,' continued Stevens, 'despite the fact that you *are* only a girl, believe me, you are *more* than capable to take on the opportunities I am going to give you.'

Peggy could have hit him.

Completely unaware of her disdain, Stevens continued: 'We're very proud of you, my dear. Your father did this firm a great service when he brought you to us. I have complete faith in your ability to take over Joseph's position.' His smile suddenly became quite fixed. 'Until he returns from active service, that is.'

By this time, Peggy couldn't hear a word he was saying. All she could hear in her mind were her own words over the breakfast table a few hours before: '*Father. Working as a clerk in a solicitor's office is not doing my bit for the war effort.*'

'As I said, this is a tremendous opportunity for you.'

To Peggy, Stevens was sounding more and more as though he was doing her a favour.

'Not only is Joseph's position more senior to your own, but it will mean a modest increase in salary.'

Peggy was dying to tell him that she knew only too well that he was only giving her this great 'opportunity' because now that so many men were being dragged off to fight the war, women were their only replacement.

In the street outside, the air was suddenly fractured by the clanging bell of a fire engine racing past. This was immediately followed by the frenzied sound of ambulance and police car bells.

Stevens waited for the noise to disappear, then turned

to Peggy again. 'Women have a great part to play in this war, Peggy,' he said. 'Firms like us won't be able to survive without them. That's why I'm so very grateful to your father for suggesting you for Joseph's job.'

Peggy looked up with a start. 'My father?' She was horrified. 'You – you've spoken to my father?'

'Why, yes,' replied Stevens, surprised by her reaction. 'We spoke on the telephone a short while ago. He told me how keen you are to do your bit. We both agreed this was a wonderful way for you to do so. It's all arranged.'

It took Peggy the best part of the day to get over the sheer audacity of the plan set up without her knowledge by her father and Stevens. How dare they? she kept asking herself over and over again. How dare they just assume that she would do anything her father wanted her to do? The moment she came out of Stevens' office, she felt physically sick and went straight to the ladies' toilet on the first floor. As her eyes looked up into the mirror above the sink, she saw her whole twenty years laid out before her, constantly dominated by having to do things that she didn't want to do. But how could she change all that? In a few months' time she was going to be twenty-one, and yet she was still incarcerated inside a family cocoon, scared to break out and make her own decisions. How much longer could she go on like this? she asked herself. How much longer could she suffer the frustration of living in someone else's shadow, of not being allowed to spread her wings and fly off into the wondrous world of her true self?

It was already dark when Peggy left the office that afternoon. Irene walked part of the way with her to the bus stop. Peggy had always got on well with Irene, for she was someone who, although more than twenty years older than Peggy, was shrewd and understanding enough to know what it was like to be tied down to a ritual way of life. Even so, Peggy had always been surprised that Irene had not so far married, for she was a handsome, if not beautiful woman, with large brown eyes and long dark brown hair, and the fact that she wore only a suggestion of make-up made her even more attractive. But as they picked their way along the blacked-out Upper Street, Peggy was unprepared for the advice Irene had for her.

'Grab the moment, Peggy,' the older woman said, 'because if you don't, you never will.'

Peggy turned to look at her. But all she could see in the dark was the silhouette of Irene's profile. 'You think I shouldn't take Joseph's job?' she asked.

'No, that's not what I'm saying,' replied Irene. 'What I'm saying is, do what your heart tells you, not your mind. It's your life, and nobody else's. As a matter of fact, I feel the same as you about this war. I want to do something to help bring it to an end.' She turned a passing look at Peggy's darkened profile. 'If I had enough guts, I'd sign up for the Land Army.'

Peggy was shocked. 'Irene! You wouldn't?'

'Give me half a chance! Anything to get away from this hellhole we're living in.'

'But just think of having to get up early in the morning, digging up potatoes and things, and milking cows, and the smell of pigswill and everything. And I heard you'd have to sleep in the same room as all sorts of girls,' said Peggy. 'Girls – well, you might not get on with.'

'What's wrong with that?' asked Irene. 'I mean, let's face it, it doesn't matter where we come from, we're all human beings – aren't we?'

Irene took her leave of Peggy, and made her way off to the Angel tube station. When Peggy reached the bus stop, she found such a long queue waiting there that she decided to try her luck at the separate tram stop in the middle of the road further along. It was now bitterly cold, for the earlier drizzle had turned to sleet, which left her totally inadequate felt hat and grey astrakhan coat sopping wet. However, the queue was much shorter than the one for the bus, and she was able to take advantage of the rear part of an umbrella being held up by a man in a homburg hat just in front of her, and which gave her just enough protection to keep her head and shoulders dry. When the number 33 tram finally approached, Peggy was relieved to see that there were still a few places available on board, even if it meant standing. It was a relief to get out of the biting cold wind, for even though the interior of the tram had no lighting or heating, the warmth of human bodies pressed close together helped to restore some life back into Peggy's frozen limbs. Also, no sooner had she found an overhead strap to hold on to than a middle-aged man, whose face she couldn't see in the dark, offered her his seat. She felt a surge of gratitude towards him.

The grand old lady trouper tram rattled off towards Islington Green and Highbury. Peggy hoped that by the time she reached the Nag's Head, the Holloway Road would be clear enough of bomb debris to allow the tram to go all the way to Archway Junction. From there, it would be no more than a short walk home.

It was an odd journey, for the darkened streets were rapidly emptying in anticipation of the wail of the siren which about this time each evening heralded the regular dusk-till-dawn air raid. Everywhere dark figures could be seen hurrying home, anxious to get themselves and their families fed and watered before settling down to a night of hordes of enemy aircraft droning across the night sky, releasing their deadly high-explosive bombs on to an innocent civilian population, and followed wherever they went by a deafening cacophony of anti-aircraft shells bursting all over the night sky of London town. For most of the journey, Peggy travelled with her eyes closed, trying hard to immunise herself against the reality of war and the situation she found herself in. She was miles away, thinking about her employer, Mr Stevens, and his offer of promotion in a job that she never wanted; thinking about her father, and the way he was trying to manipulate her life, and her mother, with no more aim in life than being a wife to her husband. And then she thought about all the things she could do that might anger her father the most. What could she do that would prove she was something more than a good middle-class daughter from Highgate Hill? How could she 'do her bit' for her country at war? Should it be the staid but courageous WVS, like Betty Desmond, or would she ever consider Irene's burning ambition, to be a Land Army girl? And then she thought about joining up. What about the ATS, the WRNS, the WAAF – any one of the women's armed services? No. That would mean learning how to fire a rifle, and marching up and down a parade ground with a whole bunch of girls from all walks of life. And as she was scared of the sight of blood, there was no way she was going to be able to train as a nurse, or even as a volunteer with the St John Ambulance or Red Cross. As she sat there with her eyes closed tight, every idea that came to her seemed far too daring and unnerving.

'Tickets, please! All tickets, please!'

Peggy's eyes sprang open. The diminutive figure of the tram conductress was hovering over her, torch beam focused directly on to Peggy's face. 'Archway, please,' she said.

'Only goin' as far as the depot, mate,' came the rough voice of the conductress. 'Yer can pick up a trolley from there.'

'Thank you,' replied Peggy primly.

Using the light from her torch, the conductress slipped

out two tickets from her ticket rack. 'Penny ha'penny, please, mate.'

With great difficulty, Peggy dug deep into her coat pocket to find the coin she had all ready for the fare.

The conductress took the coin, and held on to it. 'Ain't yer got nuffin' smaller than a froop'ny bit, mate? I'm a bit low on ha'pennies.'

' 'Ang on!' croaked a female voice next to Peggy. 'I've got a whole bunch of 'em from me barrer.' With help from the conductress's torch, the woman took out a handful of coins from her pocket, sorted out six halfpennies, and handed them over to Peggy. Peggy then sorted out three of the coins, and handed them to the conductress, who duly returned her threepenny bit.

Using her punch slide, the conductress clipped the two tickets, one penny and one halfpenny, then quickly gave them to Peggy. 'Fanks, mate.' Then she struggled her way on through the crowd of standing passengers, calling, 'Fares, please! Any more fares along there, if you please?'

'Thank you very much,' said Peggy, turning to the passenger sitting beside her.

'You're welcome, ducks,' returned the woman's voice, sniffing all the while. 'I always 'ave plenty of small change from the barrer. Tuesdays is a good day fer that. We always have a queue when we gut the rabbits.'

Peggy decided not to continue the conversation. The thought that she was sitting next to a woman who sold gutted rabbits on a barrow in Chapel Market sent her quite rigid. It hadn't occurred to her that she had moved a couple of inches on her seat away from the woman. Even so, something inside her seemed to stir. She didn't quite know what it was, except that the whole exchange with both the conductress and her fellow passenger was somehow exhilarating.

With all the other passengers, Peggy got off the tram at the corner of St John's Grove, leaving the grand old trouper to rattle its way back to its depot in Pemberton Gardens. Within the next hour or so, the main Holloway Road would be almost deserted, as shopkeepers, office and factory workers, and commuters from the city hurried back to their homes. As there were still long queues at all the bus stops, Peggy decided to walk the final half-mile or so to Highgate Hill. As she went, she passed the time by turning over in her mind how she was going to tackle her father about his blatant interference with the way she wanted to run her own life. She had now made up her mind that, despite her father's objections, she was determined to register for some kind of war work as soon as she possibly could. She would tell him that he had no right to ask favours on her behalf from Mr Stevens or anyone else. She would tell him that whether he liked it or not, mobilisation of women was now a reality, that she wanted to be part of the war effort, and that the moment she reached the age of twenty-one, in just a few months' time, she would prove that she was just as capable of filling a man's shoes in the essential services as any other woman. But by the time she had reached Archway Junction, and was in clear sight of her own home, her confidence had waned. Yes, she was perfectly capable of doing *something* for the war effort – but *what*?

At exactly five forty-five in the evening, the air-raid siren wailed out from the roof of nearby Highgate Police Station. With now only ten minutes or so before the first wave of enemy bombers appeared overhead, Peggy quickened her pace, but the bulb in her torch was gradually fading, which made walking uphill in the dark quite a struggle. She had only just reached the gates of the Whittington Hospital, when a trolley bus climbed the hill silently and without any effort behind her. As it passed by, she could see the outline of the bus conductress, hanging out from the platform, surveying the pavements alongside. It was a strange moment for Peggy. Somehow, it was exciting to see how, despite the threat of the oncoming air raid, the bus was forging its way ahead, completely oblivious of any danger it could so easily encounter, serving its passengers with almost monotonous regularity. It was a challenge – a challenge for the people determined to keep London on the move whatever the cost. And it gave her the sign, the inspiration she had been so desperately looking for.

By the time she reached the front door of number 49A Highgate Hill, Peggy Thornton knew exactly what she wanted to do with her life.

Chapter 2

Friday had been a night of real horror. Not only had London had its worst night of the Blitz for several weeks, but on the following morning, the front pages of every newspaper in the country had carried dramatic stories and pictures about the devastation of the city of Coventry by a massive German Luftwaffe air raid. Despite the Government's efforts to play down the extent of Coventry's desperate ordeal, rumours soon swept the country that amongst the widespread carnage and death caused in residential, industrial and commercial areas, the once proud cathedral had been reduced to ruins. The only compensation had been the news that large numbers of RAF planes had bombed Berlin.

Undeterred by the news that Camberwell bus garage in south London had been devastated by extensive bomb damage the week before, Peggy went ahead with her application to join London Transport as a conductress. She knew it was a rash thing to do, and for a time was tormented by the thought that she was only doing it to spite her father, who had shown that he was prepared to be quite ruthless in his determination to control her future. But ever since the start of the Blitz, the feeling had been growing inside that she had to do something more than just waste her life away in a stuffy old solicitor's office, and once she had collected the details of how to apply for a conductress's job from a recruitment advertisement on the lower deck of a trolley bus, her mind was made up. None the less, it came as quite a shock when, just three days later, a letter arrived in the post informing her that her application for an interview had been granted.

Peggy had been to Chiswick only once before, and that was when her father took her to watch the Oxford and Cambridge boat race on the River Thames when she was a small child. Even in the best of times, getting to West London from Highgate was never easy, and with daylight air raids now coming just as regularly as those at night, the journey was clearly going to be extremely hazardous. As things turned out, however, there were no real incidents en route, but the trip – which involved taking a bus to Holloway Road tube station, followed by a direct train on the Piccadilly Line to Acton Town – seemed to take for ever. Fortunately, because it was Saturday morning, the trains weren't crowded, and Peggy felt rather proud of herself that she had managed to find the London Transport Board Training School without too much difficulty. The only thing that wasn't to her liking was the fact that as soon as she entered the building from the Bollo Lane entrance, she found about a dozen girls ahead of her waiting in chairs outside the interview room. Feeling thoroughly disoriented, she instinctively averted her gaze, found a chair, and quickly sat down. But whether she liked it or not, she was soon noticed.

'Tug Wilson,' said the bright-eyed, dark-haired young girl sitting next to her.

When Peggy turned to look, she found the girl's hand outstretched to her.

'Me real name's Josie,' said the girl, in a perky East End accent, 'but they all call me Tug.'

Reluctantly, Peggy took the girl's hand, and found her own shaken so hard that she felt as though her arm was being pulled off. 'Margaret Thornton,' she replied, with a weak, lofty smile. 'Peggy,' she added, quickly correcting herself.

Tug was too affable to recognise haughtiness. 'Me an' Brenda 'ere,' she continued, nodding her head towards the slightly older blonde-haired girl sitting next to her, 'we boaf come from up Mile End Road way. If I get fru the interview, I'm 'opin' they put us in the same garage tergevver.'

'Why shouldn't you get through?' asked Peggy, doing her best to ignore the blonde girl, who had leaned forward to take a look at her. 'Surely the reason we're here is because they need us?'

'Yeah, I know,' replied Tug, moving close and lowering her voice. 'Trouble is, I ain't much good at sums.'

'Sums?'

'Yer know – 'riffmatic an' fings. I mean, when yer sellin' bus tickets an' yer 'ave ter give change, yer've got ter know 'ow ter add up, ain't yer?'

Peggy thought about that for a moment. In fact such a thing hadn't occurred to her. But for her, knowing how to do simple arithmetic was the least of her problems.

The next two hours were absolute hell for Peggy. Being shut up in a corridor with a dozen girls from all parts of London, all sharing 'fags' with each other and chatting nervously about their chances of getting jobs on the buses didn't seem to her to be what she had in mind when she'd decided it was time to do her bit for her country. No matter how hard she tried to resist her feelings, she knew only too well that she had absolutely nothing in common with these girls. They didn't speak or act like her, they didn't share the same interests, whatever her own interests were, and most of them came from homes and backgrounds that were totally alien to her own. Over and over again she kept reminding herself that she didn't even know anything about the people who lived in Lower Holloway, which, although only a short walk from her own home, was as different to Highgate Hill as anything she could possibly imagine. Were her parents right? Should she really 'keep to her own station in life', and only mix with people of her own sort? But then she remembered what Betty Desmond had told her: '*It takes all sorts to make a world.*' By the time she had been called into the interview room, she began to feel that, no matter where they came from, these girls were all much more approachable and interesting than herself.

'A bicycle?'

'It's a perfectly straightforward question, Miss Thornton,' said the unsmiling male staff superintendent, once Peggy had finally taken her turn in the interview room. 'If you are on late-night duty, a bicycle, and the ability to ride it, would be an asset.'

Peggy bit her lip. In her wildest moments, she could never have imagined that she would actually be just as nervous about an interview as all the other girls waiting outside. So much so that she became terribly conscious of her crystal-clear Highgate Hill voice replying, 'I'm afraid I've never been on a bicycle.'

The superintendent gave no hint of a reaction, and merely scribbled Peggy's response down on her application form on the desk in front of him. When he looked up again, he immediately had another question to fire at her: 'How much are five tuppence ha'pennies?'

Although the suddenness of the question took her by surprise, Peggy felt that she was now on safe ground with a question she could answer quite easily. 'Ten and a half . . . no . . .' To her astonishment, she was fumbling her reply. 'No . . . I mean . . . one shilling and a ha'penny.'

The superintendent's eyes were dark and full, his lips pressed tightly together, and he was breathing heavily through his nose, as though he had a cold. 'Are you quite sure, Miss Thornton?' he asked cautiously.

Peggy was in a panic. For a moment, she couldn't even remember the question. 'Y-yes, sir,' she spluttered falteringly. 'Five times tuppence ha'penny is . . . yes, definitely . . . one sh-shilling and a ha'penny.'

The superintendent hesitated for a brief moment, then started writing furiously on to Peggy's application form again.

Peggy was devastated. Inside she could hear a voice asking her how she could be so stupid. She, of all people, a clerk in a solicitor's office who had been offered a senior position in the firm, someone who was supposed to have a brain, who could probably run circles around all those girls waiting in the corridor outside, and yet who was totally incapable of calculating without too much effort that five tuppence halfpennies added up to one shilling and a halfpenny.

'And how much change from a ten-shilling note would you give if the fare was one shilling and fivepence ha'penny?'

Even though the superintendent hadn't looked up at her to ask his follow-on question, sheer panic prompted Peggy into giving him an immediate response. 'Eight shillings and sixpence ha'penny, sir.'

The superintendent accepted her answer without any reaction whatsoever, and merely wrote it down on the application form.

Peggy hated the man. From the moment she had entered the room and opened her mouth she could tell how much he disliked her. It was perfectly obvious to her that he had absolutely no intention at all of approving her application; she was clearly far too well bred and well spoken for that. Oh, she knew what kind of a person he was, all right, right from that first question in which he had asked why someone like her should want to do a manual job. The nerve of it! *Someone like her?* How dare he suggest that because she came from an educated background, she was unable to punch a few bus tickets each day? As far as she was concerned, she was just as capable of filling a man's shoes as any one of those girls waiting outside.

'Thank you, Miss Thornton. If you'll just wait there a moment . . . I think I have all the information I need. We shall be in contact with you within the next few days.'

So that was it. Interview over after no more than five minutes, kicked out before she'd even had the chance to show what she could do. After all, she had all the right qualifications: she was over eighteen years old, over five feet three inches in height, her weight was well under eleven stone, and she had good eyesight. True, she hadn't been in a job that meant being on her feet for hours at a time, but at least her feet were perfectly strong, and she hadn't got varicose veins. In fact, she was an extremely fit young woman, so there was absolutely no need at all to turn down her application just because she was – well, who she was. As the man sat there scribbling down notes without even the courtesy to look up at her, she felt nothing but rage and indignation, and a strong desire to ask him why he himself hadn't been called up. Why, she kept telling herself, did she ever imagine that being a bus conductress was such a good idea? Why didn't she heed her father's advice that she was destined for better things in life?

'Please take this to the medical unit – down the corridor on the right.'

Peggy did a double take. Not only was the man looking up at her, but he was also holding out a piece of paper for her. 'I'm s-sorry?' she spluttered, taking it.

'Your medical examination, Miss Thornton.' The man

actually had a hint of a smile on his face. 'Before you start work on London Transport buses, it's mandatory for you to take a medical examination.'

Suddenly Peggy was in a daze. First she looked at the piece of paper in her hand, and then at the superintendent. 'Before I start work?' she said feebly. 'You mean – I've got the job?'

Again the man smiled. 'Provided you're fit and well – and get through your training. However –' he held out his hand – 'I'm sure you won't have too many problems. As a matter of fact, I think you'll make a very good bus conductor. Good luck.'

Peggy shook his hand, and left the office in a daze. On her way home, all she could think about was how much she had liked the superintendent, and how, when he smiled, he was really quite handsome.

On Sunday morning, Peggy and her mother went to church. Thornton did not go with them, for he had an important meeting to attend at the town hall, which apparently concerned the emergency measures the Borough Council were putting into place in the eventuality of an invasion. This was no real surprise, for ever since the evacuation of British troops from Dunkirk, there had been persistent rumours that the Germans were massing along the French Channel ports in preparation for a swift massive sea and air assault on the British mainland. The church, as always, was full of worshippers, a sign that it was now only unity, faith, and determination that was going to halt the advance of Adolf Hitler's powerful and frightening war machine.

That determination was soon put to the test when, after only a quarter of an hour, the service was interrupted by the wail of the air-raid siren, which heralded the start of yet another daytime raid. The service continued, however, until the deafening roar of a fierce air battle being fought in the skies above, followed by a series of high-explosive blasts nearby, shattered the calm of the church, causing overhead chandeliers to swing back and forth, and dust and small pieces of loose plaster to come floating down on to the congregation. Although most people were huddled on the floor for protection between the pews, no one panicked, and some of the more undaunted parishioners remained stubbornly upright on their seats. As soon as the immediate danger had passed, the service continued, culminating in a rousing version of the sailor's hymn 'Eternal Father, strong to save'.

On the way home, Peggy told her mother about her interview with London Transport. To her surprise Catherine took the news with remarkable calm, as though she had been expecting something like this to happen, and Peggy even suspected that her mother secretly admired what she had done. But by the time they had got back home, Peggy had become acutely aware that her mother had more pressing problems on her mind.

'I can't understand what's happened to him,' called Catherine from the first-floor landing. 'He promised faithfully he'd be home for lunch.'

This was turning out to be one more occasion when Robert Thornton was failing to get home at the time he had indicated, and Peggy could see that it was making her mother more and more agitated. 'It must be a pretty serious meeting,' she suggested. 'Maybe the invasion is closer than we think.'

Catherine, not reassured, went to check on the Sunday lunch Mrs Bailey had prepared for them before she returned home to feed her own family, who lived in a two-bedroomed ground-floor flat in Lower Holloway.

'Why don't we telephone the town hall?' asked Peggy,

following her mother into the kitchen. 'At least we'd find out if the meeting's over.'

Catherine swung around with a start. 'Absolutely not!' she insisted, shocked by the very suggestion. 'You know what your father's like. He hates to have people checking up on him.'

Peggy was puzzled – and curious. What was so terrible about trying to find out if your husband was going to be home for lunch or not? 'What if he got caught in the air raid or something?' she persisted.

Catherine shook her head. 'If that was the case, we'd have heard by now,' she replied confidently.

Peggy decided not to pursue the subject any further. Although she was hungry, if her mother was prepared to let the Sunday lunch frizzle up in the oven, then so be it. Even so, Catherine's edgy behaviour over the previous few weeks was beginning to intrigue her, and to Peggy's mind it had nothing to do with the Blitz.

'I forgot to tell you,' she said, once they had settled down to a quiet moment together in the sitting room. 'I bumped into Betty Desmond the other day. She'd been on duty the night that bomb came down on the public house.'

Catherine pretended not to hear. She had settled down on the chaise longue to continue working on a half-completed petit point cushion cover.

'She was asking after you,' persisted Peggy.

Catherine still did not respond.

Peggy decided to wait a moment before pursuing the subject, and made her way across to an upholstered bench seat in front of the window, where she was able to watch her mother in silence from behind. Peggy hated that chaise longue. She hated all chaise longues, which she had always considered to be one of the most uncomfortable pieces of furniture ever made. In fact she didn't care much for any of her mother's tastes in furnishing, with the heavy embroidered draped curtains and blackout blinds at the windows, the unfathomably designed Persian carpet which covered the entire floor, the Victorian roll-top mahogany desk in one corner of the room, and the straight-backed Victorian dining chairs, which had been rickety ever since Peggy could remember and long in need of repair. And as if that wasn't enough, the room was cluttered with meaningless brass objects which her mother had collected over the years. Interestingly, her father's only contribution to the room appeared to be the black ebony tobacco pipe rack which nestled comfortably in the centre of the mantelpiece, and which contained a variety of specimens, including one medium-sized briar, and one or two with slightly smaller bowls.

'She's such a nice woman.' Peggy was determined not to drop the subject. 'Mrs Desmond, I mean. I'm sorry we don't see her so much these days.'

Catherine sighed irritably.

'Mother, why *doesn't* Mrs Desmond come over here any more?'

Catherine's eyes flicked up from her petit point. It was now obvious that she could no longer avoid Peggy's questions. 'Peggy,' she said, without turning, 'Mrs Desmond and I have separate lives to live. We have very little in common.'

'But you used to,' replied Peggy. 'Betty Desmond was always one of your best friends.'

Catherine tried to dismiss Peggy's questions by trying to seem absorbed with her needlework. 'There's a war on,' she said brusquely. 'People have their own ways of coping with things.'

Peggy couldn't understand what her mother was trying to say. She remembered the times when Betty Desmond and her mother had been inseparable, playing bridge together at least once a week at the Ladies' Bridge Club in Highgate Village, or visiting Wednesday matinée performances of fashionable West End plays, and they were always in and out of each other's homes, taking tea together. So what was this all about?

Through the window she suddenly caught a distant glimpse of her father getting off a number 611 trolley bus further down the hill. She got up quickly, went across to her mother, and sat beside her. 'What is it, Mother?' she asked softly, clasping her hand gently on Catherine's arm. 'What's going wrong?'

Catherine looked up with a start. 'What are you talking about?'

Peggy, careful not to hurt her mother's feelings, lowered her voice. 'Things are not the same, Mother,' she said with an affectionate smile. 'You just don't seem to be happy any more.'

Catherine pulled her arm away. 'Because I don't see Betty Desmond?' she said, trying to make light of it.

'No. Because I know something's bothering you.'

'How absurd!' said Catherine, continuing with her stitching. 'In case you hadn't heard, there's a war on. It's "bothering" everybody!'

Peggy was hurt by Catherine's response. She was more used to that kind of sarcasm from her father. It was not something she would ever have expected from her mother. 'But as long as we have each other,' she said, trying to show affection, 'there's no need to be frightened.'

Catherine slammed down her needlework. 'Who said anything about being frightened?' she snapped. 'There are far worse things going on in this war than being bombed.'

Catherine tried to get up, but Peggy gently stopped her. 'When I was little,' she said, trying hard to make eye

37

contact, 'you used to tell me that I should never keep things to myself, and that if I ever had a problem, the only way to be grown up was to talk about it. I'm grown up now, Mother. Won't you please talk about it?'

Catherine raised her eyes. It wasn't hard to see that there was pain there. She wanted to say something positive, but just when it seemed she was going to, she was distracted by the sound in the hall outside of Thornton arriving home.

'Catherine!'

Catherine immediately broke loose from Peggy, got to her feet, and threw down her needlework. 'Coming, dear!' she called, hurrying to the door. Before she went, however, she paused just long enough to throw Peggy a final brief look. Her smile, though weak, tried to thank her, to tell her something. But Thornton's movements in the hall outside quickly curtailed that.

Two weeks later, a bomb which completely devastated a row of small terraced houses in a mews just behind Chapel Street, also badly damaged not only the funeral parlour, but also the offices of Parks and Stevens on the two floors above it. Fortunately for Mr Stevens and his staff, the air raid came during the night, but eleven people in the mews lost their lives, which caused tremendous grief and heartache amongst the community who had lived there.

Peggy did not hear about the bomb until she arrived for work on Monday morning, but the moment she got there, she and the rest of the firm's staff, supervised by a distraught Edwin Stevens, set about the job of clearing up the chaos and mess. It took several days to retrieve the mountain of legal paperwork which was scattered all over the floor amidst shattered glass, plaster, broken furniture and piles of valuable books, and it soon became clear that it would take some considerable time to restore the structure of the building to anything like a safe place to work. However, as if by a miraculous sense of timing, two days before the tragedy, Peggy had received a letter from the London Transport Board to say that, following confirmation that she had successfully passed the medical examination, her application for a job as a bus conductor had been accepted, and that she had been allocated to service work at Holloway Bus Depot, following training at the Chiswick training centre, commencing at eight a.m. on Monday, 9 December 1940. Peggy was thrilled when she got the letter; at last she had a genuine excuse to give in her notice. Despite Mr Stevens' assurances that the firm would continue business as usual as soon as they had found temporary accommodation, Peggy, with her friend Irene West's support, took the plunge and left Parks and Stevens the moment she had done her bit to help clear the office of the chaos caused by the mews bomb.

On her first day at the training centre, Peggy was kitted out with her winter uniform, which included a smart grey peaked cap, a navy-blue, loose-fitting three-quarter-length overcoat, and, to her horror, two pairs of grey slacks, which had recently replaced the divided skirt which had been considered too cold for the winter. At the same time she was allocated her summer garb, consisting of two grey duster coats. The uniform, she was told, was to last her for two years, and she was expected to provide her own black flat-heeled shoes. Then, before she entered the classroom for training, she was provided with all the necessary equipment she would need, such as a leather cash-bag, a ticket rack, and a punch slide.

As there was a war on, there was a real urgency to fill the vacancies left by men who were being drafted at an alarming rate into the armed services. Consequently,

Peggy's initial training itself lasted for just three days. It consisted of learning about the ticket system, and how to complete and balance the cash total sheet. Peggy also learned about things that had never occurred to her before, such as how to deal with members of the public, especially passengers who were difficult. She was told to use her days off to get to know London, and the routes on which she was likely to work, and to be prepared for endless questions from passengers about how to get from one place to another.

But for Peggy, the greatest experience of all was going to be mixing with people from all walks of life and, by the time she was ready to go out on the road for practical training, she had surprisingly become quite friendly with Tug Wilson and her mate Brenda, the two East End girls she had met before her interview.

Holloway Bus Depot in Kingsdown Road was one of two London Transport home garages situated within a short distance of each other in the same North London area. The depot was used exclusively for the service and maintenance of petrol buses, whilst Holloway Bus Garage, in Pemberton Gardens nearby, was the base for electrically operated vehicles, such as trams and trolley buses, and since Peggy had been allocated road training on the number 14 petrol bus route from Hornsey Rise to Teddington, her three-month probationary period as a trainee bus conductor was to be an attachment to the Kingsdown Road depot.

As it was clearly going to be a long time before Robert Thornton was going to forgive his daughter for not only giving up her job with Parks and Stevens without even consulting him, but also for taking on work that was totally out of keeping with the daughter of a noted public official,

Peggy was forced into finding ways that would prevent her father from being involved in her new life. Her main problem was that her mother never wanted her husband to see Peggy in her conductor's uniform, a situation which, from the very first day, resulted in Peggy having to leave the house with a suitcase so that she could change into her uniform at work.

It was bitterly cold when Peggy arrived for her first day's road training. Long thick icicles drooped down from the high roof of the depot, their ice glistening red in the early morning winter sun. The first thing that Peggy noticed as she made her way through the vast maintenance area was the overpowering smell of petrol from the row of buses being hosed down and serviced there, and the deafening sound of Geraldo and his orchestra on the wireless, booming out from huge Tannoy speakers all over the place. Her first job was to find the ladies' rest rooms, and once she had changed into her uniform and stowed her own clothes away in a locker, she made her way to the admin office to keep her first appointment with a women's welfare supervisor, to whom, she was informed, she would always be able to refer to for help and guidance at any time during either training or in her subsequent service with London Transport.

During the next hour or so, Peggy was taken on a tour of the depot. She was shown the conductors' room, where she would return to each day to check her tickets and money with the waybill, the cashiers' counter for 'paying in', the superintendents' office, the inspectors' room, the staff canteen, and the women's dormitory, which was for the use of anyone who couldn't get home after hours during an air raid. On her tour around the depot, she was introduced to people doing all sorts of jobs – mechanics working on the maintenance and repair of bus engines, female cleaners, other bus conductors, both male and female, inspectors (who seemed to be exclusively middle-aged males), a couple of wage clerks, and two young girls (who to Peggy's surprise turned out to be conductors) who were hosing and mopping down the exterior of one of the buses. Although everyone she met treated her cordially, the moment she started to respond in her well-spoken boarding-school voice, eyebrows were well and truly raised.

The middle-aged man assigned to accompany Peggy on her first day out on the road was a conductor of long service, who had been given his present job because of his patience and tolerance with new recruits. Charlie Pipes had a reputation for being one of those people who couldn't get rattled even if his missus found him in the arms of a tart from up the 'Dilly, which was most unlikely anyway. He seemed to have a perpetual smile on his circular face, which immediately endeared him to Peggy, even if she couldn't always follow his quick patter whenever he had something important to tell her. But from the word go, he was a great comfort to her.

'Don't yer go worryin' yerself, gel,' he said, when he first saw the look of terror in her eyes. 'Yer'll soon get to know this job's a piece er cake. All yer've got ter do is ter remember that once yer're on that bus, *you're* the guv'nor, not the man up front. Anyway, Charlie Pipes'll keep an eye on yer. I tell yer – piece er cake!'

A short while later, Peggy and Charlie made their way up to Hornsey Rise, where Peggy was scheduled to take over a number 14 bus for part of the journey to Teddington. On the way, Charlie filled her in more fully about the various duties she would have to carry out along the way, and gave her some useful tips on the kind of routine she should employ, such as keeping a rough count of how many passengers who got on at each stop went up to the top deck, thereby saving her too much climbing of stairs. He also gave her a special warning about fare dodgers, especially the 'spivvy' types, who knew how to work the buses by constantly changing seats and getting off the bus before the conductor appeared. By the time they had changed crews at Hornsey Rise, Peggy's mind was reeling. It didn't help that the first driver she had been allocated to work with was someone whom most of the conductors had never been able to get on with, mainly because he spent most of his time on and off the road studying form in the *Greyhound News* and didn't like to be disturbed.

To her immense relief, Peggy's first morning as a 'clippie' turned out to be a resounding success. Only once did she give the wrong change, and that was to an elderly female passenger who had confused her by changing her mind about where she wanted to go. Apart from that – and the fact that she found the whole experience utterly exhausting – Peggy felt good. It was, of course, peculiar not sitting alongside the passengers, as she had always done, staring aimlessly out of the windows as the world passed by, for if there was one thing she had learned very quickly, it was that when she had to be on her feet all day, and collecting fares before people got off, there was no time to daydream. However, when she eventually changed crews at Tottenham Court Road, there was still one thing that troubled her.

'D'you think I talk too posh, Charlie?' she asked. 'Does it put people off?'

Charlie roared with laughter. 'That's a good one, that is!' he quipped. 'You're one of the few people I know on the buses who speaks as good as Alvar Lidell on the wireless. Posh or not, gel, I like it.'

Unfortunately, Charlie's enthusiasm didn't seem to be shared amongst others when he took Peggy in to have a midday meal at the staff canteen. When they joined a table with some of their fellow conductors, most of them hardly seemed to acknowledge her presence until Charlie made a point of introducing her. Two of the conductors, Alf and Bernie, were middle-aged men, but the third man, called Leo, was wearing dungarees, and turned out to be a mechanic. Apart from Peggy, the only female at the table was a sharp-eyed little blonde called Elsie, who, from the moment Peggy appeared, shut up sulkily, clearly put out that she was no longer the centre of attention. By the time Peggy and Charlie took their seats, most of them had finished their meals and were sprawled out at the table, smoking fags and reading the *Daily Mirror* and the *Daily Herald*. God knows, Peggy found it difficult enough to eat overcooked sausagemeat pie and boiled potatoes, but to do so in a cloud of cigarette smoke was something she hadn't bargained for. As she looked around the table at her fellow workers, she suddenly felt like a fish out of water, where she had plunged herself into a world of coarse behaviour, where ill-bred people had no time for even the most basic of courtesies. As they chatted amongst themselves, every word seemed to be 'bloody' this or 'bloody' that, and as hard as Peggy tried to ignore it, there was no getting away from the fact that mixing with people from other walks of life was not going to be easy.

'So where yer from then, mate?'

Peggy was so taken aback by the remark being addressed to her by the balding conductor with a cigarette dangling from his mouth opposite her, that at first she didn't respond. But when she suddenly caught his eye and found him and the others looking at her, she quickly replied, 'Oh – I live on Highgate Hill.'

Around the table there was an immediate exchange of looks.

'Do yer now?' jeered Alf, the man who had asked the question. 'So we need a whip round ter talk ter you, do we?'

The others grinned, sharing the joke.

'I'm sorry?' asked Peggy, suddenly feeling very self-conscious about her 'posh' voice. 'What do you mean?'

'Come off it, Duchess!' said Alf, stubbing his cigarette end out on his plate.

Peggy put down her knife and fork. She was puzzled. Why did this man call her 'Duchess'? Charlie had told them her name when he'd introduced her. Why did Alf have to call her such a silly name?

Charlie, at her side, leaned towards her. 'It's a joke, gel,' he said reassuringly. 'Just a joke.'

For a brief moment, Peggy tried to think about it. Then she returned a weak, understanding smile. 'Oh, I see,' she nodded. But she didn't see. She didn't see at all. Sadly, she had to recognise that humour had never been one of her strongest points. She picked up her knife and fork again, and resumed eating.

'Must cost a bomb livin' up there?'

Peggy looked up. This time it was Elsie talking.

'Before the war they used ter say yer 'ad ter be born wiv a silver spoon in yer mouf ter live anywhere between the Archway and 'Ighgate Village. Bet yer couldn't get a place up there on *our* wage.'

Now Bernie, the other middle-aged man, joined in. 'I bet yer could,' he said, exhaling a lungful of smoke. 'Most er them people on the 'ill moved out pretty sharpish – day war broke out.'

Peggy listened, but refused to contribute to what she considered to be a totally banal and pointless conversation. How could they talk across her like this, she asked herself, as though she wasn't even there? What had she done to provoke this kind of banter? What had she done to upset them? Did they treat all newcomers in the same way? Or was it just sour grapes because she was not only a woman, but a woman who didn't speak their kind of language? Her only hope now was to eat the rest of her awful meal as quickly as she could. The canteen was filling up fast with staff coming off the morning shift, and this would be a good excuse for her to give up her seat.

'Don't blame 'em,' said Leo, the young mechanic, who was sitting on the opposite side of the table between Alf and Bernie. 'Sittin' target up there if yer ask me – on that 'ill in the middle of an air raid.'

Peggy looked up and immediately found herself looking directly into the soft dark eyes of the young mechanic, who had a head full of tight black curls, fag drooping from his lips, his forehead smudged with axle grease. Peggy felt something stir inside. She smiled shyly, but then quickly averted her gaze and returned to her food, aware that their mutual look had lingered a little too long.

Leo, however, kept on watching her. He was riveted to her cool, mature manner, the oval green eyes, and the red bobbed hair, just visible beneath her clippie's cap, glistening in the stark light from a solitary light bulb hanging down from the canteen ceiling high above them. He watched the way she delicately cut the dried up sausage pie, chewed it several times before swallowing, then just as delicately dabbed the corner of her lips with her handkerchief. It appeared, by the way he was leaning on his elbows just gawping at her, that he was totally smitten. 'So wot sorta work yer bin doin' then?' he asked.

Peggy looked up to find the boy giving her a friendly tantalising smile. His mischievous eyes, and fresh, bright complexion, with razor nicks on his chin that couldn't have been caused by someone who had mastered the art of shaving, all suggested that he was no more than eighteen. Peggy felt a warm glow in her cheeks as she replied with a shy smile, 'I worked in an office.'

'Is that a fact?' asked Leo, his smile now so huge that his teeth were gleaming. 'Wot kind er office?'

'A solicitor's office.'

Leo scowled at the others as they let out a silly chorus of jibes: 'Ooh – get *'er*!' and 'Solicitor, eh?' and 'Good ol' Duchess!'

Peggy ignored their jibes and carried on eating.

Leo could see that she was embarrassed, so he glared at the others, leaned across the table at her, and gave her a reassuring smile. 'Don't take no notice of this lot,' he said. 'They wouldn't know a solicitor from a coster boy up Chapel Market!'

The others hooted and Alf gave him a two fingers reply.

'As yer can see,' continued Leo, ignoring his mates, 'it's a bit different round 'ere to an office job.'

Peggy met his eyes. They lingered. She smiled her gratitude for his support. Then, aware that the others were watching them, she quickly returned to her food.

'So wot's in it for yer, Duchess?' asked Alf, still baiting her. 'Wot's a good middle-class gel from 'Ighgate 'Ill doin' takin' a job on the buses?'

Peggy, eyes lowered, waited a moment. Then she suddenly flicked her eyes up at him. 'I took the job,' she taunted, 'because I couldn't resist the opportunity of working with someone like you.'

There was a split second before everyone had taken in what she had said, then to gales of laughter and applause from the others, Peggy got up from the table and left.

The afternoon was a complete disaster. Not only was there the first real snow of the winter, but, unlike in her performance on the morning shift, Peggy just couldn't seem to do anything right. It happened from the moment she and Charlie changed crews at the Knightsbridge stop, when a smartly dressed woman passenger complained about the stifling cigarette smoke that was choking her on the top deck. Although Peggy did her best to explain that most of the passengers didn't want to open a window because it was too cold, the woman used the most insulting language to Peggy, accusing her of being totally incompetent to be in charge of a bus. After that, Peggy's morale seemed to fall apart. As the bus made its way along Knightsbridge, past the Royal Albert Hall, down Kensington High Street, and on to Hammersmith Broadway, she found it difficult to cope with the number of people who were clambering on and off, complaining about having to wait endlessly in the cold for a bus to arrive, only to find three or four buses of the same number coming at the same time. Despite Charlie's constant assurances that this was only her first day and that she would eventually get used to the irritations of the travelling public, Peggy made one mistake after another, giving out the wrong change, and passing on inaccurate information to passengers about where to pick up a bus of another route. By the time they reached Teddington, Peggy was ready to quit, to admit that she had made a terrible mistake by thinking she was either physically or mentally fit to cope with the ordeals of manual work. But when she got back to the depot late in the afternoon, Charlie tried to convince her that the problems she had encountered had nothing to do with her abilities, but with the way she'd been treated during the midday meal in the canteen.

'Believe me, gel,' he said, with fatherly reassurance, 'in the long run, the ignorant ones in this world suffer most. They don't know no better.'

Charlie's words echoed through Peggy's mind as she left the depot, and made her way into Holloway Road. It was now dark and well past blackout time, and the snow that had fallen earlier in the afternoon, and which had started to thaw almost immediately, had now turned the pavements into sheets of ice, which meant that Peggy's short journey home was going to be a perilous one. As most private cars had now disappeared from the roads, the only traffic around was the odd taxi or two, an *Evening News* van, two trams passing each other in opposite directions, a number 609 trolley bus heading effortlessly and silently up towards Archway Road, and several petrol buses, loading and unloading exhausted rush-hour travellers. As always, it was hell trying to move around in the dark, with only the fading light from a totally inadequate torch bulb to guide the way. But it was the same for everyone, and whenever Peggy glanced up from the pavement, there was always a flotilla of torch beams bearing down on her, all struggling to get their bearers safely home before the inevitable evening air raid began.

Unlike a normal evening, it took Peggy a full ten minutes of hard work to reach even the halfway mark to Archway Junction. She was so nervous about slipping on the ice that she didn't notice the long queue that had formed in the dark outside the old Empire Cinema on the opposite side of the road. Even if she had it wouldn't have meant anything to her; going to such a popular place as a cinema had never formed part of her upbringing. What she had noticed, however, was how thoroughly dispirited she felt. Everything she had planned, everything she had dreamed of for so long, seemed to have disappeared during the course of one disastrous day. This is what she had wanted, she kept telling herself. This was the opportunity she had taken to prove her father wrong. And yet, for some reason or another, the one who had been proved wrong was herself. Oh, it wasn't that the work was too difficult for her – that was something she would gradually cope with. No, it was people, always people, who dragged you down. What her mind was dominated with, of course, was that gang of loud-mouthed creatures who had been so cruel and insensitive to her in the canteen. What did Charlie call them – 'the ignorant ones'? No matter how hard she tried Peggy was now riddled with doubt – doubt about them and doubt about herself. Maybe *she* was the one who was wrong, too much of a snob to mix with the lower classes – just like her father, just like her mother. Was it because she herself was as cold and unapproachable as the ice on the pavements she was walking on?

'Duchess?'

Peggy halted with a start, and turned. For a split second in the dark she couldn't identify the voice, but the moment she directed her torch beam on to the face of the young man behind her, she recognised it only too well. 'Oh – hello,' she replied, immediately warming to him.

It was Leo, the young mechanic who'd been at the same table as her and Charlie in the canteen with the other stupid bunch. 'Fawt it was you,' he said, squinting in the torchlight. 'Didn't recognise yer at first – when yer come out the depot in yer civvies.'

Peggy was puzzled. 'Civvies?' she asked.

Leo grinned, and moved closer. 'Civvies. You know – out er uniform.'

'Oh,' replied Peggy, who now understood what he meant. For a brief moment she looked at him, his head covered with a flat, peaked working cap, face and ears blood red in the biting cold. Then, fearing that he might see how attracted she was to him, she quickly turned off the torch beam. 'Once I've finished work, I prefer to go home in my own clothes,' she replied, in the dark.

'Oh, I'm not complainin',' Leo assured her, digging his hands into his duffel coat pocket. 'I was just finkin' 'ow good yer look, that's all.'

Despite the cold, Peggy actually felt herself glowing inside. No one had ever spoken to her like this before, no one had ever paid her such a compliment. 'I have to be on my way,' she said, turning on her torch again, but redirecting the beam down on to the pavement. 'Goodnight.'

'Can I walk wiv yer a bit?'

Peggy hesitated before moving. She could hardly believe what she was hearing. Although his voice was rough and so different from anything she had been used to in her own distant world, she loved the way he talked, the way he talked to *her*, to her as a person he seemed to like. And yes, she liked him too, she had liked him the moment she had set eyes on him. He may not have been cultured, but he was real, he was sincere, and even in the dark she could see those long black eyelashes and soft dark eyes that made her tremble inside. And he actually wanted to walk with her – with *her*! 'I only live at the top of the Hill,' she said. 'Where do you live?'

'Me?' Leo moved alongside her. 'Oh, I live down 'Ornsey Road, near the Nag's 'Ead.'

'Then aren't you going out of your way?' Even as she said it, Peggy wished she hadn't.

'Yeah,' he replied. 'But who cares? I just fawt yer might like a bit er company, Duchess.'

Peggy suddenly tensed. Being called such a silly name reminded her of that ghastly scene in the canteen. 'Please don't call me that,' she said, sharply. 'My name is not Duchess.'

'Sorry,' Leo said quickly. 'Don't mean any offence. I'm sorry about those stupid buggers round the table ter day.

51

They can't see no furver than the end of their noses. Though I know wot Alf means. Ter me you're a duchess. Not that I've ever seen one meself, mind yer. But you're 'ow I imagine one would look – smashin', real smashin'.'

Peggy felt consumed with guilt and wished she had bitten her tongue. This boy was so lovely. 'You don't even know my name,' she said.

Leo's spirits immediately revived. 'Peggy,' he said instantly. 'That's short fer Marg'ret, right?'

Again Peggy was taken aback. 'Yes,' she replied, her voice now clearly showing her admiration for him. 'How did you know?'

'Oh, I know all right,' said Leo, pointedly. 'When I take a shine ter someone, I like ter know lots er fings. Funny 'ow people muck around wiv names though, in't it? Peggy – Marg'ret, that sorter fing. It's like my bruvver. 'Is name's 'Orace, but everyone calls 'im Ace.'

'Ace?' Peggy found herself chuckling. 'Well, that's certainly original.'

'Yeah,' said Leo, who now felt confident enough to slowly move off with her. 'Ace loves it. Makes 'im feel like 'e's someone. 'E ain't, er course, but 'e finks 'e is.'

They both moved off to avoid a group of well-oiled men who were just crowding out on to the pavement from a pub. It was some time before their rowdy voices disappeared far enough down the road for Leo to be heard again. 'Bet you're wonderin' why someone my age ain't bin called up?'

His question took her by surprise. 'I hadn't really thought about it,' she said. 'I don't know how old you are.'

'Eighteen,' he announced proudly, then added quickly, 'practically eighteen an' a 'alf. I should've got me call-up papers on me eighteenf birfday, but 'cos er me mum, I got deferred by six munfs. She 'ad ter 'ave this operation.'

'Oh, I'm sorry.'

'Yer don't 'ave ter be,' he replied chirpily, grinning to himself in the dark. 'Between you an' me, it's a bit of a fluke. It was only a gallstone.'

By now, Peggy was growing quite fond of his cheery, natural way of speaking, which was, she recalled, completely different from the cocky way he spoke to his older mates back in the canteen.

After a slow stroll, they eventually reached Archway Junction, which was surprisingly busy with last-minute shoppers and city commuters, rushing in and out of the tube station in a desperate race to get home before the first air raid of the evening. Peggy and Leo stopped briefly on the corner of Holloway Road, where the audience was just turning out from an afternoon performance at the old Electric Palace cinema, next to the tube station. By the time they had come to a halt, Peggy regretted that they would now have to part. 'I have to go now,' she said, turning her torch beam on to his face again. 'I go up the hill, you go down.'

'That's wot it's all about, in't it?' replied Leo, his smiling dark eyes glistening in the torchlight. 'It's amazin' the diff'rence a mile or so can make.'

'I suppose so,' she replied, sadly.

There was a moment's silence between them whilst they looked at each other, he in the beam of her torch, she in the half-light reflected back at her. There was a great deal going through both their minds, and it was a moment that they wanted to savour for as long as possible.

'Goodnight, Leo,' said Peggy, softly, reluctantly.

Leo was ecstatic. 'Hey!' he cried jubilantly. 'Yer remember me name!'

His delight was infectious, and made Peggy laugh. 'Of course,' she replied. 'After all, you remembered mine!'

Chapter 3

By the end of November, Peggy had completed her mandatory ten days' road training, and also three additional days' classroom training at Chiswick, which resulted in a successful final examination. After a bumpy start, her practical work went well, and by the time it had finished, she found that she was actually starting to enjoy the job. Better still, the other conductors were gradually accepting her, and even began to exchange a few words with her whenever they were in the conductors' room together at the depot at the end of each day, checking their tickets and money with the waybills, and paying in to the cashier. To her relief, she was even beginning to make friends with some of the other female conductors, including Elsie Parker, who had previously made her feel so unwelcome in the canteen on her first day in the job. She was also surprised to discover that she was not the only female conductor who didn't share the type of background as most of the others, for there turned out to be one woman there who was not only middle-class, but also middle-aged.

The situation at home, however, was not so good. On at least two occasions, Peggy had come home in the evening to discover that her parents had clearly had some sort of a row, which had led to an intense atmosphere between them. It was a curious development, for, over the years Catherine Thornton's slavish devotion to her husband had always been somewhat tiresome to those who knew the couple, and the way she was now only speaking when spoken to, especially during meal times, was, to say the least, worrying.

Thornton himself was also behaving oddly. Having abandoned his makeshift air-raid shelter beneath the stairs in favour of the comfort of his own bedroom on the first floor, he had now taken to spending the occasional night away at his club in Holborn, where, after a jovial evening with some of his fellow magistrate friends, he was able to stay in the comparative safety of the club's well-furnished basement shelter. The only blessing to be drawn from this new strain in the Thorntons' relationship was that Peggy was no longer self-conscious about the fact that she had taken to wearing her clippie's uniform in her father's presence whether he liked it or not.

However, in an attempt to find out why her parents were behaving in such a strange way, she turned to her grandmother and grandfather, Alice and Herbert Thornton, who lived in a grand detached house called The Towers, set in its own gardens at the top of the hill, near Highgate Village.

'More than likely he's got himself a mistress,' sniffed Alice, Thornton's mother, an autocratic old woman who didn't look anything like her seventy years, mainly because she had never stopped to think how old she was. 'I remember when he was young, long before he met your mother, he had a different woman friend every month. Never held on to them for long, of course. Always too full of himself.'

'Father? A mistress?' Peggy couldn't believe what she was hearing. Her grandmother was just getting over the flu, and Peggy was sitting on the edge of the old lady's bed, sipping tea. 'He'd never do such a thing. Not someone in his position – surely?'

The old lady let out a raucous laugh. 'Never do such a thing? Not much!' she bellowed, turning to her husband, who was sitting at a card table on the other side of the room, doing his best to cheat himself at a game of dominoes. 'Eh, Herbert?'

Herbert Thornton was three years older than his wife, but looked more. Whereas Alice's hair had been coloured back to its original dark brown many times, her husband had been content to allow his own full head of hair to proceed to a glistening pure white.

'I don't think that's a very nice thing to say in front of your granddaughter, Alice,' he said, without looking up from the domino board.

'Stuff and nonsense,' croaked Alice, pulling on a Craven A cigarette, and using her teacup saucer as an ash tray. 'This girl's going to be twenty-one in the New Year. If she doesn't know about the facts of life by then, she never will!'

Peggy still hadn't taken in what the old lady had suggested. Her father with a mistress? It just didn't seem possible. And yet, in his own way he *was* still quite a handsome man, and mischievous though her grandmother undoubtedly was, it was just possible that she could be right.

'I would hate to think Father was being unfaithful,' she said wistfully. 'I always thought he loved Mother.'

The old lady looked at her granddaughter, and suddenly felt a rare glimmer of guilt. Alice Thornton had always liked the girl. She found her not only a pretty child, but someone with whom she could identify, much more than with her own son, whom she had always found stuffy to the point of boredom. What she admired most was Peggy's independent spirit. On more than one occasion she had heard her stand up to her father, which so many people seemed to be too afraid to do. In Alice's mind that could only be a good thing, because her son was too much like herself: thoroughly self-opinionated, full of himself and an absolute bore unless he got his own way.

'Of course he loves your mother,' she declared, wiping her running nose with her handkerchief. 'But that doesn't mean he can't have a mistress. God knows, your grandfather's had plenty of them in his time.'

Herbert was used to his wife's barbed remarks, so he didn't even bother to react.

Over the years, Peggy had also grown used to her grandmother's outrageous behaviour. As she looked around the bedroom, which had walls and practically everything else coloured lilac, she remembered the times when she was a child when her grandmother used to make frequent trips to France just to buy snails, which she would then bring back home, prepare and cook herself, and then eat with relish in front of the entire family and their servants. Her son, Robert, had long despaired of his mother, which was one of the reasons why to this day he rarely visited her.

'If Father *is* seeing someone else,' said Peggy stoically, 'then I think it's being dishonest and unkind.'

'Dishonest? Unkind?' The old lady pulled herself up in bed. 'To whom?'

'To my mother,' replied Peggy gallantly. 'It's no way for a husband to behave.'

Alice propped herself up against her pillows. 'Fidelity, my child,' she claimed, 'is hardly the lasting ambition of every red-blooded man. Nor is it always, I'm pleased to say, for every dutiful wife. Unless, of course, you live at the bottom of the hill, where they invariably breed like rabbits!'

Peggy turned her face away. Sometimes she felt quite ashamed of the way her grandmother talked. Somehow it showed a lack of feeling for anyone but herself. 'So what do you suggest I do?' she asked tenuously. 'Am I supposed to sit idly by and ignore what's happening between them, or am I expected to take sides?'

The old lady's eyes narrowed. 'It depends, my dear,' she

replied mischievously, 'on which one of your parents you respect more.'

'Frankly, Grandmother,' said Peggy, getting up from the edge of the bed, and putting her cup and saucer down on to the old lady's bedside cabinet, 'The way I feel at the moment, I couldn't care a damn for either of them.'

On the other side of the room, Herbert looked up from his domino game, and grinned wryly over the top of his spectacles. It was the only comment he was prepared to make.

Leo Quincey looked up the hill and wondered what all the fuss was about. The eldest of three sons born to Marge and Reg Quincey, he was undoubtedly the biggest daydreamer of them all, and despite all his bravado when he was with his mates up at the depot, he was really quite a loner, who dreamed of better things than a life of drudgery. Of late, he had thought an awful lot about Highgate Hill, and especially the people who lived there. Oddly enough, he had only been up there once in his life, and that was when, before the war, his dad took him and the rest of the family to the fairground on Hampstead Heath on an August Bank Holiday Monday. As they were only passing through on a bus at the time, all he could remember about the hill was the hospital and the big Catholic school on the left, and an assortment of posh-looking houses high up on a terrace stretched right the way along the opposite side. But as he left work at the end of his split-turn shift and paused to take a brief look up at the hill in the dark, he wondered why anyone should think such a place was any better than anywhere else. It was certainly not a patch on where he and his family lived, above the coal merchant's office in Hornsey Road, where the neighbours were real people and not just stuck-up toffs.

A few minutes later, he made his way on foot to the Nag's Head, where he was just in time to change on to a number 14 petrol bus, which was just pulling away from the bus stop outside Lavalls' sweet shop in Seven Sisters Road. As there was an air raid on, the interior of the bus was in darkness, and he was immediately blinded by a torch beam.

'Oh no! Not you again!'

Leo had a broad grin on his face as he was greeted by Peggy, who by absolutely no coincidence at all turned out to be the conductress. ' 'Allo, mate!' he replied cheekily, sitting down on the bench seat close to the conductor's platform. ' 'Ome, James! An' don't spare the 'orses!'

This was one of the bus's last few stops before the terminus up at Hornsey Rise, and most of the passengers had now got off.

'Leo,' Peggy said, shining her torch straight into his eyes, 'you don't live on this route, you know you don't. Your place is the other end of Hornsey Road.'

'Go on,' replied Leo, mockingly holding up his free PT travel pass. 'Yer don't say?'

Peggy sighed, but not too disapprovingly. 'Are you following me?'

'Yeah,' replied Leo confidently. ' 'Ow d'yer guess?'

Aware that there was still one passenger left sitting in the dark in one of the front seats, Peggy turned off her torch, and sat beside him. 'There's an air raid on, Leo,' she said, lowering her voice. 'You should get home.'

'Yeah, I know.' Leo lit a match. The flame illuminated his face, and the reflection flickered in both his eyes. 'Some people do stupid fings, don't they?' He lit the dog-end waiting in his lips, then blew out the match. 'Wot yer doin' when yer come off shift then?' he asked in the dark.

Peggy had been half expecting the question, and she

was ready for it. 'I'm going straight home,' she replied. 'Best place to be in the middle of an air raid.'

Leo came back at her immediately. 'Not entirely,' he said. 'There *are* uvver places yer can take shelter, yer know. Much better places.'

'Such as?'

'The boozer. It's a good place ter drown yer problems.'

'Who said I had problems?'

Leo paused a moment before answering. He took a puff of his dog-end, which glowed in the dark. 'It's a lucky person who ain't got 'em.'

In the dark, in the cold, Peggy could sense the warmth emanating from his body. For some extraordinary reason she found it exhilarating. 'I think you should know that I've never been inside a public house in my entire life.'

'All the more reason,' came Leo's quick-as-a-flash reply. 'Where I come from, the boozer's our second 'ome. It's just like one big 'appy family.'

One big happy family. Peggy thought about that. A happy family was something she'd never experienced. All she'd ever known were parents who cared only for status and position, and not the love and warmth that came with true family life. And as she sat there and watched Leo's dog-end glowing in the dark, she radiated with the thought that this boy was taking an interest in her. Such a thing had never really happened to her before. Oh, she had met plenty of boys in her time, but most of them were like Joe Stevens – smooth, well-off office types, who worked in sound middle-class jobs, such as in the Stock Exchange, or in accountancy, or those 'mummy's darlings' who were perfectly content just to hang around doing nothing until it was time to collect their inheritance. They were all takers, not givers. Love rarely entered their well-scrubbed lives. But this was different. For the first time in her life Peggy felt wanted.

'Why, Leo?' she asked, her voice just heard above the rattling sound of the old bus engine. 'Why do you want me to have a drink with you?'

Leo was a bit rattled by the directness of her question, and his first response was brittle. 'I'm not beggin' yer, yer know.'

Peggy suddenly felt guilty. 'Oh, Leo,' she said, clutching his arm, 'I didn't mean to sound – ungrateful. I just thought—' She stopped when she felt his hand reaching out for her own. It was freezing cold, and it took her breath away.

'I like yer, Peggs,' he said, leaning as close as he dared in the dark.

Peggy's own hand was now as cold as his. 'Why?' she asked, demurely.

Leo paused before answering. 'When I first met yer,' he replied, stroking her hand gently with his thumb, 'I knew yer was someone I wanted ter know.'

Now Peggy paused before answering. 'So how much *do* you know me?' she asked coyly.

Leo took the dog-end from his lips. 'Enuff ter ask yer ter 'ave a drink wiv me!'

They were suddenly distracted by the voice of an elderly woman who had got up from her seat and was now making her way to get off the bus. 'Go on, gel, go an' 'ave a drink wiv 'im,' she called in the dark. 'Just make sure 'e pays fer it!'

Peggy immediately leaped to her feet, and as the bus came to a halt at the next stop, she used her torch to help the old dear to get off. Then she pushed the driver's call button, and once the bus was on the move again, she turned her torch beam back to Leo. He had a huge grin on his face. 'Don't worry,' he said. 'I promise ter pay.' This made them both laugh, until, without warning, they were interrupted by a deafening explosion which rocked the bus from side to side, shattering windows, and bringing it to an abrupt halt.

'Jesus Christ!' yelled Leo, as he threw his arms around Peggy to shield her.

Terrified that the bus was about to roll over on one side, neither of them dared to move for several seconds. When the vehicle did finally settle, Peggy's first thought was to make sure that there were no passengers left on the upper deck, so with the light from her torch, she went to the foot of the stairs, and called out, 'Anyone up there?' With no response, she hurried up the stairs to find out for herself. Fortunately, most of the windows on the upper deck had been saved by the protective netting, and once Peggy was satisfied that there was no one there, she quickly went back down the stairs, and left the bus with Leo.

They were met by the driver, Nobbie Morris, who had blood streaming down one side of his face.

'Nobbie!' gasped Peggy, horrified, immediately going to help him.

'No need ter panic!' said the elderly driver, with his usual cool-as-a-cucumber manner, despite the blood he was dabbing with his handkerchief, which was gushing from a wound on the side of his forehead. 'Bit er glass, that's all. Which is luckier than some poor sods.'

All three turned to look at the sky above the rooftops on the opposite side of the road. Their faces were illuminated by the fierce red glow from a massive fire which was burning fiercely just a couple of streets away.

'Looks like it's over Fonthill Road somewhere,' said Leo.

As he spoke, all hell broke loose. The emergency services came rushing towards them from all directions – fire engines from the Mayton Street station, ambulances, police cars – the sound of bells and horns cutting through the pandemonium that had broken out everywhere. Above them, however, came a very different sound: the sinister droning of aircraft engines, gradually overwhelming the skies like a swarm of bees. Soon, the overcrowded evening sky became a kaleidoscope of searchlights, all crisscrossing each other amidst a tumultuous barrage of small white puffs of smoke from the profusion of anti-aircraft shells and tracer bullets which were targeting everything above that moved. One of the silver cigar-shaped barrage balloons suddenly burst into flames and fluttered down in the dazzling glare of the searchlights. This was followed by another, then another, all falling victim to the blaze of enemy aircraft machine-gun fire. All along Hornsey Road, eyes were turned in horror and disbelief towards the great inferno which had engulfed the entire sky.

'Let's get out of 'ere,' said Leo, hurriedly leading Peggy and her driver away to the safety of the nearest public air-raid shelter.

Although Marge Quincey's eyes were closed tight, she was not asleep. Her heart was thumping hard at the thought of what might happen if one of those sods overhead was to drop a bomb on to her and her family, who were huddled together in the back yard brick-and-concrete shelter behind the coal merchant's office. Every possibility was going through her mind. What if there was a direct hit, and the concrete roof just caved in on her and the kids? What chance would they have? But then she imagined that if it was a direct hit, then at least none of them would know anything about it because it would all be over in a flash. It was bad enough that she and the kids had to bear this nightly horror on their own, for her husband, Reg, had vowed never to go into the shelter, opting for the freedom of the street outside where he and his fire-watching mates were able to keep an eye on what was going on up above. Marge had never been able to work him out. How *could* a man who loved his wife and kids so much leave them to suffer on their own?

'I wanna pee!' As usual, young Eddie was moaning away to his mum, who was on the mattress by his side, holding him tight against her for protection.

As Eddie was only seven, utterly spoiled, and the youngest, he played it up to the full, much to the annoyance of his brother Horace, who was eleven, and who made up for being the middle son by calling himself 'Ace', which in his older brother, Leo's, opinion was a pretty pathetic way of saying that he was the best. However, one thing the two young brothers did have in common was their hatred not only of having to bunk down with their mum on two mattresses on the cold stone floor night after night, but also being wrapped up in blankets and eiderdowns, and their dad and elder brother's old overcoats.

'Yer'll 'ave ter wait till the All Clear goes, Ed,' growled his mum, pushing his face back firmly into her chest in the thick woollen cardigan she had knitted herself.

'I can't wait till the All Clear,' mumbled Eddie, pulling away. 'I wanna go now!'

'Yer're a bleedin' nuisance, Ed!' snapped Marge. 'Yer always want ter pee just when the siren goes. Wos the matter wiv yer? Can't yer 'old it in till the raid's over?'

'No!' barked the boy, getting up. 'I wanna go now!'

Marge, who still looked a bit frail after her recent gallstone operation, struggled to her feet. 'Well, yer can't go outside,' she replied firmly. 'Yer'll 'ave ter use the bucket.'

'Aw, Mum . . .' groaned Horace. 'Not again.'

Marge snapped at Eddie, 'In the corner! An' don't take all bleedin' night!'

Horace crumpled up on his mattress, and covered his ears with his hands. 'If Leo'd bin 'ere,' he grumbled, ' 'e'd 'ave taken 'im outside ter do it.'

Marge settled down on the mattress again. 'Well 'e's not 'ere,' she said, 'so stop complainin' an' get ter sleep!'

She didn't suggest how poor Horace was expected to get any sleep while bombs were exploding all over the place outside and his young brother was making as much noise as he could by peeing in the bucket in the corner.

After a pause, Horace said, 'It's all right fer Leo. 'E don't 'ave ter come out ter this smelly dump every night. Too busy enjoyin' 'imself.'

Marge sighed despondently, and tried to fix her hairnet, which had slipped off over her left ear. 'Yer bruvver 'as a job er work ter do.'

'Oh, yeah?' jeered Horace, taking his hands away from his ears and sitting up. 'I've 'eard that one before!'

Eddie finished his pee, and put down the bucket. ' 'E's probably out 'avin a leg over wiv 'is bit er skirt,' he said mischievously.

Before Marge had time to get back at him, a bomb whistled down outside, and exploded somewhere a little too close for comfort. Fortunately, Eddie had managed to leap back to his mum's side just in time before all the walls shook with the vibration. However, she waited just long enough for the dust to settle before having a go at the boy. 'If I 'ear you use language like that again, Ed, I'll get yer dad on ter yer. Right?'

Eddie sat up. 'Wot yer talkin' about?' he groaned.

'Yer know bleedin' well wot I'm talkin' about. Pam's a nice gel, and one er these days she's goin' ter be part er this family. So don't yer go round talkin' dirty about 'er, d'yer 'ear?'

'Pam?' Horace was sitting up again. 'Who's talkin' about Pam?'

Marge swung a glare at him. In the flickering light from the paraffin lamp, she could see that her middle son's long dark curly hair that she took so much trouble to comb each day was looking like a tea cosy. There and then she decided that first thing in the morning she would get the boy's father to give him a haircut.

'Wot d'yer say?' she called.

'I bet 'e ain't out wiv Pam,' said Horace, smirking in the shadows. ' 'E's out wiv 'is toffee-nose.'

' 'Er wiv the plum in 'er mouf!' added Eddie.

Both boys roared with laughter.

At that moment, a 'Chicago piano', a naval pom-pom anti-aircraft gun mounted on a naval truck roaming the streets outside, fired deafening rapid shots up into the air at the enemy raiders. All three Quinceys dived for cover, clasping their hands over their ears until the vehicle had moved on.

'Who yer talkin' about, 'Orace?' asked Marge, the moment she could sit up again and be heard. 'Wot toffee-nose?'

Horace sniggered. 'This gel on the number 14. Kenny Warren told me 'is dad's seen 'em on the bus tergevver loads er times. 'E said—'

'She talks wiv a plum in 'er mouf!'

Again both boys roared with laughter.

Marge's hand slid beneath the blankets to her gallstone scar. It had started to irritate her. She was thinking about little Pam Warner, who had been walking out with her Leo for the past six months, and who was not only pretty as a picture but, in Marge's mind, the perfect choice for a daughter-in-law. If what the kids were saying was true, if Leo was playing the dirty on her, then why? Why should he want to go mixing with toffee-noses when he'd got a good Holloway girl who'd make him the perfect wife?

'Who is she, this gel?' Marge asked Horace, trying not to show her irritation.

'Dunno,' replied Horace with a shrug.

'She's a clippie!' announced Eddie triumphantly.

Marge turned to look at her youngest. 'A clippie?'

'She punches yer tickets.' Eddie fell back on to the mattress again.

Horace did likewise, and closed his eyes. 'If she's on the number 14, she must work up the same depot as Leo.'

Marge lay down alongside Eddie, and cuddled him up to her. It was now bitterly cold, for the paraffin heater had gone out and, as there was no more paraffin available, the best thing she could do was to pull the blankets and eiderdown right up to their chins. Outside, the sound of droning enemy planes and anti-aircraft fire was gradually dying down, but if every other night was anything to go by, it would be a short respite. She closed her eyes, but sleep was clearly going to elude her for some time yet. There was too much on her mind. Could it be true – a clippie with a plum in her mouth? Why? Why couldn't Leo stick to the types he knew best, types like his own sort who knew how to muck in and be part of a hard-working family. Types like that lovely little Pam Warner. If he jilted her, he'd be a fool, a silly bleeding fool. He'd be betraying his own roots. No. It wasn't true. Horace and Eddie were trying to get her worked up over nothing. Leo loved Pam all right, anyone could see that. You could see it in his eyes. And when it was time for him to be called up, Pam would be waiting for him to return, there was no doubt in her mind about that. Or was there?

Robert Thornton surveyed the London skyline through

binoculars. The view from the roof of Sandford's, his club in Holborn, seemed quite surreal, for there were fires burning in every direction, from Acton in the west to the London Docks in the east. To make matters worse, he had been drinking, drinking quite a lot, as it happened, mainly brandy, which was allegedly in short supply, except, it appeared, in places such as a certain exclusive men's club for the legal profession a stone's throw from Lincoln's Inn Fields. Since the start of the Blitz, he had resented having to do fire-watching duties alongside the higher echelons of his profession, such as High Court judges and King's Counsels, but since every member of the club was expected to do his bit, there was no alternative. None the less, lookout duties on a night like this were always fraught with danger, for the sky had become one vast battleground.

'Must be hundreds of 'em up there!' called Edwin Stevens, adjusting his tin helmet. 'I just don't understand it. With all this ack-ack around, they should be bringing down far more of the blighters.'

It was just Thornton's luck that his lookout partner on the roster for the evening turned out to be the man whom his daughter had previously been working for. Not that he particularly disliked the fellow, but he was only too aware that Stevens only became a member of the club so that he could keep in with people like Thornton himself.

'I mean, what's happened to the RAF?'

Thornton was finding it difficult to cope with Stevens' whingeing. He pushed his tin helmet to the back of his head, puffed on his pipe, and moved back a little from the window of the rooftop fire-watching post.

'They're supposed to be defending us,' Stevens continued. 'Fine defences, I must say! Just look at that sky. Jerry's got it all to himself. If you ask me, we're losing this damned war.'

'If you don't mind my saying, Stevens,' Thornton said at last, 'I think you're being just a touch too pessimistic. If you look hard enough, you'll see that our chaps are bringing down quite a few of those planes. I'm sure the RAF are doing their best.'

Stevens went quite taut. 'Oh, I wasn't implying any criticism of the Royal Air Force, Mr Thornton,' he said, realising that he had been too opinionated. 'I was just a little concerned about the general situation, that's all.'

It was several minutes before he decided to open up a conversation with Thornton again. When he did, he carefully avoided talking about 'the situation'. 'I must say we miss that lovely daughter of yours,' he said, only half keeping a watch out through the open door of the sheltered post. 'My secretary, Miss West, was only saying so the other day. I'm sure we'll be able to move back to our own office in the New Year. The repair work is well advanced.'

Thornton merely grunted his reply.

'If she could have waited until then, we could have implemented our little arrangement without any difficulty whatsoever. Such a pity she had other plans, don't you think?'

Thornton grunted again. 'Yes, Stevens,' he said, irritated that he had been over this same point with this tiresome man time and time again. 'A great pity.'

'However, I'm glad to say that my son, Joseph, hasn't given up hope.' To Thornton's irritation, Stevens turned back to him. 'I have to say, I agree with what you said a few months ago. They *would* make such a perfect couple.'

'Did I say that?'

Stevens was a little taken aback. 'Why, yes,' he said, a little unsurely, 'yes, you did. If you remember, when we first discussed the matter, we both agreed how wonderful it would be if we could somehow – well, bring them closer together. You *do* remember – don't you?'

Thornton paused to think for a moment. 'Oh yes, Stevens,' he replied evasively. 'I remember.'

With the air unexpectedly quite silent outside, Stevens followed Thornton out on to the rooftop to see what was going on. Although the dark evening sky was still criss-crossed with searchlights, the armada of enemy aircraft seemed to have passed over, and their engines could now be heard droning in the far distance.

'Looks like they've finished for the night,' said Stevens, scanning the sky through his binoculars.

'I doubt it,' replied Thornton, also peering through binoculars. 'I'd say they're on their way to the south-east, probably the Bermondsey Docks.'

Both men waited for the droning sounds to disappear before lowering their binoculars.

'When do you expect your son to be home on leave?'

Thornton's sudden question took Stevens by surprise. But it delighted him. 'Joseph's only been gone a couple of weeks,' he explained. 'But if his training goes well, I expect it won't be too long before he gets a weekend pass. After all, Gosport isn't all that far away.'

'Let me know.'

Quite suddenly, the moon made a brief appearance from behind dark night clouds, which gave Stevens the chance to get a better look at Thornton. 'I beg your pardon?' he asked.

'Your son, Stevens,' sighed Thornton, still concentrating on the city skyline ahead of him. 'I said I'd like to know when he comes home for a weekend.'

Again, Stevens was taken by surprise. 'Oh yes – yes, of course,' he replied, with immediate enthusiasm. 'I shall most certainly do that.'

Thornton turned to look at him. 'They must get to

know each other. I'm sure they don't yet realise that they have a lot in common. Every so often young people need a push.'

'Oh yes indeed!' enthused Stevens. 'I couldn't agree more.'

'We must organise something for them, Stevens. A get-together. A Sunday tea-party perhaps. At Highgate Hill. You may bring your wife.'

Stevens was delirious with joy. This was what he wanted, what he had hoped for: a union between his son and Major Thornton's daughter, a path into a whole new world of power and position – a dream come true! 'Excellent idea, my dear Major,' he cried exultantly. 'Excellent!'

'Just one more thing.'

Stevens swung a look at him, but the moon disappeared behind the clouds as quickly as it had arrived, and once again all he could hear was a voice in the dark.

'I hope you will agree that if, with our encouragement, our scheme bears fruit, then I think we should come to some arrangement – about my daughter's involvement – in your firm.'

Stevens' exhilaration immediately disappeared. 'Arrangement?' he asked.

'Well, let's face it, Stevens,' continued Thornton darkly, 'you and I are not getting any younger – are we? We have to make sure that our children are taken care of. I'm sure you agree?'

'Oh – yes. Yes, of course,' stammered Stevens. This was not what he had been expecting. An *arrangement*? An *arrangement* in exchange for his son's hand in marriage? What could he possibly mean?

'I think you'll also agree that my daughter is quite an intelligent young woman?'

'Indubitably.'

'In which case, on your demise, she and your son would be a fine team, working together to continue the high standards you have set for your firm?'

Stevens was confused. 'A fine – *team*? You mean – a partnership?'

'Precisely. Fifty-fifty seems to me to be a perfectly logical arrangement for two people who will be spending both their married *and* their business life together?'

Stevens was beginning to panic. 'But – but Peggy – I mean Margaret – I mean your daughter – she indicated that she was no longer interested in the legal profession. She wanted to do her bit for the war.'

There was a moment's silence, which unnerved Stevens. He guessed what Thornton was about to say.

'The war will not last for ever, Stevens,' Thornton said. 'And when it does end, I'm sure that your son and my daughter will, one way and another, form a most satisfactory union.'

Peggy and Leo sipped nothing stronger than cocoa. After their near-escape in the air raid earlier in the evening, all thoughts of having a drink in the pub had to be abandoned, for their primary task had been to get the injured driver and the damaged bus back to the depot. Fortunately, there was still a member of the canteen staff left who was able to make them something hot to drink, and once Peggy had recovered from the initial shock of what had happened, she and Leo were able to relax awhile at one of the empty dining tables. For a short time, however, they sat in silence, pondering on their own thoughts about what could well have turned out to have been a night of tragedy. Since the start of the Blitz, this was the first time Peggy had been anywhere near an 'incident' as it was actually happening, and she was having difficulty coming to terms with it. It was all so different from being tucked up nice and cosy with her mother inside the Morrison shelter. What she had experienced that night was the true reality of war, and how it was affecting every man, woman and child who had become part of it.

'Wot about a fag?'

Peggy looked up to find Leo holding out a cigarette for her. She smiled gratefully, but shook her head.

'Do wonders fer yer nerves,' he said cheekily. 'Not so sure about yer lungs, though!'

This brought the first real broad smile to Peggy's face.

'Yer should do that more often, yer know.'

Peggy was puzzled. 'Do what?'

'Smile,' replied Leo. 'Yer don't know 'ow good yer look when yer do it.' He popped the fag into his own mouth and lit it.

Peggy sighed, and wrapped both her hands around the cup of hot cocoa to keep them warm. 'I'm sorry, Leo,' she said, looking across the table at him. 'It's wrong of me to be like this. I've got to learn to be stronger.'

Leo took a puff of his fag, and leaned his elbows on the table. 'Yer look strong enuff ter me – Duchess.'

Peggy looked up and gave him a sharp glare.

Leo grinned, his eyes twinkling. 'See wot I mean?'

Realising he was teasing her, Peggy chuckled and leaned back in her chair. For a moment or so, they just sat there looking at each other. At this time of night, the canteen seemed a dark and bleak place, with blackout blinds down and low-voltage lamp bulbs dangling from the white distempered ceiling, providing the minimum of light. The place also smelled of a mixture of lard, which was always used for frying chips at the midday meal, boiled cabbage, and DDT, which helped to keep the kitchens and serving areas free of cockroaches. Outside, there was now just the faint, distant rumble of anti-aircraft guns, and somewhere from the main service area they could hear some of the night-shift staff joining in with a gramophone record over the Tannoy of Victor Silvester and his orchestra playing a soothing rendition of 'Anapola'. For one brief moment, Leo's eyes met Peggy's, but she seemed embarrassed, and quickly avoided them. But it was just enough for Leo to know that his initial attraction for her was no five-minute wonder. It wasn't just her looks, though God knows with those green eyes, red hair and slim jawline, she could drive any bloke half bonkers. No, it was more than that. It was something that Pam Warner hadn't got, would never have. It was something that seemed to say, like me for who I am and not *what* I am. It was something about wanting to be free, to be let out of a cage.

And in the brief moment that Peggy met Leo's eyes, she also felt something that was more than just a mutual attraction. Leo was about as rough a type as she had ever met, totally different from anyone she had ever known. And yet, somehow, she related to him. After nothing more than a subliminal glance, she could remember everything about his looks that she had tried to erase from her mind the first disastrous time they had met – the dark, mischievous eyes and black curly hair, the fresh bright complexion with the razor nicks which were still there, even though he now had a hint of black stubble on his cheeks and chin. Why did this boy, who was a couple of years younger than herself, make her feel so comfortable? Why was he the only boy she had ever met who didn't give her the feeling that he was trying to look right inside her?

'Somebody told me your dad's a judge or somefin',' said Leo, after a long silence.

'A magistrate,' replied Peggy. 'He sits on the bench at Highbury.'

'The only fing I know about a magistrates' court is when some mate er mine got done fer sellin' black market. That was up Clerkenwell, though. Two quid fine or ten days inside the nick. Not fair really. 'E only did it 'cos 'is old man was pissed an' fell in a 'orse trough outside the boozer.'

To his surprise, Peggy roared with laughter.

This amused Leo, and he laughed too. 'Wot yer laughin' at?' he asked. 'The poor ol' geezer was on the dole fer over a munf!'

This made Peggy laugh even more.

'It's not funny, Peggs!' Leo said, sharing her laughter. 'Me mate's family could've starved!'

Peggy tried to control herself. 'I'm sorry, Leo,' she said awkwardly. 'I shouldn't laugh, I know I shouldn't. It's just that, well – I've been in court and heard my father take so many cases like this.'

Leo's laughter faded. 'So 'ow many poor geezers 'as 'e sent down in 'is time then?'

Peggy began to feel guilty. 'Actually, for all his faults, he has a reputation for being quite lenient. When I hear him in court sometimes, he can be quite fair-minded.'

'Is that a fact?' replied Leo. Then after a brief pause, he asked, 'So wot d'yer fink yer dad'd make er me?'

His question took her by surprise. 'I don't know, Leo,' she replied falteringly. 'Once he'd met you, I'm sure he'd like you very much.'

Leo grinned broadly, knowingly at her. ' 'Im an' my ol' man'd get on well tergevver then.'

Peggy was puzzled. 'What d'you mean?'

Leo stubbed his fag out in his saucer, then placed the dog-end behind his ear. 'Always ready ter listen ter reason – know what I mean? Not my ol' ma, though – set in 'er ways, that one. Once she's made up 'er mind, she's like the Rock er Gibraltar! When I was a kid once, she whacked me round the lug 'ole 'cos I said I didn't like cod's roe.'

The look on Peggy's face showed that she had no idea what he was talking about.

'Cod's roe – you know, when yer 'ave fish an' chips on Friday nights? Anyway, she was determined that there was nuffin' in the 'ole wide world was goin' ter convince 'er that I didn't like cod's roe. To 'er, it was all in me mind – that is, till she give me some an' I sicked the 'ole ruddy lot up. Rock er bloody Gibraltar – that's me ol' ma!'

It was almost two o'clock in the morning by the time Leo had walked Peggy back home. By then, the skies seemed to have settled down again, although the air-raid siren still hadn't sounded the All Clear. On the way they had to walk carefully to avoid treading on red-hot pieces of shrapnel from exploding ack-ack shells. Earlier in the evening, there had been a light drizzle, and as the temperature was now several degrees below zero, a thin film of ice had formed on the pavements making the trek up Highgate Hill on foot extremely perilous. This was the height of the Blitz and the busy main road was now quite still, and even though there were ambulances constantly entering and leaving the Whittington Hospital on the other side of the road, Peggy and Leo were far too preoccupied with each other to notice them.

When they eventually reached the gate of number 49A, Peggy felt quite sad to take her leave of Leo, for on the journey home, he had put his arm around her waist in an attempt to keep her warm.

'Can't thank you enough, Leo,' she said, once they had come to a halt.

'Fank me? Wot for?'

'For helping me get through tonight. I couldn't have done it without you.'

It was too dark for her to see that he was grinning again. 'Don't yer believe it!' he replied. 'Yer've got fings inside yer that yer don't know about. We all 'ave. Fing is, we don't know about 'em till we're up against it.'

Peggy was radiating warmth towards him. 'Good night, Leo,' she whispered, leaning towards him, and gently kissing him on his cheek.

Leo had no time to reciprocate, for she turned, opened the garden gate, and disappeared up the steps to the front door of the house.

' 'Night – Duchess,' he called, knowing that she would not have heard him. He waited there for a moment, and once he'd heard the front door open and close, he gently placed his fingertips to the spot on his cheek where Peggy had just kissed him. It was still moist, so he transferred some of it to his lips, and kissed his fingers. Then he turned up his duffel coat collar and made his way back slowly down the hill.

He was unaware that Robert Thornton was watching him from behind the blackout curtains of an upstairs window of the house.

Chapter 4

Pam Warner was, in Marge Quincey's words, 'as pretty as a picture'. Her main attributes were her lovely large blue eyes, natural blonde hair, and a honey-milk complexion that emphasised the full-moon shape of her face, which had the most appealing dimple right in the middle of her chin. She also had well-formed breasts and a small, delicate mole near the right side of her mouth, which she had darkened black with an eye-pencil, a fashion which seemed to have been set by Margaret Lockwood when she appeared in an Alfred Hitchcock thriller film called *The Lady Vanishes* just before the war. Although she was just five feet five inches tall, every dress she wore, no matter how simple, seemed to highlight her trim little figure, so much so that young Horace Quincey thought she was a real 'smasher', which had cost him many a clip round the ear from his big brother, Leo, for suggesting that if only he was a few years older, he himself would be only too ready to take her off for a good time in the back row of the Savoy Cinema. His dad, Reg Quincey, also fancied the girl, but when she was around he tried to give the impression that he was a responsible parent, whilst doing his best to conceal that he was quite obviously consumed with lust.

Leo and Pam had now been walking out for about six months. When they first met, at a chance meeting in the Caledonian Road market, Leo had felt so hot for her that all he could think about was how soon he would be able to bed her. That opportunity had come within a month, when Pam's mum, dad, and younger sister had gone away for the weekend to visit some relations in Canvey Island, leaving the third-floor council flat free for just the kind of romp the couple were looking for. But after the initial attraction, Leo was quite irritated to discover that Pam possessed not only a desirable body, but also a mind of her own.

'Well, I know wot *I* fink,' said Pam, who, by her very presence, couldn't help being the centre of attention at the Quinceys' Sunday tea table. 'I fink Churchill should get the Yanks in. We shouldn't 'ave ter fight this war on our own.'

'Well, there ain't much chance er that!' said Reg, after gulping down a mouthful of tea. 'Roosevelt ain't goin' ter get 'is lot ter go ter war just ter 'elp *us* out.'

'I agree wiv Pam,' said Marge Quincey, slicing bread to go with the cockles, cold Spam, and hot boiled potatoes. 'We need all the 'elp we can get to end this war. The Yanks wouldn't like it if Jerry was sittin' right on *their* doorstep.' She suddenly slapped Eddie's hand when he tried to nick the first slice of bread. 'Manners!' she growled. 'Ladies first!'

Reluctantly, Eddie withdrew his hand, and, with a gracious smile at him, Pam helped herself to a slice of bread.

'All I can tell yer,' continued Pam, toying with a bit of lettuce on her plate without ever actually putting it into her mouth, 'is that the girls in the hairdressers where I work say that once the Yanks get over 'ere, they'd welcome 'em wiv open arms.'

'I bet!' mumbled Leo, who had made himself a Spam sandwich, which he was eating whilst smoking a fag.

His mum gave him a disapproving glare.

Pam continued to talk whilst nibbling her piece of bread. 'Ter my way er finkin',' she said in a tiny but firm voice, 'if women 'ad their way, we could change the 'ole direction of this war.'

Reg, who was in his late forties, and, apart from thinning fine hair, looked like a twin of his eldest son, hesitated before piling a spoonful of cockles into his mouth. ' 'Ow come?' he asked, eyeing her in disbelief.

'We'd go over ter 'Itler and tell 'im that there's no way 'e can conquer the world an' get away wiv it.'

Reg nearly choked on the mouthful of cockles he was chewing. 'I fawt we'd already bin down that road wiv Chamberlain?'

Pam bridled. 'Chamberlain was a silly ol' fool!' she said assertively. ' 'E deserved ter be kicked out. Mind you, Churchill's not much better.'

'Oh?' said Reg, who, until riled, was mostly a mild-mannered man. 'Wot makes yer say that, Pam?'

'Well, it stands ter reason, don't it?' she said, putting down her knife and fork. 'Look at the mess we're in – bombed night after night, everybody gettin' ready fer an invasion, and wot does Churchill do? Smoke cigars all day. All wind an' no fire, that one. If yer ask me, 'is bark's worse than 'is bite.'

'Yeah, but yer ain't seen 'im bite yet, Pam,' replied Reg, with a wink. ' 'E's a tough ol' geezer. Real British bulldog. When I get my call-up papers, I'll be proud ter serve 'im.'

Pam smiled weakly, not at Reg, but at the lettuce on her plate she was still toying with.

'Well, yer're not goin' ter get yer call-up papers!' snapped Marge, glaring at him from the opposite end of the table. 'I'm not 'avin both my 'usband an' my son leavin' me be'ind ter cope on me own wiv *this* pair.'

Horace and Eddie munched their cockles, completely oblivious of their mum's disparaging remarks about them.

'Don't be stupid, woman!' countered Reg, wiping his mouth with the back of his hand, and searching for a dog-end behind his ear. 'I'm nearly forty-eight years old, an' I can be called up any time. So yer'll 'ave ter lump it.'

'Finished, Pam dear?' asked Marge, ignoring what her husband had said.

'Oh yes,' replied Pam, who had already put down her knife and fork. 'I'm blown out.'

'Then why don't you an' Leo go an' settle down in the front room?' beamed Marge. 'It's nice an' cosy in there. I've lit yer a nice fire. We shan't disturb yer. I'm sure you two've got a 'ole lot ter talk over.'

Pam smiled coyly at Leo. But he merely sighed, and stared at his plate.

The front room was indeed cosy. One of the advantages of living above a coal merchant's office was that, despite the fact that there was a nationwide shortage of fuel, there were always a few bags of coal available to the tenants who lived above the office. But the room itself, like the kitchen parlour where most of the meals were taken, had all the warmth and comfort of a well-loved working-class home. The furniture, although all second-hand and bought long before the war, was kept in pristine condition. Even the backs of the sofa and chairs of the velour three-piece suite, which had shown signs of fraying, had been neatly covered by crochet squares designed and made by Marge on wooden frames knocked up for her by Reg. Sadly, because the building was built with little available money for the coal merchant's office, the upstairs windows were rectangular and quite ugly, but even they were made to look more friendly by Marge's floral-patterned hand-made curtains, which helped to disguise the sombre blackout blinds behind them, and in this room there was always a huge china pot on a table in front of the window which contained a vast sprawling plant which Horace always referred to as 'the man-eater'. The front room may not have been a showpiece, but it was certainly part of a home, in fact the perfect place for a young couple like Leo and Pam to do what Marge wanted them to do, and that was their 'courting'.

'Don't see much er yer these days,' said Pam, nestling down alongside Leo on the sofa. 'Not since we went out ter the pictures on me birfday.'

Leo, arms crossed, leaned his head back on one of his mum's crocheted squares, and stared up idly at the faded white ceiling. He felt restless without actually knowing why. 'Bin quite busy at work,' was all he could say. 'We lost a coupla more buses in the raid down Moorgate way. We've got ter get them back on the road as soon as possible.'

'Yer don't 'ave ter explain ter me, Leo,' she said, taking hold of his arm and pulling it over her shoulders. 'I just wanted yer ter know that I've missed yer, that's all.' She turned herself towards him as far as she could, and snuggled up.

Leo knew she was trying to get him to look at her in that special way that he had done before when they had slept together in her own bed at home. But he just couldn't do it.

Pam decided to take the initiative. She raised herself up, closed her eyes, and kissed him full on the lips.

Leo's eyes remained wide open. He could smell the eau-de-Cologne his mum had bought her for her birthday. The kiss seemed to go on for ever. He wanted it to end, but as soon as it did, he felt guilty. So he quickly pulled her back again, and kissed her with force rather than passion.

When she came up for breath, Pam was taken aback by the intensity of his response. 'Yer're a dark one, you are, Leo Quincey,' she panted.

'Wos that s'pposed ter mean?'

She gently licked her own lips. She could taste him. 'It means, yer've got 'idden depths,' she said seductively.

This irritated Leo; it sounded too much like the woman talking in the romantic picture he'd taken Pam to. He gently eased her away, took a dog-end from behind his ear, and quickly put it between his lips.

Far from being put off, Pam sat up with him at the same time. Then she kicked off her shoes, and pulled her feet up so that she was facing him, with one leg folded beneath the other. 'Yer mum's a sensible woman,' she said. 'If yer ask me, she's a bit of a psychic. She *knows* 'ow we feel about each uvver.'

Leo turned to look at her. ' 'Ow *do* we feel about each uvver, Pam?' he asked, the unlit dog-end drooping from his lips.

Pam smiled at him. 'Well, we've bin tergevver now fer six munfs,' she said. 'It must mean *somefin'*.' She buried her head in his chest.

Leo thought about this. He thought about all the times he'd been with her since they'd first met. He thought about what it was that attracted him to her, and how many times he'd wondered whether she was the girl he wanted to spend the rest of his life with. He wondered why he wasn't able to see clearly, to start settling down to the kind of relationship that his mum craved so much for him. As he glanced down at Pam's head, her face pressed against his chest, he had so many questions buzzing through his brain, so many doubts and illusions. She was a girl he liked a lot – down-to-earth, sexy and with all the right ideas to make a go of it. And yet, the more he looked at her, try as he may he just couldn't see who he really *wanted* to see.

'Takes longer than six munfs ter get ter know someone,' he eventually said bravely.

Pam looked up with a start to find him lighting his dog-end. 'Takes a lifetime,' she replied quickly. 'But yer 'ave ter start somewhere – don't yer?'

Leo hesitated a moment, then smiled affectionately at her. ' 'Course,' he replied, leaning forward to give her another kiss. Unfortunately, even whilst his lips were pressed against hers, he felt nothing, absolutely nothing.

* * *

The number 14 bus was full. It had been like that ever since it left Kensington High Street, where hordes of passengers had embarked after a morning's Christmas shopping. On the lower deck, the maximum number of people allowed to stand was making it a hard job for Peggy to collect all the fares, and her task wasn't helped by a party of rowdy adolescents who seemed hellbent on not only making as much noise as possible, but also on obstructing her progress through the bus. To make matters worse, during her busiest period between Knightsbridge and Tottenham Court Road, her ticket punch had jammed, and it took all her ingenuity to clear it with the use of a sharp-pointed pencil. Nor was she prepared for the unexpected appearance of the passenger who got on board in Shaftesbury Avenue.

'Peggy – my dear! How lovely to see you.'

Betty Desmond was one of the last people Peggy expected to see on her bus. It wasn't that she felt ashamed to be recognised, but somehow she had never considered the possibility that her mother's friends found it necessary to use public transport during wartime, just like anyone else.

'Hello, Mrs Desmond,' Peggy said, as she tried to regulate the queue of people crowding on board. 'See you in a minute!' However, it wasn't until the bus had alighted a good number of its passengers at King's Cross that Peggy was able to have a few words with her. 'Nice to see you again,' she said. 'Have you been shopping too?'

Betty, who had eventually found a seat at the back of the bus on the top deck, was already on her second cigarette. 'Not exactly, dear,' she said. 'I've just come from a funeral.'

Only then did Peggy realise how smart Betty was looking, dressed in a long black fur coat, with matching fur hat. 'Oh – I'm so sorry,' she said. 'Is it anyone I'd know?'

Betty shook her head, and pushed her metal-rimmed spectacles gently back on to her nose. She wasn't a particularly attractive woman, but her elongated face, thick red lipstick, and well-powdered cheeks gave her a certain style which was very different to the homespun tweed suit, red jumper, felt hat and overcoat she wore in the WVS. 'Jackie Hailswood,' she said, without her usual jokey delivery with which Peggy always associated her. 'She was an old friend of mine. We used to go to the same school in Hampstead. We even joined up for the WVS together.' She paused a moment, then took a quick deep puff of her cigarette. 'She was killed on duty last week. A parachute land mine in a street near the Angel. She was handing out tea to some of the fire service boys. Blown to pieces – eight of them. She's left a wonderful husband and three teenage daughters.'

Peggy felt the blood drain from her. 'Oh God,' she replied. 'How absolutely awful.'

Betty shrugged her shoulders. 'All part of the job, I suppose,' she said, trying to put the best face on it. 'Life has to go on.' She suddenly took hold of Peggy's hand, squeezed it affectionately, and smiled up at her. 'What about your mother and father? They must be very proud of you doing this job?'

Peggy raised her eyebrows. 'Not exactly, I'm afraid,' she replied caustically. 'A daughter in uniform – any kind of uniform – is a little too undignified for them.'

'Balderdash!' growled Betty, summoning up her spirits again. 'Somebody's got to take over from the men, otherwise everything is going to come to a grinding halt. And in any case, what you're doing is far better than slogging it out in that dreary old Stevens office. I only wish to God you could persuade your mother to do something as useful.'

Peggy leaned forward, and lowered her voice. 'That's

something I could never do,' she said, suddenly intense. 'But *you* could.'

Betty did a double take. '*Me?*'

Before Peggy could continue what she wanted to say, the bus pulled up at a stop, and she had to wait for one passenger to get off, and another to get on. But once she had pushed the driver's call button, and the bus had moved off again, she came back to rejoin Betty. 'Mrs Desmond,' she said, with some urgency, 'something's happened at home, between my parents, and I'm not quite sure what to do about it. The one thing I do know, however, is that my mother has got to get out of that house and do something positive. She's spent so much of her life seeing my father off to work in the mornings and waiting for him to come home at night that she's forgotten what life is like in the outside world.' Before continuing, she briefly glanced around the passengers to check that no one was listening to her. 'I know we talked about this the other day, but I think you should have another go at asking her to volunteer for the WVS.'

'Peggy!' gasped Betty, astonished.

'Yes, I know it's a lot to ask,' she said, 'but . . .' She was distracted for a moment by the passenger who had just got on and was now taking his seat nearby, and once she had collected his fare, she went straight back to Betty. 'Look, Mrs Desmond,' she said, kneeling on the spare seat at the side of her, 'I don't know why you and my mother have stopped seeing each other, but I happen to know that if there is one person in the world she can trust, if there is one person who could knock some sense into her, it's you.'

Betty was shaking her head.

'Believe me, you can, Mrs Desmond!' insisted Peggy. 'Whatever you may think, Mother still regards you as the best friend she's ever had.'

Betty was still shaking her head. 'No, Peggy,' she said,

87

taking a deep puff of her cigarette, and then stubbing it out with her heel on the floor. 'You're wrong. I'm afraid you don't know just *how* wrong. What has happened between us is too deep. She could never forgive me, and if I were in her position, I would feel the same.'

'Forgive you?' asked Peggy, now alarmed rather than just intrigued. 'Forgive you for what?'

Betty slowly looked up at her. 'Don't ask me, my dear,' she said with immense difficulty. 'Promise me that you'll *never* ask.'

Robert Thornton left his court in Highbury shortly after four. As a stipendiary magistrate on a regular wage, he was on duty each day from Monday to Friday, and owing to the emergency powers imposed by the Government at the start of the war, for most of the time he was obliged to sit on the bench alone without the participation of any fellow magistrates. This, however, was no hardship for someone like Major Thornton, for during his term of military service in the army during the previous war, he had loathed the experience of serving at general courts martial on active duty, where men were sentenced by a panel of three or more senior officers, especially when so many of the offenders were guilty of little more than sleeping or being drunk when on sentry duty, or being involved in scuffles with any of their fellow soldiers. 'Judgment by committee', was his opinion at the time, and he never liked it. As far as he was concerned, his own decision was the one that really counted. But he was not without ambition, and was always letting it be known to people like Edwin Stevens that by the time the war had come to an end, he would be moving into a far more influential position on the judiciary.

Outside the court building, Thornton climbed into a taxi which was waiting for him, and asked the driver to take him to Clerkenwell Road. A taxi was one of the last few perks left available for a man in his position, for there was an acute petrol shortage, which meant that most private cars had disappeared from the roads, leaving public transport as the only means of getting around. Along the route, blackout curtains were drawn everywhere, but there were still plenty of people on the streets, struggling with hand torches to get around in the dark. Despite the regular threat of an air raid at this hour, the shops in Upper Street were quite busy, for Christmas was only three weeks away, and everyone was scrabbling around, desperate to find something to buy before the wartime shortages got any worse.

Thornton had a lot on his mind. His wife, Catherine, his daughter, Peggy – what had happened to them both? Why were they treating him as though he was some kind of monster? Hadn't he always tried to give them everything they ever wanted? They had money, position, a good home – what more did they want? Whatever Catherine thought about him, she was wrong. He was just as devoted a husband now as he had ever been, and he had no intention of changing – not unless, unless . . . He briefly took off his bowler hat, and gently stroked his forehead with gloved fingers. He had a headache with the worry; all this domestic complexity was getting him down. And as for Peggy . . . Who was this man who brought her home the other night? It was bad enough that she had humiliated him, her own father, by getting a job on the buses, but getting herself involved with someone, someone like whoever it was he saw her with that night – that was not only deceitful, it was despicable. None the less, his mind was made up. Despite his daughter's ingratitude, he would *not* turn his back on her, he would *not* allow her to ruin her life – war or no war.

The taxi came to a halt outside a rather smart-looking

block of flats, and once he'd paid the fare, Thornton made his way to the front entrance hall, where he took a lift up to the third floor. As he walked along the corridor, there were different smells of cooking, the strong odour of disinfectant, and the sound of small children playing and yelling at each other. Thornton stopped at flat number 307, which was approximately halfway down the corridor. He checked either side of him to make sure no one could see him. Then he knocked.

The door was opened almost immediately. Standing there was an attractive woman in her forties, smartly dressed in a brown woollen dress. She looked taken aback.

'I have something I want you to do for me,' Thornton said curtly.

The woman opened the door further to let him enter. Then she nervously checked the corridor, went back inside, and closed the door behind them.

Leo Quincey woke up early to find that his two young brothers had already left for their school lessons at a neighbour's house. Their actual school had been closed since a few days after the outbreak of war, and as most of the pupils had been evacuated, one or two of the teachers had volunteered to provide some of the basic lessons for those children whose parents had decided to keep their kids with them. Fortunately, this was one of the rare mornings that Leo didn't hear Ace and Eddie leave. Usually, the moment they came up from the back yard air-raid shelter, all thought of a lie-in was out of the question, for their arrival invariably meant a battle-to-the-death pillow fight. However, although Leo was on split-turn shift and didn't have to be at work until twelve noon, the fact that there had been no air raid overnight to exhaust him resulted in his waking up automatically at the same time that his brothers descended on him each morning.

When Leo came downstairs for breakfast in the first-floor parlour, Marge was out in the scullery doing the washing. The place was full of steam from the bucket of water which was boiling on the gas stove, and sweat was pouring down Marge's face as she toiled with a pair of Reg's trousers on the scrubbing board at the aluminium bath on the well-worn scullery table.

'Yer bread's under the grill,' she said, wringing out the trousers. 'Yer'll 'ave ter turn it on. Ain't got no marge till termorrer, though. Tea's still 'ot if yer want some.'

' 'Ere, let me give yer an 'and,' said Leo, taking the pair of trousers from his mum and helping her to wheel them through the mangle.

'Wot time yer due at work then?'

Before answering his mum's question, Leo waited until his father's trousers had been drained of water through the rollers. 'Split turn,' he said. 'Don't 'ave ter get in till twelve.'

' 'Ow yer gettin' there?'

Leo was puzzled by her question. She, probably more than anyone else in the house, knew his work routine. Since Reg only ever earned a pittance from his bricklaying job, Leo was, after all, the principal wage earner in the family. 'No idea,' he said curiously. 'The 609, 611 – whatever bus comes first. Why?'

'No reason.' Marge took the trousers, folded them, and put them on top of the pile of the other washing waiting to be hung up on the overhead drying rack in the back parlour. 'Not goin' up on the 14 then?' she asked casually, whilst drying her hands on a towel.

Leo spun her a look. Now he was really puzzled. 'The 14?' he asked querulously. 'The 14 bus don't go up 'Olloway Road, yer know that. Wos this all about?'

Marge gave him an equally puzzled look. 'I was only

wonderin', that's all – knowin' 'ow much yer like travellin' on that route.'

Leo froze.

Marge calmly lit the grill to toast the two slices of bread that were waiting there. Leo went to her, but before he could say anything, she asked, 'Who's this gel then?'

'Mum—' said Leo, trying to object.

'I'm only askin'.'

Leo sighed. 'Look,' he said, beginning to lose his patience, 'I don't know wot yer've bin 'earin', or who yer've bin 'earin' it from, but it's no one's business but me own. Right?'

Marge kept her eyes on the toast under the grill. 'Wot about Pam? I fawt yer was keen on 'er?'

Leo, agitated, ran his fingers through his curly hair. 'Pam's a nice gel, Ma—' he said.

Marge didn't allow him to finish. 'So why bovver wiv someone else?' she asked, careful not to raise her voice to match his.

' 'Cos I *want* to, Ma!' he snapped. ' 'Cos I've got every right ter go out wiv whoever I please!'

'Even if they ain't one er yer own kind?'

Once again Leo was frustrated from replying to her immediately, for she had to deal with the toast, which was beginning to smoke. So he waited for her to take the two slices out from beneath the grill, and put them on to a plate. 'Mum—' he said, trying to reason with her. But she eased past him and took the plate of toast into the kitchen. Before following her, he tried to take control of himself. This was not the first time he had had this type of exchange with his mum. Ever since he was a kid she had been the dominant force in the family, and even though his dad had a bit of a temper, his mum nearly always got her own way, quietly, sometimes hardly noticeably, but always her own way. 'Wot *is* me own kind, Mum?' he asked, with restraint, as he followed her into the parlour.

Marge was at the breakfast table, pouring two cups of tea. 'Tea's not all that 'ot,' she said, feeling the teapot beneath the cosy, and ignoring his question, 'but it's drinkable.'

'Wot *is* me own kind, Mum?' Leo repeated.

Marge put down the teapot, and looked at him. But she had that sickly, righteous smile on her face which always told Leo that he was about to receive some of her self-styled wisdom. 'Yer own kind, son,' she began calmly, 'is someone who shares the type er life yer've bin brought up into, someone who's prepared ter get down on 'ands an' knees an' work fer a livin'. Someone like your Pam.'

Leo sighed, and sat down at his place at the table. 'Pam don't belong ter me, Mum,' he said. 'She's a friend, just a good friend. We ain't a couple. We've never bin a couple.'

Marge sat opposite him. 'Believe me, son,' she replied, trying to engage him in a smile, 'that's gel's a gem, a real gem. She's one of us – one in a million.'

Leo stared down despondently at the plate of toast in front of him, then slowly looked up. 'Some day she'll make someone very 'appy,' he replied. 'But not me, Mum. D'yer understand wot I'm sayin'? Not me.'

Marge's face stiffened. Her eyes flicked away, and when they looked back at him they had lost any sign of warmth. 'Then *who*, son?' she asked tersely. 'Wot woman in this world is goin' ter make *you* 'appy?'

Leo hesitated. 'I dunno, Mum,' he returned awkwardly. 'I'm only eighteen years old. In a coupla munfs' time I'll be in the army; I'll be out in some front line, not knowin' if I'll ever get back ter civvy street again. So 'ow can I know, 'ow can I possibly know who's out there waitin' who I want ter spend the rest er me life wiv?'

Marge realised that her whole body was taut so she tried

to unwind by taking a sip of lukewarm tea. 'Yer'll 'ave ter sooner or later, yer know,' she said. 'Yer won't be in the army fer ever. Yer'll 'ave ter find *someone* ter settle down wiv.'

Leo's eyes were lowered again. 'Don't push me, Mum,' he said calmly but firmly. 'If I'm old enuff ter fight, I'm old enuff ter make me own decisions.'

'Of course, son,' replied Marge, sitting back in her chair, eyeing him carefully over her cup of tea. 'You do wot yer want wiv yer life. It's every person's right. An' don't yer worry about me an' yer dad. We'll back yer. Wotever yer do, we'll back yer ter the 'ilt. That is, of course, as long as yer don't make a fool er yerself.'

Peggy was helping Mrs Bailey to prepare the table for dinner. The old retainer had cooked a pot roast of ham with onions, carrots and parsnips, and, despite the cold evening outside, the Thorntons' kitchen was stifling with heat from the busy gas cooker.

'I 'ope yer mum feels like eatin' somefin' ternight,' said Lil Bailey, busy mashing potatoes at the stove. 'I 'ad ter practically go down on bended knees ter get this bit er 'am from me butcher. 'E only let me 'ave it 'cos 'e fancies me!'

Peggy laughed. Mrs Bailey was the one ray of light in the house. Nothing and no one could ever dampen *her* spirits. 'Oh, I'm sure she won't be able to resist this, Mrs B,' Peggy assured her. 'I should think the smell of cloves alone must be driving her mad. She loves them.'

'Yes, well, you tell 'er from me, if that air-raid siren goes before she comes down ter dinner, she's ter take that pot roast ter the shelter wiv 'er. I don't want 'er wastin' away when there's good food around.'

A few minutes later, Mrs Bailey went off to catch her bus. Fortunately, there had been no air raids at all for the last few nights, mainly because there had been extensive cloud cover over the whole of London, which under normal circumstances was depressing for it brought either freezing winter drizzle or even snow showers, but anything that could thwart another night of carnage was received with relief and gratitude by Londoners.

Peggy decided to go upstairs and see if her mother was ready to come down to dinner. Although it was an elegant house, Peggy always felt that it had no heart. For a start, it was far too dark and dismal, due mainly to the fact that, for some weird reason, her father preferred dim lighting throughout. Even the wallpaper above the narrow staircase was brown, with dark stained woodwork, and over the years Peggy had often felt the urge to take a brush to the whole place and paint it white.

On the way upstairs she thought about what Mrs Bailey had said. It was certainly true that, of late, Catherine Thornton had shown very little interest in food, and this could only be because she was unhappy. And yet, after the way the poor woman's husband had been playing fast and loose with her, it seemed understandable that Catherine had lost her appetite for not only food, but also life itself. By the time Peggy had reached the first-floor landing, she had decided that she could no longer be indifferent to her mother's dilemma. From now on, she was going to help her mother to do as she herself had done: stand up and defy the man who had dominated their lives for far too long.

'Mother?' she called, tapping gently on Catherine's door. 'Are you ready for dinner?'

'Come in, darling!'

Peggy went in, and was a little surprised but delighted to see her mother sitting at her dressing table applying her make-up.

'Two minutes, and I'll be with you,' said Catherine, who

had not only put on her favourite simple black cocktail dress, diamond brooch and earrings, but was also applying more lipstick than Peggy had ever seen her use before.

'There!' she said brightly, with a huge beaming smile. Then she got up from her stool, and proudly showed how good she looked.

Peggy was completely taken aback by the transformation. She hadn't seen her mother look so good for years. 'You – you look wonderful.'

Catherine, still smiling, came across to her. 'Well, don't look so surprised, darling,' she said, pecking Peggy gently on her cheek. 'I know I'm your mother, but I'm not ready for senility just yet!'

Peggy watched in astonishment as Catherine went back to the dressing table, and checked her lipstick with one finger. 'Isn't this a lovely brooch?' she asked, turning back towards Peggy to show off the elephant-shaped diamond brooch pinned to the lapel of her dress. 'Your father gave me this when he came back from a trip to Ceylon soon after the last war. Whenever we went out, he always loved me to wear it.' She turned again to look at it in the mirror.

'It's lovely,' said Peggy, still unable to take in why her mother had perked up so much. 'But – why? Is anyone coming to dinner?'

'Yes,' replied Catherine. 'Your father.' She picked up an expensive-looking ring from the dressing table, and slipped it on to her forefinger. 'I haven't been very fair to him. He always liked me to look nice. I've let him down for far too long. But things are going to be different now.' She was looking at her reflection in the mirror, as though she was talking to her husband rather than her daughter. 'From now on, Robert will have a wife he can be proud of.'

Chapter 5

By December, the Luftwaffe air raids had become few and far between. For the citizens of London, it came as a welcome relief after the intensity of the nightly attacks, which had been going on virtually nonstop from September to November. No one quite knew why they were being given such a respite, except that the weather for the past few weeks had been fairly foggy. It was therefore no surprise that in the build-up to Christmas, shops everywhere were increasingly busy, with everyone scrabbling around to find anything they could, because unofficial rationing seemed to have started already by the very fact that most things were too expensive to buy.

Holloway Bus Depot was in the grip of Christmas fever, for there were seasonal decorations draped everywhere, the staff canteen, the recreation room, the administration offices, the conductors' room, and even in the vast parking and maintenance area. There were rumours that, despite the shortage of meat, for those on Christmas Eve and Boxing Day shift work, the canteen would be serving roast turkey and Christmas pudding, one of the few remaining luxuries during these increasingly austere times. None the less, the party spirit was in full swing, with plenty of after-work get-togethers in the Holloway Tavern, the local pub. Peggy got her first glimpse of what the inside of a pub was like when, one evening during the second week in December, Leo took her there to have a drink with him and some of his mates. She found it an unnerving experience, and felt totally out of her depth. It didn't help that some of the bus crews were still calling her 'Duchess', and seemed amused every time she opened her mouth to say something. Leo tried to convince her that being teased by a bunch of blokes was their way of accepting her, and that she should just take it as all good fun. But Peggy's hackles rose.

'How would you feel if you were being "teased" by a crowd of drunken girls?' she asked cuttingly.

Leo broke into another of his broad grins. 'Depends wot they looked like!' he replied.

Peggy was not amused. There was still a great reserve of Highgate Hill embedded within her. She also found it difficult to cope with everyone drinking beer. In the world she had moved in, people either drank wine or spirits, and on special occasions champagne. But then she felt a great deal of remorse that she'd made the comparison when she remembered that it wouldn't be long before most of the men in the pub that night would be eligible for call-up. It was a depressing thought. Even so, she now realised that mixing with people from such different backgrounds from her own was not easy, and she couldn't help wondering if she had made the right decision. Was her father right? Was the gulf between 'them and us' insurmountable?

'Not such a good idea after all, was it, mate?'

Peggy looked up with a start from her shandy to find that Leo had turned his back on the crowd they were with and was standing close to her. 'Oh – no – I mean yes,' she replied falteringly. 'Actually it's not bad at all. What did you say was in it? Beer and lemonade?'

Leo smiled. 'I wasn't talkin' about the drink,' he said, putting his arm protectively round her shoulders. 'I meant bringin' yer ter a place like this.'

She smiled back at him. 'I'm sorry, Leo,' she said guiltily. 'Am I giving you a hard time?'

Leo shook his head. 'I just don't want yer ter feel out er place,' he said. 'I won't 'ave anyone 'urt you.' He leaned forward, and gave her a light kiss on the lips.

There were immediate jeers from the crowd.

Peggy was taken by surprise. She blushed at the idea of being kissed, no matter how lightly, in front of so many people. 'Could we find somewhere to sit down?' she asked. 'My feet are killing me.'

Leo looked around. The pub was packed to suffocation, but he spied a spare bench seat at a table in a corner on the other side of the bar. Putting his arm around her waist, he gently led Peggy through the crowd, but by the time they had got there, a girl had already been pushed on to the end of the bench by her soldier boyfriend. However, there was just enough room left for Leo and Peggy, so they squeezed up close together.

Peggy stiffened when Leo again put his arm around her shoulders. 'Don't you ever get embarrassed?' she asked.

Leo leaned towards her. 'Embarrassed?' he asked. 'Wot about?'

Peggy was fumbling for words. 'Well – what you did back there . . . in front of all those people . . .'

Leo was puzzled. 'Why should I be embarrassed just 'cos I give yer a bit a kiss. They're my mates. Wot's it ter them?'

Peggy shrugged.

He moved as close to her as he could. 'I'm sorry if I upset yer, Peggs,' he said, directly into her ear. But there was a great deal of laughing and shouting going on over at the bar, which meant that he had to raise his voice more than he wanted. 'I just couldn't resist it, that's all.'

The girl next to him smirked at her soldier boyfriend, who immediately pulled her towards him, jealous that she was paying more attention to Leo than to himself.

'I want ter see more of yer, Peggs,' continued Leo. 'I don't just mean 'ere an' now, I mean – I want ter see more of yer.'

Peggy suddenly noticed that the elderly man and woman sitting opposite them were straining to hear everything that Leo was saying. Embarrassed, she swung around on the bench so that her back was turned towards them. 'I don't know what you see in someone like me,' she said.

Leo's back was also now turned on the old couple. For a brief moment, he just looked at Peggy. 'We're not really so diff'rent, yer know,' he said, trying to make himself heard against the background roars of laughter coming from various groups of well-oiled customers. 'D'yer know wot me gran used ter say?'

Peggy shook her head.

'She used ter say that the only diff'rence between the top er the 'ouse an' the bottom was the floors between.'

Peggy smiled. 'What about all the stairs you have to climb?'

'Reckon I could cope wiv that,' replied Leo, 'as long as I don't smoke *too* many fags.'

They shared a gentle laugh, then sipped their drinks. A great pall of smoke suddenly floated across at them from behind. When Peggy turned to look, the old man was puffing madly on his pipe, much to the amusement of his missus. Peggy gave them a wry smile, then strained to look through the haze of thick blue fag smoke that had engulfed the crowded bar, to where Leo's mates had started a game of darts. She was impressed, but at the same time despondent, to see how well the men were getting on with some of the clippies, who were clearly having a great time with them.

'D'you think they'll ever accept me like that?' she asked, turning back to Leo.

Leo took a quick look over his shoulder. 'Why?' he asked, turning back to her again.

'I just wish I could be like them, that's all.'

'Why?' asked Leo, puzzled. '*Why* d'yer wanna be like them? You're far better than all this lot put tergevver. You're *you*, an' yer shouldn't try ter be any uvver way.'

'Easier said than done,' said Peggy. 'When I'm with some of those girls back at the depot, there are times when I feel like I'm way out of my depth. They know so much about life. I know absolutely nothing.'

Leo was shaking his head. 'Yer know your trouble, don't yer, mate?' he said. 'Yer take yerself too serious. Wos it matter where yer come from? I like yer just the way yer are.'

'Try telling that to that lot,' said Peggy, with a nod across towards his mates, who were enjoying some horse-play with a balloon and some Christmas paper-chains that had come unstuck from the bar ceiling.

Leo gave them no more than a quick glance. 'Stop worryin', will yer?' he said reassuringly. 'They'll get used ter yer sooner or later.'

'Perhaps,' replied Peggy. 'But how soon will I get used to *them*?'

'Hello, Peggy dear.'

Both Peggy and Leo turned with a start to find a middle-aged woman standing directly in front of them. She looked neat rather than smart, in a blue knee-length topcoat, which had a stylish hood lined with grey wool.

'Irene!' Peggy immediately got up and threw her arms around her. 'Leo, this is Irene. We used to work together. Irene, this is Leo – Leo Quincey.'

Irene offered him her hand and a generous smile. 'Irene West,' she said, pulling back her hood with the other hand.

Leo looked a bit baffled, but shook her hand vigorously.

'Pleased ter meet yer,' he replied with gusto.

'What are you doing here?' yelled Peggy above the deafening sound of the rowdy high spirits coming from the pre-Christmas revellers on the other side of the bar.

Irene shrugged. She couldn't hear a word Peggy was saying. To make matters worse, one of the regulars, an elderly man, who was himself half cut, starting thumping on the upright piano. From then on, the whole place erupted into the start of what was clearly going to be a series of singsongs.

'Why don't you two gels move inter the private?' yelled Leo, having to compete with a thunderous version of 'She'll Be Coming Round the Mountains'. 'Yer'll be able ter talk in there!'

Peggy nodded in agreement, then allowed Leo to lead her and Irene through the rowdy customers into the adjoining private bar. 'I'll bring some drinks,' called Leo as they went. 'Wot'll it be, 'Rene?'

'Oh, anything,' called Irene, straining to be heard. 'A medium sherry?'

Fortunately, the private bar was not so full, and once the door to the saloon bar had closed behind them, they were at least able to hear themselves talk. Whilst Leo went straight to the counter to order the drinks, Peggy and Irene found a table for the three of them in a quiet alcove near the fireplace, above which was a large mirror on which the words, 'MERRY XMAS' had been stuck with cotton wool. And on one side of the counter was a tall Christmas tree, decorated with fairy lights, tinsel, and all the other seasonal paraphernalia which had clearly been brought out regularly at this time of the year since goodness knows when.

'How on earth did you know I was in here?' asked Peggy, the moment she and Irene had settled themselves at the table.

'I didn't,' replied Irene, trying to massage some life back into her cold hands in front of the log fire. 'It was the people up at the depot. They told me to try here. Clearly it's a popular place to unwind after work.'

Delighted to be in the company of her old office friend again, Peggy stretched across, and squeezed Irene's hand. 'I can't tell you how lovely it is to see you again, Irene,' she said affectionately. 'I've missed you.'

Irene returned the smile. 'I've missed you too,' she said. 'I've been up to try and find you several times over the past couple of weeks. I wanted to know how you're getting on. It just hasn't been the same without you, especially since we moved into the temporary office in Liverpool Road. Things are in such a mess. Nobody can find anything. It needs your touch.'

Peggy was puzzled. 'But wasn't Mr Stevens supposed to be getting in someone to replace me?'

'Oh yes,' replied Irene dismissively. 'An office clerk straight out of school. A sweet boy, but absolutely no idea of law whatsoever.' She delved into her handbag and brought out a packet of Craven A cigarettes. 'D'you mind?'

'Of course not,' replied Peggy, curious that she had never seen Irene smoke before.

'And what about you?' Irene asked, lighting her cigarette. 'How's life on the buses?'

Peggy shrugged. 'Ask me at the end of the war!' she joked.

Both chuckled.

'But really?' asked Irene.

Peggy shrugged again. 'At least it's different,' she replied caustically. Then she corrected herself. 'No, that's not quite true. In a strange kind of way, I'm enjoying it. It's just that mixing with some of the people I have to work with takes quite a bit of getting used to. They're pretty much set in their ways. They don't really take too easily to "gels" who come from – shall we say – another part of town.'

Irene smiled. 'There seem to be *some* advantages, though,' she added, casting a quick glance towards Leo, who was in the middle of a group of customers all struggling to get served at the counter. 'He's very good-looking.'

Peggy lowered her eyes shyly. 'Yes,' was all she was prepared to say.

'Is that all?' pressed Irene. 'Just – *yes*?'

'It's hard to tell,' replied Peggy, reluctantly. 'I've only known him for a few weeks. But he *is* different, I can't deny that. For some extraordinary reason he's really looking after me. He won't let anyone say anything unpleasant about me – not in my presence anyway. I tell you, Irene, if it wasn't for Leo, there's no way I could cope with working on the buses. I've never met anyone quite like that before. It makes me feel,' she shrugged, 'good.'

Irene took a quick look back at Leo over her shoulder, then returned to Peggy again. 'Does your father know?' she asked cautiously.

'Father?' replied Peggy, a bit taken aback by Irene's question. 'No. Why should he? It's none of his business. What makes you ask?'

'Oh – no reason,' said Irene, casually flicking the ash from her cigarette into a large glass ash tray.

The singsong in the saloon bar was getting more boisterous, and with the door between the two bars suddenly left open by someone passing through, the whole pub was beginning to reverberate to the sound of 'Nellie Dean'.

'Actually, he seems rather nice,' said Irene, once the offending door had been closed by the landlord. 'Leo, I mean. Where does he come from?'

'Holloway,' replied Peggy. 'Lives at home with his parents. He's got two young brothers.'

'Oh, really? How old is he?'

'Eighteen. Well – eighteen and a half.' Peggy's eyes fixed firmly on the flames crackling in the fireplace. She felt a little self-conscious talking about Leo. 'He's been deferred from call-up – just until his mother gets over an operation. He could go any day now.'

'Do you mind?'

When Peggy looked up, she found Irene staring at her. 'Do I mind that he's being called up?'

'No,' replied Irene. 'I mean, do you mind that's he's younger than you?'

Peggy was again taken aback by her friend's question. 'D'you know, it's never occurred to me,' she said with apparent surprise.

Irene seemed agitated, and rolled the cigarette between her fingers nervously. 'Some people might say that two years can make quite a difference,' she said.

Peggy was about to reply, when Leo returned with the drinks.

'Sorry about this, gels,' he said, balancing the three glasses in his hands until he landed them safely on the table. 'That guvnor's as pissed as a newt.' He raised his glass. 'Cheers!'

'Cheers,' said Peggy and Irene, both taking sips of their drinks.

Leo took a gulp from his pint of bitter and wiped the froth from his lips on the back of his hand. 'I must say, 'Rene,' he said, collecting the usual dog-end from behind his ear, 'it makes quite a change ter meet one er Peggs's mates. All she ever sees round 'ere are tin-'eads like me.'

By the way Irene was discreetly eyeing him over the top of her glass of sherry, she was clearly inquisitive about him.

'I'm sure you're no such thing, Leo,' she replied reassuringly. 'It must take an awful lot of mechanical skill to keep the buses in good condition.'

Peggy and Leo exchanged a brief, puzzled look. 'How did you know Leo is a mechanic?' Peggy asked her.

Irene swung her a startled look. 'Oh,' she replied cagily, 'they mentioned him in the office at the depot, when I went to ask where I could find you.'

'Ha!' said Leo, perfectly happy to accept her explanation. 'Din't know I was so famous!'

Peggy wasn't quite so sure. For some reason, she felt uneasy. 'Any more thoughts about going into the Land Army?' she asked.

For a moment Irene looked vacant. 'The Land Army? Oh – no. Not for the time being, anyway. I thought I'd wait until the firm has moved back to Upper Street, give old man Stevens time to find a replacement. By the way, he told me to wish you a Happy Christmas.'

Again Peggy was somewhat surprised. 'He knew you were coming to see me?'

This time Irene was not quite so cagey. 'I told him I was going to try to look you up before Christmas.'

Peggy smiled.

Irene felt a bit uncomfortable, especially as Leo seemed to have his eyes on her. 'Joe was asking about you the other day. He was home on a weekend pass.'

'Oh really?' said Peggy. 'How's his officer training going?'

Irene shrugged. 'God knows,' she replied, after taking more than a sip of her sherry. 'Mind you, by the sound of things they're trying to push all the cadet training through as fast as they can. I suppose with all the ships we've been losing in the Atlantic, they need all the conscripts they can get.'

' 'Ornsey Road!'

Both women turned with a start to find Leo staring directly at Irene.

'I'm sorry?' asked Irene, puzzled.

' 'Ornsey Road,' he repeated. 'That's where I saw yer the uvver day. I knew I'd seen yer somewhere before. You was walkin' up terwards the bridge.'

'Hornsey Road?' Irene asked, alarmed. 'Where's that?'

'I live down there,' replied Leo, confidently. 'I'm sure it was you I saw walkin' up terwards the—'

Equally confident, Irene answered firmly, 'I'm afraid you must be mistaken. I have no idea where Hornsey Road is.'

Irene turned with a faltering smile to look at Peggy, but Peggy's eyes avoided her. They were fixed determinedly on the table in front of her.

By the time Peggy got home that evening, she was too late to sit down to dinner with her parents, and so once she had been upstairs to her bedroom to change out of her uniform, she went straight to the sitting room to join them. When she got there she found her father in his usual chair by the fire, behind *The Times*, which he always read voraciously from cover to cover each day, and her mother sitting at a small card table which was covered with small pieces of china from the vase that had been a victim of the bomb blast some weeks before, and which she was now attempting to glue together.

'Mrs Bailey's left you some liver and onion casserole in the oven, dear,' said Catherine, as she greeted Peggy by accepting a peck on the cheek. 'It's a little tough, but the sauce is really quite delicious.'

'Thank you, Mother,' Peggy replied, casting a casual glance across at her father, who hadn't looked up from his newspaper. 'I'll eat a little later. I'm not too hungry.' She looked back at the skeleton of the vase her mother was working on, and saw that, despite the patchwork of small and large pieces stuck together, the shape was gradually building up. 'You're doing very well,' she said. 'I don't know how you have the patience.'

'As it was one of your father's wedding presents to me,' simpered Catherine, 'I'm not going to abandon it without a fight.'

Peggy was amazed how glamorous her mother was looking these days. For years, Catherine had seemed to let herself go, dressing only practically, without any real sense of pride in how she looked. But everything had now seemed to have changed, for there was hardly an evening when she hadn't come down to dinner looking immaculately groomed and dressed. It was as though she had worked it out in her mind that if her husband was seeing another woman, then she, Catherine, was responsible – responsible because she had allowed herself to become dowdy and unattractive, which was enough to make any husband lose interest. After more than twenty years of marriage, a man had a right to expect something more to come home to than someone who no longer cared about how she looked. Peggy knew only too well that this was what her mother was thinking, and she found it deeply disturbing.

She looked across to her father, who was still immersed in his newspaper. 'Are you going to listen to the nine o'clock news tonight, Father?' she asked.

'Possibly,' he replied, with only a cursory glance at her. 'Why?'

'If you don't mind, when it's finished, I'd like to listen to the *Postscript* programme.'

Thornton immediately returned to his newspaper. 'I think not,' was his only response.

'But someone at work was telling me that J. B. Priestley is a fascinating speaker,' she said. 'He's apparently a wonderful writer, and talks very perceptively about the war.'

'Thank you, young lady,' replied Thornton, glancing aimlessly at his newspaper. 'I'm well aware just how "perceptive" he is.'

Peggy looked to her mother for some kind of explanation, but she was clearly determined not to be drawn into the conversation. 'I don't know what you mean, Father,' she persisted.

Quietly exasperated, Thornton dropped the newspaper to his lap. 'What kind of political education did they give you at Highfield?' he asked, removing his reading spectacles. 'Did they never teach you anything about the radicals in society?'

Peggy had a blank expression. 'Radicals?'

'Priestley is a radical, a Bolshevik, a troublemaker,' replied Thornton, turning round in his chair to look at her. 'That fifteen minutes after the news each night is nothing more than spurious propaganda.'

'Everyone at work says he's a very nice man, very homely.'

Thornton was becoming quietly irritated with her. 'Homely?' he jibed, collecting the newspaper from his lap and throwing it on to the small table beside his armchair. 'And which of your knowledgeable new work colleagues informed you of *that* tantalising piece of information?'

Although Peggy was taken aback by his reaction, she was determined to speak her mind. 'Father,' she said, still standing alongside her mother, 'I'm not interested in politics. I never have been.'

'But you *are* prepared to listen to political propaganda?'

'I am prepared to listen to other people's opinions as well as my own. Surely that is everyone's democratic right.'

Catherine suddenly intervened. 'Peggy, my dear,' she said breathlessly, 'you'll be delighted to know that I have decided to do my bit for the war effort.'

Peggy didn't respond. Her eyes were still locked in conflict with her father's.

Catherine persisted. 'I've agreed to knit mittens and socks for the troops,' she said, rising from her chair, and sliding her arm affectionately around Peggy's waist. 'It appears there's a terrible shortage of such things. Something to do with all the supplies they had to abandon at Dunkirk, I imagine.'

'Catherine, my dear,' said Thornton, quietly assertive, 'would you be kind enough to allow me a few words alone with Margaret?'

Catherine was about to object, but he spoke again before she had the chance.

'Please.'

Catherine hesitated, then smiled weakly at Peggy. 'I'll go and see to your dinner,' she said. Then she turned and reluctantly left the room.

Once she had gone, Thornton said, 'Margaret, I think it's about time we talked one or two things over.' There was calm reasoning in his voice, and even a weak attempt at a smile. He got up from his chair, went to the window, folded his hands behind his back, and looked out. 'I want you to know that I don't like the distance that has grown between us,' he said, keeping his back turned towards her. 'It seems so utterly unnecessary.' He looked back at her. 'You're the only child I have, and I want us to be friends.'

Peggy had resisted the urge to sit at the table where her mother had been, choosing instead to stand and face him with arms crossed. 'I'd like us to be friends too, Father,' she said, without raising her voice. 'But I'm no longer a child. I need to follow a life of my own.'

'I quite agree,' replied Thornton, amiably. 'We can hardly expect you to remain a child for the rest of your life. But your mother and I still have the right to be concerned for your wellbeing.'

'I'm not sure I know what you mean.'

Thornton shrugged his shoulders. 'Making decisions.'

'My *own* decisions?'

'The *right* decisions,' replied Thornton, resisting the urge to raise the tension. He casually strolled back to the fireplace, and sought out his favourite pipe on the mantelpiece. Whilst he was doing so, his eyes fixed momentarily on a framed photograph of Peggy when she was a child at Highfield Girls' School. 'I've learned from experience that just one mistake can affect you for the rest of your life.' He turned from the photograph to look at her. 'I've made too many mistakes in my life, Margaret. I hope you won't do the same.'

'If I do,' replied Peggy, 'I'll have no one to blame but myself.'

'By then it could be too late.'

Peggy was becoming irritated. It was something she was prone to, without ever stopping to realise that it was a trait inherited from her father. 'Father,' she said, holding on to the back of her mother's chair, 'what is it you're trying to say to me?'

Thornton had found his tobacco pouch, and was filling his pipe. 'I'd like to know why you've decided to drift towards people who've never played a part in your life before.'

'Because I like them,' she replied quite effortlessly. 'Because they're just as much a part of this world as you and me.'

'They're a breed apart.'

'Perhaps. But I have a right to try to find out who and what they are,' persisted Peggy.

'Stuff and nonsense! How much do they know about you, or me, or your mother? How much do they know about learning how to better themselves, to educate themselves so that they can make something of their lives instead of drinking in their public houses every night, resenting anyone who has more money in their pocket than someone else?'

'And how much do *we* know about *them*, Father?' Peggy was in despair. She had heard him talk like this so many times before, and it made her feel aggressive. 'You, me, Mother – all the people we've ever mixed with in our lives – why do we keep them at arm's length? What have we to be afraid of? Why do we smile and say thank you very much for doing menial jobs for us, and then treat them with condescension as though they're only worth the fee we pay them? You call them a breed apart, well, maybe they are. But let me tell you something, Father. There's a war on, and if we're going to win it, we've *got* to get on with each other; we've got to make the effort – both them and us.' Worked up, she turned and made for the door.

'Well, you're certainly doing your bit,' Thornton called after her.

Peggy stopped dead, and turned to look back at him.

'Judging by the company I saw you with outside this house the other night,' said Thornton, calmly lighting his pipe, 'I'd say you're certainly doing your bit for this war.'

Peggy was stung. She'd heard some pretty nasty remarks from her father in her time, but this was the worst. She turned to leave, but he called again.

'Whoever he is,' he warned, 'I advise you to keep well away from him.'

Peggy refused to respond, and quickly left the room. In the hall outside, she paused to calm herself down. From the sitting room, she could hear the deep-throated sound of Big Ben, booming out the start of the nine o'clock news.

* * *

Reg Quincey wanted a cuddle. Ever since the start of the Blitz, his wife had been forced to leave their bedroom in order to sleep with the kids in the back yard air-raid shelter. It had been a frustrating time for him, and he was fed up with waiting. But there hadn't been a heavy air raid for almost two weeks, and now that he and Marge were able to sleep together again in their own bedroom, he reckoned it was high time he resumed getting what he was entitled to. To his disappointment, however, Marge was not very co-operative. For the past few nights she had resisted most of his advances and just lay there like a lump, staring aimlessly up at the ceiling in the dark. Every time he tried to get on top of her, she made one excuse or another, either that her rheumatism was playing her up, or that she was still feeling weak after her gallstone operation. Even when he tried to give her a good smacking kiss, one of her hair curlers suddenly prodded him in the eye, her feet were always ice cold, and she always insisted on tucking her flannelette nightdress tightly between her legs. Hardly the most romantic relationship, he kept telling himself. How he longed for a real slap and tickle with some buzzy blonde. The way he felt, anything or anyone would do, and if that person happened to be Leo's bit of fluff, Pam Warner, he certainly wouldn't complain! What was wrong with his missus? he wondered. Does honest-to-goodness married life *have* to come to an end just because you've got three kids? Well, try as he may, tonight he just couldn't sleep, and after a great deal of tossing and turning, he searched for a dog-end in the ash tray on the bedside table, found it, and lit up. For ages, he just lay there, smoking himself to death, listening with rage and anger at two moggies who were battling it out with a yelling match on the back yard wall outside.

In desperation, he finally spoke. 'You awake?'

There was no response from Marge.

Irritated, he stretched his hand across and prodded her. 'Marge?' he growled.

'Yer've got ter do somefin' about it.'

'Wos that?'

'Leo,' she grunted, totally immobile where she lay. 'Yer've got ter talk ter 'im.'

'Huh?' Reg was nonplussed.

The sheets rustled as Marge pulled herself up, and leaned her back on the headboard. 'It's gone too far,' she said with a sigh. 'It's not fair, I tell yer, it's just not fair.'

Reg was now convinced she'd gone bonkers. He was well used to his wife sorting out all her problems at bedtime, but this was now going a bit far. 'Wot's not fair?' he asked.

'The way 'e's treatin' that gel. Poor Pam. She's everythin' a man could ever want.'

Reg agreed with her about that.

'An' now 'e's goin' ter lose 'er. 'E's a fool, a bleedin' little fool!'

'Lose 'er?' Reg pulled himself up in bed. 'Wotcha talkin' about?'

'Leo!' yelled Marge. ' 'E's gone an' got 'imself anuvver gel – some stupid stuck-up little cow from up 'Ighgate.'

'Wot?' Reg was now taking some interest. 'Wot gel? Who is she?'

'She's a clippie on the 14s. Pays in up at the same depot.'

'Is that a fact?' said Reg, beginning to enjoy himself. ' 'Ow come I ain't 'eard about all this?'

'Yer're about the only one in the 'ouse who 'asn't! But yer've got ter do somefin' about it.'

'*Me?*'

Marge got out of bed, slipped her feet into her house

slippers, and went to the window. As the electric light was hardly ever turned on in the bedroom, the blackout curtain hadn't been drawn, so she was able to look out of the window through the net curtains. It was quite a foggy night, and she could only just make out the outline of the brick air-raid shelter where she and the kids had spent so much of their time over the past few months. 'Yer've got ter tell 'im wot a silly bleedin fool 'e's makin' of 'imself. Yer've got ter tell 'im that 'e's got ter do the right fing by that gel.'

Reg smoked his dog-end, and scratched his head. 'I don't see wot business it is er ours,' he said. 'If 'e don't fancy the gel, an' 'e's found someone else, wot can *we* do about it?'

Marge turned on him. 'We're 'is mum an' dad, ain't we? We've got a right ter tell 'im wot we fink!'

'We can tell 'im, but 'e don't 'ave ter listen.'

Marge was furious. It was at times like this that she could give Reg Quincey a right fourpenny one. Why was it always her who could see the dangers their kids were getting themselves into? This is the way it had always been throughout their long marriage – it was always her who had to do the running, her who had to have the guts to speak her mind and get things done. 'Leo's under age, Reg,' she said forcefully. 'Until 'e's twenty-one, 'e can't do nuffin' wivout our permission.'

'Don't be bleedin' stupid, woman!' rasped Reg. 'In a few weeks' time the boy'll be goin' in the army. Under age or no under age, there ain't nuffin' we can do about that!'

'I don't want 'im gettin' mixed up wiv a gel like that!'

'A gel like what?' growled Reg. In weary desperation, he threw back the bed sheets and eiderdown, and sat on the edge of the bed. 'How d'yer know wot she's like?'

'Becos I know!' snapped Marge, shaking her fist. 'She's

a different class er person ter us. She comes from moneyed people, people who don't care whose life they ruin. I could never like anyone like that, never.'

'Yer know, it's a funny fing,' said Reg, getting up from the bed and going to her. 'I fawt we was talkin' about Leo – not you.'

Marge went taut. 'I won't 'ave a son er mine going around wiv someone like that, I just won't.' She made her way back to bed, got in, and pulled the covers over her. 'An' if *you* won't do somefin' about it, then *I* will!'

116

Chapter 6

London had come to a standstill. The culprit this time, however, was not the Luftwaffe, but blinding, grey, choking fog. It was, of course, a seasonal hazard, hardly surprising when coal fires were pumping out thick black smoke from practically every household chimneypot throughout the capital, but its effect was catastrophic, not only for the elderly and those who suffered from severe bronchial problems, but also for the thousands of people who were unable to go about their normal everyday business. Commuters were particularly hard hit, both during the early morning rush hour, but more particularly during the evening, when the combination of fog and the wartime blackout restrictions made getting to and from work a major challenge. Transport was the main casualty. Bus and tram drivers had no idea where they were going, for at times, visibility was down to no more than a few yards, and their only way of making any progress at all was to have the conductor walking in front of the bus, lighting the way with a torch. Peggy's first ordeal in such conditions came halfway through her week of split-turn shift work, when her new regular driver was 'Frosty' Morris, an affable middle-aged cockney from Bow.

'Try and keep the light down, gel!' shouted Frosty, through his open side window. All he could see of Peggy through the murk ahead was a dim outline behind a flickering torch beam. 'I can't see a fing if yer 'old it too 'igh!'

'Sorry!' called Peggy, whose voice sounded flat and crushed, as she tried to walk backwards holding the torch to guide the bus. 'I've no idea where we are.'

'Gotta be in the Cally by now!' returned Frosty. 'We passed over 'Olloway Road more than twenty minutes ago.'

'Are we goin' ter get a refund?' yelled a young clever dick, whose face was pressed up against the window of the driver's compartment on the lower deck. 'We could walk in 'alf the time!'

Keeping his eyes on the torch beam through the front windscreen, Frosty answered cuttingly, ' 'Elp yerself, mate! Don't expect us ter come an' look fer yer!'

The young bloke got what he asked for, and quickly returned to his seat, leaving the other passengers to sigh and grunt, which was the only way they could vent their frustration.

When the number 14 bus had set off from its stand at Hornsey Rise, the fog had been threatening, but still vague enough to allow a reasonably clear view of the road ahead. But by the time they had reached the Nag's Head bus stop in Seven Sisters Road, a real pea-souper had descended so quickly that at one time they were unknowingly crawling along the middle of the main road. Although the handful of passengers had settled back and accepted the inevitable delays ahead, sitting in the dark with no views through the windows other than a blank dark mass was, even for the hardy, an unnerving experience. The only relief came as Frosty finally managed to manoeuvre the vehicle around the junction of Holloway and Caledonian Roads, where, with the lack of any concerns about an air raid, some enterprising locals had lit a pavement bonfire as a makeshift beacon.

However, when the visibility became so bad that Frosty could no longer make out the beam from Peggy's torch, he decided to pull the bus to a halt. Sliding back the conductor's access window to the lower deck passengers, he called, 'Sorry, folks! This is as far as we go!'

To loud groans from the passengers, Peggy went alongside Frosty's door as he climbed out. 'What happens now?' she asked.

' 'Ang on 'ere a minute,' he said. 'I've got an idea where we are. I'll be right back.'

'For God's sake, don't get lost!' called Peggy, as her driver disappeared into the murk. With no response, she found her way back on to the bus, and by the light of her torch, addressed the passengers.

'I'm sorry about this, ladies and gentlemen!' she called, loudly enough for both upper and lower deck passengers to hear. 'I suggest we all stay put until the fog clears. There's no way we can move on at the moment.'

'*Sorry about this, ladies and gentlemen!*' called one female voice in the dark, imitating Peggy's accent.

'So wot're we expected ter do?' asked the clever dick young bloke. 'All kip down fer the night or somefink?'

'I've got ter get my kids 'ome ter bed!' complained a young woman, whose young child was grizzling in the dark.

'Typical London bloody Transport!' yelled a bombastic male voice from the upper deck.

'Fer chrissake leave the poor gel alone!' called an elderly woman from the lower deck. 'The wevver ain't 'er bleedin' fault!'

Peggy turned off her torch and sat down, relieved that there was at least one person on the bus who had come to her defence. It was at times like this that she realised how unreasonable some people could be. As the old lady had said, the state of the weather could hardly be blamed on either her, her driver, or indeed London Transport. If anyone was to blame it was all those people at home, sitting comfortably in front of their huge coal fires, whilst the rest of the city choked in the deathly black smoke they emitted. As she sat there alone, anxiously waiting for Frosty to return, it occurred to Peggy that she must be mad ever to have imagined that being stuck on a bus in the middle of a fog was 'doing her bit'. Her mind went back to that nice warm paraffin stove in the firm's office in Upper Street, and the nice hot cup of tea that her friend Irene always had waiting for her when she arrived for work every morning. But then she got to thinking about Irene herself, and the way she had unexpectedly turned up at the pub where she and Leo were having a drink together the other evening. It was such a little thing to stick in her mind, but every time she had thought about Irene since then, she had puzzled over Leo's insistence, and her denial, that on some previous occasion, he remembered having seen her near his home in Hornsey Road. If it was true, then why *was* she denying it, but even more mysteriously, what was she doing down there, so far away from her own flat in Clerkenwell?

'We're just outside the cop shop!'

Peggy leaped up with a start, relieved to hear Frosty's voice calling to her from the pavement outside. She turned on her torch and rushed out to join him. 'What's happening?' she asked anxiously.

'The bobbies reckon this 'as set in fer the night,' he said, shivering with the cold, hands tucked under his arms, and looking like an Eskimo in his woollen Balaclava and uniform cap stuck on top.

'There's no way we can move on in this muck.'

Peggy was beginning to panic. 'What are we going to do with this lot?' she asked desperately.

'Don't you worry yer pretty little 'ead about that, my gel,' said Frosty, sensing her nervousness. 'I've bin on these buses fer the best part of me life, an' if there's one fing I've learned, it's never ter let the payin' customers get me down.'

'But they're getting quite obstreperous.'

Frosty went blank. 'Come again? Oh – oh, I see wot yer mean. Well, let 'em. You leave it ter ol' Frosty. We'll take 'em round ter Sid an' Mabel's place. They'll soon cheer 'em all up.'

Peggy hadn't the faintest idea what he was talking about. 'Who?' she asked.

'*Who?*' he repeated, astonished at her ignorance. 'Don't tell me yer 'aven't 'eard about our Sid an' Mabel? Blimey. An' yer call yerself heducated?'

Although the 'FRYING TONIGHT' sign in the blacked-out window wasn't entirely visible from the pavement in the fog outside, the seductive smell of cod, haddock, eel, rock salmon, and chips, bubbling in boiling hot lard, hardly disguised what succulent things were going on inside the shop. But then, Sid and Mabel's place wasn't just a shop, it was an institution, a Mecca for addicts of good working-class food and, in wartime, one of the few places where a queue formed even before the door opened for business. However, the fog had taken its toll of business for this evening, and so it was a great relief when Frosty turned up with his clippie and a handful of customers.

'Come an' get it, folks!' he called to them all. 'All 'ot an' luvely!'

'Speshul ternight!' proclaimed Sid, a jovial, rotund man, famed for eating more of his own cooking than he should. 'Ninepence fer fish an' a pennyworf er chips!'

Peggy watched in astonishment as the half-dozen or so passengers jostled to form a queue at the counter. She wasn't used to taking meals in such a place. 'Frosty, what a marvellous idea,' she said. 'Do you always think of things like this?'

Frosty chuckled. 'Trick er the trade,' he replied, lowering

his voice. 'Got ter keep the customers 'appy in an emergency.' Then with a wink, he added, 'An' you an' me get a free meal frown in!'

A few minutes later, the passengers had settled down at the few tables at the back of the shop beyond the counter. Frosty and Peggy left them to it, preferring to keep to themselves by eating their free cod and chips out of newspaper standing up at the opposite counter. The place now reeked of vinegar, and Peggy couldn't get over seeing her driver demolish two pickled onions with his meal.

'Salt er the earf – Sid an' Mabel,' Frosty said. 'D'yer know Mabel's 'ad six kids, an' just look at 'er – don't look anywhere near 'er real age, do she?'

Peggy looked across at Mabel, who gave her a smile and a wave. She was certainly a sweet-faced woman, pretty as a picture despite her bloated face and almost spherical body, which was much the same shape as her husband's. But what was really surprising Peggy was how good the fish tasted, and even the chips, which she had smelled cooking in similar shops she had passed on the street so many times before without ever having the courage to go in.

'I'm surprised your bloke ain't brought yer in 'ere before,' said Frosty, who had the brightest blue eyes, which were a striking contrast to his snowy white hair. 'Young Leo's mad about this place.'

Peggy was a bit taken aback to hear Leo referred to as 'her bloke', but she let it pass. 'He has good taste,' was all she was prepared to say.

Frosty had a mischievous twinkle in his eye. 'Yer can say that again!' he said with a chuckle, nudging her.

Peggy blushed, and concentrated on eating the fish with her fingers.

'Good ter see 'e's come ter 'is senses, say I. Young feller like 'im needs ter pull 'is socks up sooner or later.' Frosty leaned his head back, and with a great deal of huffing and puffing to cool it down, dropped a hot chip into his mouth. 'I must say, I've never fought much of 'is choice in the past.'

Peggy flicked her eyes up and down, trying not to show that she had registered what he had said. Behind her, Mabel rang up the cash till to give some change to a customer who had just paid.

'Nuffink up 'ere, them type er gels!' Frosty persisted, pointing to the side of his forehead. 'Just up fer one fing.'

'Leo and I are not really – you know – it's not like that,' Peggy said awkwardly. 'We're just very good friends.'

Frosty swallowed his chip, and turned to look at her. 'That's not wot '*e* finks,' he said, with an artful grin. ' 'E reckons yer the cat's whiskers, an' I must say I don't blame 'im. I reckon yer're tops.'

Again Peggy was embarrassed, so she quickly returned to picking at her fish.

Ever since they'd entered the shop, the steam rising from the boiling lard had merged with the thin film of fog which had drifted in from the street outside every time the front door opened, and which had now tinted the air a sickly yellow colour in the dim glow of the overhead lights. In the back room, the bus passengers were so busy devouring their fish and chips that they had almost forgotten the predicament they were in, and one or two of them had even taken to praising Frosty and Peggy for taking such good care of them.

'Well, at least that muck outside keeps jerry away,' said Mabel, as she brought over two cups of tea, for Peggy and Frosty to wash down their greasy meal.

After Mabel had gone, Frosty took out a narrow tobacco tin from his jacket pocket from where he extracted the last of several fags he'd rolled for himself earlier in the day. 'Course, I know 'is dad.'

'I'm sorry?' Peggy asked. 'Who?'

'Reg Quincey,' replied Frosty, lighting his fag. 'Young Leo's dad. Used ter work up the trolley garage in Pemberton Gardens. Got the push fer – *you* know . . .'

Peggy was puzzled. She didn't know.

Frosty held up his hand to mime drinking a pint. 'Too much booze,' he said, voice low. 'That's why he had ter go freelance brickie. Can't be easy when yer've got a wife and three kids ter look after. I was sorry fer 'im. He's a good bloke, really, but not much up 'ere.' He pointed to his head. 'Funny fing was, 'e 'ad it all goin' fer 'im. 'E was a first-class mechanic – one er the best. 'E could've 'ad a job fer life. When they give 'im the push, 'e cried like a baby. Life ain't fair ter some folk, is it? Why does it 'ave ter pick an' choose who it likes best? Mind you, I've always liked boaf Reg an' 'is boy. Yer get wot yer see wiv the Quinceys – honest as the day is long. The ol' boy too – Leo's granddad – straight as a die, never owed any sod a penny till the day they carried the poor old git out in 'is box. No, the Quinceys are fine. The only problem wiv that family 'as always bin '*er* – Marge Quincey.'

Peggy glanced up briefly from her fish and chips. 'Really?' she said casually.

'Oh yes,' Frosty said gloomily. 'She don't suffer fools gladly, that one. Rules that 'ouse wiv a rod er iron. Wot Marge says goes, and no bugger better say any diff'rent. That's where young Leo gets 'is moods from.'

'Moods?' asked Peggy, surprised. 'What kind of moods?'

'Loses 'is temper at the drop of an 'at,' he replied, now on a roll and prepared to speak his mind. 'It's all 'er fault, er course. From wot Reg used ter tell me, there are times when she bosses the boy about so much, he rushes straight out er the 'ouse, finds the first empty milk bottle 'e can lay 'is 'ands on, and frows it as far as 'e can. I once saw 'im bash the daylights out er a bloke just becos 'e called 'im a mummy's boy. Terrible!' He turned to look at Peggy. 'Why can't people just leave their kids ter get on wiv their own lives?'

Peggy had lost her appetite, so she rolled up what was left of her fish and chips in the newspaper. 'And what about you, Frosty?' she asked. 'Do you have a family of your own?'

'Me?' he asked, breaking into a broad smile. 'Oh yes, I've got a family all right,' he purred proudly. 'Got the best little missus in the 'ole wide world. It's our Ruby next year – forty years! An' I've got two lovely married daughters, Gord bless 'em. But I'll tell yer somefin', Peggs,' he said, leaning close so that he could not be overheard, 'if I 'ad a son like young Leo, I'd be the proudest man on earf. If yer'll take my tip, yer'll 'ang on ter 'im, gel.'

The Quincey family were listening to *ITMA*. It was their favourite wireless programme, and that of millions of other listeners throughout the country, for not only did it appeal to young and old alike, but its special brand of zany humour was raising the morale of everyone during the dark days of the Blitz. The one to whom it appealed least, however, was Marge Quincey, who always sat in her usual utility chair at the side of the dresser in the kitchen parlour, knitting multicoloured pullovers for Horace and Eddie out of spare balls of wool, and smiling only when Mrs Mopp appeared, greeting her irrepressible boss, Tommy Handley, with her stock catch phrase, '*Can I do yer now, sir?*' The kids, of course, knew every character's catch phrase, and every time they were sent off to bed at the end of the show, they assumed the role of the two broker's men, Claude and Cecil, bowing to each other as they passed through the kitchen door, muttering, '*After you, Claude,*' '*No, after you,*

Cecil.' Both Reg and Leo hated listening to the nine o'clock news, and so once the *ITMA* half-hour had come to an end and the kids had been packed off to bed, they left Marge to it, and escaped to the front room for their usual nightcap of brown ale.

'So wot's all this I 'ear about this new gel?' asked Reg, as he watched his eldest son pour two pint glasses from a quart bottle. 'All over wiv Pam, is it?'

Leo was taken aback. He had grown used to having to put up with his mum's carping on about the subject, but he didn't expect it from his dad. 'Come off it, Dad,' he replied, handing over one of the glasses. 'I don't wanna talk about it.'

'Oh, it's all right, son,' replied Reg. 'I couldn't care less who yer go wiv. But yer know wot yer mum's like. She's set 'er eyes on gettin' 'er first grandchild.'

They exchanged a knowing look, which turned into a smirk. They held up the glasses and toasted each other. 'Cheers!'

When Reg had taken his first gulp, there was a rim of froth on his lips, which he immediately wiped away with the back of his hand. 'So – who is she?'

Leo also wiped his lips with the back of his hand. 'Just someone I met up the depot.'

'All right, is she?'

For a split second, Leo looked tormented. 'Bloody marvellous,' he replied. He offered his dad one of his fags. Reg took it, and let his son light up for both of them.

'Is this it then?' asked Reg, inhaling deeply. 'Are you two goin' ter make a go of it?'

Leo sighed. ' 'Ow can I tell, Dad?' he replied. 'I've only known 'er fer five minutes. All I can say is, she's not like any girl I've bin out wiv before.'

'Wot's so speshul about 'er? Good-looker, is she?'

Leo shrugged. 'Yes and no. I've seen better. It's not 'er looks. It's – the way she is.' He took a quick puff of his fag, and exhaled. 'I fink it's got somefin' ter do wiv the way she listens ter me. She's a t'rrific listener. An' *when* we talk, she talks *wiv* me, not *at* me.'

'Sounds like a bit of a toff.'

Leo came back at him immediately. 'No – she's not like that. Well, she is – and yet she ain't.'

Reg settled back in his chair by the fireplace. 'Seems ter me only toffs 'ave the gift er the gab,' he said.

'Don't you believe it,' said Leo. 'I can 'old me own, don't you worry!'

Reg smiled. 'Oh, I'm quite sure about that. All I meant was, I wish I was like that. Ever since I was a kid, every time I meet someone that speaks well, I get tongue-tied. Bit of an inferiority complex, I reckon.'

Leo looked across at his dad. He felt a surge of affection for him. 'There's nuffin' inferior about you, Dad,' he said. 'And don't yer let no one make yer fink uvverwise.'

Reg came round briefly from his reflective mood, and gave the boy a wink. 'So wot 'appens about Pam?' he asked.

'Wot d'yer mean?'

' 'Ow's she goin' ter take ter this? I mean, you two've bin walkin' out tergevver fer six munfs, ain't yer?'

'We 'ave not bin walkin' out, Dad!' snapped Leo, springing up from his chair.

'That's not wot yer ma finks.'

Leo went to the window, gulping down his brown ale. 'I don't care a monkey's *wot* she finks!' he snapped, fed up with a lifetime's interference from his mum. 'She ain't me ruler, she ain't me boss! I do wot I want, an' I don't 'ave ter ask 'er bleedin' permission!' He swung round and shook his half-empty glass at his dad. 'Pam an' I've bin knockin' around. That's all there is to it, that's all there's ever bin to it! She couldn't care less if we never saw each uvver again!'

'Yer know that, do yer?'

Leo's impulse was to answer straight back, but something stopped him. He went to the window and, despite the blackout restrictions, peered outside into the fog.

'Let me tell yer somefin', son,' said Reg, easing himself out of his chair. 'I know 'ow yer feel about yer mum, an' 'ow she interferes.' He strolled across and stood with Leo at the window. 'But she ain't all bad; she ain't wivout *some* knowledge about wot's right and wrong. She cares about yer, son. She cares a lot fer this family. Now maybe she overdoes it – at times, I know she does. But yer stop an' ask yerself wevver she's got a point or not.'

'Dad,' said Leo, turning round calmly from the window, 'I fink I'm in love with this gel. Don't ask me 'ow it's 'appened as quick as this, but it 'as, it just '*as*.'

Reg sighed. 'Fair enough,' he said. 'But remember this. Before yer do anyfin' stupid, make sure. Yer owe that ter Pam. Yer owe it ter hurt 'er as little as yer can. She's a 'uman bein', son, a 'uman bein' just like you, like me, like yer mum. No matter 'ow wrong yer fink she is fer you, she 'as the right ter be treated as an equal. Don't keep 'er 'angin' around, son. Once yer've made up yer mind, go an' tell 'er in as nice a way as yer can. But be sure, be bloody sure yer know wot yer're doin', or yer're goin' ter 'urt an awful lot er people on the way.'

The two kids on Peggy's bus were bawling their heads off. They'd had their fish and chips at Sid and Mabel's, they'd had nearly two hours of forced sleep, and now they were letting their mum know that they'd had enough of the fog and wanted to get home. The rest of the passengers were fast asleep when Frosty finally announced that the visibility had cleared enough to let them get on their way, but after making a telephone call to the depot from the nearby cop shop, he had been instructed to abandon the journey and get back as soon as possible. Needless to say, this did not go down well with the passengers for most of them were going as far as King's Cross or thereabouts, so it meant that they were left with the alternative of either waiting for another bus, which might not make the attempt to get through for several hours, or return with Peggy and Frosty to the depot until the fog had cleared. In the event, the more hardy passengers decided to try to continue their journey on foot, whilst one elderly married couple, together with the young mum and her two bawling kids, opted for the safety of a return to the depot, and perhaps a long wait until the fog had cleared.

Despite the fact that the fog had thinned enough to allow Frosty to move the bus, manoeuvring such a large vehicle around in the middle of Caledonian Road was a risky task, which meant that Peggy had to use her torch to guide him. To make matters worse, a middle-aged drunk suddenly appeared from nowhere and tried to get on the bus, but when he turned out to be a bit on the aggressive side, Peggy was relieved that he hitched a lift instead on the back of a brewer's cart, which was being pulled by a large black and grey work horse. The horse seemed to be the only one completely unperturbed by the weather conditions, disappearing into the fog at a slow trot as though nothing was different from normal.

To Peggy, the return journey down Caledonian Road seemed just as perilous as when they had crawled along the same route nearly two hours before, and although she could now just see the road on either side of her, in the dark the normal, everyday images that one took for granted became quite sinister, and sent a cold chill down her spine. To her consternation, by the time the bus had finally reached the junction with Holloway Road, the blanket of fog had changed its mind and come down again, which meant that, as before, she had to get out and walk in front of the bus with her torch. Fortunately, the local residents' bonfire was still burning on the corner outside the council flats, so she had at least some sense of which direction to head towards. It was also increasingly hazardous, for not only did she have a difficult task keeping Frosty from mounting the pavement as they went, but she also had to keep her eyes open for any other vehicles that had been abandoned along the kerb. The slow crawl along Holloway Road was turning out to be a nightmare, and it didn't help that the fog was now so biting cold that Peggy's face had gone quite numb. She just wished someone would suddenly appear from the mist, and help her through this misery, a knight in shining armour perhaps, who would relieve her of all the responsibility.

She had no idea why Leo came to mind. But then Frosty had been talking about him so much, she couldn't really get him out of her mind. What was it Frosty had said – '*If I 'ad a son like young Leo, I'd be the proudest man on earf. If yer'll take my tip, yer'll 'ang on to 'im, gel*'? Hang on to him? Why should she hang on to someone that she hardly knew, someone who was from a different world from everything she had ever known, someone who apparently had a vile temper when provoked. After all, wasn't Mr Stevens' son, Joe, more capable of looking after her and giving her the type of life she was destined for? One day he would be a naval officer, and she quite fancied herself as the wife of someone like that. Or did she? No, of course she didn't! That was rubbish, absolute rubbish! It was just that 'type' of life she was trying to get away from. She wanted a life where she could do things for herself and not rely on others to do them for her. So why then was she suddenly thinking so much about Leo – thinking about him more than she could possibly understand? Was he infatuated with her? Or was she just another pick-up to give his mates a bit of a laugh? No, not that. She didn't believe that. Oh God, why was he on her mind so much? Was it perhaps she who was the one that was infatuated, or was it something more than that? Was it possible? Was it possible to have such feelings for someone she had only known for just a few weeks, or was it because this working-class boy was the only real, the only positive thing that had ever happened to her in her entire life?

'Oy! Watch out, mate!'

An angry voice shouting out from the fog ahead abruptly reminded Peggy that she had allowed her concentration to wander, and that she was leading the bus straight into a parked goods van. Frantically waving at Frosty with her torch, and with a loud yell of 'Over! Over!' she managed just in time to avoid a nasty collision. 'Oh God, Leo!' she asked herself. 'Why can't you be here?' The fact that the only person she could think of at a time like this was Leo, led her to the conclusion that she was falling in love with him.

Catherine Thornton was in the loft, searching for a party dress she had discarded several years before. The loft was a fairly large and airy space, and she often went up there when she felt depressed and wanted to be on her own. There was a window set in one half of the sloping ceiling, through which could be seen magnificent views of London in one direction, and the wide open spaces of Hertfordshire beyond the Archway Road and Finchley. Catherine loved this place; she thought of it as her 'inner sanctum', mainly because this was where she stored all her past, memorabilia dating back over the years right to when she was a child.

Her childhood had always been her happiest days, for she had come from a family who cared – cared for her, and for who she was. But even in those days she had been lonely, for, like Peggy, she had been an only child, and always longed for a brother or sister to keep her company. Many a time she had come up to the loft, desperately trying to recapture the past by trying on dresses that she had worn on special occasions with Robert over the years, admiring herself in a tall full-length mirror, remembering the event, nostalgic for those times, for she had retained her slender figure, and looked elegant in anything she wore. Tonight, however, the loft was freezing cold, and the thick blanket of fog that had obliterated all views outside had somehow filtered through the sides of the blackout blinds at the window, creating an eerie glare beneath the glow of a single light bulb dangling down at an angle from one side of the sloping ceiling.

Eventually, Catherine found what she was looking for, a green velvet three-quarter-length dress, which she immediately held up against her in the mirror.

'It suits you.'

Catherine turned with a shocked start. Thornton had come quietly up the stairs, and was watching her.

'You should wear it more often,' he said, approaching her. 'You're still a very beautiful woman, Catherine.'

Catherine was embarrassed, turned away, and quickly put the dress back into the trunk from where she had taken it.

He went to her and pulled her round to face him. 'Why won't you ever let me admire you?' he said. 'Every woman likes to be admired.'

Catherine felt brave enough to smile. 'Thank you, dear,' she replied gratefully.

To her surprise, he leaned forward and kissed her gently

on the lips. 'You have a lot of memories up here, Catherine,' he said softly. 'We've shared many fascinating times together. You must never forget them. Am I right?'

She smiled weakly, put her arms around his neck, and kissed him more passionately than he had kissed her. When he responded, she felt revived, invigorated. It hadn't been like this for such a long time. He was back to how he used to be, loving, admiring, caring. Whatever he had done, whatever mistakes he had made, if he was going to be like this, come what may, she was going to forgive him.

He pulled away, held her at arm's length for a moment, and looked at her. He was still smiling. 'Where is our daughter this evening, Catherine?' he asked.

The question took her by surprise. It disappointed her, for she was expecting more affection. 'She's on split turn,' she answered feebly.

'Split turn? What does that mean?'

Catherine shrugged her shoulders. 'She goes to work late in the morning or something, and finishes halfway through the evening. I'm not really too sure.'

Thornton looked at his watch. 'It's after ten,' he said pointedly. 'She should be home by now.'

'It must be difficult. The fog is very thick tonight.'

Thornton registered what she had said, but without reaction. He turned and leaned one hand on a high stool nearby. 'I think you should know that I'm very concerned about that girl. We're losing her, Catherine, and it's wrong.'

She was puzzled.

'She's seeing someone,' he said, turning round to look at her. 'Did you know that?'

'Seeing someone?' she asked naively.

'A boy from that bus depot. I saw him bring her home one night.'

If Catherine did know anything, she wasn't going to

show it. 'But he's probably just an acquaintance,' she replied. 'Peggy's had boyfriends before, Robert, you know she has. She's a very attractive girl. Now that she's almost come of age, it's only natural she would want to go out with boys.'

'Not with this one,' said Thornton, his visible breath showing how cold it was in the unheated loft. 'Not with a boy half her age, a manual worker in a bus garage, the son of a bricklayer in Hornsey Road – Hornsey Road, Catherine, at the bottom of the hill.'

Catherine sighed in despair. 'Does it matter, dear?' she asked tentatively. 'I mean – does it matter *who* she chooses to go out with?'

Without realising it, Thornton was grinding his teeth. 'It matters to me, Catherine. It matters that a daughter of mine – my only daughter – is throwing away all the advantages in life you and I have struggled to give her. A good home, good education, the chance of an excellent career with a reputable firm of solicitors – thrown away, all, all thrown away. I do have *some* reputation in this world, you know. If she has to go touting on the streets for a husband, why the devil can't she stick to her own kind?'

Catherine went to him. 'You mustn't upset yourself about this, Robert, my dear,' she said, cupping his face in her hands affectionately. 'I'm sure it's just a passing phase.'

Thornton pulled her hands away. 'Passing phase or not, I won't allow her to ruin my life and her own. I know an awful lot about this boy, and the more I hear, the more determined I am to get rid of him. If Margaret doesn't put a stop to this liaison, then *I* will!'

With Peggy's help, Frosty finally managed to edge the number 14 bus into the depot in Kingsdown Road. It had been an appalling journey every inch of the way, and to her, it seemed a miracle that they had got there at all, for all along Holloway Road drivers had just surrendered their vehicles to the fog wherever they had come to a halt, unable to proceed without putting themselves at tremendous risk. At one location near the Nag's Head, a trolley bus had ended up on the wrong side of the road, the poles having been dewired from their overhead cable, leaving the driver and conductor in a desperate position as they wrestled to restore the connection with their regulation-issue bamboo pole. Further along the road, a taxi had been in collision with a milk float, which had left a sea of milk running down the gutter into the drains. Chaos everywhere.

'All part of a day's job!' said Frosty, as he finally climbed down from the driver's cab.

Peggy, however, was absolutely exhausted. Her first experience of being caught on duty in such relentless weather conditions had been an initiation of fire, and she prayed that it wouldn't be too soon before she had to walk with her torch again in front of the bus. None the less, her efforts earned her a pat on the back from Frosty.

'Well done, gel!' he said comfortingly, as she led the few remaining passengers into the comfort of the staff waiting room. 'Yer've got real cat's eyes, an' that's fer sure!'

Once she had paid in, Peggy returned to the forecourt, which was now crowded with buses and their crews, all unable to get out on the road until the fog had cleared. Although she had doubts about trying to make for home on foot, she decided that, tired as she was, she had to make the effort.

On the street outside, she could hardly see a hand in front of her. Shivering with the cold, she paused a moment, and turned to look back at the bleakness of the depot behind her, its huge interior overhead lights hardly visible in the grey, swirling mass. As she stood there, she wished that she didn't feel so alone, so isolated. The war was one thing, but being entombed in a choking, soulless fog was something quite different. She pulled up the collar of her uniform coat, and briefly closed her eyes. In her mind's eye, she could see a warm fire, a hot cup of tea – and Leo. Leo? Was she going mad or something? She shook her head, and opened her eyes, hoping to restore her sanity. But as she did so, she caught sight of a movement in the fog directly in front of her. It was the shape and outline of someone gradually emerging from the fog. At first it scared her, and she automatically stepped back, ready to escape into the safety of the depot, but as she strained to see who the figure was, a voice called to her.

'Duchess?'

She stopped dead. As it approached, the figure was holding out its arms. 'Leo!' she gasped. 'Oh God, Leo – you . . . !'

Leo rushed at her, threw his arms around her, and held her tight.

Peggy pressed her head against his chest. Even through his duffel coat she could feel his heart beating. 'Oh God, Leo,' she said, her arms wrapped around his waist. 'It's so good to see you . . . so good!' She looked up, but could only just make out his face grinning down at her. 'What are you doing here?' she asked breathlessly. 'How did you know I was—'

'I've bin waitin' fer yer,' he whispered. 'But I ain't waitin' any longer . . .'

He pulled her towards him, and kissed her forcefully on the lips. She responded passionately, and for several moments, they just stood there, locked in each other's arms. Then he opened his duffel coat, wrapped it around her, and then led her off into the dark, murky night.

Chapter 7

Leo got his call-up papers the day before Christmas Eve. It came as quite a shock, for he was under the impression that he still had five weeks left of the six months' deferment he had been granted by the army following his mum's gallstone operation. However, he still had a week left before he had to report to Aldershot barracks in Hampshire, and so, defying the mounting opposition now coming from both their families, he and Peggy decided to make the most of every precious spare moment they could spend together. Their first opportunity came soon after Peggy had come off her early morning shift at noon. Hardly aware that she had been on duty since four o'clock that morning, she arranged to meet Leo outside Selfridges department store in Oxford Street where they would do some last-minute Christmas window shopping together. Peggy decided to take the tube to get there, and when she got out at Oxford Circus underground station, she found it difficult to imagine that there was a war on, for the famous West End street was throbbing with crowds, all desperate to complete their last-minute shopping in the last remaining hours before the stores closed for the Christmas holidays. She, like everyone else, was only too grateful that the Luftwaffe seemed to have granted them a respite from their regular nocturnal visits, and this new-found freedom had certainly permeated through the crowds, spreading a feeling of seasonal exuberance and joy.

Leo was waiting for her in the grand front entrance of Selfridges, and when she first caught a glimpse of him, he had his hands tucked into his duffel coat, a thick woollen scarf wrapped around his neck, and he was shifting from one foot to another to keep warm in the icy drizzle of a cold afternoon. The moment they came together, they just stood there briefly, smiling, searching out each other's eyes.

'Wotcha,' he mouthed inaudibly.

'Wotcha,' she replied, reading his lips in mock affection.

Then, completely oblivious of the crowds who were jostling all around them, they hugged and kissed.

Wandering around inside Selfridges was a strange experience for them both, for the store had been badly hit during the early part of the Blitz, but even though there wasn't much to buy, everyone seemed to be grabbing anything they could lay their hands on. Peggy stopped briefly from time to time to take a passing glance at what remained of the jewellery counters, where so much had been lost in the air raid, and the toiletries section where, to her delight and amusement, Leo forked out a shilling for a bar of luxury soap, which was more than he had ever paid for such a thing in his entire life. The biggest scramble, though, was in what was left of the food department, where a surprise consignment of Christmas puddings and mince pies suddenly appeared on one of the counters. Peggy and Leo were nearly trampled in the rush, for such items had almost totally disappeared from the shops, and anyone who managed to include them in their shopping basket was clearly going to give their family a real Christmas Day treat. Looking around the store, however, was a cheering sight, for despite the awful austerity of war, Christmas trees, lights and decorations had transformed every floor into a glittering seasonal wonderland, and even Father Christmas was there in his 'iceland ghetto', playing host to a long queue of wide-eyed children, who were all brimming with excitement about the long night ahead of them.

Stumbling out into the street again, Peggy and Leo found themselves caught up in the frantic rush to buy anything before the shops closed. In a few hours' time, Oxford Street would be utterly deserted, plunged into darkness as the blackout restrictions took their nightly grip on a beleaguered rush hour. Behind Selfridges store, Leo found a small café, where he and Peggy ordered roast chicken, boiled potatoes, cabbage and carrots, which seemed to be the only dish left on a very limited menu. But there was more on their mind than food, for they spent most of the time staring into each other's eyes, and holding each other's hand on the table in front of them.

After a while Peggy stretched across and, with the tips of her fingers, gently cleared one of the curls hanging down on to Leo's forehead. 'Calling you up just before Christmas is fairly brutal,' she said with a sigh. 'I shall miss you.'

Leo gave her a characteristic grin. 'Oh yeah?' he teased. 'I bet yer tell that ter all the boys.'

'You can talk,' she replied jokily. 'From what I hear, you're quite a one with the girls.'

Leo immediately pulled his hand away from hers. 'Who told yer that?' he snapped.

'Ah!' she laughed, unaware that he had taken her seriously. 'Wouldn't you like to know?'

'Whoever it is, I'll smash 'is bloody face in! Who told yer that? *Who?*'

Peggy was taken aback. His aggressive reaction had alarmed her. 'It was only a joke, Leo,' she replied awkwardly. 'Just a joke.'

Realising he'd assumed she knew more than he wanted her to, Leo calmed down and sat back in his chair. 'Sorry,' he said with a sheepish smile. 'It's just that there are so many loud moufs up that depot, they could put the dirty in on anyone.'

Peggy was curious. 'Is there any reason why they should want to do that?' she asked.

'No way!' he replied quickly, in an attempt to laugh it off. 'Where's this grub, then?' he said, raising his voice, looking around impatiently for the waitress. He was clearly agitated. 'I should've brought yer somewhere better than this,' he babbled. 'Just look at it – bleedin' awful dump. Can't even put up a few paper chains fer Christmas!'

For a moment, Peggy watched him closely as he took out a packet of fags from his coat pocket and started to light up. Briefly, she was wondering whether what Frosty had told her about Leo's temperament was true. 'It doesn't matter, you know, Leo,' she said, stretching across for his hand again. 'It doesn't matter that you've had other girlfriends. I don't mind, really I don't. That's all part of life. I've had boyfriends in my time – not many, but some. One thing I can say though is, none of them have been quite like you.'

The match Leo had just struck was still burning in his fingers. 'An' so I should 'ope,' he replied lightly. His grim look gradually dissolved into a guilty smile. He blew out the match, took the unlit fag from his lips, and put it back into the packet. 'Sorry,' he said.

'You don't have to apologise to me, Leo,' said Peggy. 'If we're going to love each other, the past makes no difference at all.'

Leo looked up at her with a start. This was the first time she had said it, the first time she had actually mentioned the word love. Across the table they looked deep into each other's eyes. They were both searching for the answer to the question they wanted to know: was it really possible that they were falling in love? With their eyes still fixed on each other, their hands slowly, simultaneously, crept towards the centre of the table until they finally met and locked together. Then

Peggy broke into a warm, loving smile.

Leo smiled back at her and squeezed her hands. But it didn't come easily. He had other things on his mind.

It was a good thing Reg Quincey had a head for heights, for the type of work he was expected to do, perched on top of the remains of what used to be an old textile warehouse in City Road, required nerves of steel. When the building received a direct hit from a high-explosive bomb during the first week of the Blitz, everything inside the place was so inflammable that it went up in a ball of fire, bringing down the roof, ceilings, and practically every interior wall. However, although the skeleton of the structure remained, it posed a danger to both pedestrians and traffic, for it was situated right on the busy main road. The firm who had received the contract to demolish the building employed any good men they could get to do the job, and although Reg was now a bricklayer by trade, taking on work as a labourer came as no real hardship, for the money was good, and he had no fear of heights. In any case, he was casual labour, and in wartime beggars could hardly be choosers. The part of the wall he was now carefully dismantling with a pickaxe was about fifty feet from the ground, and from the top he had a perfect view of St Paul's Cathedral, and the City of London, which was looking very battered after the hammering it had taken night after night since the air raids began back in September. He also had a good view of his workmates, who were either chipping away at other parts of the skeleton or collecting the rubble for transport elsewhere.

'Reg! Get down 'ere!'

As the December weather was bitterly cold, with a freezing drizzle making work conditions even more treacherous than normal, Reg was not really listening out for the message one of his mates was suddenly yelling up at him. 'Wos up?'

he yelled back as loud as he could. 'Wot d'yer want?'

'Visitor! Get down 'ere!'

'Visitor?' he yelled back irritably. 'Who?'

' 'Ello, Mr Quincey!' called a tiny female voice. 'It's me!'

Even from that height there was no mistaking the diminutive figure of Pam Warner, waving frantically from the pavement below.

'Pam?' yelled Reg. 'Wos up?'

'Can I see yer fer a minute, please?'

Reg reckoned she must have gone bonkers or something, calling on him at work like this, but after pulling his flat cap on tight, he made his way down a series of ladders which took him down from scaffold platforms on three different levels. The moment he reached the pavement below, he was aware that he was being watched by his foreman.

'Wos up, Pam?' he asked as she approached him. 'Wot yer doin' 'ere?'

'I'm sorry, Mr Quincey,' she said. All dolled up in a white woollen topcoat, headscarf, white boots, and carrying a skimpy umbrella, she looked like a chorus girl from a Hollywood musical film. 'I'm really sorry ter bring yer all the way down, but I'm worried about Leo.'

'Leo? Wot about 'im?'

As she moved close so that they could both share her umbrella, some of Reg's workmates gave her a few wolf whistles. 'I 'aven't seen 'im fer ages – not since I came ter tea with yer all that Sunday.'

Reg let out an exasperated sigh. 'Blimey, Pam!' he said. 'Yer brought me all the way down 'ere just ter tell me that? It's Chrissmas Eve. We'll be knockin' off in an hour.'

'It's important, Mr Quincey, honest it is. Yer see, Leo 'asn't bin 'imself just lately, an' I need ter know wot's wrong, an' I was wonderin' wevver yer could tell me?'

'Me? Why don't yer go an' ask my missus? She's the one

who knows about this sort er fing.'

' 'Cos I know yer're the one Leo's fond of, Mr Quincey.
'E respects everyfin' yer say. Please tell me. 'As 'e said
anyfin' to yer – about 'im an' me, I mean?'

Reg pushed back his cap and scratched and shook his
head. 'Look, Pam,' he said awkwardly, 'I 'ave no idea wot
goes on between Leo an' you. It's yer own business, no one
else's.'

'But 'e must've said *somefin*'. 'E's bin so moody, 'e don't
talk ter me no more – I mean, not properly, like I meant
somefin' ter 'im.'

Over her shoulder in the distance, Reg could see his
foreman watching him impatiently. Fine Christmas this
would turn out to be, he thought, if he were to lose this job
just because he was gabbing too much. And yet, something
inside him told him that it wasn't right for him just to send
the girl away. As he had told Leo, Pam was a human being,
and the boy had no right to just kick her around like a
football. 'All I can say, Pam, is 'e'll be goin' away soon.
Yesterday mornin' 'e got 'is call-up papers.'

'Oh no!' Pam gasped.

'So yer see,' Reg continued, 'who knows wot the future
'olds – fer 'im, you, or any of us.'

Pam was close to tears. From the other side of the site,
the remains of a bonfire, dampened down by the icy cold
drizzle, was sending an undulating wave of black smoke
towards them. 'I just want ter know where I stand, Mr
Quincey,' Pam said, with a huge lump in her throat. 'That's
all. I just want ter know.'

Disregarding the glares he was getting from the foreman,
Reg took pity on the girl, and put a comforting arm round
her. He found it difficult to control his own feelings as he
caught the powerful aroma of the cologne she had clearly
smothered herself in. 'Yer know wot *I* fink yer should do,

Pam?' he said reassuringly. 'I fink you an' 'e should get tergevver an' talk fings over. When 'e gets 'ome ternight, I'll get 'im ter come round an' see yer. Would yer like that?'

'Oh, Mr Quincey,' replied Pam, tears streaming down her full little cheeks, 'I'd be so grateful. I really would.'

'Right then,' he said. 'That's settled!'

To his astonishment, Pam suddenly kissed him on the cheek. 'It's funny,' she said, 'in some ways, yer're so like Leo. But then – 'e's not a bit like you. Merry Chrissmas, Mr Quincey.' She turned and strolled off.

Reg, in a daze, watched her go. 'Merry Chrissmas, Pam,' he called.

As she made her way towards the end of the road, Pam's tears dried up very quickly. At least she had set her bait, and Reg had taken it. Now all she had to do was to wait for Leo's response, then tell him the truth about herself. It wasn't going to be easy but, thanks to Reg Quincey, her job was going to be made much easier. As she reached the end of the road, she wanted to take one last wave at him, so she came to a halt, and turned to look up. Reg had reached the second platform, and was already climbing up the third ladder on the last leg of his journey back up to the wall he had been demolishing. But he too stopped to take a look down at Pam, who had now returned to being a tiny figure in the distance. She looked quite extraordinary, dressed all in white like a snowdrop, with a thin curl of black smoke slowly drifting towards her from the dying bonfire.

Pam was waving frantically at Reg, so he did likewise. Down below, the foreman, clearly agitated, was again watching him, so he quickly resumed his climb. But the moment he started doing so, his attention was so diverted by Pam in the road below that he missed his foothold, and in his panic to hold on, caused the ladder to fall away from the wall.

Pam's screams echoed out across the vast expanse of the demolition site, as she watched Reg's helpless body, almost as if in slow motion, tumbling out of control towards the ground below.

At the Marble Arch Pavilion, the matinée performance of *The Thief of Baghdad* was about to begin. Under normal circumstances Leo would have moaned like hell at having to queue for nearly forty-five minutes in the rain to get in, but as he was with Peggy, he hardly noticed the time, especially as they had a variety of regular queue entertainers to keep them amused whilst they waited. The only thing he did moan about, however, was the price of admission to a West End cinema. 'Two an' six ter go ter the pittures!' he grumbled, after he'd bought the tickets at the box office. 'It's bleedin' 'ighway robbery, I tell yer! We can get in fer a tanner down the Marlborough!'

Peggy loved his grumbles, and linked arms with him as they made their way from the grand foyer towards the auditorium. For her, this was an enormous excitement, for it was in fact her very first visit to a cinema, and the whole experience, especially on the arm of someone she felt so utterly happy and secure with, was the best Christmas treat she could ever wish to have. On the way in, they stopped briefly to look at the photographs of the silent screen star Rudolph Valentino, who had once been mobbed by a huge crowd of women fans when he made a personal appearance at the cinema, and, as a footnote on the wall informed them, had had to be rescued from a back entrance by the police.

Once they had taken their seats in the back row of the grand circle, Peggy marvelled at the luxury and grandeur of the auditorium, with its red plush curtains and a huge chandelier hanging down from the middle of the high ornate ceiling, complete with dozens of tiny electric light bulbs. For Peggy, it was such a strange feeling to be in such a place, for the moment she walked in there was an atmosphere of warmth and friendliness that she had never experienced in the concert halls to which her father had always taken her and her mother with such overbearing enthusiasm.

Leo couldn't wait for the lights to go down, but when they did, and a trailer for *Foreign Correspondent* directed by the greatly admired Alfred Hitchcock had appeared, everybody's high spirits gradually evaporated as they watched the Gaumont-British News reminding them that there was a vicious war going on, and giving Peggy a sinking feeling in her stomach as she realised that Leo would soon be in that same army that was helping to defend the country in a struggle for survival. Only when they had settled down to the glitter, colour, spectacle and magic of the feature film did she relax again. Leo didn't have to say anything, but in the flickering light from the screen, she knew he was looking at her. When he slipped his arm around her shoulders, she leaned her head against his chest. Then, with one hand, he gently raised her chin, turned her face towards him, kissed her on the lips, then leaned his head on the top of hers. For this moment at least, there seemed to be no one in the whole wide world for each except the other, and the fact that they were snuggling up together in a cinema on Christmas Eve was as magical, and as far detached from reality as they had ever dared to hope.

Leo's young brothers, Horace and Eddie, were in the kitchen parlour playing conkers. Their mum had just given them their bath together in the scullery, and as she was still struggling to bucket out the dirty water from the tin bath down the old stone sink, she was unaware of the rumpus they were causing. However, she was relieved to get another chore over and done with; at least the kids would be clean when the family went to spend Christmas Day over at Gran and Granddad's place in Bethnal Green. The only problem was that neither of her sons much cared for their maternal grandparents, and despite the welcome presents they always got from their relations, Horace and Eddie usually teamed up with their equally as boisterous cousins to play merry hell during the family festivities, which more often than not ended in tears. Marge was pondering all this and emptying the last bucket of water from the old tin bath when she suddenly heard a loud crash coming from the kitchen.

'Wos goin' on in 'ere?'

The thunderous appearance of their mum at the door, with dress sleeves rolled up ready for a barney, threw the two boys into a panic. Whatever they had been up to, they had somehow managed to untie the overhead clothes-drying rack and bring it crashing down to the floor.

'It wasn't my fault, Mum!' pleaded Eddie, getting in first before his brother. 'Ace was larkin' about wiv it!'

'Liar!' protested Horace, grabbing his young brother by the hair and pulling him. '*You* did it! Yer know yer did!'

Marge had to break up the scuffle by shaking them, and giving them a token clout each behind their heads. 'Pack it up!' she yelled, until she had managed to separate them. 'This ain't the bleedin' school playground! Just look at my clothes! D'yer fink I've got all day ter keep clearin' up after you two?' She released the pair of them, and they quickly retreated into separate corners. 'You wait till yer dad gets 'ome. Yer'll be sent straight ter bed, Chrissmas Eve or no Chrissmas Eve!'

As they watched their mum picking up damp clothes from the floor and replace them on the drying rack, the two boys made obscene gestures to each other behind her back.

'It beats me 'ow yer can't even play a game of conkers wivout smashin' the 'ole place ter bits,' growled Marge.

'We ain't got no more conkers,' complained Eddie. 'Ace broke the last one. It's not fair. 'E 'ad a king – a really big one!'

'I din't!' snapped Horace.

'Yer did!'

'Shut up, you two!' yelled their mum, who was trying to unravel the home-made paper chains that had also been brought down with the drying rack. 'Why ain't yer got no more conkers left? Wot've yer done wiv 'em all?'

'Leo said 'e was goin' ter bring more when 'e came 'ome,' said Horace.

'Well, 'e'll be 'ome from work soon,' snapped Marge, getting more flustered and irritated with them. 'Yer'll 'ave ter wait till then!'

' 'E *won't* be 'ome soon,' replied Eddie, defiantly. ' 'Cos 'e *ain't* been ter work terday!'

Marge immediately stopped what she was doing. 'Wos that?'

Eddie suddenly felt quite superior. 'I said 'e ain't bin ter work terday.'

Marge, sweat still pouring down her face from emptying the bath water, gave Eddie a look of thunder. 'That's not true,' she said, trying hard to convince herself. 'Leo's on speshul Chrissmas Eve shift terday. 'E's due ter finish at four.'

Eddie ignored her, and returned to his broken conkers on the kitchen table.

Marge turned to Horace. 'Ace?' she asked sternly. 'Is this true?'

Being more loyal and discreet than his young brother, Horace hesitated before answering. 'I'm not really sure, Mum,' he replied sheepishly. 'All 'e said ter me wos as 'e's goin' inter the army after Chrissmas, 'e wants ter 'ave a bit of a last fling.'

Marge came close and glared at him. 'A last fling? Wot does *that* mean?'

Terrified, Horace shrugged his shoulders.

Marge waited a moment whilst she took in what she suspected. Then she quietly replaced the last of her washing on the clothes rack, pulled it back up to the ceiling, and fastened it to the hook on the wall below. When she turned around, both boys were watching her nervously. 'Go and get yer pyjamas on,' she said calmly.

Usually the boys would have automatically protested, but tonight they were on dangerous ground, so they were relieved to have an excuse to leave the room, which they did in record time.

Once they had gone, Marge sat at the kitchen table and, using her apron, wiped the sweat from her forehead. Then she idly looked around the tiny room, taking in, as she had done so many times before, that the place needed a damn good coat of paint. She couldn't remember how many times before the war she had asked Reg to do it, but somehow he always had an excuse not to. If you want something done, she said to herself, do it yourself. But there was a war on now, and paint and wallpaper were almost impossible to buy, and even if they were, she was only too aware that there weren't enough minutes in the day for her to do anything more herself. Even the old kitchen dresser, wedged up against the wall by the door, which she'd got from her own grandmother after she had died, was falling apart, and its dark brown varnish only made the room look even gloomier than it already was. But her mind was not on the old dresser. The clock on the mantelpiece above the oven range was showing that Leo should be home by now. This was Christmas Eve, and for most people it was a half-day holiday. So where the hell was he? Why had he lied to her? Where was he? What was he up to? Then she cursed Reg for not speaking to the boy. Did she have to do absolutely everything herself?

Just then she realised that she was squeezing something hard in the palm of her hand. When she looked, she found that it was one of the kids' conkers, which had been cracked in two. In a sudden fit of rage, she threw the conker with enormous force straight at the oven range, smashing the remains of the conker into pieces. 'Bloody little fool!' she cried.

At that moment, the front door bell downstairs rang. Automatically assuming that it was Leo who had forgotten his front door key, she got up from the table, stormed out of the room, and hurried downstairs.

Before she had reached the front door, the bell rang again, this time continuously.

'Bloody wait!' she yelled. 'Wot d'yer take me for?'

But at the very instant she managed to get the door open, Pam Warner rushed straight in, and threw her arms around her. 'Oh God, Mrs Quincey!' she sobbed hysterically. 'I'm sorry! I'm so sorry . . . !'

Marge was completely shocked. 'Pam!' she gasped. 'Wos up?'

Only then did she discover that the girl was not alone. Stepping into the passage from the early evening darkness of the yard outside was the tall figure of a police constable.

When Peggy and Leo left the cinema, it was already dark, but as most people were now hurrying home for the Christmas break, there was no queue outside, and in any case since the start of the air raids, afternoon performances were considered safer to attend than those in the evening. In Oxford Street, they wandered hand in hand, dodging in and out of the busy kaleidoscope of torch beams which were bouncing along the pavements in the dark, hurrying towards the nearest bus stop or tube station. For Peggy, however, it was a sorry sight, for she remembered this street only too well in happier days before the war, when at this time of year the multitude of shoppers were greeted with brightly lit windows, Christmas trees and fairy lights and, despite the seasonally cold weather, a real feeling of warmth and joy. But as they passed the burned-out shell of the badly bombed John Lewis Department store, she felt nothing but despair for the pure futility of war. Although the Peter Robinson store at Oxford Circus had also been damaged, it had reopened within a few days, and as they passed close by, Leo's torch beam suddenly picked out a news vendor's poster, with its ominous quote from the evening's headlines: 'CHURCHILL: ENEMY GAS ATTACK WARNING.' It was depressing stuff, and Peggy did her best to ignore it.

In Piccadilly Circus, they paused awhile, sitting on the steps of what in times of peace had been the Eros statue and its fountain. For its protection from air raids the statue had been removed and replaced with advertising billboards, which robbed this thriving thoroughfare of its very heart. Leo smoked a fag whilst they sat in silence, watching the last remnants of the working population making their wild dash home for Christmas with their families. Even the old flowerseller had sold the last of her chrysanthemums, and had packed up for the holiday. When Leo put his arm around Peggy's shoulders, she responded by snuggling up close to him and leaning her head against his shoulder. There was very little left to see, no neon lights, nor cockney sparrows picking around for discarded crumbs of bread, nor cars, nor lorries – only taxis and buses, and a horse-drawn coal cart on its way for a final delivery. The stone steps they were sitting on were ice cold, but they could feel nothing except the warmth of their own bodies.

'You know something?' Peggy said quite suddenly. 'If somebody asks me in twenty years' time where I was on Christmas Eve 1940, they're not going to believe me. In fact, I'm not sure I believe it myself. The night before Christmas has never meant much to my family.'

Surprised, Leo looked down at her.

Peggy glanced up at the evening sky, where dark night clouds were tumbling over each other to cover the bright winter moon. 'When I was a child,' she said, 'year after year I was told that there was no such person as Father Christmas, that such things were only for poor children, who were brought up to believe in fantasy, and that only God was the giver of riches and rewards. I remember one Christmas Eve, waking up in the dark in the middle of the night, and wondering if I could hear someone coming down the chimney. So I quickly got out of bed, went to the window, and frantically searched the sky, desperate to see those beautiful reindeer I'd read about so much, trotting across the rooftops, pulling a sleigh behind with a great big fat man with white whiskers and a red coat. In some ways I *could* see him, because I wanted to, because I could then prove that everything my father had told me wasn't true. But it wasn't like that. All I could see were the moon and a sky full of stars – a bit like tonight, in some ways.' She felt for Leo's hand, and held it. 'If there was such a person as Father Christmas,' she said, 'if he was on my roof, I'd have known it. But it doesn't matter really. Regardless of what my father thinks, I do *still* believe, because I *want* to. Silly, isn't it?'

Leo leaned down and kissed her gently on the top of her head.

She waited a moment, then asked, 'Do *you* still believe, Leo?'

'In Farver Chrissmas?'

'No. In us.'

Leo turned to face her. Although he could only really see her features when the moon popped in and out of the clouds, he used the tips of his fingers to trace gently the outline of her lips. 'I've believed in us ever since I first set eyes on yer,' he said.

'It's not going to be easy,' she said softly.

' 'Cos I'm goin' away?'

'No, Leo,' she replied. 'Because people don't want this to happen.'

Leo bridled. 'People? *Wot* people?'

'Your family – and mine.'

'Now look, Peggs—' he protested.

She interrupted him. 'We can't ignore the fact, Leo,' she said. 'We're different people, we come from totally different backgrounds. Officially you're still under age. Your family can stop this whenever they like. So can my father. He has such a jaundiced view of life.'

' 'E can't stop us lovin' each uvver, Peggs,' he said firmly. 'No one can do that.'

'Got a fag, mate?'

Both turned, startled, to see the outline of a down-and-out figure hovering over them.

'Piss off!' snapped Leo angrily.

'Leo,' pleaded Peggy softly. 'Please . . .'

Irritated, Leo dug down deep into his duffel coat pocket, found his packet of fags, and pushed them into the man's hand. 'Take the packet!' he growled, eager to get rid of the tramp.

'Gord bless yer, mate!' gasped the elated old man, shuffling off and calling as he went, 'Merry Chrissmas ter yer boaf!'

Leo waited for the man to disappear, then turned his

attention back to Peggy. 'Look, Peggs,' he said, 'I've got one week before I have ter report fer call-up. Durin' this week, I wanna prove ter you that wot I feel fer yer ain't some shot in the dark. I want yer ter know that wot I feel fer you is nuffin' any family can take away from us – yours nor mine. I love yer, Peggs. I know that may sound stupid ter yer after only a few weeks, but it's true – honest ter God, I mean it. If yer'll wait fer me, if yer'll just 'old on, I promise yer I'll let no one stand between us, not now, not never. D'yer believe me, Peggs? Do yer?'

Peggy believed everything he said. She believed him because she felt exactly the same way. Until she had met this boy from a world she hardly knew existed, she had thought that the love she had always craved for was only for other people but not herself. Yes, she believed him, and if necessary she would wait for him until eternity. As the moon made one of its fleeting, seductive appearances from behind the clouds, she could see Leo's pleading eyes glistening in the soft, pale light. Without saying a word, she leaned forward and gently kissed him.

It was after nine o'clock in the evening when Leo finally left the tube at Holloway underground station, and made his way back home along Hornsey Road. As he walked, it didn't seem possible that tomorrow was actually Christmas Day, for the streets were dark and deserted, and not a light could be seen at any window. But although the night was bitterly cold, and the pavements glistened in his torchlight, Leo felt confident enough to stride out with new-found assurance that he was at last beginning to sort out his life. His only regret was that for the next forty-eight hours, he would be parted from Peggy whilst they both played the charade of spending Christmas at home with their respective families. He wondered if the day would ever come when their two lives would be so inextricably woven together that separation at such a time would be a thing of the past. Would it ever happen? Could he foresee a day when he would be sitting down to a meal at the Thornton family table, or Peggy doing likewise with his own family in Hornsey Road? Well, whether they all liked it or not, he was determined that his future was going to remain with the girl he loved, and with this in mind, he had decided to follow his dad's advice. Before he left home for call-up, he would make a point of being completely honest with Pam Warner. As far as he was concerned, whatever their relationship had ever been in the past, it was now well and truly over.

As he passed under the Hornsey Road railway bridge, a goods train was making what must have been its final journey before the Christmas holiday, which probably accounted for the added zest with which the old rolling stock rumbled along the well-worn tracks. Leo often wondered how amazing it was that the bridge had so far survived the air raids, for, being so close as it was to the family's home, a direct hit would be calamitous. Just before he turned into the coal merchant's yard, he paused briefly to listen to a good old singsong coming from one of their neighbours' houses just along the road, where even Father Christmas himself would have felt like joining in the rousing chorus of 'Good King Wenceslas'.

The moment he opened the front door, Leo knew something was wrong. The place was in silence, which seemed more than odd considering this was the time when the kids were allowed to stay up and play games with their dad before turning in and dreaming of what Christmas presents they might find in their socks early the following morning. However, no sooner had he closed the door behind him and adjusted the blackout curtain draped over it, than his two young brothers came bursting out into the passage from the kitchen parlour.

'Leo!' yelled Horace, clearly upset. 'Where've yer bin?'

'Mum's bin waitin' fer yer!' reprimanded Eddie. 'Yer was s'pposed ter be 'ome hours ago!'

'Wos up?' asked Leo, astonished by all the fuss. But when he entered the kitchen parlour, he was even more astonished to find Pam Warner waiting there.

'Oh God, Leo!' sobbed Pam, dissolving into tears, and rushing forward to hug him. 'Wher've yer bin? We fought yer'd never get 'ome!'

'Pam!' spluttered Leo. 'Wot yer doin' 'ere? Where is everyone? Where's Mum?' His eyes were frantically searching the room. 'Where's Dad?'

At the mention of his dad, Pam dissolved into tears again.

'Dad's 'ad an accident,' said Horace, who was also tearful.

Leo froze.

' 'E fell off this buildin',' added Eddie. ' 'E's in the 'ospital.'

'It was my fault,' sobbed Pam. 'It was all my fault.' She looked up at Leo, her make-up streaked all down her chubby cheeks. 'I shouldn't've gone ter see 'im at work. 'E told me not to. 'E told me it was the wrong place ter talk. But I 'ad ter tell 'im. I 'ad ter tell 'im about you an' me.' The tears were flowing fast now as she added, 'I shouldn't've done it, Leo. I shouldn't've done it . . .'

Leo was totally shocked. 'Where's Mum?' he asked gravely.

No sooner had he mentioned her name than Marge Quincey appeared in the doorway. She was still in her hat and topcoat, and her face was torn with anxiety and tension.

'Mum?' said Leo, going to her.

Marge fixed him with a thunderous glare and, before he could say another word, she raised her hand and, with all the force she could muster, slapped him hard across the face.

Chapter 8

Peggy felt strange working on Christmas Day. Her special holiday shift was scheduled from seven in the morning until four in the afternoon, and this involved two return journeys from Hornsey Rise to Putney. As it turned out, however, she rather enjoyed herself, for not only were her passengers full of good seasonal banter, but Frosty, her driver, gave her a Christmas present of a small porcelain Morris dancer.

'Saw it in this shop in the arcade down the Nag's Head,' he said, chuckling as he gave it to her. 'My ol' woman reckons I've got the worst taste of any man she knows!'

Peggy disagreed. As far as she was concerned, it was the most wonderful present anyone had ever given her, and all the more so because it was so totally unexpected.

Despite the devastating scars of war on practically every street, Peggy thought that for just a few days at least, dear old London was looking at peace with itself. As the familiar red painted double-decker chugged its contented way along the deserted streets of Islington, Westminster and Kensington, Peggy had her first real opportunity to take in the views that she could on a normal working day only glimpse whilst running up and down the bus stairs collecting fares. In Tottenham Court Road she suddenly noticed a tall, narrow, nineteenth-century building that had clearly once been an elegant town house, but which in recent times had been squeezed between two much larger modern office structures. At first sight the old house seemed no more than a fleeting image on a much larger

157

landscape, but as the bus slowed to a halt at the nearby traffic lights, she realised that every outside window ledge of the entire building had been taken over by a profusion of sparrows and pigeons, who were all haughtily preening themselves in the early Christmas morning sun. Behind them were the charred remains of a completely gutted interior.

In Kensington High Street, Peggy collected quite a few new fares, for the congregation of St Mary's Roman Catholic Church were just filing out into the street after the early Christmas morning Mass. There were several families amongst them, and the children were beside themselves with excitement as they clutched presents they had either received in their socks or stockings overnight, or were taking on to their grandparents' home for the start of the family's Christmas festivities. Inevitably, there were plenty of high spirits, and Peggy found it difficult to cope with the sudden demand for change from ten-shilling notes, especially when the fare was for no more than tuppence or threepence ha'penny. She was relieved when, at Hammersmith Broadway, the bus practically emptied again, but even before they had reached the far side of Hammersmith Bridge, she found herself hurrying to the aid of an elderly woman whose poor old arthritic limbs found it quite a challenge to climb on to the platform.

'Not as young as I used ter be, ducks,' she laughed, as Peggy helped her to a bench seat close to the baggage compartment beneath the stairs. The old dear prefaced practically everything she said with a little chuckle or a hoarse laugh.

Peggy waited for the bus to move on before returning to her elderly passenger. 'Where to, madam?'

The old dear wasn't used to such respect, and it brought a huge grin to her face. 'All the way, ducks!' she returned chirpily. 'All the way ter dear ol' Putney. Wouldn't miss me Chrissmas treat fer the world!'

Peggy took the sixpenny piece the old dear was holding out for her, dug deep into her own leather coin pouch, returned tuppence-ha'penny change, then punched a ticket. 'So where are you off to for your Christmas treat then?' she asked, as she handed over ticket and change.

'Where?' asked the old dear, surprised. 'Why, it's 'ere, ducks,' she said, holding up the ticket Peggy had just given her. '*This* is me treat. A ride on me favourite bus ter Putney an' back. Just the job!' She pinched the dew drop from her nose, and rubbed it into her fingers. 'Just fink of all the marvellous fings I can see on the way,' she chuckled, her face positively beaming with excitement. 'Crossin' over the bridge, a nice walk down by the river, watchin' all the people rushin' off ter 'ave Chrissmas wiv their folk. Luvely!'

Peggy was completely taken aback. 'You mean, you're spending Christmas Day riding back and forth on the bus – to Putney?'

'*Every* Chrissmas Day, ducks! Once in the mornin', once in the afternoon. Bin doin' it fer years.'

Peggy could hardly believe what she was hearing. 'But – don't you have any family to go to?'

The old dear burst into laughter. 'Course I 'ave!' she roared, the remains of her pure white hair just visible beneath a neat well-used felt hat. 'But who wants ter see *them*? *I* don't, I can tell yer! Why should I? They don't want ter see me – not one of 'em, not me daughters nor their 'usbands, nor me grandchildren. So why should I want ter see *them*? No – ever since my 'ubby went I made up me mind ter do wot *I* wanna do wiv me life. So if I do it wrong, I've only got meself ter blame.'

When the old dear finally got off the bus at Putney Bridge, Peggy leaned out and watched the tiny figure go.

Neatly dressed in her Sunday best, her chubby old face blood red with the cold, and a thick woollen scarf wrapped tightly around her bony neck, she slowly made her way in the direction of the Putney embankment. The bus pulled away from the stop, and Peggy's final view of her extraordinary old passenger was of a distant silhouette gradually disappearing towards the winter sun, which was now a dazzling reflection in the fast-flowing waters of the River Thames.

Leo spent Christmas morning at his dad's bedside in the Royal Northern Hospital in Holloway Road. But although Reg's accident had resulted in serious bone and internal injuries, he had had a miraculous escape from death. To Leo's intense irritation, his mum insisted that the reason her husband had survived was because she had built up his constitution over the years by feeding him well and looking after him.

The Christmas parties that were taking place in the adjoining wards brought little cheer or comfort to Leo, who spent much of the time in the corridor outside, listening to his mum castigating him for not being around when she needed him most.

' 'E could've died fer all *you* cared!' she ranted over and over again. 'An' where was you when yer dad was fightin' fer 'is life? Well, I'll tell yer. Yer was out wiv yer bit of skirt from up the 'ill – right?'

'Stop it, Mum!' Leo turned away. He'd had just about all he could take from her. 'Dad's 'ad an accident, an' it's no use tryin' ter blame it on me!' He suddenly swung round. 'It's all Pam's fault,' he growled, eyes blazing. 'If *she* hadn't've gone up ter that site—'

'You leave Pam alone!' roared Marge, her shrill voice echoing along the hospital corridor. 'That poor gel's gone fru quite enuff becos er you!'

Leo suddenly felt that he was talking to a mad woman. 'Wot the 'ell are yer talkin' about?' he asked with incredulity. 'I wasn't the one who went ter the site. I wasn't the one who caused Dad ter fall off that scaffold!'

'Don't you go blamin' that on Pam!' barked Marge, squaring up to him.

'She 'ad no right ter be there, an' you know it!'

Marge was so infuriated she looked as though she would slap his face again. 'Wot's up wiv yer?' she asked, staring him straight in the eyes. 'Where d'yer get this chip from? Why d'yer always 'ave ter be number bleedin' one?'

Exasperated, Leo turned away from her again, and took a dog-end from behind his ear. 'I don't 'ave ter listen ter this,' he replied.

'No, of course yer don't, son,' persisted Marge. 'Yer don't 'ave ter take anyfin' 'cos yer don't want ter know. Yer don't want ter know nuffin' about no one except yerself! Yer don't want ter know 'ow yer're breakin' that poor gel's 'eart. Yer don't want ter know that she can't believe wot yer're doin' to 'er!'

Leo swung round on her. 'Wot d'yer mean, wot I'm doin' to 'er? Fer Chrissake, Mum, Pam's not my steady. She never 'as bin, she never will be!'

'Then why've yer bin stringin' 'er along?'

'I 'ave *not* bin stringin' 'er along!'

'Well, that's wot *she* finks!'

'Then that's *'er* problem, not mine!'

Marge watched him walk away from her again, and light his dog-end. 'So that's it, is it?' she asked, without expecting an answer. 'Pam's out, is she? Dumped – just like that?' She found her way to the visitors' bench alongside the ward door, and sat down. 'An' fer wot? I'd like ter know. Wot's 'Ighgate 'Ill got that 'Olloway 'asn't?'

This time Leo smoked his fag without turning to look at her. 'I don't know where yer get yer information from, Mum,' he said cuttingly, 'but yer don't know wot yer're talkin' about.'

'Oh no?' asked Marge, spitefully. 'Yer'd be surprised wot *I* know.'

Leo paused, considering her words, then calmly dropped his freshly lighted dog-end on to the lino floor, and screwed his heel into it. He now knew that there was very little more he could say to her. Ever since he was a kid, his mum always had to have the last word; it was the way she lived her life, the only way she knew – no argument, no discussion, no compromise. But this time she was wrong, and there was no getting away from it. He faced her one last time.

'Mum,' he said, calmly but firmly, 'I'm just as upset as you about Dad's accident, and I'm sorry I wasn't around ter support yer when it 'appened. But there's somefin' yer must know, somefin' yer've got ter understand.' He went across and stood in front of her. 'I can't do wot yer want me ter do. I can't be made ter love someone *I* don't love. I'm sorry, but that's 'ow it is – sorry fer Pam, an' sorry fer you.' He turned, and made for the exit.

'Number one, eh, son?'

His mum's voice caused him to stop briefly by the exit door, but without turning to look at her.

'Always number one.'

Leo angrily punched open the double doors with both his hands, and made off. As he did so, he bumped into an elderly hospital doctor who was dressed up in a fairly crude scarlet and white Father Christmas costume.

'Merry Christmas!' beamed the festive doctor, struggling with a heavy sack of gifts for the children's ward.

'Yeah!' returned Leo dismissively, pushing him aside.

Leo sprinted down the stairs. He just wanted to get out

of the place, away from the sour hospital smells, away from his mum's paranoia. When he finally made it to the yard outside, the Christmas morning sun was like a tonic, and he breathed in the crisp fresh air to rid his mind of the stifling atmosphere inside. As he left the side entrance of the hospital and made his way along Manor Gardens, he could hear the nurses' choir singing 'O come, all ye faithful' from one of the wards inside. Even that irritated him, so he quickened his pace until he found himself breaking into a run. He only came to a halt when he had reached Seven Sisters Road at the corner of Axminster Road with its long smart rows of solid Edwardian houses. There he paused just long enough to pull himself together, light up a fresh fag, and listen to the sounds of family Christmas celebrations coming from the front rooms all along the road. Everyone sounded so lively, so together. He quickly crossed over the main Seven Sisters Road, and started a brisk walk home. On the way, he passed a great gap where only a month or so earlier an aerial torpedo had ripped through a terrace of shops, causing immense devastation, death and injury. Once he had passed by, his pace slowed, but, for some reason, his mind was racing.

He came to a halt, and found himself staring into the window of a delicatessen-type shop, renowned in better times for its sixpenny pigs' trotters. But when he looked in the glass window, it wasn't his own reflection Leo could see there. Peggy. Suddenly, her face was there before him, first in the café behind Selfridges on Christmas Eve, and then in the back row of the picture house at Marble Arch. Why? Why was she there in his mind? What did it mean? He came to, and looked along the Seven Sisters Road. A number 14 bus was approaching from Upper Hornsey Road. Whether this was the mental connection with Peggy or not, he couldn't be sure, but it made him want to see her. He *had* to see her – now, that very minute. Even though he knew that Peggy was probably on the other side of London on her earlier shift, he quickly retraced his steps and made an impulsive dash towards the nearest bus stop.

He just managed to jump on to the platform as the number 14 was moving off, but the moment it had crawled just a few yards, it was suddenly held up at the traffic lights. He had only enough time to find a seat, when, again impulsively, he leaped up and off the bus just as it was pulling away. 'Make up yer mind, Leo!' yelled the conductor, who was one of Leo's mates from up the garage. Leo hardly acknowledged the call. He just turned away, and made off along one of the quiet back streets towards home. Why had he got off that bus? Wasn't it Peggy he wanted to see, Peggy that he wanted to hold tight in his arms? So why was it another face that suddenly dominated his mind? Pam Warner? Poor, put-upon Pam, who meant nothing to him, nothing at all. Why her? Why not Peggy? He had absolutely no idea.

Peggy got to The Towers at about six o'clock on Christmas evening. By then she had managed to go home, have a bath and change out of her clippie's uniform into something more suitable for Christmas dinner with the family at her grandparents' house at the top of Highgate Hill. Fortunately, the war had somewhat dimmed the Thorntons' enthusiasm for formal dress at dinner, so Peggy chose a simple plain dark green dress. When she got there, the festivities, such as they were, were already in progress. This involved three frenzied games of whist, played at separate tables in the large, ornate sitting room, followed by drinks, and then the grand Christmas family dinner itself. Peggy timed her arrival perfectly, for by the time she walked in, the whist tables had just been folded away, and drinks were being served by a maid and a manservant.

'Workers of the world unite!' mocked Alice Thornton, the moment Peggy made an appearance. 'And how many fares have you collected today, my brave little comrade?'

Peggy's inclination was to ignore her grandmother's silly jibes, but she wasn't going to give the old woman the satisfaction of knowing that she was irritated by her remark. 'Actually, it was a quiet day,' she replied, giving her grandmother the mandatory peck on her cheek. 'I imagine most people were at home having Christmas lunch with their families.'

Alice put a brave face on her failure to provoke a spirited response. 'I imagine so,' she replied, pulling on her usual Craven A.

Once she'd toured the room, greeting the rest of the family, Peggy took her place on a chaise longue alongside her maternal grandmother, Nora Tyler, whom Peggy had always felt more comfortable with than her father's own autocratic mother. Nora's second husband, Arthur, a podgy little man in a grey three-piece suit, with a gold watch and chain in his waistcoat and a golf club tie, had taken up his usual position in front of the crackling log fire, warming his rump with both hands, a habit which always infuriated Alice Thornton. The room itself was snug enough, but more of a showpiece than a home, with heavy velour curtains draped across the tall bay windows, a rather bland Persian carpet which covered most of the floor space, and heavy mahogany furniture which had been inherited from Alice's own father, who had had the stuff shipped back from India during his tour of military service out there.

'Tell me something, Peggy, my dear,' Alice persisted. 'What happens when the war's over? Will you continue your career running up and down the stairs of a bus each day?'

Peggy smiled back at her graciously. She was ready for

her. 'Who knows, Grandmother?' she replied instantly. 'If the prospects are right, I may well consider it.'

'Prospects!' Alice nearly choked on a mouthful of sherry. 'On a bus?'

Again Peggy smiled graciously. 'Why not?' she asked.

To everyone's surprise, Robert Thornton roared with laughter. It was a deep-throated booming sound, for whenever Thornton laughed he always wanted to make sure that he was drawing attention to himself. 'Really, Mother!' he said, his whole body shaking up and down as though someone had just said something unbelievably funny. 'If you don't know what a young rascal your granddaughter is by now, you never will! This is just a little bit of fun for Peggy, her way of contributing to the war effort. When this damned war is over, she'll be doing something that is far more suitable for her abilities.' He gave Peggy a lingering, expectant smile. 'Isn't that so, my dear?'

All eyes turned towards Peggy. After a pause, her reply for her father was, for him, tantalisingly frustrating. 'We shall have to wait and see, Father,' she said. 'When the war's over, I imagine things are going to be different – for *all of us.*'

As she spoke, an antique brass Swiss clock, which had not got the time right in twenty years, chimed the hour. To Peggy, it sounded like a laugh. But not to Thornton, who had a grim, fixed smile on his face.

Grandmother Nora moved uncomfortably in her chair. 'Well, I do hope this wretched war comes to an end soon,' she said. 'It's playing havoc with my nerves.' Unlike her daughter, Catherine, Nora was a dumpy, dithery little woman, whose face was lined with perpetual anxiety.

'Oh, don't worry,' announced her husband, Arthur, confidently. 'It'll all be over by the New Year.' He didn't have a hair left on his head, but he did have a bushy white moustache which he hoped made up for it. 'You mark my words, Hitler's got the wind up. Took on more than he could cope with. Didn't think us bulldogs could take care of ourselves. Well, he knows now, that's for sure. That's why we shan't get any more air raids.'

As usual, everyone listened in silence to Arthur, but never believed anything he said. Arthur, a businessman who had gone into textiles after coming a cropper in insurance, was generally accepted in the family to be a bit of a know-all; he invariably had plenty of opinions, but very little substance.

It was Catherine who broke the embarrassing silence following his remark. 'I hope you're right, Father,' she said nervously. 'Remember what Mr Churchill said the other day. We can't be complacent.'

Peggy put a comforting arm round Nora's shoulders and gave her a reassuring smile.

'Churchill!' snorted Alice. 'That stupid old fool! He's more interested in his brandy and cigars than keeping the huns out of our skies!'

'I think that's a bit unfair, Alice,' said Arthur, careful not to ruffle her feathers too much. 'We need a strong leader like Churchill. If that buffoon Chamberlain was still in charge, we'd have collapsed like a pack of cards.'

Over by the window, Herbert Thornton slammed his own pack of cards down on to the card table. He was bored out of his mind. 'I'll go and see how the dinner's coming along,' he said, getting up from his chair and leaving the room.

Peggy watched him go. She wished she could join him. The others, however, hardly noticed that he had left. Despite the huge, beautifully decorated Christmas tree in one corner of the room, there was no feeling that today was any more special than any other day of the year. Here, in this room, in this musty old house which was far too big for its two sole occupants, Peggy felt a sense of decay, as though everyone had gone to sleep with their eyes open. Is this really what happens to people who are well off? she asked herself. Although her paternal grandparents were not rich in the true sense of the word, they had never had to suffer, to scrimp and save. Did having a lot of money mean that you were a better person than most, she wondered; did it make you feel good inside? Had it made her grandparents or her parents feel 'good' inside? Had it drawn them closer together, helped them to love and to cherish each other? As she looked around the room at the bland faces of her family, she doubted it. Money. How extraordinary it was to think that little pieces of paper and grubby coins should be allowed to determine so many people's lives.

'Now tell me, Robert,' said Alice Thornton, suddenly sitting up in her red plush armchair. 'Have *you* ever travelled on an omnibus?'

'Don't be ridiculous, Mother,' replied Thornton, irritated. 'Of course I have – many times. Especially in my younger days at college.'

'And did you enjoy the experience?'

'*Enjoyed* is hardly the word I would use.' Thornton got up from his seat, and went across to the baby grand piano, where he idly flicked through some music sheets.

'Well, *I* went on an omnibus once,' said Alice, clearly determined to develop the conversation as a means of teasing her granddaughter. 'It was years ago, of course, when I was just a young girl at finishing school.' She looked around the room for reactions when she added with a twinkle in her eye, 'Actually, I quite enjoyed it.'

Nora accidentally caught her eye, and smiled back nervously.

'It was a dare,' continued Alice, who accepted Nora as a captive audience. 'Mainly because my father had told me not to. It was a horse-drawn vehicle. We went through Trafalgar Square. I remember the driver bringing us to a halt at a water trough to let the animal have a drink. It was hilarious, especially when it fouled the kerb. The horse I mean, not the driver!' She roared with chesty laughter as she simultaneously laughed at her own feeble joke and pulled on her Craven A. 'The only part I didn't like was the person sitting next to me. A dreadful old woman – looked as though she'd come straight out of the poor house. Smelled like it too! She positively reeked of pickled onions!'

Peggy felt nothing but despair as she listened to her family sniggering self-consciously at her grandmother's banal story. It was so condescending, so totally unamusing. But it did bring a smile to her face when she recalled that other very different old lady, who had been a passenger on her bus that morning: '*This is me treat. A ride on me favourite bus ter Putney an' back. Just fink of all the marvellous fings I can see . . . Crossin' over the bridge, a nice walk down by the river, watchin' all the people rushin' off ter 'ave Chrissmas wiv their folk. Luvely!*' It seemed such a long way from sherry and playing cards on Highgate Hill. A few minutes later, she left the room to look for her grandfather.

Herbert Norton was taking refuge in the old summerhouse at the bottom of the garden. When Peggy caught up with him he was huddled up in his warm garden duffel coat, thoroughly enjoying a pipe of his favourite tobacco.

'Is this a private party,' asked Peggy, 'or can anyone join?'

Although it was too dark to see her features clearly, Herbert smiled, and made room for her on the wooden bench seat next to him. As Peggy was only in her thin cotton dress, he immediately untagged his coat, which allowed her to snuggle up close to him. For a moment or so, they sat there in silence, shielding themselves from the biting cold, staring up through one of the last remaining windows towards the dark night sky above, which was already overcrowded with a profusion of shimmering bright stars all vying for attention.

'Hard to believe it's Christmas night,' said Peggy, her voice only just audible, but still cracking the utter stillness of the moment. 'D'you think it was like this when it all began?'

'Christmas night, you mean?' asked Herbert, an undulating funnel of smoke filtering up from his pipe. 'Up there – yes. Not sure about down here, though.'

For a moment they remained in contemplative mood until Peggy suddenly asked, 'Grandfather, why don't you ever smoke your pipe inside the house? Is it because Grandmother won't let you?'

Herbert smiled to himself. In the dark he could feel her head leaning gently on his shoulder. 'Not really,' he replied, putting his arms around her shoulders. 'I just choose not to, that's all. Better to put out a fire before it starts,' he added.

From the house, they could hear the start of the Thorntons' traditional Christmas pre-dinner musical soirée. Accompanied by his wife on the baby grand piano, Robert Thornton, whose only really likeable feature appeared to be that he had a rich baritone voice, was launching into a stirring rendition of 'Come into the Garden, Maude'.

'D'you think he loves Mother?' asked Peggy, reflectively.

'Your father?'

'Yes.'

Herbert hesitated a moment before answering. 'I think

he's not capable of loving in the same way that we think people *should* love,' he said. 'But that doesn't mean he doesn't love your mother in his own way. I know my son only too well. Admitting that he cares for someone would seem to him like failure.'

Peggy was puzzled. 'Failure?'

'Failure because it would reveal a soft interior. Robert couldn't do that. But beneath all that bravado, I think he does love your mother. He'll just never have the courage to tell her so.'

Although most of the shattered windows of the summerhouse had been boarded up after bomb blasts, there were still one or two panes of glass left through which you could watch the dark night clouds as they rushed impatiently across the luminous white light of a seductive half-moon.

'And what about you, young lady?' asked Herbert, after taking several puffs from his pipe. 'D'you feel like telling me about *your* young man?'

Peggy was surprised by his unexpected question, but because there had always been a close bond between them, she was perfectly prepared to answer it. 'Nothing much to tell really,' she replied casually. 'He's just – very nice, that's all.'

'Why?'

'Why is he nice?'

'Why do you *think* he's nice?'

Peggy took a moment to think about that. 'Because he brings out something in me that I didn't know existed. We also love being in each other's company.'

'Well, that's not a bad start.'

'No, it's more than that, Grandfather,' continued Peggy. 'He's encouraged me to start questioning myself, to find out who I am, and what I want to do with my life. It's funny, but these days there are times when I feel as though

171

I'm walking around with my eyes wide open. It's never really been like that before.' She snuggled her ice-cold face into the warm fleece lining of his coat. 'Leo doesn't know all this, of course,' she said. 'But that's how I feel.'

They returned to another brief moment of silence, broken only by the unmistakable sound of Robert Thornton's baritone voice booming out one of his favourite Christmas carols from the drawing room, and harmonising nicely with the howling of a disapproving dog in the distance.

'Grandfather,' said Peggy, having to raise her voice slightly to be heard, 'is it really possible to love somebody who's so completely different to yourself? I mean, somebody who has had hardly any education, who never reads a book, uses bad language and smokes too much, and who couldn't tell the difference between a dessertspoon and a soup spoon?'

Herbert's affectionate smile was clearly visible as the moon suddenly emerged from behind a vast night cloud and flooded his face. 'Well, I'm not exactly an expert in matters of the heart, my dear,' he said, looking down at her, 'but as a layman I'd imagine it isn't about cutlery and books. It's about *who* and not *what* you are.'

'But you love Grandmother,' said Peggy, 'and you're very different from her.'

'Am I?' he asked. 'I wonder.' For a moment, he leaned his head on the high back of the bench seat. 'As a matter of fact,' he continued, 'I *don't* love your grandmother. In fact, I don't think I ever have.'

Peggy was shocked. 'Grandfather!' she gasped.

'Oh, you mustn't be too shocked.' He pulled his coat tightly around her shoulders. 'Alice is a bully. She always has been. It's in her blood, you see. Just like her father. Has to be in total control of everyone and every situation she's involved with. Oh, she has a quick tongue all right, ever ready with a sharp response, a clever jibe, always the matriarch, the queen pin of the family. But the poor woman has a centre that's as hard as nails.'

'And you still feel the same way about her – after all these years?'

'Oh yes. More so if anything.'

'But if you've never loved her, why did you marry?'

Herbert breathed a sigh of despair. 'Because at that time I believed that marrying her would give me the one chance I'd ever have of getting away from parents who just couldn't let go. Ever since I was a child I felt totally dominated by a forceful mother and an indifferent father. Your father takes after his mother. They're both tyrants. Whatever my parents did, I had to follow – follow, and never lead. You know what it's like to be trapped in a cage, Peggy. Well, that's what it was like with me. Oh yes, whenever my parents were away, there were other women, quite a few of them as a matter of fact. I fell madly in love with one of them, but I didn't have the strength of character to hold on to her. Yes, Peggy, I was weak. I've always been weak. That's why I married your grandmother. When I first met her, she was beautiful, composed, accomplished and such good fun. I thought I loved her, but I was wrong. I blame myself. Alice can only ever be the person she is. But she's not the person I should have spent the whole of my life with, and I'll always regret it.'

From the house, the musical soiree seemed to be gathering momentum.

'Don't ever let the same thing happen to you, Peggy,' said Herbert, who leaned closer so that she could hear. 'Make no mistake, I love my son. I love Robert very much. But if he's given the chance, he'll destroy you. He's like his mother. He wants control, total control. He can't help it.

It's in *his* blood too, in his family's blood. What I'm trying to tell you is that if you love this boy, whether he comes from the top or the bottom of the hill, then hang on to him. Because if you let him go, your father will make quite sure you'll never get the same chance again.'

Robert Thornton's rendition of his favourite carol was building to a climax with the final chorus. It was a curious choice for someone like him.

> 'Christmas is coming,
> The geese are getting fat
> Please to put a penny in the old man's hat
> If you haven't got a penny, a ha'penny will do
> If you haven't got a ha'penny, a farthing will do
> If you haven't got a farthing, God – Bless – You.'

It hadn't been much of a Christmas Day for the Quincey family. Most of the time had been spent taking turns visiting Reg in hospital, which meant that the usual Christmas Day get-together with Reg's widowed father, brothers and cousins, had to be abandoned. However, since his mum was determined to spend most of the day at Reg's bedside, Leo did his best to look after his young brothers, playing football with them in the coal yard in front of the office block outside, helping Horace to assemble the model Spitfire kit his parents had bought him for Christmas, and encouraging young Eddie to make stink bombs with one of his presents – a home chemistry set. At about six o'clock in the evening, Marge popped home briefly to put the chicken in the oven, and although Leo didn't know the first thing about cooking, he agreed to keep an eye on it, and put the potatoes in the roasting pan after about three-quarters of an hour. By the time Pam turned up, soon after seven, the pungent smells wafting in from the scullery were driving

Horace and Eddie mad with hunger. To distract their cravings until their mum got home, they were packed off to their bedroom to get acquainted with the few sparse wartime Christmas presents they'd found at the end of their beds that morning.

'I've bin up the 'ospital wiv yer mum,' said Pam, who seemed nervous about what kind of a mood Leo would be in. 'She said it'd be all right if I looked in on yer.'

'I bet she did,' replied Leo tersely. He was fully aware that she was looking as pretty as a picture in a powder-blue coat and cotton headscarf, but he wasn't going to show it. Turning his back on her, he went to the tiled mantelpiece, and found himself the remains of a dog-end.

'It's a terrible thing to 'ave 'appened,' said Pam tentatively. ' 'Speshully at Chrissmas.'

When Leo turned back to look at her, she was sitting at the kitchen parlour table. 'Wot d'yer want, Pam?' he asked coldly.

Pam looked as though she wanted to cry, but couldn't. 'I just wanted ter say sorry,' she said, eyes lowered. 'I shouldn't've gone ter see yer dad up the site.'

'Then why did yer?'

To steady her nerves, Pam took a deep breath before answering. 'I 'ad ter know. I 'ad ter know if it was true.'

Leo tried unsuccessfully to make eye contact with her. 'Wot yer talkin' about?'

'About if yer're seein' someone else.'

Leo felt himself tense. 'Who told yer that?' he growled.

'No one told me,' replied Pam, her face still red from the cold evening air outside. 'There are some fings people know wivout 'avin' ter be told.'

Leo didn't answer her. He merely found a box of matches, put the dog-end in his lips and lit it.

Pam was determined to get an answer from him.

'So?' she asked apprehensively. 'Is it true?'

Leo remained defiantly silent.

'I've got a right ter know, Leo,' pressed Pam.

'Yer've got a right ter know nuffin', Pam!' he snapped. 'We're not a couple. We're not engaged, we're not married. Yer've got a right ter see who yer like – an' so 'ave I! Is that right, or ain't it?'

Pam still didn't have the courage to look up at him. 'Yes, Leo.' Her response was barely audible.

As he watched her sitting there, hands dug deep into her coat pockets, he felt one brief moment of remorse. After quickly inhaling an agitated puff from his dog-end, he said, 'Look, Pam, 'ave I ever tried ter make yer fink that I wanted us ter spend the rest of our lives tergevver? 'Ave I?'

'No, Leo.'

'Then wot's this all about? Why are you an' me muvver gangin' up on me, tryin' ter make me do somefin' that I don't want ter do?'

'We're not gangin' up on yer, Leo.'

'No? Then why's she blamin' *me* for me dad's accident?'

'Because she knew 'ow much I felt fer yer.' For the first time, she looked up directly into his eyes. 'An' I do, Leo. I still do – despite everyfin'.'

Leo felt trapped. As he looked into those big blue eyes, they immediately filled him with guilt. It was, after all, those same eyes he had stared into on that one fateful night they had slept together. 'Pam,' he said, trying hard to make some kind of effort, 'wot we done in the past ain't got nuffin' ter do wiv 'ow two people *feel* about each uvver. It was somefin' that 'appened, that's all – becos fings like that 'appen between people all the time.'

Pam lowered her eyes again. She felt as cold as ice.

'Yer're right,' said Leo, turning to stare into the dim

glow from the coke fire in the grate. 'I *am* seein' someone else. An' I do love 'er.'

Pam stirred inside. But it wasn't pain.

'I don't know 'ow it's 'appened – or why – but that's the way it is.' He turned round to find that Pam had risen from her chair. 'I'm sorry,' he said. 'I'm truly sorry. I don't wanna 'urt yer, Pam. I don't wanna 'urt no one. Maybe I'm just all mixed up – I don't know. But I've got ter do fings *my* way. Yer do understand that, don't yer?'

Pam smiled bravely. 'As long as I know,' she replied. She turned, and made her way slowly to the door. When she got there, she took one last look at him. 'G'bye, Leo,' she said.

Leo wanted to say one final thing to her, but she had already gone.

On the landing outside, Pam paused just long enough to get her breath back. She felt very odd, torn between relief and rejection. But there were no tears, no regrets. She wasn't that sort of person. She was her *own* person, and now that she knew where she stood with Leo, she knew that she had to think again about what she wanted to do. Taking a deep breath, she made a sudden dash down the stairs, moving as fast as her legs would carry her. But before she had reached the front door, she realised that Leo was rushing down behind her. To her absolute astonishment, he threw his arms around her impetuously and hugged her tight.

'I'm sorry, Pam,' he whispered in her ear. 'I'm really sorry.' Even as he spoke, the words stuck in his throat. How could he do what he was doing, he asked himself? How could he betray Peggy, the only woman he loved, the only woman he would ever love? But, torn apart by despair and uncertainty, after what had happened to his dad, he couldn't betray his family either. Whatever he thought of his mum's bullying ways, there *was* such a thing as duty – duty to his family, and a duty to do what he hoped was right. He pulled away and smiled weakly at Pam. 'I'll do me best,' he said, with difficulty. 'I can't promise it'll work, but I'll do me best.'

As he moved in to kiss her firmly on the lips, Pam's eyes widened. It was just as well that Leo couldn't take in her expression, for it was one of disbelief and shock. This was not what she had wanted. This was not what she had wanted at all.

Chapter 9

Christmas couldn't end quickly enough for Peggy. It meant that she had no more family commitments to tie her down, no more having to listen to her grandmother holding court over her household, and no more pretending that she was part of a loving, united family. But the most important thing for Peggy was that it meant she would see Leo again, even if it was for just a few more days before he left for the army. But when she turned up for work the day after Boxing Day, she was not expecting the news that awaited her.

'Leo's bin deferred fer anuvver munf,' announced Charlie Pipes, who met Peggy just as she was signing on in the conductors' room. 'Apparently 'is ol' man 'ad an accident. Fell off the scaffold on the site where 'e works.'

'Oh God!' gasped Peggy. 'Is he seriously hurt?'

Well, 'e ain't too speshul by the sound er fings. But 'e's on the mend, so Alf Grundy says. They took 'im to the Royal Northern down 'Olloway Road. Poor ol' Reg. 'Ate ter see it 'appen ter someone like 'im. Real salt of the earth, that one.'

Peggy felt a wave of anxiety. 'When did all this happen?' she asked.

'Chrissmas Eve.' The answer this time came from Elsie Parker, the young conductress who, with her mates, had given Peggy such a rough time in the canteen on Peggy's first day at work. 'Alf said Reg fell off the scaffold after some gel went ter see 'im.'

'Girl? What girl?'

Elsie shrugged and winked mischievously. 'Probably some fancy bit 'e's 'avin' on the side!'

Her raucous laughter at her own attempt to be funny fell on deaf ears. Charlie Pipes, for one, was not amused. 'Reg Quincey ain't that sort er bloke,' he said, without so much as a fleeting glance at Elsie. 'I've known 'im fer years. When 'e used ter work up 'ere, 'e often did as much overtime as he could get just ter make ends meet. But I'll tell yer somefin': that man's bin a number-one 'usband an' farver ter 'is family. One er the best.'

Elsie could have bitten off her tongue. 'I didn't mean nuffin',' she said guiltily to Peggy. 'Honest ter God I didn't.'

Peggy gave her a reassuring smile. Despite the unpleasantness of their first encounter, Peggy had started to get on quite well with Elsie, so much so that they had recently taken to sitting with each other in the canteen between shifts. Peggy had also come to realise that Elsie herself had had a crush on Leo, which had clearly never developed into anything.

The conductors' room was now getting quite busy, with people coming and going, getting chits signed, opening and balancing their cash total sheets, collecting the day's stock of tickets, and checking up on any road delays that would affect their routes.

'Can't've bin much of a Chrissmas fer young Leo,' said Charlie, who was just preparing to go out on the road with a new trainee conductor. 'If I know anyfin' about that mum of 'is, she's blamed everyfin' on 'im regardless.'

Peggy was puzzled. 'What do you mean?' she asked.

'Leo's 'er punch-bag,' explained Elsie. 'Rules over 'im wiv a rod er iron. If the poor sod don't do exactly wot she wants, she gives 'im wot for. Real tyrant, that one!'

Peggy was finding it hard to take all this in. 'I don't understand,' she said. 'Leo always says how well he gets on with his father. Surely Mr Quincey knows how to deal with his own wife?'

Charlie and Elsie exchanged wry smiles.

'Yer don't know Marge Quincey,' said Charlie. 'I'm afraid she's a very spiteful woman, Peggs. She don't care who she upsets, or wot she says ter 'er folk in front er people.'

'Yer can say that again,' agreed Elsie. ' 'Ere, Charlie, d'yer remember that time she come up 'ere ter see Leo when 'e was just knockin' off from work – said 'e ought ter be 'ome lookin' after his bruvvers instead er spendin' all 'is time in the boozer wiv 'is mates?'

'I remember,' said Charlie, shaking his head with a sigh. 'I also remember 'ow she walloped the daylights out er 'im when 'e told 'er ter bugger off an' mind 'er own business.'

'Bloody cow!' growled Elsie. 'They ought ter lock 'er up an' frow away the key!'

Peggy was listening to all this in a state of sheer disbelief. Was it possible? Leo – beaten up by his own mother – and in front of other people? It sounded incredible. This wasn't how she'd imagined Leo lived his life. Surely this wasn't how working-class people treated their own kith and kin. Surely it was only people like her own sort who lived their entire lives wanting their own way.

'Can anyone tell me Leo's address?' she asked.

'I wouldn't if I was you, Peggs,' warned Charlie, grave-faced.

'Keep away from that place,' added Elsie. 'It won't 'elp Leo – or you.'

A short while later, Peggy was back on the conductor's platform of the number 14 with Frosty as her driver. It was a fairly uneventful journey with the exception of a middle-aged male passenger who found he hadn't a penny on him to pay for his ticket. Peggy knew precisely why. She could smell the beer on his breath before she'd even climbed the stairs to the upper deck. But as she was in no mood to tell him to get off the bus, she paid the penny ha'penny fare herself, and gave him a ticket. She realised that it was a foolish thing to do for if she did the same for other passengers she would end up bankrupt. She made a mental note not to do it again.

The bus had only reached Caledonian Road when the air-raid siren sounded. As the Germans had proclaimed a suspension of air raids during the Christmas period, none of the passengers on the bus took much notice, and were quite content to continue on their journey. As it turned out, however, the siren was a false alarm, and before they had even reached King's Cross station the All Clear was blasting the air all over London.

For most people Friday was back-to-work day after the Christmas break, which meant that the streets were once again bristling with shoppers, office clerks and manual workers. Piccadilly Circus looked as though everything had remained open during the Christmas break, for there were already queues forming outside the London Pavilion for the morning show of *Goodbye Mr Chips*. In the West End the bus collected more passengers than anywhere along the whole route, mainly window shoppers looking out for bargains in the forthcoming New Year sales. There were also plenty of soldiers home on brief passes, doing the sights with their girlfriends, trying hard to forget that there was still a war on and likely to go on for a very long time. Amongst the passengers Peggy picked up en route were two middle-aged women who were on their way home from their cleaning jobs at offices above the St Pancras Hotel, and who, in the short time that Peggy had been on the buses, had become her 'regulars'. Nicknamed 'Gert and Daisy' after the popular music-hall entertainers, they kept Peggy's spirits up all the time with their cockney banter, which invariably included some fairly bawdy jokes at the expense of Adolf Hitler.

The bus terminated at Hammersmith Broadway, and turned around ten minutes later. During that time Peggy and Frosty just had time to snatch a quick cuppa at the London Transport mobile canteen at the roadside, and catch up on how both had spent their Christmas and Boxing Day evenings. But whilst they chatted, Frosty became aware that Peggy's mind was miles away.

'Looks like you got boyfriend trouble, my gel,' he said, with a shrewd twinkle.

'Oh, I'm sorry, Frosty,' said Peggy. 'I don't know what's wrong with me today. Too much of Father's port last night, I think!'

She chuckled nervously, but Frosty merely smiled. 'Wos up, mate?' he asked. 'Is it Leo?'

Peggy nodded. 'Frosty,' she said, 'I've been hearing such extraordinary things about him. Apparently his father's had an accident and although it had nothing to do with Leo, his mother's taking it out on him.'

'Nuffin' new about that,' said Frosty gloomily.

'Is she really the kind of person they say she is?'

Frosty sighed. 'She give 'im a black eye once,' he said. 'When 'e turned up fer work the next day, he tried to make out he'd 'ad a barney in the pub. But we all knew. When she was up the garage once, I saw 'er wiv me own eyes punch 'im right in the stomach.' He touched his own stomach as though he could feel the blow himself. 'I tell yer, it was a terrible fing ter see.'

Peggy was horrified. 'But *why*?' she asked. 'Why does she do things like that? Why does her husband *let* her do things like that? And to their own son?'

Frosty shrugged. 'Not much poor ol' Reg can do about it,' he replied. '*She's* the boss in that family, make no mistake about it. If yer ask me she's 'alf round the bend.'

On the return journey, Leo was constantly on Peggy's mind. It seemed incomprehensible to her that for someone who was so obviously more than capable of defending himself in a rough and tumble against any man, he appeared to be completely incapable of standing up to his own mother. And yet, was it so different to her own homelife? True, she didn't have parents who beat her up, but she did have a tyrannical father who was just as self-willed and dominating as Leo's mother.

In Euston Road, a young soldier got on to the bus carrying all his army gear on his back. Peggy helped him to stack it into the baggage space under the stairs, then let him go off to take his seat. After the boy had got off at the Offord Road stop, a middle-aged male passenger spoke to her from a bench seat near the bus platform. 'Forgot something, haven't you, miss?'

Peggy looked up with a start. 'I beg your pardon?' she replied.

To her surprise the man, who was wearing a navy-blue overcoat and trilby hat, suddenly produced a London Transport identity card from his pocket. Peggy didn't have enough time to look in detail at the card before he put it back into its wallet, but she saw enough to know that the holder was a 'Spots Man', who travelled incognito on the buses to check that the conductors were being honest. 'Are you aware that when a member of the armed forces gets on board without paying for his ticket, you are supposed to ask to see his travel pass?'

'Well, yes,' foundered Peggy, 'but I thought it was obvious he was in the army.'

'Obvious or not,' continued the man, taking out a small, intimidating notebook from his pocket, 'LT rules are there to be acknowledged – and obeyed. How could you be sure that he wasn't an imposter?'

Peggy did a double take. 'Imposter?' she spluttered. 'But he was in uniform.'

'Thornton. Is that right?' The man was checking her registration number with a list in his book.

Peggy couldn't bear his nasal voice, which sounded as though it was a talking machine. 'Yes,' she replied, flustered. 'Yes, it is.'

'New recruit – right?'

Peggy swallowed. 'Yes.'

'Right.' The man closed his little book. 'I'm prepared to overlook the matter on this occasion, miss, but please remember that London Transport's rules are there for everybody – you *and* me.' He got up from his seat just as the bus was pulling up at the next bus stop. But before getting off, he called back: 'And also remember – you're still on three months' probation.'

The man got off, Peggy rang the bell, and Frosty drove off, leaving his conductor to flop down on to the empty bench seat, astonished by the warning she had just been given.

Reg Quincey was not a pretty sight. Apart from being swathed in bandages, his left arm was in plaster and so was his left leg, which was partly suspended on a hoist. Fortunately, he was now off the critical list, for it had been almost three days since the accident, but judging by his appearance, it would be some time before he would be up and about again. Matters were made no better by the fact that there had been a steady stream of visitors during the day, including one or two of his cousins whom he couldn't bear, together with one of his workmates from the building site where he had had his accident. Marge had also brought Horace and Eddie in to see him, but the two kids had made such a racket that the ward sister had asked them to leave after just ten minutes. Despite Reg's condition, Marge had spent the best part of the afternoon visiting hour nagging him into demanding compensation from his employer for their negligence in not making the working conditions on the site safer.

Reg breathed a sigh of relief when she finally left, and was only too pleased when Leo turned up to see him in the evening. Reg waited for the nurse to freshen up his pillows before showing the first real sign that he was getting back to his old self. 'Yer can come an' do this fer me at my place any time yer like, darlin',' he joked cheekily, though it was an effort for him to talk.

Leo laughed. The nurse grinned. 'Better ask your missus first!' she said, before leaving.

Once Reg had watched the nurse disappear down the ward, he turned and winked at his son. 'If I was twenty years younger . . .' he said.

'You ain't doin' so bad, mate,' replied Leo, drawing as close as he could to his dad's side.

'Be better if I 'ad a fag,' said Reg.

'Come off it, Dad,' said Leo, with a grin. 'Yer know yer can't smoke in 'ere.'

Reg grunted. 'Too many rules an' regulations,' he said. 'Too many people tellin' me wot I can't do.' He looked up at Leo, who was still a bit out of focus. 'Bin like that nearly all me life. Well – ever since I met yer mum.'

This prompted Leo to take a chance. Making quite sure there were no nurses around, he quickly took the dog-end from behind his ear, and lit up. Then after another fleeting look to check that the coast was clear, he gently put the dog-end between his dad's lips. ' 'Ave ter make it quick, Dad!' he said. ' 'Urry up!'

Reg's face beamed as he took a laboured puff.

Leo fanned away the smoke with his hand, whilst he

waited for his dad to take in another puff. Then he quickly retrieved the dog-end, and pinched it with the tips of his fingers, sending a small amount of ash to the floor, which he covered with his foot. 'Yer'll get me bleedin 'ung, drawn an' quartered,' he said, still fanning the smoke away with his hand.

'Sometimes yer 'ave ter take a few risks in life,' replied Reg, lying back, eyes closed, with a contented look on his face. 'I took a risk when I married yer mum, yer know.'

This remark surprised Leo. But he decided not to react.

Reg opened his eyes to find Leo with his head bowed. 'But if I 'adn't, I wouldn't'a 'ad a son like you, would I?' he said. He reached out with his unplastered right hand, and placed it affectionately on Leo's arm. 'I only ever wanted one kid,' he said. 'Did yer know that?'

Leo shrugged.

'It was yer mum's idea ter 'ave the uvver two, not mine,' he continued. 'Not that I regret 'avin' 'em. They're good boys. But I only wanted one. I told 'er that, the night we got married. But yer know wot she's like.' He sighed, and closed his eyes again. For a brief moment he just lay there in silence, his hand still lightly clutching Leo's arm. 'I should've put me foot down,' he said airily. 'I shouldn't've let 'er do the fings she's done ter you. I don't know why she does it. I don't know wot gets into 'er. Some people are like that. They just 'ave ter 'ave someone ter take it out on.' His eyes slowly opened, and once again he tried to focus on Leo. 'Don't let 'er blame this on you, son. It wasn't yer fault.'

Leo shrugged again, and looked away. 'Who cares wot *she* finks, Dad,' he replied. 'I can take care of meself.'

With effort, Reg slightly raised his head from the pillow. 'Can yer, son?' he asked wearily.

Leo did everything to avert his dad's gaze, but even

though his eyes were darting all over the place, he didn't really notice the Christmas paper-chains that were still draped across the ward ceiling. During those few seconds, he thought about what his dad had said. Was he really capable of taking care of himself? Was he really capable of standing up to his mum, and if so, why had he let her dominate him all these years? Why had he allowed her actually to beat him, to humiliate him in front of his own workmates? For one brief moment he felt as though he was living in a nightmare world.

'Of course I blame meself.' When Leo turned back to look at his dad, Reg's head had sunk on to the pillow. 'Yes. I should have put me foot down years ago,' said Reg, eyes closed again. 'I should've told 'er that yer can't get nowhere by bullyin' people.' His eyes sprang open. 'So why didn't I? 'Cos I love 'er, I s'ppose. Stupid in't it? But I *do* love 'er – despite everyfin'. Gord only knows why.' He slowly licked his parched lips. 'An' yet I'll tell yer somefin'. Sometimes she's right about fings – not always, but sometimes. An' when she *is* right, it sometimes don't make sense till long after.'

Once again, Reg's eyes closed, and within seconds he had nodded off to sleep. Leo waited by his bedside for a moment to see if he would stir, and when he didn't, he got up, and just looked down at his dad's face, which was now prematurely lined after years of turmoil and suppression. How *could* a man go on loving a woman like that, he wondered, after all she'd done to him? Marge Quincey didn't deserve a husband like his dad. He was pure gold, and she wasn't worth a light beside him. Like it or not, however, what his dad had said was true. His mum was a shrewd woman, and there were times when she *did* talk sense. But was he right to have done what she expected of him, to give up something that he wanted more than anything else in the whole wide world? Was he really trying to climb a tree in the wrong part of the woods? Only time would tell. But as he left his dad's bedside, and slowly made his way out of the ward, the only picture Leo could see in his mind was of the one girl he had ever really cared for.

So far, it hadn't been much of a day for Peggy. Apart from her encounter with the Spots Man on the bus during the morning, she had got into such a muddle with her cash sheets at the paying-in counter that Alf Grundy, one of her fellow conductors, who had been one of those who had initially shown her such derision, had to come to her rescue. On top of that, she mislaid two tuppenny ha'penny unsold tickets, which was not received well by the stock clerk when she came to return her ticket rack for the day. And if that wasn't enough, she received a message to say that a date at the end of the month had been set for her first routine interview with an official from the Board, at which she was now convinced she would receive her marching orders. God, is it worth it all? she asked herself. Eighty-three shillings and eightpence a week, and that included the fifteen shillings war wage! And yet, most girls considered that to be a great improvement on what women were paid before the war, and which had only come about because there was now an acute shortage of men. Even so, Peggy felt she had sacrificed more than she had ever realised since leaving the warm confines of Messrs Parks and Stevens.

Once she'd been home and had a quick dip in a bath of lukewarm water that was restricted to a miserable six inches, she changed into a warm dress and joined her mother and father for a meal. As soon as the meal was over, however, she surprised them both by announcing that she had to go back to the depot as she had mislaid her purse, and had a feeling that she had left it in her locker in the female conductors' room.

Thornton only pretended to believe her story until such time that his contact had provided further detailed information on her movements.

A number 611 trolley bus was just pulling up at the stop near the house when Peggy came out, so she quickly caught up with it, and hopped on board. The journey to the Nag's Head was no more than a few minutes, so she had very little time to think of what she was about to do. When she got off, she felt as though she was in a different world. Although she had passed through the area many times on her way to her office in Upper Street, a fleeting glimpse from the top of a bus was somehow quite different to actually being there, and especially on a cold, dark December evening when most people were at home in front of their fires, listening to the wireless. She decided to get off two stops on from the Nag's Head, at Jones Brothers Department Store, which was much closer to where she wanted to get to. She knew exactly in which direction she was heading, for after a great deal of persuasion Peggy had managed to get the address from Elsie Parker. But as her torch lit her way down Tollington Road, which was lined on either side by terraces of elegant four-storey Edwardian houses, and Shelburne Road school – now closed for the duration of the war, and taken over by the Auxiliary Fire Service – she felt apprehensive about calling on Leo at his own home. After all, she'd been warned about the kind of woman Leo's mother was, and the kind of reception she could expect to give to any friend of her husband or son she didn't approve of.

By the time she had reached the junction with Hornsey Road, Peggy was beginning to wonder whether she was making a big mistake. So she came to a gradual halt, and paused briefly to think things over. Why was she coming here, she asked herself? Was the real reason because she had been so upset to hear about Reg Quincey's accident, or was it because she had received no contact from Leo since Christmas Eve? In a sudden change of mind, she turned round and started to retrace her steps. But then she stopped again. What was she so afraid of? Was it such a crime to visit someone she loved? She turned again, and continued on her way.

Even in the blackout, Peggy could tell that Hornsey Road was no match for the leafy lanes of Highgate and Hampstead. In the dark, the light from her torch beam could just pick out the regimented row of sombre-looking houses, most of which were in dire need of repair and a good coat of paint. And the sour smell of cat's urine was everywhere, despite the wonderful attempts by so many residents to grow a few plants in their tiny front gardens, a cherished dream of fresh fields and open-air countryside, which many of them were unlikely to get a chance to experience for the duration of the war. She walked on, the synthetic fur of her thick coat collar wrapped snugly around her neck, her footsteps echoing along the stark stone pavements. As she approached the yard entrance to Milson's Coal Merchants, a train rattled slowly across the nearby railway bridge, and the crisp evening air was once again pierced by the smell of urine, this time from the men's lavatories beneath the bridge on the other side of the road.

Inside the bare concrete yard, Peggy's torch beam picked out two empty coal carts, which looked lost without their loyal dray horses and their daily sacks of coal, and Peggy hoped that the noble creatures themselves were stabled in a nice warm barn somewhere, tucking into a hearty feed of hay. As she stood there in the dark, she could hear the sound of laughter coming from a wireless set on the first floor of the purpose-built office building, which she assumed was where the Quincey family lived. Suddenly her legs felt like giving way beneath her, but after taking a deep breath she moved towards the ground-floor entrance, where her torch beam soon picked out a bell button on the side wall which had a small scrawled nameplate above it showing: 'QUINCEY'. She rang the bell, and waited. The audience laughter from the variety show on the wireless upstairs continued, and was joined by the sound of two young boys who were listening to it and clearly thoroughly enjoying themselves. After a time, she imagined that the bell hadn't been heard, so she pressed the button again, this time keeping her finger on it for longer. The wireless upstairs was suddenly turned off. The deathly silence that followed seemed like an eternity to Peggy, and when she suddenly heard somebody hastily thumping down the stairs inside, she found herself taking two paces back. The door was suddenly flung open, and a stream of light from the long narrow staircase inside flooded on to her.

'Yer're 'is fancy gel!'

Because the light was blinding her, Peggy couldn't see the face of the small boy who had greeted her. All she could tell was that he was wearing a woollen vest and trousers down to his knees held up by a pair of braces.

'You must be Eddie?' she asked.

Eddie ignored her question. 'Yer're 'is bit er fluff. I saw 'im wiv yer once – up 'Olloway Road.'

Peggy was a bit taken aback by his cheek, but amazed by his instant recognition of her. 'Can I see Leo, please?' she asked.

' 'E ain't 'ere!' Eddie grunted, scratching his head. ' 'E's gone down the boozer!' With that, he slammed the door in her face.

The boy's brusqueness took her breath away. She immediately rang the bell again.

The door opened. 'Wot d'yer want now?'

'Can you tell me *which* – boozer your brother's gone to?'

' 'Ow should I know? I don't drink.'

This time Peggy prevented him from slamming the door by holding it open with her hand. 'Could I speak to – to your mother?' she asked tentatively.

Eddie was just as brusque as before. 'She ain't 'ere eivver. She's gone ter see Auntie Flo.'

From the road, a man's voice yelled out, 'Put that light out!'

Peggy hardly had time to react when Eddie abruptly slammed the door on her again. Standing there helplessly in the dark, she wondered what else she could do. But when she heard Eddie's feet rushing up the stairs again, and the wireless set being turned on the moment he reached it, she realised it was futile to try again. She turned, and made her way out of the yard.

However, she had only gone a short way, when a young boy's breathless voice called to her from the dark behind: ''Scuse me, miss.' Taken aback, Peggy swung round. In her torch beam was the serious-looking face of Horace, the elder of Leo's two brothers. 'If yer wanna find Leo,' he panted, ''e's up The Eaglet.'

'The Eaglet?'

'End er this road, corner of Seven Sisters.' His hasty message delivered, the boy turned quickly and rushed off.

'You're Ace, aren't you?' she called, trying to stop him.

Horace kept on running.

'Leo told me all about you,' she shouted. 'It's what everyone calls you!'

She held the small figure in her torch beam until it

finally disappeared through the open gates of the coal merchant's yard.

The Eaglet pub was always full on Friday nights. After all, it was pay night and most blokes wanted to down a few tubs to celebrate getting through yet another hell of a week. You could always tell the place was full the moment you went in, for the rush of fag smoke could knock you off your feet. Leo was on his third pint and his sixth fag of the evening, and there was still two or three hours left before closing time. He was just finishing off a game of darts with his mates when he saw her.

'Hello, Leo,' said Peggy.

Leo hadn't seen her come in, but when he turned round and saw her standing right behind him, his face automatically lit up, and his immediate response was to want to hug her. But then his stomach suddenly tensed, and his smile faded. 'Wot you doin' 'ere, Peggs?' he asked.

Peggy's own warm smile also waned. It was the first cool response she had received from Leo since they first met. 'I heard about your dad,' she said, trying to be heard above the raucous high spirits throughout the public bar. 'I wanted to know if there was anything I could do to help.'

Leo suddenly realised that all his mates were watching him. 'Come on!' he said to Peggy. Throwing his darts down on to a nearby table, he slipped his arm round her back, and to the accompaniment of jeers and cheers from his mates, practically frog-marched her out through the bar. 'What the 'ell d'yer fink yer're doin', Peggs!' he snapped angrily, the moment they got outside.

'What are you talking about?' Peggy replied, completely taken aback. 'What have I done wrong?'

'Yer shouldn't've come 'ere,' he said, stomping up and down in front of her. 'I don't know who told yer wot pub I used, but yer shouldn't've come. This is *my* neck er the woods, not yours. There's nuffin' down 'ere fer you – nuffin'!'

Peggy watched in disbelief as he threaded the tips of his fingers agitatedly through his hair. 'I'm sorry,' she said, hurt by the sudden, inexplicable change in his feelings towards her. 'I had no idea our relationship had anything to do with which neck of the woods you live in.'

He stopped pacing, looked over his shoulder to make sure no one was watching him, and then stood as close as he could, facing her. In the blackout, he could only see the outline of her face, and it immediately gave him a feeling of deep yearning, of deep despair. 'I've not bin fair to yer, Peggs,' he said reproachfully. 'I shouldn't've led yer on.'

'Led me on?' asked Peggy, incredulously. 'I'm not a dog on a lead! What's this all about, Leo?' she asked again. 'The reason I came to find you is because I heard about your father's accident, because I was concerned for you.'

'I know, I know . . .'

'Then stop treating me as though I'm a complete stranger.'

Leo tried to reach out and touch her arm. She pulled it away. 'Yer're not a stranger, Peggs,' he replied painfully. 'Yer're a gel in a million.'

'Is that why you failed to contact me?'

Leo hesitated. 'Fings've 'appened at 'ome, Peggs,' he said with difficulty. 'Fings that I 'aven't bin able ter keep under control.'

'Are you talking about your mother?' she asked acidly.

There was a brief silence from Leo. 'I've got responsibilities, Peggs,' he replied. 'Fings I just can't turn me back on. Fings I can't explain.'

'Don't worry, Leo,' said Peggy haughtily. 'I can assure you, you have no need to explain to me about *anything*.'

She left him and walked off.

'No, don't, Peggs,' he called, hurrying after her. 'Please don't.'

Peggy strode on, ignoring him.

'Listen ter me, Peggs – please.' In the dark, he took hold of her arm and brought her to a halt. He waited a moment in the hope that she would be responsive, that she would turn to face him. 'I've never known a gel like you – 'onest. In these past few weeks, yer've given me more than I could ever dare 'ope from anyone. It may sound stupid ter you, but ever since I met yer, I 'aven't bin able ter get yer off me mind. I couldn't understand what anyone like you could see in someone like me. We're diff'rent as chalk an' cheese – an' yet – some'ow – we clicked. It made me feel so good.' He sighed. 'But it can't work, Peggs. You an' me know there's no way it could work. You're a mover – I'm not. I don't 'ave the right ter 'old yer back.'

'If you're trying to find an excuse to get rid of me, Leo,' replied Peggy, 'please don't bother. I'm a grown-up girl. I know more about life than you think.'

'I'm not tryin' ter get rid er yer, Peggs,' said Leo. 'I could never do that – not ter *you*.' He reached out in the dark and gently tried to touch her face. She let him do so, even though all her instincts were telling her not to. 'If it wasn't fer who I am an' where I come from, fings could be so diff'rent.' He gently slid his hand behind her neck, and slowly eased her towards him. 'I don't want ter let yer go, Peggs,' he whispered. 'Not now, not never.' Their lips were now so close to each other it seemed inevitable that they would kiss. But just when their lips were about to do so, Leo's face was suddenly caught in the beam of someone's torch.

'Leo?' called a girl's voice. 'Is that you?'

The moment Leo heard Pam's voice, he pulled away

from Peggy. 'Pam!' he gasped, completely taken aback.

'Sorry I'm late,' she said. 'I went wiv yer mum ter yer Auntie Flo's.' She switched the torch beam to Peggy's face. 'Sorry if I'm disturbin' anyfin'.'

Peggy backed away and then, in one quick movement, turned and rushed off.

'Peggs . . . !'

Leo's voice echoed along the darkened main road. But Peggy had already gone, and his last view of her was of a distant figure leaping on to a number 14 bus at the nearest bus stop.

Chapter 10

Irene West got off the tube train at Bank station. Outside in Threadneedle Street she was greeted by a glorious day, with ancient grand buildings all flooded with a rush of morning sunlight which cascaded down from the high rooftops, and illuminated the dark narrow back lanes behind the Mansion House and Guildhall. But that day Irene found it hard to believe that this was the famous 'square mile', for this was the Saturday morning after Christmas, and the City streets were practically deserted, which was clearly the reason why Robert Thornton had agreed to meet her there. In Throgmorton Street she found the place she was looking for, the austere British Restaurant, run by the London County Council, and as good a place as any to avoid the prying eyes of anyone who might know either her or the man she was meeting.

Thornton had arrived ahead of her, a full ten minutes before the appointed time, and sat with his back to the window at a table partly obscured by a flight of stairs which led to the overfill section upstairs. Fortunately, the restaurant was empty but for three or four clerks from the Stock Exchange, who looked miserable enough to show that they had been dragged in against their will to do some urgent work during the Christmas break. Thornton had already collected two cups of tea from the self-service counter, one of which had a saucer covering the cup to keep its contents warm.

'Sorry I'm late,' Irene said, sitting down opposite him at the table.

Thornton accepted her apology with a slight nod of the head. Before saying anything, he watched her slide off her gloves, put them on the table, and remove the saucer from her cup. 'So what's this all about?' he eventually asked.

Irene was used to his lack of pleasantries. It was always straight in with a direct question. 'I'm going away,' she said, with more verve than she usually had the courage to show him. 'I've applied to join the Women's Land Army.'

Thornton listened to her without response. He just watched her over the top of the cup of tea he was holding up to his lips.

To steady her nerves, Irene took a quick sip of her own tea. It was almost cold. 'I've talked to Mr Stevens about it,' she said. 'He wasn't too happy, of course, but I think he understood.' She replaced her cup in the saucer. 'I'm hoping to leave early in the New Year.'

Thornton lowered his eyes, and sipped his tea. Then he looked up at her again, quite content – for the time being – to let her do all the talking.

His reaction was making her all the more nervous. 'I – I wanted you to know,' she said, sub-consciously touching the crucifix around her neck, 'that I can't go on doing – what you want me to do any more.'

Thornton replaced his cup in the saucer. 'I wish you good fortune, my dear.'

Irene was astonished by his sudden, calm reaction, and even more astonished when he made a move to get up. 'You – don't mind?' she asked incredulously.

Thornton froze. 'Mind?' he replied, in what appeared to be an understanding smile. 'Why should I mind? My dear, you're an adult. You have a right to make your own decisions.'

For some reason, Thornton's reaction was now unnerving Irene more than if he had lost his temper with her. As she stared up into his blank dark eyes, the massive height of his tall frame towering over her, her mind briefly returned to the fateful day almost a year before when they had first met. She could see him now, entering the front office at Parks and Stevens, an immaculate figure in bowler hat and the long black overcoat with silk lapels. And in those few brief seconds, she recalled how, when their eyes met, she had become completely infatuated with him, with everything about him. But now, she said to herself, things had gone far enough. She could no longer go on betraying someone whom she liked, someone who had always trusted her.

'I just hope you won't forget me, that's all.'

She looked up to find him staring straight through her. His cold, piercing voice had crushed any feeling of comfort.

'I hope you won't forget what knowing me has meant to you.'

Now it was Irene's turn to respond with silence.

Thornton hesitated before sitting down again. 'You know, this war has had an extraordinary effect on people,' he said. 'It makes them do things that under normal circumstances they would never even contemplate.' He leaned across the table, and lowered his voice. 'When we first met,' he said, staring deep into her eyes, 'we both felt a mutual attraction. I found you – I still find you – a very attractive woman, a woman of bearing and substance. For the last twenty-five years, I have lived through a marriage that has survived only through habit, and not desire. For me, our first few weeks together were a tonic. I felt like a different kind of man, someone who was wanted for love and not position. I trusted you. I trusted you more than anyone in my entire life. You gave me hope.' For one brief moment, there was a glimmer of affection in his eyes. But it disappeared as quickly as it had come. 'But that hope was misplaced.' He leaned back in his chair again. 'Misplaced, Irene,' he added scornfully, 'from the moment you told me that you were carrying another man's child.'

Irene's face crumpled. She covered it with both hands.

Thornton waited a moment before continuing, 'It hardly mattered to me that you didn't want the child. What hurt was that you didn't really want me either.'

Irene immediately lowered her hands. 'That's not true, Robert,' she protested.

'Oh, but it is,' he quietly insisted. 'You used me, Irene. You used me because I was the one person who could help you keep your secret. I was the one person who could get you out of your sordid little mess.' He leaned towards her again. 'I don't mind, Irene, really I don't. In some ways it was a blessing – *I* help you get rid of a child you didn't want, a child that would have caused you immense shame and embarrassment with your family, relations and friends, and *you* make me realise what a fool I've been, make me realise that the only person I really want a relationship with – is my own wife.'

'It's not fair,' said Irene, tears gradually welling in her eyes. 'I love you too, Robert. I always have – from the moment I set eyes on you.'

'That is *your* problem, my dear,' replied Thornton, with a glimmer of a smile. He leaned back in his chair again. 'Love comes at a price. Especially your kind of love.'

It was such a cutting response that Irene felt her stomach tense.

'I can't let you go, Irene,' continued Thornton, draining the last of his tea. 'You agreed to my price, and I intend to keep you to it.'

'But I can't continue spying on Peggy,' replied Irene, agonised. 'She's my friend. She trusts me.'

'I trusted you too.'

Irene hesitated before answering. Her mind was torn between two levels of trust. How could she go on betraying someone like Peggy, someone who had never done her any harm, and who had always been such a loyal friend? Why *should* she go on following her everywhere she went just because this man wanted to keep a hold over his own daughter, to prevent her from forging her own destiny? Fully aware that what she was about to say was taking a huge risk, she said: 'I think Peggy's in love with this boy.'

Thornton's look hardened. After a pause he replied, 'I expect you to keep our bargain.' He got up from the table, collected his hat from the empty seat beside him, and started to go.

'Surely we both have reason to be discreet?' asked Irene boldly.

Thornton stopped dead. 'I think *I* am able to cope with a difficult situation better than you, my dear,' he replied with a wry smile. 'Wouldn't you agree?' With that, he put on his bowler hat and left.

Irene watched him as he passed by the window where they had been sitting, and made his way briskly along the street outside. Never before had she felt so much like a caged animal.

Frosty Morris was quite concerned about Peggy. Ever since she'd first become his regular clippie, he'd taken a real shine to her. But today she wasn't herself. Of course, working over a weekend was never much fun for the crews, for like everyone else they'd much sooner be at home with their families, and as this was the last Sunday before the New Year, he and the others at their table in the canteen reckoned it was making her feel a bit down in the dumps.

'Post-Christmas blues, gel,' he said, as he tucked into a snack of baked beans on toast before they set out on their evening shift. 'That's wot yer've got.'

Peggy looked up from her cheese sandwich, suddenly aware that her lack of conversation was being noticed. 'Sorry, Frosty,' she said, trying to put a brave face on it, and sipping her tea.

'Don't you apologise, Peggs,' said Elsie Parker, who had finished her tea and was using her hand-mirror to freshen up her lipstick. 'We're all in the same boat. It's not fair we 'ave ter work over 'oliday weekends when everyone else can put their feet up.'

'Wot *you* goin' on about?' grumbled Effie Sommers, one of the canteen servers, who was hovering over them with her usual fag dangling from her lips. 'I've bin on duty every day fer the last week – Chrissmas and Boxin' Day included!'

'Yeah,' said Alf Grundy, who was just finishing off a fairly stale rock cake. 'An' takin' 'ome all that luvely double time!'

To Effie's intense irritation, the others laughed and jeered. 'Bleedin' cheek!' she growled. 'Unlike you lot, I don't get a penny extra, an' you know it, Alf Grundy! London Transport don't give me somefin' fer nuffin'!'

'Don't listen to 'im, Eff,' said Elsie, putting a comforting hand on Effie's arm. 'It's all sour grapes 'cos 'is ol' woman's in the family way again!'

'Blimey!' said Sid Pierce, the other conductor at the table, looking up from reading form in the *Greyhound News*. 'Not anuvver one!'

' 'Ow many's that, Alf?' asked Frosty. 'Four?'

'As a matter of fact, it's five,' sniffed Alf haughtily.

'Five!' said Elsie.

'Wot you after then?' joked Sid. 'A bleedin' football team?'

The laughter this provoked at last succeeded in bringing a smile to Peggy's face. Frosty was the first to notice this.

'An' we fink *we've* got problems, eh?' he said.

Peggy smiled, and returned to her sandwich. The others exchanged knowing looks. They all guessed what was wrong, but left it to Frosty to try to draw Peggy out. 'Wot news of Leo?' he asked, as casually as he could.

Peggy avoided looking at him. 'No idea, I'm afraid,' she replied.

'Wonder 'ow poor old Reg's gettin' on?' ventured Alf, directing his question straight at Peggy. 'Must be feelin' pretty rough.'

Peggy merely nodded back.

Frosty and Elsie exchanged a look.

'Well,' said Elsie, 'let's just 'ope Reg's accident gets Leo off doin' 'is call-up fer good. The way this war's goin', we'll 'ave none er our boys left. It scares the daylights out er me.'

Sid chimed in, 'They say once us young 'uns've gone, they're goin' ter pick on you ol' fogies.'

'Well, that includes you, mate!' sniped Alf, to jeers from the others.

'Come off it!' protested Sid. 'I'm only twenty-nine, fer chrissake!'

'Twenty-nine!' exploded Effie. 'Yer've bin twenty-nine since the day yer was born!'

A few minutes later, Peggy and Frosty left the canteen and made their way out towards their bus, which was parked waiting for them in the garage forecourt. It was a wonderful end to a day which had been bathed in crisp morning sunshine and a cloudy afternoon, and as the empty, darkened bus chugged its way down Holloway Road en route to its starting point at Hornsey Rise, Peggy was able to look up at a sky that was now a vast crimson quilt, broken only by the first glimpse of a crystal-clear bright winter's moon, and the first shimmering star of a rapidly approaching night.

Before the bus set off for its first journey of the evening, Frosty still had enough time to go back into the cabin to join Peggy for a chinwag and a fag.

'So wot's the New Year goin' ter do fer yer, Peggs?' he asked. 'A lot er good fings, I 'ope?'

'I doubt it,' replied Peggy solemnly.

'Bad as that?'

'Positive.'

Frosty lit his fag, and sat beside her on the bench seat. The only passenger who had so far got on went straight upstairs to the top deck. 'Wanna talk about it?' he asked. 'You an' Leo?'

Peggy hesitated before answering. 'There's nothing to talk about, Frosty,' she said, trying to dismiss the subject as quickly as possible. 'Nothing matters very much any more.'

'Matters ter me,' replied Frosty. 'I got kids er me own – remember?'

Peggy thought about this. Yes, if she could trust anyone ever again, it would be Frosty. He was turning out to be like a father she wished she'd had.

'Bin playin' around, 'as 'e?'

Again, Peggy hesitated before answering. 'I wouldn't mind, if only he'd told me. What I can't bear is the deceit.'

'Yer must've known wot yer was gettin' yerself into?'

'No, Frosty, I didn't,' she replied. 'I'm afraid I'm a simpleton in this kind of game.'

'Game? Mmm.' He took a puff of his fag; the red glow from it was already a tiny beacon in the blackout. 'If I was you, I wouldn't take it ter 'eart,' he said. 'That gel ain't nuffin' ter write 'ome about.'

Peggy swung him a look. 'Girl?' she asked, surprised. 'What girl?'

'Pam Warner,' replied Frosty. 'Gel 'e's bin knockin' around wiv fer ages. Dumpy, blonde – right?'

Peggy was too taken aback to answer him straight away. 'You mean – you knew?'

'Course I knew. We all did. She's bin 'angin' round 'is neck fer munfs. Dunno 'ow 'e could put up wiv someone like 'er, ter be frank. Not a brain between 'er ears, if yer ask me.'

Peggy suddenly felt let down. 'Frosty, if you knew,' she replied, 'if you *all* knew, why didn't you tell me?'

'Becos we knew it was 'is ol' woman's idea – Ma Quincey's. Like we told yer, *she* wears the pants in that 'ouse'old.'

'Oh, come now, Frosty,' protested Peggy. 'You can't blame the woman for everything. Leo's got a mind of his own. He wouldn't walk out with someone he didn't want to.'

Frosty leaned back on the padded bench, turned to her, and rested one elbow on the ledge behind. 'Yer know,' he said, 'my youngest bruvver was a bit like Leo when he was 'is age. Drifted on from gel ter gel, never knowin' 'ow ter pick the right one an' settle down wiv 'er – that is, not till 'e got 'er in the family way an' *'ad* ter marry 'er. 'E didn't want to, though. But me dad insisted. Real thumper, that one – thump yer if yer didn't agree wiv everyfin' 'e said. Some people are like that, Peggs. Can't make decisions; always 'ave ter rely on someone else ter force yer ter do fings. Trouble is, pushin' people inter doin' fings can ruin 'em fer the rest er their lives. Me bruvver was as miserable as sin fer over ten years fer bein' married ter someone 'e din't want. It ended up wiv 'im leavin' 'is woman an' kid, an' runnin' off wivout so much as a by yer leave. None of us 'ave seen 'im from that day ter this.'

Peggy sighed. 'It doesn't make it any easier, Frosty,' she said. 'In a way, perhaps it's a good thing this has happened. What use is there in being involved with a man who can't even stand up to his own mother? You see, I don't believe it's all her fault. If Leo really felt anything for me, he'd tell her to mind her own business.'

'Ha!' laughed Frosty. 'You don't know Ma Quincey. Fink yerself lucky yer don't 'ave someone like 'er pushin' an' pullin' yer all fru life!'

Peggy waited whilst Frosty got up and made his way back to the driver's cabin. It wasn't until the bus was on its way that she fully took in what he had said: '*Fink yerself lucky yer don't 'ave someone like 'er pushin' an' pullin' yer all fru life!*' She was thinking now, thinking very hard indeed. Not about Leo, nor his mother. She was thinking about her own father.

Marge Quincey was dead on her feet. Despite the fact that it wasn't washing day until tomorrow, she'd done some bits and pieces and got them dried in front of the fire. Then she spent the afternoon at Reg's bedside while Leo took Horace and young Eddie to the Sunday pictures. As soon as she got home she then cooked them all their Spam and chips for tea, and it wasn't until a quarter-past five in the evening that she finally managed to sit down. Even so, when it came to working out ways to manipulate her family, she had boundless energy.

'I'm so pleased ter see you an' Pam friends again,' she said to Leo, as she helped him clear the dirty tea-time dishes from the kitchen table and follow him out with them to the scullery. 'Yer're a sensible boy, Leo. I'm very proud er the way yer've put fings right wiv 'er. She does so idolise yer. Anyone can see that.' At the sink, she put her arms round his waist and hugged him. 'I'm yer mum. I know about these fings.'

Leo tried not to listen. He'd done what she wanted, so what more could he say?

'I've got somefin' I want ter tell yer,' she said, lowering her voice and checking to see that Horace and Eddie were not around. She went to the scullery door, closed it, then returned to the sink where Leo had started washing up. 'I wasn't goin' ter tell yer till yer dad came out er 'ospital but – ' she lowered her voice to a whisper – 'I've bin puttin' a little bit er cash aside fer yer, fer when you an' Pam name the day.'

Leo gritted his teeth, and briefly stopped what he was doing. 'Mum,' he said calmly, 'Pam an' I 'aven't even talked about gettin' married yet.'

'I know, dear, I know. But yer will. An' when yer do, I don't want ter be caught nappin'.'

Leo sighed, and carried on with the washing-up.

Marge picked up a tea cloth and starting drying the dishes. She was watching him closely all the time. 'I feel ashamed er meself,' she said. 'I admit it. I shouldn't've talked ter yer the way I did. I shouldn't've blamed yer fer wot 'appened to yer dad. I'm sorry, son.' She stretched out her hand, gently touched his cheek, and turned his face towards her. 'Fergive yer silly ol' mum?'

Leo was embarrassed. 'Can we get the washing-up done, Mum, please?' he asked, pulling his face away.

Marge gave him a simpering smile, and returned to drying the dishes. She waited a moment or so before pursuing what she wanted to say. 'I know yer don't always fink much er me, son,' she said out of the blue. 'I know yer fink I'm just an interferin' ol' cow, who should just pipe down an' mind me own business. But I don't mean ter be like that, son.' She hesitated whilst she took a plate from him. 'The fact is,' she continued, 'I don't want yer ter make the same mistakes as I did – when I married yer farver.'

Leo suddenly looked up at her.

'Oh, don't get me wrong,' she explained. 'I love yer dad.

Always 'ave, always will. But 'e's not a pusher, 'e don't stand up an' get on wiv fings.' She realised that Leo was looking hard at her. 'I'm lonely, son,' she said.

Leo found it hard to comprehend what she was trying to say. 'Lonely?' he asked.

'Tired. Tired er tryin' ter make somefin' er this family all on me own.'

'Mum,' replied Leo, 'yer don't need ter make *anyfin*' of this family. We can do fings fer ourselves.'

Marge sighed deeply. 'Oh, I wish that was true, son. I wish ter God it was true.'

Leo returned to the washing-up.

Once Marge had finished drying the plate she was holding, she piled it up on top of the others, then opened the small window in front of the sink to release the acrid smell of the lard which had been used to fry the chips. 'Yer know,' she said, 'sometimes I wish I'd bin born a man. I've got the stamina – that I do know. But if I *was* a man, there'd be so much I could do. I wouldn't sit round waitin' fer things ter come ter me – I'd go out an' get 'em fer meself. Unlike yer dad, I'm a born pusher, Leo – not fer meself, but fer everyone else. That's why I get so frustrated. Yer 'ave ter be one step ahead in this world, 'cos if yer ain't, the world'll walk right over yer.'

Despite his attempt to ignore what she was rabbiting on about, Leo listened to every word. Oh yes, she was a pusher all right, and didn't he know it? But she only ever wanted to push things the way *she* wanted. That's why both he and his dad always felt like ants squashed under her feet. But why? Why had he never bothered to find out what it was that turned such a basically ordinary woman into a conniving, possessive wife and mother?

'Yer made the right decision. Yer know that, don't yer, son?'

Leo flicked her a brief look. He didn't know what the hell she was talking about.

' 'Er from up the 'ill. Yer madam!'

'Don't call 'er that, Mum,' pleaded Leo, firmly. She's an 'ard-workin' gel – just like anyone else.'

'Really?' Marge finished the last plate she was drying, put down the tea cloth, and turned away. ' 'Ave yer ever looked at 'er 'ands?'

' 'Er wot?'

She turned back to him. 'People who 'ave ter scrub floors an' bring up three kids on a few bob a week – they're the ones who do the *real* 'ard work – not the grand ladies on 'igh who spend most er their time bein' waited on 'and an' foot.'

Leo sighed. 'You're getting it all wrong, Mum,' he replied, wiping his hands on the tea cloth. 'Peggy's not like that.'

Marge's face stiffened at the first mention of Peggy's name. 'Oh, yes,' she said, trying not to sound too caustic.

Leo took a dog-end from behind his ear and lit it.

Marge knew she was now on dodgy ground, so she went to him cautiously. 'Look, son,' she said, trying to sound as reasonable as she was able, 'you'd never be able ter mix wiv people like that. They're too lofty, too full er themselves. 'Ow d'yer fink they'd take ter a navvy's son from the bottom er the 'ill? Yer'd be like a fish out er water.'

Leo slowly turned to look at her. 'An' 'ow d'yer fink *she'd* get on down 'ere, Mum?' he asked. 'Greeted wiv open arms?'

Marge's expression hardened. She sat down at the scullery table.

'Anyway, wot does it matter now?' said Leo. 'It's over an' done wiv. I've done wot yer want. So why don't we call it quits?'

If Marge felt put down, she wasn't going to show it.

'Course, son,' she replied, with a sickly smile. 'As yer say, wot does it matter now? Yer've done all right fer yerself, I've no doubt in me mind about that. So don't yer go worryin' yerself. From now on, times are goin' ter be good fer you an' yer Pam. You leave it all to yer mum. I'll always be 'ere ter give yer a bit of a push.'

The smoking lounge at Sandford's men's club was already filling up. Although it was not yet five thirty in the evening, Sunday was a favourite time for the members to have their drinks and a cigar before going home for dinner with their wives. Robert Thornton was already on his second brandy before Edwin Stevens joined him on the leather-covered sofa. Once again it was their turn for fire-watching duties on the roof, and a warming drink before standing around in the freezing cold for half the night was a necessity.

'If you ask me, this is all a waste of time,' said Stevens, downing his whisky quicker than he should. 'There hasn't been an air raid for almost a week. It's ridiculous to imagine it's going to start all over again.'

Thornton only tolerated Stevens because he had to. The man was an absolute bore in Thornton's eyes, and if it wasn't for the fact that he was going to be useful to him, he'd avoid him like the plague.

'Never underestimate the enemy, Stevens,' replied Thornton, in his commanding military voice. 'I've no doubt there's a plot being hatched somewhere in Berlin.'

Stevens' eyes widened. 'I say, d'you think so? D'you really think so?'

Thornton shrugged, and sipped his brandy.

'I must say, it's been quite beastly since it all started in September. People spending the night in air-raid shelters, on tube platforms – it's a terrible way to have to live.' Stevens took out a fat Havana cigar from a leather cigar case inside his coat pocket, clearly purchased on the black market like most of the drink on sale in the club. 'What about Mrs Thornton and Peggy?' he asked in between lighting up in a cloud of smoke. 'Are they still sleeping in the Morrison shelter?'

'Not at the moment,' replied Thornton, disdainful that Stevens should have asked him such a personal question. 'My daughter,' he added curtly, 'has been working quite late.'

Stevens was a touch embarrassed, and masked his disapproval behind his whisky glass. 'Don't you ever worry about her?'

'Worry?'

'Working into the night, getting home late on her own? I would have thought it was quite dangerous for a young girl to walk out alone in the blackout?'

'I'm sure you know my daughter well enough to realise,' said Thornton, collecting the butt of his own cigar from the ash tray, 'that she is of an independent spirit, and perfectly capable of taking care of herself in any situation.'

Stevens was flustered. 'Oh, I wasn't suggesting anything, my dear fellow,' he replied quickly. 'I'm sure what you said about her is absolutely true. It's just that I was concerned for her.'

'If you are concerned, then may I presume that you have news to give me?'

For one brief moment, Stevens was perplexed. 'Oh – about my son – about Joseph. Yes, as a matter of fact I *do* have news – splendid news!' Conscious that he could be overheard, he leaned closer to Thornton and lowered his voice. 'He's coming home on a weekend pass. Not until after the New Year, though.'

Thornton's eyes lit up. 'Ah,' he purred.

'Apparently he's doing remarkably well on his course.

His commanding officer says he's perfect officer material. I'm so proud of him!'

A white-coated waiter appeared, and replaced their ash tray with a clean one.

Stevens waited until he had moved away. 'Would you like me to arrange a meeting?' he asked, his chubby little face already starting to flush with the whisky. 'I'm sure Joseph would agree to it.'

Thornton's expression was stiff, his eyes as cold as stone. 'I would think my daughter is the one who should decide that,' he replied icily. 'Wouldn't you?'

'Quite so, Major,' replied Stevens, quickly taking a nervous gulp of his whisky and soda. 'Quite so.' He dabbed his wet lips with the back of his forefinger. 'I remember you did once suggest that a Sunday tea-party might be a good idea – at Highgate Hill, I think you said.'

Thornton felt that Stevens was sitting too close to him, so he discreetly put some distance between them. 'May I suggest,' he said, deliberately ignoring Stevens' remark, 'that the moment you have a date for your son's weekend pass, you notify me as soon as possible?'

'But of course, Major,' returned the only-too-willing Stevens, delighted that they were plotting together something that was mutually beneficial. 'I'll arrange with my wife to organise a nice afternoon tea-party for them.'

'That will not be necessary,' replied Thornton, haughtily. 'I suggest that their meeting should be entirely of their own choice. We have no right to interfere.'

Stevens was surprised. 'But I would have thought—'

'That's your trouble, Stevens,' said Thornton. 'You think a little *too* much.' He downed the remains of his brandy. 'Young love must be allowed to flourish unhindered. All that is required of us – is a little encouragement.'

* * *

Frosty Morris had only just brought the number 14 to a halt at the stop outside the Ritz Hotel in Piccadilly when the air-raid siren suddenly wailed out across Green Park. As it was Sunday evening, there were only a handful of passengers on the bus at the time, but as it was mandatory for the bus crew to give anyone the opportunity to get off, he and Peggy paused for a moment or so. In any case, they were a few minutes early, and the last thing they wanted was to be torn off a strip by some overzealous inspector waiting to pounce on them somewhere en route. As soon as he heard the siren, Frosty climbed down from his cabin, to be met by Peggy, who came round to meet up with him. 'I thought it was too good to be true,' she said.

Frosty didn't answer her for a moment or so; his eyes were too busy scanning the cloudless evening sky.

'What is it, Frosty? Something wrong?'

'Too clear,' he answered distantly. 'I 'ate this sorter night.'

Peggy looked up at the sky with him. There were no dark night clouds to obscure the profusion of stars, and the light from a three-quarter-size moon was casting a bright luminous glow on to the endless terraces of grand buildings, and also helping to spin a web of eerie shadows from the huge sycamore and plane trees lining the park alongside the road ahead of them. 'It's probably just another false alarm,' she said, her voice only just audible, as though she was worried that someone might be listening to her. 'It's probably a good thing to keep us on our toes. Mr Churchill warned us not to be too complacent.'

'No,' replied Frosty, still mesmerised by the sky.

Peggy was getting worried by his lack of communication. 'Can you hear something?' she asked.

'No,' he replied. 'But it ain't good.'

'Here we go again!'

The chirpy girl's voice caused Peggy to turn with a start,

when she found another clippie calling to her from the number 19 double-decker that had just pulled up behind. Peggy didn't know the girl by name, but she had passed a few words with her on a couple of occasions before when they had paused en route at the same stop.

'Good ol' Jerry,' squealed the girl, who was in her twenties, and whose voice carried boundless energy. 'Probably goin' ter give us 'is New Year present.'

'I hope not,' countered Peggy.

'Oh, I don't care any more,' said the girl. 'I've 'ad so many near misses since I've bin doin' this job, I feel like a cat wiv nine lives!' She laughed at her own joke, but then thought better of it. 'Don't wanna see any more of me mates killed,' she said solemnly, looking up at the ominous sky. 'It's 'ard ter believe, in't it? It's over three munfs now since all this began. When I fink er everyfin' we've gone fru – all those buildin's comin' down, all those people we've lost . . . Poor ol' London town – *our* London. We don't deserve all this. Yer know, sometimes I fink it's just one long, 'orrible nightmare, an' when I wake up it'll all be back ter 'ow it used ter be.' She suddenly turned back to Peggy again. 'Coo, listen ter me! Bein' so cheerful as keeps me goin'!' She laughed, and started to move off. 'Don't worry,' she called. 'I don't fink nuffin'll come of it. Not ternight. Safe as 'ouses!' She reached the platform of her own bus and, climbing aboard, called back one last time, 'By the way, me name's Vera – you know . . . *We'll meet again* . . . !' She giggled again as she sang the first line of the popular Vera Lynn song.

'I'm Peggy.'

'Nice ter meet yer, Peggy! Be seein' yer!'

Peggy watched as the driver of the number 19 started up, and moved off, overtaking the number 14. As it went, Vera leaned out from the platform, waving madly. 'Mind how you go!' Peggy called to her.

'I will!' returned Vera. 'Can't keep a good clippie down, yer know!'

Peggy waited for the bus to disappear along Piccadilly towards Hyde Park Corner. For the first time that day, she had actually forgotten all about Leo. In fact, Vera had actually brought a smile to her face. But when she turned back to Frosty, she still found him staring up at the sky.

'What is it, Frosty?' she asked quietly. 'Tell me.'

As though being woken from his sleep, Frosty perked up, and looked at her. 'Nah,' he said. 'It's nuffin'. All in the mind, in't it?' With that, he returned to his cabin, and Peggy got back on to the platform. She rang the bell, and the number 14 continued on its way.

As it did so, the air was gradually filled with the familiar droning sound of aeroplanes. Although they were still some way off, their sinister, menacing engines could be heard quite clearly as they cut through the dark evening sky of the last Sunday of a quite extraordinary year.

Chapter 11

Leo was in the saloon bar of The Eaglet when the first bomb fell. Nobody took much notice because it seemed distant enough for them to carry on drinking. Only when young Horace rushed into the bar in a state of panic did everyone finally realise that something was up.

'Mum says yer've got ter get 'ome right away!' gasped the boy. 'There's a load er planes comin' over. We're all in the shelter!'

'Get that boy out er 'ere!' yelled the angry landlord. 'Yer want me ter lose me licence?'

Leo grabbed hold of Horace behind the neck and virtually frog-marched him out of the place. 'Stupid little bugger!' he growled. 'Yer know yer're not allowed in places like this! Yer'll get me banned again!'

'It's bad, Leo!' protested the boy, as Leo pushed him through the door. 'It's really bad!'

'Out!'

Leo's attitude changed the moment they were on the pavement outside. 'Christ!' he yelled, as they were greeted by the deafening throb of plane engines.

The entire sky looked as though it had been invaded by a massive flock of birds of prey, wave after wave of them, and all oblivious of the crisscross of dazzling white searchlight beams which picked them out for the anti-aircraft guns on the ground. Leo couldn't believe his eyes, for already two barrage balloons had been fired upon and were exploding into flames and fluttering down in pieces back to their anchored positions in Finsbury Park just up

219

Seven Sisters Road. High above them, the bright light of
the moon had been absolutely overwhelmed by a plenitude
of small white puffs of smoke from the thousands of anti-
aircraft shells that were shooting up at the raiders. Even in
the few seconds they were standing there, Leo and Horace
counted at least two planes that had been hit and were
spiralling to the ground in flames.

'Let's go!' yelled Leo.

Horace didn't have to be told twice. In a flash he was
running off along Lower Hornsey Road with his big
brother, and overtaking him almost immediately. They
seemed to fly like the wind, only stopping briefly to get
their breath back at the corner of Tollington Road, where
Leo gasped in horror at the massive red glow coming from
the distance in the direction of the City. As they hurried
across the main road, two open-back army trucks raced
past them, with mounted ack-ack guns pumping a stream
of tracer bullets up into the sky. Scared as he was, Horace
was mesmerised by the action, and had to be dragged away
by Leo.

They had almost reached the railway arch when a salvo
of heavier gunfire nearby heralded the start of an intense
cacophony of sound which was provoked by a series of
deafening explosions from different types of bombs all
around them.

Horace suddenly screeched out: 'Me foot! Me foot!'

Leo rushed to his aid, to find that the boy had keeled
over after treading on a jagged piece of white-hot shrapnel,
which had pierced right through the sole of his plimsoll.
'It's OK, Ace! It's OK!' he yelled reassuringly, as he grabbed
the boy up in his arms and made a quick dash for the
family's brick shelter in the coal merchant's yard.

As they did so, a cluster of incendiary bombs rained
down on to the railway bridge just above them.

* * *

Robert Thornton and Edwin Stevens were also taking shelter. On fire-watching duty on the roof of Sandford's, they could see fires beginning to break out all over London, but in particular, in the square mile of the City.

'They're not ours,' called Stevens, holding on to his tin helmet as he crouched down in the relative safety of the rooftop shelter.

Since the sky was absolutely brimming with enemy raiders, all raining bombs down on to the streets, Thornton considered it would be futile even to respond to Stevens' pathetic observation.

They both ducked as an explosion a couple of streets away rocked the buildings all around them.

Thornton was first to re-emerge. Leaving the shelter and rushing straight across to the edge of the rooftop terrace he yelled out: 'Looks like they've copped the Barratt chambers!'

'My God!' returned Stevens, unwilling to risk stepping out on to the rooftop.

'It's on fire!' called Thornton. A fierce red glow from the flames reflected on to his face. 'That'll finish off all the court archives. There won't be much left after they've put *that* out!'

'Don't stand out there, Major!' yelled Stevens. 'The shrapnel!'

He was right. The sound of dozens of pieces of jagged white-hot shrapnel tinkling down on to the rooftop from the ack-ack shells overhead was deeply alarming.

For once, Thornton took Stevens' advice, but just as he was about to make a dash for the shelter again, there was a blinding flash as a Molotov cocktail of incendiaries plummeted down from the sky with a thud on to the roof close by them.

'Thornton!' yelled Stevens, in a panic, shielding himself again on the floor of the shelter.

'I'm all right!' returned Thornton, who had thrown himself flat on his stomach. 'Christ!'

Behind him, the cocktail had burst open, dispelling its deadly contents of magnesium canisters on to the red-paved roof of the club building.

In one of the most daring acts he had ever performed, Stevens rushed out of the shelter and helped Thornton to his feet. 'Hurry!' he gasped breathlessly. 'Let's get out of here!'

'Don't be a fool, man!' snapped Thornton, holding on to his tin helmet as a huge piece of shrapnel came down with a thud beside him. 'What d'you think we're here for?' With not a minute's thought, he found his way straight to the row of water buckets lined up against the wall of the shelter, collected one of the stirrup pumps, and started to assemble it. 'It's now or never!' he called.

Stevens was paralysed with fear as the cluster of incendiaries suddenly burst into life with a glittering metallic white shower.

Alice Thornton was defiant. Ever since the real Blitz had started back in September, she had prided herself that she had never deserted her household during a night-time air raid. But tonight was different. When Herbert came rushing into her room shortly after six thirty, not only was the sound of droning war plane engines overwhelming the calm and tranquillity of Highgate Village, but the sound of fire engines racing back and forth outside was beginning to get on her nerves. 'I do not intend to leave this house and spend the night in a damp, mice-infested shelter!' she barked, at even the suggestion of the idea.

Herbert was just as adamant. 'If you don't,' he warned,

'then don't blame me for the consequences. If you'd care to look out of the window, you'll notice that the whole of London is under attack. It's not safe to stay in a house as vulnerable as this.'

Alice eased herself up from her favourite armchair, and went straight to the telephone.

'What are you doing?' asked Herbert, exasperated.

'I'm checking with Robert,' she snapped irritably, picking up the receiver. 'He's on fire-watch at Sandford's tonight. If *he* says things are looking bad, then I'll take his word for it.'

'Frankly, my dear,' returned Herbert, losing patience with her, 'I don't care a damn for Robert's word!'

'Well, you should!' yelled Alice, dialling. 'He's your son, for God's sake!'

Herbert was not prepared to waste any more time with her, so he left the room.

'Hello! Hello!' Alice was shouting into the unresponsive receiver. 'Blast!' she barked. 'What's the matter with everyone this evening . . . ?'

She had hardly slammed down the receiver when an explosion rocked the house to its foundations, all the lights went out, and the glass in the bow windows behind her shattered against the heavy blackout blinds. With a scream she threw herself to the floor.

'For Christ's sake, Alice!' yelled Herbert, from the open door. 'Now will you believe me?'

The distant explosion in Highgate Village was heard down the hill at number 49A, where Catherine Thornton had already taken refuge in the Morrison shelter. She didn't take too much notice for it was turning out to be just one of many worrying explosions that seemed to be taking place all over London. At least she felt safe, for unlike a lot of people who usually waited until the enemy raiders were directly overhead, she and Mrs Bailey had taken cover in the dining-room shelter the moment the air-raid siren had sounded. However, Catherine was only too aware that she was taking a chance by allowing her domestic to share the confined space with her, for if Robert knew what she was doing, he would surely hit the roof. But Catherine felt that this was an emergency, and class and position had no place at such a time even though it was a bit of an ordeal, for Mrs Bailey smelled of carbolic soap and starch.

'If yer ask me, that one was a bit too close fer comfort,' professed Mrs Bailey. 'Me ol' man'll be doin' fairy lights if 'e finks I'm anywhere near that.'

'I do hope your husband won't be too worried that you can't get home?' asked Catherine, who was crouched on the far side of the mattress with as much distance between her and Mrs Bailey as she could manage. 'I should have sent you home much earlier.'

'Now, don't yer go worryin' yerself about fings like that, Mrs Fornton,' replied the old girl. 'Me ol' man can take care er 'imself – an' so can I!' With great difficulty she was sitting cross-legged on the mattress, face peering through the protective metal grille, looking for all the world as though she'd been locked up in the cooler. 'Anyway, I'm glad I'm 'ere. I don't like the idea of you bein' caged up in this contraption all on yer own. I know it's none er my business, but I'd say it's yer 'ubby's duty ter be wiv yer at a time like this.'

If it wasn't for the fact that Catherine knew that her domestic meant well, she would have taken umbrage at such an impertinent remark. 'My husband has more important duties to consider, Mrs Bailey,' she replied defensively.

'Oh yes,' replied the domestic, acidly. 'Fire-watchin' at 'is club, yer mean?'

Before Catherine had a chance to answer, a salvo of ack-ack gunfire outside caused the entire house to vibrate.

'That's it, boys!' yelled Lil Bailey, as though the ack-ack crews could hear her. 'Give them bleedin' Jerrys a kick up the arse fer us!'

Catherine tried not to show her distaste at such comments. In fact, in her real heart of hearts, she agreed wholeheartedly with Mrs Bailey's sentiments.

For several minutes after this, both of them said nothing. Despite Mrs Bailey's frivolous remarks, both women were really quite unnerved. All hell had broken loose outside, and it was difficult not to speculate on what was happening – and where. The cacophony of deadly sounds suggested that this was the worst air raid of the war so far, and it made Catherine sick with worry about the safety of both her husband and her daughter. Deep down inside she dreaded the thought that Peggy was caught up somewhere in all the mayhem. Yes, she was a strong-willed girl all right, and perfectly capable of taking care of herself, but this was a particularly savage night, and unlike in the last war, the Germans were clearly intent on targeting the civilian population. Crouched there in the dark with the electricity supply cut off, and nothing but the sound of death and destruction raining down from the sky, all Catherine could think about was Peggy, her darling girl, educated, cultured, loving – and now cutting herself down to size by doing manual work on the buses in the middle of an air raid. It seemed incredible, thought Catherine, absolutely incredible that a child of hers could have turned out to be so capable of standing up for herself, against anyone, against the world – but, most of all, against Robert. She was indeed special, but, oh God, if anything were to happen to Peggy, she, her mother, would never forgive herself.

'So 'ow's Peggy gettin' on wiv 'er young gentleman friend then?' Mrs Bailey's voice only came when there was the briefest lull in the barrage of ack-ack fire outside.

'Gentleman friend?' asked Catherine, with guarded surprise. 'Who would you be referring to?'

'You know,' said Mrs Bailey, who was perfectly aware that she was being mischievous. 'That bloke from the depot where she works. I've seen 'em 'and in 'and a coupla times on me way 'ome from work. Good-lookin' boy. Bit of a pasty face, though.'

Catherine was careful in her reply. 'I know nothing about him, Mrs Bailey,' she replied vaguely. 'Peggy's personal life is her own business.'

This puzzled the old girl. 'But yer're 'er mum,' she persisted. 'Yer must be nosy enuff ter want ter know wot kind of a feller yer daughter's goin' ter get married to?'

'Married?' Catherine did a double take. 'Has Peggy discussed such a thing with you?'

'No, course she ain't. But she's old enuff ter fink about it, ain't she? Same age as my eldest when she did the same fing. *She* tried ter keep it from me too, but I knew – oh yes, I knew all right. I knew the moment she met 'er bloke. It was that look in 'er eyes. Yer kids can 'ide anyfin' they like from yer, except when they get that look in their eyes. I'n't that right, Mrs Fornton?'

Fortunately, another close salvo of ack-ack fire outside prevented Catherine from having to reply. But what her domestic said had certainly made her think . . .

Peggy and Frosty were in the thick of it. By the time they reached Hammersmith Broadway, the mass air raid that had started soon after they left Piccadilly had gathered so much momentum that they only had two alternatives: either abandon the bus and take shelter, or turn around and get back to Holloway depot as fast as the roads would carry them. In the event, they chose the latter, and in so doing, they were experiencing the most hazardous journey of their lives. On every main thoroughfare they came to, fires were blazing in office buildings, factories, shops, department stores, houses and residential blocks of flats. As the bus crawled along at a snail's pace, people were either running to take cover in the nearest public shelter, or struggling as best they could with their bedding in a frenzied attempt to reach the safety of a tube station. In a blacked-out Piccadilly Circus, on the return journey the defiant double-decker slowly made its way around the boarded-up plinth that had once housed the statue of Eros, and in the heart of West End theatre land in Shaftesbury Avenue, Frosty had quite a job to dodge large pieces of rubble that had tumbled from the rooftops on to the road ahead of them. In the small backstreets alongside and behind the theatres, residents, shopkeepers, pub customers and even scantily dressed chorus girls from the Windmill Theatre were frantically helping firemen and servicemen home on leave to tackle fires caused by incendiary bombs showering down on to the entire area. The air was constantly fractured by the droning sound of enemy aircraft, and the returning ack-ack gunfire was now relentless. When they reached the normally busy Cambridge Circus roundabout, a bus inspector was waving mad signals to them from the protection of the portico entrance of the Palace Theatre.

'Get out of there!' he yelled. 'Fer chrissake, take cover!' But both Frosty and Peggy pretended not to see him, and ploughed on staunchly into Charing Cross Road.

In Tottenham Court Road the bus was brought to a dramatic halt by a huge fire that started in a department store and was threatening to spread to other shops nearby.

The Paramount Cinema had already been evacuated, but some of the male patrons were helping the firemen to open the fire quadrants and unravel the endless lengths of hose. Quickly grabbing his tin helmet, Frosty jumped out of his cabin to find the entire area ankle-deep in freezing cold water. 'If we don't get out of 'ere soon,' he called to Peggy, as she came down from the bus platform to meet him, 'we're goin' ter be stuck 'ere all night!' Completely ignoring the danger of falling masonry and ack-ack shrapnel, which was now falling around them every few seconds, Peggy, also now wearing a tin helmet, immediately joined him and the emergency services to start the arduous task of removing as much of the debris as possible. It was a race against time.

Another battle was taking place on the roof of Sandford's club, where Robert Thornton and Edwin Stevens were now joined by other members, fighting to control the flames that had spread from the roof to the top floor of the building below them. Using stirrup pumps and buckets of sand, the middle-aged men were desperately trying to contain the blaze in the one small area where the cluster of incendiary bombs had smashed a hole through the tiled roof, creating a cavity nearly four feet deep.

'Keep those stirrups on the move!' commanded Thornton, his voice booming out through the barrage of ack-ack fire above. He rushed across to deal with one of the incendiary bombs which was still sizzling with magnesium. 'Get some sand over here – quick!' he yelled.

Although the other members resented being treated as though they were other ranks under Thornton's military command, the emergency confronting them at this moment was far too serious for them to take issue with him.

Everyone rallied round, and even some of the waitresses from the restaurant downstairs came out on to the roof to help refill buckets of water from the mains tap on the wall of the firewatch look-out shelter.

On the opposite side of the roof, which overlooked the garden square below, two other men were busy dousing flames with water from the emergency fire hose. Fortunately, they had now virtually got the blaze under control, but the water pressure, which until that moment had been very low, suddenly cut off. 'Water's gone!' they yelled simultaneously.

Thornton, Stevens and the others turned with a shocked start.

'Tap's dry too!' called one of the waitresses. 'What shall I do?'

Thornton stared in disbelief, first at the dribbling hose mouth, then at the trickling water tap. Without saying another word, he surveyed the smouldering cavity in the roof nearby, then looked out with deep foreboding at the skyline beyond them. He was stunned. For as far as the eye could see, there were fires burning out of control everywhere, the reflection of their flames flickering recklessly in the eyes of the exhausted group staring out in horror at them. It seemed as though the whole of London was on fire.

In a state of complete shock, Stevens asked: 'Does this mean we've lost the war?'

Marge Quincey nearly had a fit when Leo burst through the door of the family's air-raid shelter carrying young Horace in his arms.

'Christ! What's 'appened?' she gasped, grabbing the boy from him. She let out a cry of anguish when she saw blood seeping through one of Horace's socks.

'It's all right, Mum!' insisted Leo, helping her to put the boy down on the lower bunk. ' 'E trod on a bit er shrapnel. It's only a flesh wound.'

This prompted Horace to yell out in pain.

'It's all right, son, it's all right!' said Marge, stroking the boy's forehead. 'Mum's wiv yer.' But when she carefully removed his plimsoll and sock, he burst into tears. 'Oh, my poor boy,' she wailed, the moment she saw the gash under his foot. With great urgency, she snapped at Leo, 'Go an' get the iodine! It's upstairs in the scullery. The cupboard over the sink.'

Leo made a dash for the door.

'An' bring me a clean tea cloth from top of the mangle.'

Leo was halfway out the door.

'An' a pair er scissors!'

The moment he was outside again, Leo heard his young brother yelling out in pain from inside the shelter. The sound hurt him almost as much as if he himself had trodden on that piece of shrapnel. Using his pocket torch, he quickly retrieved the front door key which was always suspended from the letter box inside, and went in. He sprinted up the stairs to the first floor, went straight to the scullery, and found the iodine, tea cloth and scissors. On the way down, however, he stopped dead when he suddenly heard voices calling out.

'The bridge! The bridge!'

Without a moment's hesitation, Leo leaped down the stairs two by two, and was outside in the yard in a flash. When he looked up, he was horrified to see several ARP men struggling to contain a fire on the railway bridge which crossed over Hornsey Road just above him. He rushed back into the shelter, and practically threw the iodine, tea cloth and scissors at his mum.

'I'll be right back!' he called desperately.

'Where yer goin'?' Marge yelled after him, but he'd already disappeared.

It took several minutes for Leo to find his way up the emergency ladder on to the bridge. When he got there, he found a team of men tackling an incendiary blaze which had set fire to a good stretch of the tar-covered sleepers along the railway track.

Somebody yelled: 'Sand! We need sand!'

Everyone was too busy to take notice, trying to stamp out the flames with anything they could lay their hands on: shoes, coats, shovels, even the remains of a discarded wooden apple crate, which for some reason had remained at the side of the track since God knows when.

Leo suddenly remembered there were two buckets of sand down in the coal yard, so he rushed off back to the ladder. But just as he was about to climb down, two curious sounds caused him to stop right where he was. The first was the approaching whistle from a train engine.

One of the ARP men yelled: 'Train!'

Somebody else yelled: 'Stop him!'

Leo turned, and looked along the track, where, to his horror, a train was approaching at speed from the direction of Highbury. But there was no time for him even to think about what to do next, for simultaneously, he heard the crack of machine-gun fire as an enemy aircraft came skimming across the rooftops, strafing everything in its path.

Alice Thornton couldn't remember the last time she'd been down to the cellar. As far as she knew it was a damp, dark space, which was only useful for coal and her hoard of wine and spirits. But after her near miss upstairs in her bedroom a few minutes before, when she was only saved from being cut to pieces by the blackout blinds covering her windows, she had allowed Herbert to bring her down to the shelter.

'I'd have preferred to die in my own room upstairs than spend the night in a filthy hole like this!' she grumbled, sitting on the edge of her Put-u-up bed, puffing away tetchily on her Craven A. 'If this is what the human race has come to, I want no part of it!'

'Think yourself lucky, Alice,' replied Herbert, who was trying to get some sleep on his own bed. 'There are thousands of poor souls all over London who have to carry their own beds down to the tube every night. Just imagine what those platforms are like tonight.'

'I'd sooner die than travel on the tube!' grunted Alice. Despite wearing a winceyette nightdress and a warm dressing gown, she still felt the cold, so she got up from the bed, and stood over the paraffin stove which, with a power cut in progress, was the only form of heating available. 'Nasty smelly thing!' But at least she was able to warm her hands over it. She was distracted by the sound of another distant explosion, and the volley of ack-ack shots that followed it. 'Go away!' she yelled up at the cellar door, as if anyone but Herbert could hear her. Then, irritated that he was trying to sleep through it all, she turned on him. 'Is that all you're going to do?' she snapped. 'Sleep?'

'Unless you have a better idea,' Herbert returned, deliberately turning away from her.

Alice snorted gruffly. She stood there, with one hand propping up the opposite elbow, cigarette poised in the other hand, doing everything she could to find something around her that would take her mind off the ordeal she was having to endure – the empty suitcases against the wall, Herbert's huge garden tool box, the bare brick wall, a spider's web draped across one corner of the cellar, a step ladder, a mountain of coal piled up high beneath the pavement access cover, and a perambulator which had been used successively by both Robert and Peggy when they were babies. The only thing that really brought her any real comfort, however, were the three rows of wine racks, whose contents were gradually proving too hard to resist. Fortunately, her train of thought was suddenly broken when another explosion close by sent dust and cobwebs from the ceiling fluttering down on to her nightcap.

'Damn the Boche!' she spluttered, spitting out bits of plaster.

'Why don't you get to bed, Alice?' sighed Herbert. 'At least you're safe down here.'

'Safe?' she growled. 'If this is what you call being safe, I'd sooner be dead!'

'You wouldn't feel like that if you were out on the street right now.'

'If people are stupid enough to be out on the street at a time like this,' she snapped, 'then they deserve all they get!'

Although Herbert still had his back turned towards her, his eyes slowly opened. 'Does that include your granddaughter?' he asked.

Alice swung a startled glare at him. 'What are you talking about, you stupid old fool?'

Herbert rolled over and, in the flickering light from the paraffin lamp, replied, 'You may have forgotten that Peggy has just started a week of night shifts. As I remember, Catherine told us so when she came to tea this afternoon.' With that, he rolled over and turned away from her again.

Cold as she was, Alice suddenly felt as though her entire body was on fire. Automatically, her eyes moved across the cellar and came to rest on the old perambulator. She went to it, stared at it in puzzlement for a moment, then gently caressed the handle. Peggy? she thought. But she's only a child, a baby . . . She bent over, and looked beneath the fringed awning. For one fleeting moment, she felt as though she could see that baby lying there, eyes only half open, podgy little hands grabbing at the air, two active feet and legs thumping the tiny mattress. *No, not Peggy.* Suddenly, a life was being played out right there, before her very eyes. It was as though she was drowning: Peggy romping around the floor of her grandparents' sitting room; Peggy as a five-year-old sitting next to her father on the piano stool; Peggy in tears as she came to say goodbye before leaving for boarding school; Peggy at home with her mother, learning how to crochet; Peggy the baby, the child – and now the woman. *No, not Peggy!*

When Alice eventually emerged from the deep recess of her past again, she found that she was standing directly beneath the coal access cover. Above her, she could hear the nonstop barrage of ack-ack fire, the vibration from which brought down a thin scattering of coal dust directly on to her closed eyes and upturned face. Her heart was pounding, the cigarette had been discarded, and her hands were locked together in silent prayer. *No, not her, not my Peggy,* cried her inner self over and over again. *If it has to be someone, let it be me,* she pleaded. *But not my darling, not my dear precious Peggy . . .*

Peggy was exhausted. For the past ten minutes she and Frosty had toiled away with dozens of other people to clear fallen debris which had blocked the road, making it totally impassable. There were fires blazing in tall buildings on each side of them and falling fragments of ack-ack shrapnel had already claimed two victims, who had been attended by a St John Ambulance crew and then rushed off to the Royal Free Hospital in Gray's Inn Road. Further down the road, a trolley bus had been struck by an incendiary bomb and was blazing. Peggy couldn't believe this was happening to her. What was she doing out here in the middle of a terrifying air raid when she could be tucked up nice and warm and safe with her mother in the Morrison shelter back home? Was she mad?

'Why don't yer go off ter the tube, Peggs?' croaked Frosty, who was helping a Home Guard volunteer to carry a heavy piece of masonry back on to the pavement. 'This is no place fer a gel like you.'

Although she knew Frosty meant well, she resented his implication. 'If *you* can do it, Frosty,' she called back, 'so can I!'

'Oy! Move yer arse, gell!' yelled a fireman who, with one of his mates, was trying to direct a fast-flowing hose pipe up on to the blazing first floor of a shop nearby.

Peggy got absolutely soaked in the move, but quickly leaped out of the way. She rubbed her eyes; the mixture of smoke, water and sweat was making it difficult to see. Then she quickly joined two Red Cross nurses who were struggling to carry an injured young child out from a blazing block of flats to an ambulance that was parked further along the road. It was only when the three of them had finally managed to get the child on to a stretcher that Peggy realised the little girl was dead. It was her first sight of death, and she felt quite numb. As the nurse closed the ambulance doors from the inside, the other girl glared angrily up at the sky, then quickly hurried back into the driver's seat and drove off. As she watched the ambulance disappear down a side street, Peggy, her face now blood red from the heat of the fires burning all around her, looked pleadingly up towards Heaven. The sky seemed to be on fire.

'Messerschmitt!'

'Take cover!'

'Down! Down! Down!'

With the frantic calls of police and fire crews piercing her ears, Peggy swung round with a horrified start to see the menacing dark shape of a German fighter plane flying at a low level over the rooftops, heading directly towards her and the emergency team, its machine gun blazing a trail of bullets along what was left of the debris-strewn road.

'Down! Down! Down!'

Peggy felt someone dive at her, and bring her flat down on to her stomach. In the fear and chaos of the moment, she had no idea who it was, and didn't have the courage to find out. All she could do was to lie there, covering the top of her tin helmet with her hands, almost too paralysed with fear to move. *Leo! For God's sake – where are you?* In those few seconds, as the machine-gun bullets came ricocheting towards her, the only face she could see in her mind was someone whom she had only known for five minutes, who had deceived her, but whom she wanted by her side more than ever before. Why wasn't she praying to her mother, to her father – or to God Himself? But as the first wave of lethal bullets finally popped in the debris towards her, there was only one person who really mattered to her.

With the incendiary fire on the railway bridge above now under control, and the train that was in danger of collision with the fire watchers on the track now safely at a halt, Leo was finally able to return to the family air-raid shelter. When he got there, however, he found his mum trying desperately to cope with Horace's screams of pain, and young Eddie cowering on the upper bunk, sobbing with fear.

'We've got ter get this boy ter the 'ospital as quick as we can!' insisted Marge, the lap of her coat covered in blood from Horace's injured foot. 'We don't know wot was in that bit er shrapnel.'

'We can't go out there just yet, Mum,' said Leo. 'They're chuckin' down everyfin' they can at us. We'll 'ave ter try an' 'ang on till mornin'.'

'Don't be bleedin' stupid!' replied Marge. ' 'E might get blood poisonin' or somefin'!'

Horace again squealed out in pain.

'Yer see!'

'No, I don't see!' Leo yelled back at her. 'D'yer wanna get 'im killed? D'yer wanna get us *all* killed? I tell yer it's too dangerous ter put one foot outside till this fing's over!'

Marge raised her fist as if to punch him, but she quickly thought better of it. 'If anyfin' 'appens ter this boy, I'll 'ave yer guts fer garters!' she snarled.

There was a sudden banging on the shelter door. Leo got up quickly to see who it was.

A torch beam appeared first, then a head popped in. It was Max Harris, the local special constable. 'Everyfin' all right in 'ere?' he called.

'Oh, fank God it's you, Mr 'Arris!' spluttered Marge, immediately starting to lift Horace up in her arms. ' 'Orace stepped on a bit er shrapnel. Could yer 'elp me ter get 'im ter the 'ospital?'

'Blimey – no way, gel!' replied the constable, alarmed. 'It's like an inferno out there. They've bin droppin' fire bombs all over the place. I've never seen anyfin' like it in me life! If I was you, I'd wait till the All Clear. It's just not worf takin' the chance.' His head disappeared again, but reappeared almost immediately. 'By the way, there's a real mess up Tottenham Court Road way. It just come up on our field telephone. There's a double-decker on fire.'

Leo rushed out before the constable could leave. 'Wot number?' he gasped frantically.

'D'you wot?' asked the constable.

'The number?' asked Leo, impatiently. 'What number bus got 'it?'

'Dunno, mate,' replied the constable. 'One of our blokes said it was a number 14, but I couldn't say fer cert.'

Leo left him immediately, and rushed back into the shelter. 'I'll be back soon as I can!' he said.

'Don't you dare!' warned Marge, eyes blazing. 'Don't you dare!'

But Leo ignored her, and rushed out.

Marge sat there alone, and in disbelief. She wanted to cry, but the tears wouldn't come. All she could do was to stroke Horace's head gently, to try to soothe away the pain as much as she could. But gradually her anxiety turned to frustration, and then to anger. The more she thought about Leo rushing out into the night to look for that madam from up the hill, the more she hoped that she would be dead before he could reach her. But just when her bitterness was in danger of overpowering her, a few moments after Leo had left, the door opened again, and in he walked.

For a moment or so, they just stared at each other's blank expressions. Then Leo took a dog-end from behind his ear, lit up, and sat down on the lower bunk at the side of his mum.

Chapter 12

The All Clear siren was wailing across what was left of the rooftops of London, but the light of a new day was only just breaking when Peggy arrived back home on the pillion of a fire brigade motorcycle. Once she'd thanked the girl rider who'd given her the lift, she opened the front garden gate, and made her weary way up the steps to the front door. Apart from two broken windows, she was relieved to see the place still standing. She had her key all ready but didn't have to use it, for her mother, arms outstretched, was waiting at the top of the steps to greet her.

'Thank you, God!' said Catherine tearfully, as she hugged Peggy to her. 'I thought I'd lost you.'

'You won't get rid of me as easily as that,' replied Peggy, playfully. 'What about Father?'

Catherine took a deep breath to steady herself. 'The club was badly damaged last night,' she said. 'He's lucky to be alive. He's upstairs sleeping.'

They went inside and straight to the kitchen, where, because Mrs Bailey had only just managed to go back to her own home, Catherine made the tea. Only when she had sat down at the table with Peggy did she notice how terrible the girl looked.

'I can't believe you've been out all night in the middle of all that,' she said. Then she reached across and placed her hand on Peggy's. 'It must have been appalling.'

Peggy smiled as best she could, and nodded. 'If you don't mind, Mother,' she said, 'I'd sooner not talk about it now.'

Catherine poured the tea, and Peggy let her mother do most of the talking. 'It must have been bad,' Catherine said. 'I heard about it on the six o'clock news this morning. They said it was a mass raid, a fire-bomb raid. They don't say exactly how bad, but I can guess.'

'It *was* bad,' was all Peggy would say.

For a moment or so both women sat in silence whilst they sipped their tea. Catherine watched her daughter carefully; she could see the strain in the girl's eyes, eyes that had seen so much during the past hours, but which Peggy would not yet be ready to talk about. But she was very proud of her. 'Would you ever think about giving it up?' she asked.

Peggy looked up. She was puzzled.

'This job? On the buses?'

Peggy shook her head.

'It scares me,' persisted Catherine. 'It's so dangerous.'

Peggy rested both hands on the table in front of her. 'It's all part of the job, Mother,' she replied. 'There are plenty of people doing far more dangerous things than me. Just think of what our boys had to go through at Dunkirk.'

'Soldiers expect to take risks,' said Catherine, 'but not young girls working on the buses.'

'This war is a battle for survival, Mother,' replied Peggy. 'When it comes to a fight, young girls are no different to young men. We all have to do what we can.' She took a sip of her tea. 'I saw the face of a dead child last night,' she continued solemnly. 'It seemed so unreal – and so pointless. I mean, what does a five-year-old girl have to do with people who want to kill her just because she happens to be there? She hasn't had time to learn anything about life. She only knows about playing games with her brothers and sisters or her friends. She only knows about listening to what her parents tell her to do. She only knows that she wants one day – to grow up.' She had to steel herself by taking another sip of her tea.

Catherine waited a moment before speaking. Then she asked tenderly, 'Tell me about your young man.'

Peggy looked up with a start.

'Mrs Bailey says he's very good-looking. She's seen you with him a couple of times.'

Peggy perked up. 'Mrs Bailey's an old busybody!' she snapped. 'I don't know what she's talking about.'

'Darling,' said Catherine, again reaching out for Peggy's hand, 'it doesn't matter, really it doesn't. You have a life of your own to live. In a few weeks' time you'll be twenty-one. You'll be legally entitled to have a relationship with whoever you choose.'

Irritated, Peggy suddenly got up from the table.

'Darling!' Catherine got up with her. 'Please don't be angry. All I wanted you to know was that I'll support you in whatever you do. And I'm sure your father will too – in time.'

'Mother!' replied Peggy. 'I know you mean well, but I can assure you that whatever Mrs Bailey has told you is not true. I'm having a relationship with no one – no one at all. As far as I'm concerned, I have far more important things to do with my life, so I hope you'll not bring up the subject again. If you'll excuse me, I'm desperate for a bath.'

Catherine watched in complete bewilderment as Peggy turned away, and left the room.

In her bedroom upstairs, Peggy quickly changed into her dressing gown and made for the bathroom. She took a passing glance at herself in the mirror there, which confirmed what she had already suspected, that she not only felt like hell, but looked like it too. She turned on the bath taps, then took off her robe. Although there was only a trickle of water both hot and cold, she decided there was

241

enough for her to have her rationed six inches. The first thing she noticed as she stepped in was that the hot water wasn't hot at all, only lukewarm. But she ignored this, and lay down, waiting for the two taps to produce at least enough water to cover most of her thighs. Whilst she was lying there, she thought about what her mother had just said to her, about having a boyfriend. '*Darling . . . you have a life of your own to live . . . All I wanted you to know was that I'll support you in whatever you do. And I'm sure your father will too – in time . . .*' She chortled to herself. Oh yes, I bet he will! She could just see her father sitting down to tea with her and a boy from Lower Hornsey Road! How stupid Mrs Bailey was, she told herself. How stupid her mother was too for believing such nonsense. But then she thought back to those days which now seemed like a lifetime away, when she and Leo were indeed not at all afraid of being seen walking hand in hand together down Holloway Road. The meagre trickle of lukewarm water was now becoming more tepid than ever, and with no heating in the room Peggy felt a cold chill throughout her body. She lay back, and closed her eyes. Immediately she could see him. Leo. Damn! How could she have allowed herself to be taken in by someone so fickle? After all, what was so special about a boy that she'd only known for so little time, and who had virtually swept her off her feet the moment they had met? But the more she thought about it, the more she realised that Leo wasn't entirely to blame. She blamed herself for falling in love with him. Gradually, she felt despair. The yearning was still there. She could still see his face, and no matter how hard she tried, it just wouldn't go.

She was drifting off to sleep. But a sharp thumping, bubbling sound suddenly caused her to sit up with a start and open her eyes. The taps! No water! She was lying in just an inch of almost cold water, and there was nothing coming out of either of the taps except for a few measly drops. 'Sod it!' she yelled out loud.

It was the first time she had ever used a swear word in her entire life. Now she knew for certain that she had at last succumbed to the hard reality of working-class life.

Monday turned out to be mopping-up day. In the bleak light of morning, those in London who had managed to sleep, woke up to find that their city had been quite literally torched. Although most of the destruction appeared to be in the square mile, nearly all parts of the capital had suffered fire damage, which in many cases had gutted buildings so that they were in danger of crumbling to the ground. Charred wooden beams were exposed in burned-out houses, shops and offices, and even the Royal Northern Hospital, which was now overflowing with air-raid casualties, had to move in-patients to more secure, temporary accommodation.

Having spent half the morning with his young brother Horace in the out-patients' wing at the hospital, and the rest in a ward upstairs with his father, Leo now felt relieved and confident enough to go in to work.

When he arrived at the depot he found that it too had not escaped the effects of the previous night's fire-storm, and the first thing he did was to join his workmates who were busily clearing up the debris from shattered glass and tiles on the roof of the garage. Amongst them were Shorty Biggerstaff, an engine fitter from Yorkshire, who at the start of the war had been mad enough to come to London to seek a better-paid job, and Elsie Parker, who was in dungarees and Wellington boots, hosing down the dust and other muck that had rained down on the parked buses.

'Anyone get hurt last night?' Leo was almost afraid to ask, as he immediately set to work checking the engine of a number 29 that had been towed off the road at the Nag's Head after losing most of its windows in a high-explosive bomb blast.

'Two of the lads in't workshop,' called Shorty who was flat on his back repairing the exhaust system underneath the same bus. 'Fanlight come in on 'em. But they're not too bad, just a few cuts 'ere an' there.' He poked his head out. 'Oh – Nobby 'Ancock took one too.'

Leo turned with a shocked start. 'Nobby? Route inspector?'

'Bit of a wall fell on 'im while 'e was on duty outside the Palace Theatre up Cambridge Circus. Concussion. They took 'im ter Charing Cross 'Ospital.'

'Bleedin 'ell,' gasped Leo, carefully disguising the real news he was looking for. 'Did I 'ear somefin' about one er our lot coppin' it – up Tottenham Court Road or some- where?'

At the mention of this, Elsie turned off her hose. 'It wasn't one of ours,' she said. 'It was a trolley – 653.'

Leo tried not to show how relieved he was.

'Got completely gutted, though,' called Shorty, whose broad Yorkshire voice was now calling from underneath the bus again. 'Incendiary. Set the body paint on fire – went up like a flash of lightning. Everyone got out just in time – no thanks ter Adolf!'

'Peggy was up there too, Leo,' said Elsie, lowering her voice as she joined him. 'She an' Frosty got caught in the middle of it all. Some soddin' plane come down an' machine-gunned them. They're lucky ter be alive. But Peggs is pretty shook up.'

Leo came out from under the open bonnet. 'Christ!' he gasped. 'Where is she now?'

'She's sleepin' it off at 'ome,' she replied. 'Why don't yer go over an' see 'er?'

Leo shook his head guiltily. 'I can't do that, Else. Yer know I can't.'

Elsie took him to one side. 'Wot's 'appened between you two, Leo?' she asked softly. 'I know it's none er my business, but I like Peggs. I like 'er a lot. She's too nice ter be kicked around.'

'I'm not kickin' 'er around,' he replied firmly, without believing a word of what he was saying. 'It's just that – well, it's not goin' ter work fer us. It can't.'

'Why not? She loves yer. She fought yer loved 'er too.'

Leo shrugged awkwardly. 'Fings don't always turn out the way yer expect 'em to.'

'Especially when yer've got someone else in tow at the same time.'

Elsie's remark stung him. 'I don't commit meself ter no one, not till I'm ready,' he snapped pointedly. 'I never 'ave, Else. Yer know that.'

'Oh yes,' smiled Elsie. 'I do know that – only too well. But Peggs is different. She's not the person I fawt she was. She's become one of us – just like you an' me. Fer someone who's come from where *she's* come from, she 'as a lot er guts.' She turned to go, but stopped. 'Peggs is worf somefin', Leo,' she said, with a poignant smile.

Leo watched her put down the hose, go to the mains tap and turn it off, then disappear through the doors of the female crew changing room. For a moment he just stood there, pondering on what Elsie had said, torn by indecision and guilt. Then he slammed down the bonnet of the engine he had been working on, and quickly moved on to the next bus.

Peggy woke up at about two in the afternoon. She was glad that her mother had let her sleep on, for she felt as though she had been dragged through a hedge backwards. Still in a bit of a daze, she went to the window, drew back the curtains and raised the blackout blind. The light outside was blinding, not from the sun but from a heavy fall of sleet which had temporarily settled on the garden lawn. As her bedroom overlooked the back gardens, she could only see superficial damage to the rooftops opposite, but beyond them there were clear signs of fires that were still smouldering from the previous night's fire blitz. Fortunately, when she went into the bathroom she was relieved to find that the water supply had been restored, so after a more successful attempt to have a bath, she got changed into her clippie's uniform, and went downstairs.

On the way down she could hear her mother and father having what sounded like a heated argument in the sitting room. She stopped on the stairs for a moment to listen.

'No, Robert!' insisted Catherine, who was clearly very het up. 'It's wrong, it's just wrong. And even if I did agree, I'm absolutely positive that Peggy would not.'

'Peggy's agreement is of no relevance whatsoever,' replied an implacable Thornton. 'I presume that I do still have *some* part to play in deciding what is and what isn't right for my own family?'

'It's my family too, Robert,' Catherine reminded him, in a rare show of contradiction. 'And don't forget, Peggy comes of age in a few weeks. We can't force her to do anything she doesn't want to do.'

'We shall see about that,' replied Thornton.

'See about what, Father?'

Thornton and his wife turned with a start to find Peggy standing in the open doorway.

'Peggy!' said Alice Thornton. 'Thank God you're safe, child!'

Only then did Peggy realise that her grandmother was also in the room. 'Grandmother?' Surprised to see the old lady sitting in an armchair by the coal fire, she went straight to her, and pecked her on both cheeks. This was one occasion when Alice couldn't disguise how drained and tired she was.

'Is anything wrong?' Peggy asked.

'Grandmother's coming to stay with us for a while,' Catherine said quickly. 'The Towers was badly damaged by a fire bomb last night.'

'Oh my God!' gasped Peggy, immediately kneeling beside the old lady. 'What about Grandfather?' she asked anxiously. 'Where is he?'

'Don't worry,' replied Alice, a little jealous of Peggy's concern for her husband. 'He's still with us – *just*!'

Peggy looked to her mother. 'An incendiary device of some kind hit the roof,' explained Catherine. 'It burned its way right through the house, from top to bottom.'

Peggy, horrified, clasped a hand to her mouth.

'Thank God they were both in the cellar, or they could both have been—'

'Well, we weren't!' rebuked Alice. 'So stop fussing, Catherine!'

'But where is Grandfather now?'

'He's up at the house with the servants,' replied Alice, irritated, 'or what's left of it. He's supposed to be retrieving some of our possessions, but I suspect all he's really interested in is his wretched garden!'

Peggy immediately got up. 'I'll go and see if I can help,' she said, making for the door.

'Plenty of time for that later,' said Thornton, speaking for the first time since Peggy had entered the room. 'We want to talk to you first.'

Peggy exchanged a brief, concerned look with her mother. 'About what?' she asked, with deep suspicion.

'About the danger of my womenfolk living in London at

a time like this,' replied Thornton, with just a hint of self-doubt. 'About facing up to the grave challenge that lies ahead of us.'

Peggy glanced from one face in the room to another. Both her mother and her grandmother were avoiding her look, so she returned to her father. 'I would have thought that's what we're already doing,' she ventured.

'No, Peggy,' said her father, who was still in his dressing gown after sleeping most of the morning. 'After last night, the situation is far more serious than it was. The City of London was virtually burned to the ground. And this is just the start. My information is that most people are trying to get out of the built-up areas as fast as they can.'

Peggy pulled a face. The people on the street she'd spoken to overnight seemed more determined than ever not to abandon their homes. 'If you don't mind my saying, Father,' she replied, 'I think that sounds a bit unlikely. In my experience, when their backs are up against a wall, Londoners don't usually give in that easily.'

Thornton deliberately refused to exchange a look with his wife. 'Peggy,' he said, as he slowly made his way across the room to her, 'I want you and your mother to go to Canada.'

Peggy was thunderstruck. 'What!'

'I have contacts there – a friend of mine from my college days. He has a charming wife and three grown-up children – two boys, and one girl who is married with a child of her own. They live in Toronto. It's a pleasant city. There are many English people there. You'd be made most welcome. But most of all, you and your mother would be away from all this.' He moved closer to her, and tried to show concern. 'It would be a great relief for me to know that you'll be safe and well looked after.'

Peggy continued to stare at him in disbelief. 'And what

about you, Father? Where will *you* go?'

Thornton looked across to his mother, and attempted an affectionate smile. 'I shall stay here with your grandmother and grandfather,' he replied. 'If things get too bad, we shall all leave Highgate, and make our way north to stay with Uncle Percy and Aunt Jessica in Huddersfield. As you know, they have a large house. There's plenty of room for us all.'

'If that's the case,' asked Peggy, acidly, 'then why do Mother and I have to go all the way to Canada?' As he moved away, she followed him, asking, 'Is there any particular reason why you *want* us to travel so far, Father – across the Atlantic, at the mercy of enemy U-boats? Or hadn't you heard that the Germans have been sinking British shipping at an alarming rate?'

Thornton swung round on her, but only just managed to control his anger. 'British evacuees have been sent regularly to Canada ever since the war started,' he said. 'They always travel under the protection of the Royal Navy.'

Peggy nodded. 'I'm glad to hear it.'

'There's a ship leaving from Liverpool on the eighteenth of next month. It's officially already overbooked, but I have several contacts in the P & O Line. I'm sure they could find accommodation for you both somehow.'

'How convenient, Father,' replied Peggy, walking away from him. 'Because regardless of your contacts, I for one have absolutely no intention whatsoever of travelling to Canada – or anywhere else!'

Over by the fireplace, Alice Thornton couldn't contain her admiration for her granddaughter. 'Ha!' she chuckled approvingly.

Thornton glared at her, then returned to Peggy. 'Why are you behaving like this?' he asked, in an attempt to sound uncharacteristically reasonable. 'Why can't you see that what I and your mother are suggesting is for your own good? Why can't you see that I care for you both, that if anything happened to you during this ghastly bombing, I would never forgive myself?'

Peggy slowly turned to face him. 'I'm very touched by your concern, Father,' she said calmly. 'But I have a job to do, and I intend to go on doing it.'

Thornton's approach hardened. 'And is that your only reason?' he asked, his face grim and taut. 'To do your "job" in the middle of an air raid, running up and down the stairs of a bus, punching holes in tickets for miserable passengers. Or is there some other attraction that perhaps makes it all so worthwhile?'

For only one brief moment, Peggy stared disbelievingly at him. 'The only *attraction*, Father,' she replied, 'is that I intend to stay and fight this war – in my own way.' With that, she turned, and left the room.

As she went, Alice Thornton applauded gleefully. 'Game, set and match!' she proclaimed, triumphantly.

The Towers was a sorry sight. When Peggy got there she found what had once been an elegant double-fronted Victorian detached house was now still smouldering from the previous night's fire which had threatened to gut the place completely. Fortunately, however, the fire brigade had somehow managed to rescue the building from total destruction. 'Only just in time, though,' said a rather disconsolate Herbert Thornton, whom Peggy had found, as her grandmother had complained, doing his best to clear up the burned-out mess that had been his treasured back garden. 'If they'd arrived any later, we could have said goodbye to The Towers for ever.'

'I'm so sorry, Grandfather,' said Peggy, linking her arm comfortingly through his, and shaking her head in despair at the flattened remains of his much-loved summerhouse. 'Don't worry. We'll all help you to build it again.'

'I'm not sure I want to,' he replied. 'You can't recapture something just by doing it all over again for a second time. I think I'll just stick to my memories – and the snapshots, of course.'

They smiled gently at each other, then wandered back into the house. There were still one or two firemen scraping out the charred remains of some wall beams in the main entrance hall, making quite sure that they would not reignite the moment the men had left. The place smelled of burned furniture, and following the fire-fighters' desperate struggle to bring the flames under control, in every room they found themselves ankle-deep in water. However, although the house was unfit for habitation, some parts had escaped relatively unscathed, except for the fact that every mattress, every sheet and eiderdown cover, every curtain and every item of upholstery was black with smoke, and would clearly have to be replaced.

Peggy couldn't recognise the sitting room. There was a gaping hole in the ceiling where the incendiary device had burned its way through from the roof right down through every floor of the house, the heavy brocade curtains and blackout blinds were hanging in shreds at the shattered windows, the furniture was sopping wet through strenuous attempts by the fire-fighters to save them from the spreading flames, the paintwork everywhere had frizzled up in the heat, and even the elegant William Morris wallpaper had been scorched so much that great patches of plaster were now cruelly exposed. Strangely enough, however, the one sight that saddened Peggy more than anything was the baby grand piano, now a sad and sorry sight in the afternoon gloom, its glistening dark varnish burned off and white keyboard stained and cracked with fallen ash, an elegant musical instrument reduced to a shell of its former self. Peggy couldn't understand why she should feel such nostalgia for something that only recalled unhappy memories of her mother playing it, with her father at her side, his confident baritone voice booming out in melody that defied criticism from anyone. Watched by her grandfather, she went to the keyboard, and pressed a note; the sound was tinny and pleading. 'Will it ever play again?' she asked.

'For someone else, I hope,' replied Herbert. 'Probably not us.'

For the next few minutes, Peggy helped him to retrieve some of the small ornaments, framed photos and pictures which were lying in several inches of water. It was a painstaking job, for everything had to be dried and put into the empty suitcases which had to be brought up from the cellar.

Once the last two firemen had left, Peggy had her first real chance to talk to her grandfather. 'The only good thing about all this,' she said, 'is that you'll be coming to stay with us.'

'Well, your grandmother is,' replied Herbert.

Peggy stopped what she was doing. 'What do you mean?' she asked, puzzled.

'Too many Thorntons under one roof is more than I could take,' he replied, with a sly wink. 'But I'm sure I shall be leaving your grandmother in safe hands.'

Peggy was still puzzled. 'But – what about you?' she asked. 'What are you going to do?'

'Until this house is put together again, I shall be staying with my brother, George, in Hertfordshire. I've been wanting an excuse to get away for years.'

Peggy was now fearing the worst. 'You don't mean – for good?'

Herbert smiled at her ominously. 'Who can tell?'

Peggy watched him retrieve a framed wedding photograph of himself and Alice. It was already heavily distorted by the hose water, so he threw it back where it came from. Peggy found it distressing to see how disenchanted her grandfather had become. She had always considered him such a worthwhile person, and hated the thought that he would be spending the last years of his life without the comfort of a loving relationship.

'Did you know they want to send me to Canada?' she said quite suddenly.

Herbert looked up at her. 'Ah!' he replied. 'I wondered when that would come up.'

'Did you know?'

'I heard your father and Alice hinting about it on Christmas afternoon. For your own protection would be the excuse, I imagine?'

'I have no intention of going.'

Herbert grinned. 'I didn't think you would.' He continued sorting through the water on the floor. 'If you'll take my tip, you'll get that nice boyfriend of yours to make an honest woman of you.'

Peggy stopped what she was doing, and moved away.

Herbert looked up, surprised. 'Oh dear,' he said. 'Have I said the wrong thing?'

'Not at all,' Peggy replied, turning back to him with a false smile. 'I just feel that I'm not ready for a relationship.'

Herbert looked across at her. She had that same kind of look on her face that reminded him of a time once when she'd been a small child, when she'd tried to pretend that she wasn't really hurt after falling off her bicycle in the street outside, a bicycle that he himself had bought for her birthday. 'The last time we spoke, you were quite smitten.'

'Not really,' replied Peggy, trying to pass it off lightly. 'I mean, people come and people go. How can you possibly expect to know someone when you've only just met them?'

Herbert shrugged. 'It happens,' he said, 'sometimes.'

They exchanged a knowing look, which gradually turned into a smile.

'I'd better be off,' said Peggy, going to him. 'I'm on late shift.'

'Yes, I know,' he replied, with a feeling of deep unease. 'Please be careful, my dear little one.' With one finger, he gently eased a curl of her straggly red hair back over her ear. 'Things are going to get worse before they get better. Be careful – please.'

Peggy gave him a reassuring smile, kissed him on the cheek, hugged him, and then left.

Herbert watched her go. The light from a gloomy day outside was gradually fading, and the remains of what was left of the sitting room were becoming hard to see. He went to the battered window and saw Peggy making her way back down the hill. She had a long night ahead of her, many long nights. He prayed she would survive them better than he ever had.

Leo had been waiting for almost an hour. He knew that Peggy usually got into work at least half an hour before she was due out on the road, and he was determined to get to talk to her during that time. It was almost five o'clock when she finally arrived. The sun had already gone down, and it would soon be time for the blackout. With the possibility of a resumption of the same kind of ferocious air raid that they had experienced during the previous night, everyone at the depot was on tenterhooks, for news had been coming in during the course of the day that several members of bus crews had lost their lives during incidents in different parts of London, which, naturally enough, had created a very sombre mood with their colleagues through-out the entire London Transport network.

When Leo caught sight of Peggy, he waited until she had checked in at the conductors' room, then followed her into the canteen, where she joined Frosty, Elsie and Sid Pierce, who were gloomily sipping their tea in silence at their usual table. Leo decided to wait a few more minutes until he felt the time was right for him to go across and join them.

'Terrible about that number 19,' said Sid to the others, just as Peggy was joining them with her cup of tea.

Frosty was too upset to answer.

'Don't,' said Elsie, nodding her head. 'I can't bear ter fink about it. Them poor devils.'

'A 19?' asked Peggy, sitting at the table. 'What's happened?'

'Took a packet on its way back ter 'Ackney last night,' agonised Elsie.

'UXB,' said Sid. 'Unexploded bomb. Suddenly went off when they was nearly back at the garage. No warnin' – just whoosh!'

'Killed both the crew an' four passengers,' added Elsie gloomily.

'They shouldn't've bin out on the road!' growled Frosty, suddenly breaking his silence.

Peggy was surprised he was in such a mood. This was the first time she had seen him angry.

'It was a stupid fing ter do!' he continued. 'They should've just left the bloody bus an' gone ter the nearest shelter!'

Peggy stretched across to him, and clutched his arm. 'The same thing could have happened to us, Frosty,' she said, trying to comfort him. 'We were just lucky that we managed to get out alive.'

Frosty slowly looked up at her. 'That 19,' he said, close to tears, 'it was the one that stopped be'ind us outside the Ritz. That clippie – she was the gel who come up an' spoke to yer.'

Peggy stared at him. For a moment she found it hard to grasp what he was saying. *'By the way, me name's Vera – you know . . . 'We'll Meet Again . . . !'* The words were suddenly ringing in Peggy's ears. She could still hear that young voice calling to her, so full of fun, so full of life. *'. . . Can't keep a good clippie down, yer know!'*

' 'Allo, Peggs.'

For a moment or so, Peggy sat quite motionless, until Leo's voice brought her out of her daze. When she looked up, she saw him standing beside her.

'I 'eard about wot 'appened last night,' he said tentatively. 'Fank God yer din't get 'urt.'

Everyone watched Peggy carefully, as she got up and left the table.

Leo felt embarrassed by the reproachful heat of their glares, so he rushed off after her.

Peggy had only just left the canteen when she heard Leo call her. 'Peggs – please!'

She stopped, but didn't turn round.

'Don't take it out on me, Peggs,' he said. 'I don't know why I do the fings I do, but I want ter tell yer that I've bin caught up in somefin' that – just seemed ter 'appen.'

Peggy slowly turned to face him. They were now standing in the semi-dark, so it wasn't easy for her to see his features. 'Things always seem to "just happen" to you, don't they, Leo?' she said. 'I wonder if the day will ever come when you'll have a mind of your own?'

'That's not fair,' he protested.

'Isn't it?'

'I came 'ere ter tell yer I'm sorry.'

'Did you ask your mother's permission?'

'I made a mistake an' I know it.' He tried to move closer, but she stepped back a pace. 'Look, Peggs, I've got deferred from call-up for anuvver munf. 'Cos er wot's 'appened ter Dad. Just give me time, Peggs. Give me time, an' we can sort fings out, I know we can.'

'Let me tell you something,' said Peggy. 'The day I met you, I really convinced myself that love at first sight wasn't so impossible after all. I was prepared to sacrifice an awful lot to be in your company. Being with you made me feel good. I don't know why, but I trusted you. I really believed that even though I came from the top of the hill and you from the bottom, that we had a lot in common, and that we were both capable of standing up to people who wanted to get in our way. But not any more, Leo.' She started to move off, but then stopped. 'You've destroyed a lot inside me, Leo,' she continued, not looking back at him. 'For one fleeting moment, I thought I loved you. But now I know I never could.' She turned briefly to him just one last time, and called, 'Happy New Year, Leo.'

Leo was left alone in the shadows. He knew there was no sense in going after her.

Chapter 13

Pam Warner made her way along Seven Sisters Road as fast as her tiny feet would take her. It was already nine o'clock, and she was worried that her employer, Reuben Koenitz, would once again have to reprimand her for being late for work. Fortunately, there had been no air raid overnight, mainly because of the windy weather and the heavy clouds, so most shopkeepers along the main road had had time to sweep the glass from their shattered front windows into the kerb after the intense fire blitz twenty-four hours earlier. As soon as she reached Estelle's ladies' hairdressing salon, she knew she was in for it because the front door had already been unlocked.

'Good morning, Miss Warner!' was the welcome she received from the proprietor the moment she appeared. 'How generous of you to honour us with your presence.'

'I'm awful sorry, Mr Koenitz,' said Pam, quickly taking off her coat and headscarf, and going into a cupboard at the back of the shop to hang them up. 'I 'ad ter make breakfast fer the family terday. Bein' stuck down that Anderson shelter night after night's given me mum terrible rheumatism.'

Koenitz bowed graciously to her. 'Please convey my commiserations to your mother,' he replied, in a fractured Polish accent tinged with a touch of Seven Sisters Road's style of cockney. 'But please tell her that if her daughter is late once more, she will be available to make breakfast for the family *every* day of the week.'

Pam didn't hang around to offer any more explanations.

Within a very few minutes she had joined the other two assistants, Josie and Babs, as they quickly readied the place for the first customers of the day. As she did so, every so often she would sneak a look at Mr Koenitz in one of the styling mirrors. She frequently asked herself if there was anyone in the whole wide world who was as ugly as he, with his huge paunch, double chin, baggy eyes, and a black toupee that just did not fit properly. But she was impressed with his glistening white teeth, which always reminded her of the crocodile Tarzan grappled with at the pictures. 'Silly ol' bugger!' she called him to the other two girls, but only once he'd disappeared to his flat over the shop upstairs for his usual cup of Camp coffee with chicory.

' 'E was checkin' the appointments book,' said Babs, the eldest of the three girls, who was tall and thin, wore heavy-rimmed spectacles, and who had an irritating habit of scratching her nose every few minutes. ' 'E wanted ter know who was 'ere first.'

' 'E can mind 'is own business,' said Pam haughtily. But thinking twice about it, she asked, 'Yer din't tell 'im, did yer?'

Babs shook her head.

'Wot yer goin' ter do if 'e finds out yer're doin' it fer free?' asked Josie, the youngest.

'I'm not doin' it fer free,' replied Pam, who was idly tidying up her own hair in a mirror over one of the sink basins. 'I'm goin' ter put the money in meself.'

The two other girls exchanged a puzzled look.

'Well, why shouldn't I?' asked Pam, talking directly to their reflections in the mirror. 'After all, she is s'pposed ter be me future muvver-in-law.'

Peggy was up quite early, which meant that after an undisturbed night's sleep, she was able to get out of the house before her grandmother came down to breakfast. Although the old woman had only been staying with them for less than twenty-four hours, she was already proving to be quite a handful.

The temporary offices of Parks and Stevens were situated in a rented Georgian terraced house in Liverpool Road, a busy residential area which ran from Lower Holloway Road all the way through to Upper Street at the Angel, Islington. When Peggy got there, she found that this area too, like practically all the roads she had passed on the tram on the way, had not escaped the ravages of the fire blitz twenty-four hours or so before. There seemed to be shattered and boarded up windows all the way down from Upper Street, and she passed three houses which had collapsed completely and were now nothing more than a pile of rubble. The offices, such as they were, were spread over the first two floors of the house, the two rooms on the top floor being used for the kitchen and for Edwin Stevens' personal use, which usually meant he had somewhere private to nod off during the afternoon. However, when Peggy pressed the front door bell, she was surprised to see it answered by a pimply-faced youth, who coloured bright red the moment he saw someone actually standing there.

'My God!' said Irene, the moment she set eyes on Peggy. She seemed more shocked than delighted to see her. 'W-what a lovely surprise,' she added, after a not-unnoticed pause, then quickly rushed forward to peck Peggy on the cheek.

'I thought I'd come and wish you and Mr Stevens a happy New Year,' returned Peggy, who was sad to see the place piled high with documents and nowhere to file them.

'Mr Stevens won't get in much before eleven,' said Irene. 'That fire at his club completely unnerved him.'

'I'm not surprised,' replied Peggy. 'Father says it was

touch and go.' For a moment, they exchanged brief smiles. Peggy was only too aware that Irene these days was looking decidedly drained and uneasy.

Irene suddenly noticed that the youth was watching them with awed fascination from his makeshift desk tucked away behind two battered wooden filing cabinets. She called across to him, 'Monty, how about making Miss Thornton and me a nice cup of tea?' The youth didn't have to be asked twice. Blushing profusely again, he got up from his seat, and rushed straight out of the office.

After he'd gone, both women sniggered. '*Monty?*' asked Peggy.

Irene lowered her voice. 'His real name's Montmorency Butterworth,' she said. 'I think you can understand why he prefers to be called Monty!'

Again they sniggered. Then they sat down together, Irene at her small work-table by the window, Peggy in a chair opposite her. 'I must say, you look wonderful,' said Irene awkwardly. 'Looks like punching bus tickets suits you.'

Whether Irene meant to put her down or not, Peggy was not prepared to be cowed. 'There's more to the work than that, Irene,' she said, unruffled but reproving.

Irene quickly reached out and covered Peggy's hand. 'I didn't mean that the way it sounded,' she said. 'Actually, Peggy, I have nothing but admiration for you. You're quite amazing.' She patted Peggy's hand, then withdrew it. 'How's Leo?' she asked.

For some reason, Peggy wasn't surprised by her friend's question. In fact, she had been quite expecting it. 'Leo?' she asked casually.

'Come on now, Peggs,' returned Irene, hastily searching for a Craven A from the packet on her table. 'That nice boy you introduced me to in the pub on Christmas Eve. You don't have to hide things from me.'

'Why should I want to do that?' asked Peggy.

'What?'

'Hide things from you.'

Irene was flustered. 'I don't mean "hide" exactly . . .' she said, nervously lighting her cigarette. 'I mean, you don't have to be embarrassed.'

'Embarrassed?' asked Peggy, surprised. 'Because I was having a drink with someone in the pub?'

Irene shrugged. 'I just thought you looked – well, pretty close, that's all.'

Peggy decided to let it pass – for the moment. 'Tell me,' she asked, sitting back in her chair, 'are you still thinking about joining the Land Army?'

'I'm not sure,' Irene replied vaguely, taking a deep puff on her cigarette. 'Up until a few days ago I thought I'd go ahead with it, but – I'm not too sure – just at the moment.'

'So what's changed your mind?'

Peggy's direct question took Irene by surprise. Things were made worse by the fact that Peggy was sitting with her back to the window, so the watery sun outside was shining straight into Irene's eyes. 'It's not that I've changed my mind—' Irene started to say.

Peggy interrupted her. 'I thought the last time I asked you, you'd already decided not to join up – not until the office had moved back to Upper Street.'

Irene was taken off guard. 'Did I?' she replied. 'Oh yes, yes, that's right. That's what I've decided to do. No point in rushing into things.'

Peggy watched her carefully as she got up to find herself an ash tray. She had so many questions she wanted to ask Irene, like how she seemed to have known so much about Leo when they last met, and why Leo thought he had once seen her out walking near the coal merchant's yard where he lived in Hornsey Road. Irene was puzzling her. In all the time she had known her, she had always found her to be quite secretive and withdrawn, but not to this extent. Why did she feel uneasy about her? Why did she feel that Irene was hiding something? Was it because she was having to take the strain of looking after the office practically single-handed, or was it because she had something to hide about her *own* personal life?

'Did I tell you that Joe's coming home on leave?' said Irene, as she returned with an ash tray she'd collected from the mantelpiece.

'No, you didn't,' replied Peggy, without much interest.

'We're expecting him any time,' Irene continued, sitting on the edge of the table this time so that she could get a clearer view of Peggy's reactions. 'Just a weekend pass, of course. Apparently he's been doing very well on his officers' training course or whatever it is.'

'Good.'

'If I was you I'd watch out,' said Irene. 'I've no doubt one of the first things he'll want to do is to see you.'

'Why should I want to watch out?' asked Peggy.

This again took Irene by surprise. 'Well – I thought – I presumed . . . with your boyfriend and everything . . .'

'I don't have a boyfriend, Irene,' replied Peggy. 'Where did you get such an idea?'

Irene was too taken aback to answer.

Estelle's salon was now very busy. All three styling chairs were occupied, and two other women customers were waiting to take up their appointments in the small waiting area behind a red plush curtain at the rear. Josie was in the middle of curling up the grey hair of one elderly customer, who insisted on smoking her Weights fag whilst it was all going on, but Babs was relieved that her first appointment was a young girl who, in the middle chair, was eagerly watching every movement in the mirror ahead of her as Babs gave her the nearest thing to a 'Betty Grable' cut. In the background, the inimitable Charles Shadwell and his orchestra were also busy, dishing out 'Yes, sir, that's my baby' on the wireless for the morning's regular *Music While You Work* programme, which was setting everyone's toes tapping, especially Babs's customer. By this time, Mr Koenitz had reappeared, and had already taken up his favourite position at the cash till by the door. He passed the time by browsing through his copy of the *Daily Sketch*, leaving the pre-war issues of women's magazines for his customers. Fortunately, he was just out of range to hear what conversation Pam was having with Marge Quincey, her customer on the end chair, for the one thing Mr Koenitz never encouraged during working hours was his employees engaging in too much idle chitchat with his customers.

'You're a good gel, Pam,' said Marge, amazed to see in the mirror her hair taking some kind of shape after years of doing it herself. 'One of the best.'

'Not really, Mrs Quincey,' replied Pam, who was having a difficult time cutting and untangling Marge's hair, which was as tough as old rope. 'Don't do no 'arm ter 'ave a spruce-up once in a while. Anyway, yer do a lot of nice fings fer me – the least I can do is ter give yer a bit of a treat ter start the New Year. By the way, got any New Year resolutions?'

'Me?' asked Marge. 'Oh yes, I've got resolutions all right.' She looked directly up at Pam's face. 'I wanna make sure I can 'elp you an' Leo make a real go of it.'

For one split second, Pam stopped cutting. When she caught Marge winking at her in the mirror, she smiled back weakly at her, then carried on cutting.

'D'yer fink my son really means business this time?' Marge asked, watching carefully for Pam's reaction.

' 'Ard ter tell, Mrs Quincey,' replied Pam evasively. 'You know Leo better than I do.'

'But 'e don't see that madam no more?'

' 'E's 'ardly likely ter tell me if 'e is, is 'e?' With her thumb and forefinger, Pam held up a lock of Marge's hair. 'I'm goin' ter fin it out a bit,' she suggested, peering with Marge into the mirror. 'OK?'

Marge was looking at Pam, and not at her own hair. 'Wot's she like?' she asked, ignoring the question.

'Who?' asked Pam.

' *Er!* Madam on the number 14!'

Pam let the lock of hair go. 'Honest ter God, I don't know, Mrs Quincey.'

'Yer saw 'er, din't yer? Outside The Eaglet that night?'

Aware that Babs's customer in the next chair was straining to hear their conversation, Pam leaned down to Marge's left ear and lowered her voice. 'I can 'ardly say I *saw* 'er,' she whispered. 'It was pitch-dark at the time.'

'Pity *I* wasn't there,' said Marge. 'She'd've got a piece er my mind, I can tell yer!'

Pam was getting worried, and not just about Mr Koenitz, who was peering at her over the top of his newspaper. 'Yer know,' she said, continuing to cut and comb, 'p'raps Leo ought ter be left ter make up 'is own mind.'

Marge looked up sharply. 'Wot yer talkin' about?' she snapped.

'Well,' continued Pam, after taking a quick glance across to make sure that Mr Koenitz had returned to his newspaper, 'yer can't *force* someone ter commit themselves unless they mean it, can yer? If Leo's really keen on this gel, well, there ain't much anyone can do about it. In any case, yer never know if *I'm* goin' ter meet someone else, do yer?'

Marge suddenly sat bolt upright, and swung round to

look at her. 'Wos that?' she growled, eyes blazing. 'Someone else?'

Pam suddenly panicked. 'I'm not sayin' I've got someone,' she said quickly. 'I only meant *if* I should.'

'Well, you'd better not, Pam Warner!' warned Marge. 'After all I've done fer yer!'

'Is there a problem here, madam?'

Pam looked up with a start to see the reflection of Mr Koenitz standing behind her in the mirror. 'Oh no, Mr Koenitz,' said Pam, quickly answering for Marge. 'There's no problem. Is there, Mrs Quincey?'

'I wouldn't know,' answered Marge, staring straight at her. '*You* tell *me!*'

Alice Thornton had never much cared for her son's taste in décor. She had always despised brown as a colour, and number 49A was absolutely full of brown varnish paintwork. Even the wallpaper had autumn colourings, which, to her mind, made living through summer very depressing indeed. And as for the curtains! They would not look out of place in a workhouse – nasty cheap-looking things, supposed to be silk but clearly nothing more than cotton. The place was also pretty dusty, and needed a thorough springclean. If she, Alice, were her son, she would dismiss that impertinent domestic at the first opportunity. Of course, she blamed it all on her daughter-in-law. Catherine was such a useless girl. She knew from the first day that she had set eyes on her that she was weak, and totally incapable of organising a decent household. All this was on the old lady's mind as she puffed away on her Craven A in her son and daughter-in-law's sitting room.

'D'yer want some more coal on the fire then?' rasped Mrs Bailey, who was doing her best to sweep and clean the carpet around the new lodger.

'Since this room has the temperature of an igloo,' returned the old lady haughtily, 'I would have thought the question was quite irrelevant.'

'Never lived in an igloo meself,' sniffed Mrs Bailey, 'so I wouldn't know.' She had never taken a shine to the old girl, not since the day, some years before, when she had referred to Mrs B's mince and carrot pie as 'quite tasteless'. The thought that she was now going to have to put up with both Thornton and his old dragon of a mother under the same roof, did not bode well for her. 'I'll be back in a minute,' she growled, glaring at Alice, and grabbing the empty coal-bucket from the fireplace. On the way out, she grunted as she passed Thornton coming into the room.

'I have to go to court for an hour or so, Mother,' he said, going straight to the fireplace.

'It's New Year's Eve!' Alice protested.

'Yes, I know,' Thornton replied, collecting a cigar from his humidor on the mantelpiece. 'There are no sittings today. I just have to clear up some paperwork, that's all.'

Alice watched him tuck the cigar into the inside pocket of his jacket. 'I don't intend to stay here for ever, you know,' she said. 'As soon as The Towers is habitable again, I shall go straight back – Blitz or no Blitz.'

'It could take quite a long time,' said Thornton.

'I shall nag the builders night and day until it's done.'

This brought an amused smile to Thornton's face. 'I'm sure,' he replied.

'In any case, it's neither fair nor wise to encroach upon family life. Especially *your* family.'

Thornton swung her a resentful look. 'I don't know what you mean, Mother,' he replied.

'Don't you?' Remaining seated, Alice supported both

her hands on the handle of her walking stick. 'I can't imagine being welcome for too long in a house where there's clearly a lot of – discontent.'

Thornton, puzzled, stared at her.

With the help of her walking stick, Alice gradually eased herself up, and went to him. 'I really can't understand why you can't persuade your own wife and daughter to do what is so obviously good for them. I'm sorry to have to tell you, my dear,' she continued, with a wily eye, 'but you seem to have very little influence in your own house.'

Thornton was irritated with her. 'If you're referring to Canada—' he grunted.

'Canada or boyfriends – what difference does it make?'

'Boyfriends?'

'Isn't that what this is all about?' asked Alice cunningly. 'Isn't this the reason why Peggy refuses to leave the country – because she's found someone who's become far more important than her own family?'

'Mother, you're talking nonsense!' said Thornton, turning away.

'Leo,' returned Alice.

Thornton stopped, slowly turned, and looked at her.

Alice smiled to herself, revelling in the thought that she was able to pass on the disturbing information to her son that she had accumulated after several careful sessions listening behind half-open doors to conversations between her granddaughter and Alice's adversary, Mrs Bailey. 'His name is Leo,' she continued, carefully watching her son's reaction. 'He lives with his family down the hill – in Holloway. But I don't have to tell you all this, do I, my boy? I'm sure it's something you've already known for a long time.'

'How do *you* know all this?' demanded Thornton, doing his best to conceal that he was not ignorant of what his daughter had been up to.

'*How* is immaterial,' continued Alice. 'The point is that your daughter has a working-class boyfriend, and it would seem that no one in the world is going to keep her from him. Of course, it's none of my business, but I would have thought it's an unfortunate situation to say the least.'

Until this moment, Thornton thought he knew everything there was to know about his mother. Ever since he could remember, there had been an unspoken understanding between them, as though each of them knew what the other was thinking; two minds that thought and acted alike. But this was different. Alice was one step ahead of him, and he didn't like it. Therefore, he had to pretend, pretend that he was fully in control of the situation. 'I think you're forgetting something, Mother,' he said. 'Peggy is a young woman now. She has the right to make her own decisions, and to make friends with whomsoever she pleases.'

Alice watched him carefully, pulled just once more on her Craven A, and then twisted the stub hard into an ash tray on the small table beside her. She was glowing inside in the knowledge that she was about to reveal what she had gleaned from a private telephone conversation between her son and a mystery caller whom he nervously addressed as Irene. 'If you feel that way, darling,' she asked, 'why have you had her followed?'

Peggy was filled with doubt and apprehension. As she left the offices of Parks and Stevens and made her way along Liverpool Road, back this time towards Holloway Road, her mind was dominated with thoughts about Irene, about her uneasiness, about some of the things she had said, but most of all about how much, in so little time, she had changed. Peggy needed this walk. She needed it to clear her head, to try to think straight. She was so preoccupied that she hardly noticed the kind of road she was in. It seemed to stretch forever, flanked on either side by such an array of lower middle-class two- and three-storey houses and working-class residential Victorian blocks, and the last remaining signs of tracks which had once carried trams from one end of the road to the other. She had also found it hard to believe what Irene had just told her about the kind of district this had once been in the old days – middle-class, well-to-do homes, and those who came from out of town to savour the comforting delights of the local spring water spas.

When Peggy finally brought her surroundings back into focus, she realised that she had reached the tall iron gates of a churchyard. She wasn't quite sure why she had stopped, but quite instinctively that is what she had done. The gates were open, so she walked in and found herself strolling along a narrow cement path that led to a rather ugly red brick church, which like so many other buildings in the neighbourhood, had suffered a great deal of bomb blast, and was in need of urgent repairs. As she strolled, she passed one or two other people who, like herself, were out for a quiet stroll. One girl, who seemed far too young to be pushing a baby in a pram, even gave her a passing smile, but an elderly man and woman, wrapped up like Eskimos in the biting cold, were far too intent on directing their eye-line to the path they were walking along, and hardly noticed her.

Before making for the exit signposted Madras Street, Peggy decided to take a short detour off the main path, and wander amongst the scattering of neglected grave-stones, most of which were overgrown with dead grass and weeds. The remains there seemed mainly to have been interred within the last hundred years or so, but there were one or two more contemporary ones that captured her attention, including one headstone upon which had been carved the head of a mongrel dog, with an inscription that read:

> *Emily Wonter, spinster*
> *10 January 1847 – 23 August 1934*
> *Devoted friend of 'Duke'*
> *who sadly predeceased me*

The inscription brought a smile to Peggy's face. She imagined that someone who loved a dog enough to put his name on her own gravestone must have been quite a person.

She moved on.

Nearby, she paused again. This time she had found what looked like a newly dug grave, for the protruding mound of earth contained the withered remains of bunches of flowers, with message cards still attached. Unfortunately, it was almost impossible to read them, for rain and sleet had smudged them until they were almost illegible. But when she crouched down, she was just able to decipher the three simple words that had been scrawled on one of them: '*Missin you, Mum*'. There was no signature.

'That's my mum.'

Peggy looked up with a start to find a small girl of about eight or nine standing over her. She was wearing only a pullover, short trousers, a Balaclava, and Wellington boots that were far too big for her.

'I'm sorry to hear that,' replied Peggy tenderly.

'Oh, it's all right,' said the child. 'Me dad said she's gone back ter where she came from.'

'Your dad's right,' replied Peggy.

The child wiped her nose with the back of her hand. 'She got killed in a bomb,' she said. 'Come down on our 'ouse. She was there on 'er own at the time. Dad was at work. Me an' my sister, Minn, were round at Gran's.'

Peggy bit her lip. She had no idea what to say. 'What's your name?' she finally asked.

'Janey,' replied the child. 'My mum's name was Gladys. Everyone used ter call 'er Glad. She always used ter smile. She was forty-two.'

Peggy steeled herself.

'Me dad says fings ain't always as bad as they look,' said the child. 'D'yer fink that's true?'

Peggy smiled, but with difficulty. 'I'm sure it is,' she replied, without conviction.

'Me dad says, "*Don't believe all yer see, 'cos if yer do yer'll only get fed up.*" ' For one brief, brief moment she looked down at the mound of earth, and then, as if it was the most natural thing to do, she said, 'Cheerie-bye, Mum!' She kissed the tips of her fingers, and waved them at the mound of earth, calling quite casually, ' 'Appy New Year!' With that, she turned, and hurried off.

Peggy got up from her crouched position, and watched the girl rejoining what must have been her dad and young sister, waiting for her in the distance. Then they quickly passed out through the main churchyard gates, and disappeared along the Liverpool Road.

For a moment, Peggy just stood there. The churchyard itself was now deserted, and a slight but icy cold breeze whistled through the leafless trees, bringing with it a chorus of contented, ethereal sighs. Peggy listened to it all, and allowed the breeze to swirl around her feet. All she could really hear now though was a small child's voice: '*Don't believe all yer see, 'cos if yer do yer'll only get fed up.*' The funny thing was, Peggy didn't feel fed up at all. Not any more. In fact, even the thought of Leo brought a warm smile to her face.

On his way home from work, Leo popped in to see his dad in the Royal Northern. Propped up with three pillows, Reg was now feeling well enough to sit up in a comfortable armchair in the day room, where he was able to relax and smoke a fag away from the prying eyes of the staff nurse. 'I asked 'er if she'd like a dance wiv me at New Year,' he joked. 'She said by then I'll be packed up tight wiv a biscuit an' a cup er cocoa!'

Leo laughed.

On the other side of the room, an elderly patient who was being visited by his wife, was filling the place with thick palls of tobacco smoke from his pipe, so much so that two other middle-aged women who were visiting their brother, coughed and spluttered, and constantly turned to glare at him with deep disapproval.

'So 'ow's yer mum then?' Reg asked, not for one moment expecting a positive response.

Leo shrugged indifferently. 'She's bin ter 'ave 'er 'air done,' he replied, grinning. 'Pam did it buckshee for 'er. If yer ask me yer missus wants ter give yer a New Year's Eve bunk-up!'

Reg roared with laughter. 'Cheeky bugger!' he said, nearly choking on his fag. When he had recovered, he signalled to Leo to draw closer. ' 'Ow's yer mum takin' it?' he asked, voice low. 'About – you know . . . ?'

Leo was puzzled. 'What?'

'What d'yer fink, yer knuckle-'ead!' spluttered Reg. 'Your gel! Yer clippie on the 14!'

Leo flopped back into his chair. 'Lay off, Dad!' he sighed.

'Well, yer'll 'ave ter 'ave it out wiv 'er sooner or later,' persisted Reg. 'She won't give yer any peace till yer do.'

'There's nuffin ter 'ave out,' insisted Leo. 'It's all over wiv Peggs an' me.'

'Wot!' Trying to lean forward, Reg suddenly gasped in pain.

'Dad!' Leo rushed to help ease him back into his chair again. 'Fer chrissake watch it!'

Once he'd got his breath back, Reg laid into the boy again. 'The last time we talked about 'er,' he said, 'you was all over 'er. So wot's goin' on?'

Leo sighed. 'It's not goin' ter work, Dad,' he replied. 'I should've known it all along.'

'Yer mean, yer mum knew it all along?'

'No, Dad,' Leo replied firmly. 'I've only got meself ter blame. I made a mistake. That's all there is to it.'

'Oh – so yer mean yer don't fancy 'er no more?'

'I din't say that.'

'So yer do?'

'Wot is this?' asked Leo, slumping back in his chair again. 'A bloody cross-examination or somefin'?'

Reg looked across and smiled at the two middle-aged women who were glaring at them. They immediately turned their backs on him. Once again he signalled to Leo to come closer to him. Reluctantly, Leo did so. 'I wanna tell yer somefin', son,' Reg said, grave-faced. 'I know yer mum. I know wot she's capable of when she wants somefin'.' He stretched out his hand, put it on Leo's shoulder, and drew him closer. 'When Pam Warner come ter see me on Chrissmas Eve, she was tryin' ter tell me somefin'. She was soundin' me out, Leo. I know a two-faced woman when I see one. She an' yer mum've got it all worked out between 'em. It's you they want, an' they won't let go till they've got yer.' He drew Leo so close that he was now talking directly into the boy's ear. 'The only fing is, Pam 'as ideas of 'er own – know wot I mean?'

Leo looked at him, puzzled.

'Mark my words, son,' Reg continued, 'our Pam ain't as dumb as she looks. Make no mistake about it, that gel's got somefin' up 'er sleeve all right. An' believe me, yer mum ain't goin' ter like it. She ain't goin' ter like it at all.'

Chapter 14

For most Londoners, New Year's Eve turned out to be a bit of a damp squib. After the devastating fire attack forty-eight hours before, there was very little appetite for too many celebrations, and those that were held took place in air-raid shelters, along tube platforms, and anywhere else where it was safe enough to spend the night. Ironically, by New Year's Day there had been no further raids, which was mainly thanks to bad weather over the English Channel, but even so, no one was taking any chances. Peggy was relieved to be back on day shift again, for at least it meant that she could be saved from the ordeal of being on duty out on the road during an air raid. However, she was completely unprepared for the challenge that awaited her when she found herself summoned to her first meeting of the New Year with her divisional superintendent.

'Transfer?' asked Peggy, who had been taken completely by surprise. 'But where to?'

'Oh, just across the road,' replied the quietly efficient middle-aged woman sitting at the desk opposite her. 'To the trolley bus depot in Pemberton Gardens.'

'Trolley bus!'

'A few weeks, that's all. We need someone to fill in whilst we bring in some new recruits. I'm afraid quite a lot of our boys over there have now been called up. It's been quite difficult to keep things on the move.'

Peggy was in a daze. The idea of learning how to cope with a totally different type of bus was daunting, especially as she'd only just managed to come to terms with the conventional type.

'There's nothing to worry about, Peggy,' said the woman. 'Petrol and electricity – there's very little difference really, except the trolley is much smoother – and quieter.'

'But surely there's so much more to learn?' asked Peggy, quietly panicking inside. 'I mean – all those gadgets, the pole and overhead wires and – all sorts of things. It must take ages to learn to do all that.'

'Four days,' said the woman.

Peggy slapped her hand to her mouth. 'Four *days*!' she gasped. 'Is that all?'

'Under normal conditions it would be somewhat longer,' replied the super, as she was known. 'Unfortunately these are not normal times, and desperate times call for desperate measures.' She took off her tortoiseshell spectacles and gave Peggy a reassuring smile. 'I think you should know that we're all very proud of the way you've coped with – well – all you've had to cope with since you joined us. I must say, the incidents you and your driver have been involved in have been a bit of a baptism of fire – in every conceivable way.'

Unconsciously Peggy glanced up at the two posters on the wall of the tiny office behind the super. One was a colour picture of a more familiar, and in Peggy's mind, more friendly, petrol bus, and the other was of the gleaming new monster held together with two challenging-looking poles connected to the monster's overhead umbilical electric wires. 'I shall miss Frosty – my driver,' she said.

'It's just a few weeks, Peggy,' said the super, getting up from her desk. 'I can promise you he'll still be here when you get back. And don't forget,' she continued, coming round her desk as Peggy got up from her seat, 'I shall always be here if there's anything that's worrying you.' She walked with Peggy to the door.

'When do I start?' Peggy asked timidly.

'Next Monday, the sixth,' replied the super. 'It's a brand-new year, Peggy,' she said, with another of her encouraging smiles. 'Despite everything, I'm sure you have a lot of good things to look forward to.' She held out her hand. 'Good luck.'

Peggy shook the super's hand. 'Thank you,' she replied – unconvincingly. 'I'll need it!'

'The trolleys? Bleedin' 'ell!' Frosty wasn't at all pleased to hear Peggy's news. On two occasions they'd threatened to put him on trolley bus training, and every time, so far, he'd managed to wangle his way out of it. 'Deff traps, them fings!' he insisted. 'I can't tell yer 'ow many times I've seen blokes – an' gels – tryin' ter get them poles back on the wires. A nightmare, mate! A bleedin' nightmare!'

'You're not making it easy for me, Frosty,' sighed Peggy, as the two of them made their way to the bus they were about to take out on the road on their morning shift. 'The whole thing scares the life out of me.'

Frosty suddenly realised that he was unnerving the girl, and he quickly changed tack. 'Nah,' he said, putting a fatherly arm around her shoulders as they walked. 'Take no notice of me. I'm no good at new-fangled fings, so I always make it sound worse than it is. Fank Gord yer're a bright gel. Yer'll pick it all up in no time.'

Peggy sighed again. 'I hope you're right, Frosty,' she replied. 'I really do.'

As they approached their bus, Peggy suddenly noticed Leo working on the engine of a single-decker that had been brought in for some specialist repairs after being involved in an incident up at Muswell Hill during the big fire blitz a couple of nights before. She was relieved that he hadn't noticed her, so she quickened her pace, forcing Frosty to keep up with her. But suddenly, she came to an abrupt halt.

'Wos up?' asked Frosty.

'Give me a few minutes, Frosty?' she asked.

Frosty took a sly look at where Leo was working, then smiled. 'Plenty er time,' he replied, before moving off and leaving her to it.

Peggy waited for him to go, then slowly turned round. After a brief moment to convince herself that she was doing the right thing, she went across to Leo, who was just sliding himself out from underneath the bus. 'Hello, Leo,' she said in a calm and friendly voice.

Leo looked up with a start. He couldn't believe she had actually spoken to him. 'Peggs!' he replied, quickly getting to his feet.

'How are you?' Peggy asked.

He was even more astonished. 'I'm – fine,' he replied, bewildered. 'You?'

Peggy smiled and nodded. She didn't know what to say next, and neither did he. For a brief moment they just stood there awkwardly, totally self-conscious, the yellow light from the naked electric bulbs dangling down from the asbestos roof high above them, casting uneven shadows across their faces. Eventually, she plucked up enough courage to ask, 'How's your father now?'

Leo was grateful for being given the chance to say something. But he was still tongue-tied. 'Oh – Dad – yes, 'e's gettin' on fine,' he spluttered. 'Should be 'ome in the next day or so.' Again he was at a loss for words. 'Reckon the 'ospital needs the beds,' he continued.

'I imagine so,' replied Peggy. She paused a moment, briefly looked down at her feet, then back up at him again. 'Look, Leo,' she said, 'I'm sorry about the other night. I had no right to say the things I said to you.'

'Oh, yer did,' replied Leo. 'Yer 'ad every right. I'm a chump. I always 'ave bin, an' I always will be.'

Peggy smiled. 'None of us are perfect.'

There was another brief silence, then Leo took the risk of moving a step towards her. 'I've got – so much I wanna tell yer,' he said. 'If yer'd just give me the chance ter explain—'

'Let's not spoil it,' Peggy said quickly, but not unkindly. 'There's no reason why we can't be good friends.'

Leo felt dejected when she stretched out her hand for him to shake. Reluctantly he wiped his greasy hand on his dungarees, took hers, and shook it. But for one instant he imagined that she had allowed it to linger just a little bit longer than she had intended. But he didn't mind. He didn't mind at all. The warmth from her hand immediately flowed though his entire body.

'See you around then,' she said, once their hands had parted.

' 'Ope so.'

Peggy smiled, turned and went off to join Frosty.

Leo watched her climb on to the platform of the bus, and disappear into a seat on the lower deck. His eyes followed the bus as it slowly pulled out of the garage forecourt, and set off for its morning shift down Holloway Road. For one brief moment at least, the start of the New Year had turned out better for him than he'd expected.

Robert Thornton knew his mother was watching him from the spare bedroom on the first floor. Ever since she had come to stay at the house she had watched him leave every single time. He wondered what she was hoping to see, whether she had some reason for keeping an eye on his movements. After hearing how much she had found out about his own activities in keeping track of Peggy and her working-class boy from Holloway, he was a worried man. Worried in several ways, but primarily because he was proving to be so much like his mother – shrewd, questioning and, above all, possessive. He had once heard his father call his wife a witch. Oh yes, she was that all right. Alice Thornton always had a good brew for curiosity.

Making his way down the hill on foot, Thornton stopped briefly to look up at the sky. Over the past few days it hadn't been really advisable to do such a thing, for the weather had been so dreadful, with heavy low-hanging clouds and a mixture of mist, fog and rain, which cast a relentless grey gloom over the entire city. Striding on at a good pace, he looked every inch the military man. Although his bowler hat, cane, and long dark overcoat were his winter trademark, it was his highly polished leather shoes which always seemed to attract the most attention when he was entering the main entrance of the magistrates' court. Glistening in the weak morning sunlight, they were a reminder of what he always used to tell the men under his command: 'If you can see your face in your shoes, then you can really call yourself a soldier!' Thornton was a soldier to his fingertips – and his toes.

At Archway corner he went straight to his local taxi rank. Owing to both petrol rationing and the fact that a third of London's taxis had been commandeered by the Auxiliary Fire Service, he had to wait a few minutes before one was available. When one eventually came, he got in and asked to be taken to the Nag's Head. To his way of thinking, it was the kind of place that he would only ever expect to ask for in a nightmare.

Seven Sisters Road was brimming with people out shopping. Owing to the incessant power cuts, street traders seemed to be doing a roaring trade in torches and candles, and another stall was quite literally bulging with small paraffin lamps, which was a little odd considering that there was now an acute shortage of paraffin, wicks and the matches to light them with. Thornton wandered amongst the shoppers, an incongruous sight in not only what he was wearing, but also his height, for his bowler-hatted head towered above nearly every other. At Hicks the greengrocers, he turned a blind eye to the cajoling of the assistants, who shouted out loud an offer to him of 'Best King Edwards, five pounds a penny!' And adding, to gales of laughter, 'Penny 'a'penny ter you, sir!' At the delicatessen shop next door, he stared in disgust at the large lump of pork brawn on show in the window, and the long queue of shoppers who were hoping to get a few slices or so on their coupons. Once he had reached the junction with Hornsey Road, he came to a halt, and stared all around him. He felt like he was standing in an alien world. Everywhere he looked, there were people of all shapes and sizes, people in shabby coats and ridiculous hats or headscarves, women wearing hairnets over curlers, men in flat caps and dungarees, irksome children running all over the place, weaving in and out of the human traffic, shouting and yelling, wiping their dripping noses on the backs of their hands, and making life generally quite intolerable. And then he smelled beer, stale beer, close by, as though he were drowning in the stuff. Thank God The Eaglet pub he was standing outside was not yet open; at least he was spared the debilitating sounds of drunken laughter and obscene songs.

Thornton turned the corner into Hornsey Road. It was pretty much as he had expected, a sordid place of run-down shops with poky living accommodation above. Another smell drew his attention to the other side of the road – a butcher's shop called Dorners, where some sort of cooking was going on in the window. He had to put on his long-sighted spectacles to read what the notice on the door said: 'Hot saveloys and the best pease pud in Holloway.' 'God,' he gasped to himself, 'what kind of muck do these people eat?' He moved on, carefully avoiding the attention of a few shoppers who were inside Evans the dairy, queuing for milk and their weekly ration of butter and eggs. But when he paused briefly outside a grocery shop simply called George's, he took the impetuous, bold decision to go inside.

To his surprise, he was immediately greeted with: 'Good mornin', guv! Be wiv yer in just one minute.'

Thornton smiled back an acknowledgement as graciously as he knew how. But he hoped the chattering young woman in front of him, buying dried peas, broken loose sweet biscuits, a tablet of carbolic soap and a bundle of kindling wood, wouldn't take all day.

'Now, guv,' said the shop man, whom Thornton presumed to be the proprietor, 'wot can I do fer yer?'

Thornton cleared his throat majestically. 'I'm wondering if you can direct me to a coal merchant's office somewhere along this road,' he said. 'I'm afraid I don't know the name of it.'

'Ah!' replied George, whose cheery smile was one of the main reasons he had so many loyal customers. 'That'll be Milson's. Got a bit of a walk ahead of yer, though.'

'I'm told it's somewhere near a railway arch,' said Thornton.

'That's the place!' George replied confidently. 'Ain't bin fer donkey's. Can't be easy for 'em these days, though. Wiv this ruddy war, yer can't get the coal yer used to.'

'Perhaps you'd know,' said Thornton, ignoring George's irrelevant chitchat, 'the people who live above the offices there?'

'Quinceys?' asked George. 'Cor blimey, 'course I know 'em. Known the 'ole family since they moved in a long time ago. Reg's always poppin' in 'ere fer a fag an' a moan. I tell yer, if ol' Churchill'd only get Reg an' me ter run the war, we'd 'ave 'Itler on the run in no time at all. Only fing is,' he sighed, 'it's terrible about Reg's accident. Lucky 'e wasn't killed when 'e fell off that scaffold.'

'Quite so,' replied Thornton, who reluctantly tipped the brim of his bowler, adding, 'I'm obliged to you.'

'My pleasure, guv!'

Thornton squirmed as he left the shop. He hated being addressed as 'guv'.

After hurrying past a furniture shop on the corner of Mayton Street, he took only a passing glance at what he thought looked like a grubby little sweet shop called Pop's, where he could see what looked like an ancient man serving a group of lively young children, who clearly had no ration coupons left to buy whatever real sweets were available, and were undeterred by the laxative content of the liquorice slices on offer.

As George the grocer had indicated, it took Thornton all of six or seven minutes to walk the length of Hornsey Road to the coal yard. After he had passed the back gates of Pakeman Street School, he virtually closed his mind to his surroundings; they only confirmed to him that this was no sort of world for a daughter of his to live in.

When he finally reached the coal yard, a fully loaded horse-drawn cart was just pulling away.

'Quincey?' Thornton called to the driver, as though the man had a duty to respond.

'Whoa there!' called the driver, drawing the reins in on his horse. 'Up top!' he replied, with more courtesy than he'd been shown, and nodding to the Quinceys' rooms above the office. 'But they ain't at 'ome.'

'D'you know where they've gone?' asked Thornton imperiously.

The driver shrugged.

'I'm obliged,' replied Thornton, starting to move off.

'Shall I tell who called?'

Thornton waved without looking back. But then he changed his mind, stopped and turned. 'Tell them they had a visitor – a visitor who will undoubtedly call again.'

With his cane resting on one shoulder as if it were a rifle, he marched off briskly, back in the direction from which he had just come.

Unknown to either, along Hornsey Road, he and Marge Quincey passed each other on the street.

Betty Desmond hadn't ventured on to Highgate Hill for quite some time. In the old days that weren't that long ago, she used to call on her friend Catherine Thornton whenever she was passing, and she was always greeted with a smile and a cup of tea. Then there were the bridge parties, which usually involved several of their other friends, who all took turns hosting them. But these days it wasn't like that. Betty hadn't seen Catherine since they had had their quarrel, that painful quarrel which had certainly distressed Betty, and caused what had proved to be an irreversible break in their long friendship. Or at least that's how Betty saw it at the time. Now she was wondering what she could do to bring them back together again. A few weeks before, Peggy had practically begged her to ask her mother to join the WVS, saying that it would not only give Catherine something to occupy her mind, but would also be a wonderful contribution to the war effort. But would it work? Was it worth a try? Yes, it was, Betty had decided, but only after she had cleared the air of the stupid, unjustified accusations that Catherine had made against her.

Despite the fact that she had dressed smarter than she had done for months, Betty felt self-conscious about her entire body as she approached the front gate of number 49A. Apart from one or two boarded-up windows, the house looked remarkably unscathed from the ravages of bomb blast, which was a different story from the extensive devastation that had been caused to so many other parts of the area. As she climbed the narrow stone steps to the front door, her legs suddenly were so weak from anxiety that she felt sure they would give way before she got there. However, she managed and, taking a deep breath, she rang the door bell. After a moment, she heard Catherine's voice inside calling, 'It's all right, Mother – I'm here.' And then the door was opened.

'Happy New Year, Catherine.'

Catherine did a doubletake when she saw Betty was standing there on her doorstep. For an instant, she couldn't say anything, but finally asked coldly, 'What do you want, Betty?'

Betty was stung. 'That doesn't seem a very nice way to greet an old friend,' she replied.

Catherine didn't answer.

'I – want to know how you are,' said Betty awkwardly. 'It's been such a long time.'

'What's the point?'

Betty was sensing defeat. 'I miss you,' she shrugged.

Catherine hesitated a moment, then opened the door and stood back to let Betty in.

As she entered the hall, Betty felt an overwhelming surge of nostalgia. How many times had she stood in this very same hall, gossiping with Catherine and the other women, putting the world and all their absent friends to right, smelling the cucumber sandwiches and tea cakes that Mrs Bailey always rolled out for those Wednesday afternoon bridge parties? But that was such a long time ago, and now there was a war on, and everything was *so* different.

'My mother-in-law is staying with us,' said Catherine, who was a little tongue-tied. 'Her house was hit by bomb blast. She's sleeping late in her room upstairs.'

Betty tentatively followed her into the sitting room. The air reeked of Craven A smoke, and even though it was late morning, the curtains and blackout blinds were still drawn. Catherine went straight to the windows and drew them back. When she turned round, Betty was watching her wistfully.

'You haven't changed a bit,' Betty said.

'Thank you,' said Catherine, embarrassed. 'But I don't think that's entirely true.'

'Oh, but it is,' insisted Betty. 'This war is turning most of us into shrivelled-up lunatics, but, if anything, you look younger than the last time I saw you.'

Catherine ignored what she had said, and motioned Betty to the sofa. Catherine then sat opposite her in the red plush armchair now used by her mother-in-law. 'You're not working today?' she asked.

'I work every day,' replied Betty. 'In fact I don't think the WVS members have worked so hard since the day they were inaugurated. You wouldn't believe the number of people we have to look after who've been bombed out of their homes. The emergency services are bulging at the seams trying to cope.'

There was another awkward silence between them until Betty calmly leaned forward and asked, 'What happened between us, Catherine?'

Catherine was too restless to sit, so she immediately got up again. 'I find it hard to believe that you don't know,' she replied. 'If you go around spreading malicious rumours about people, what do you expect?'

'I have never ever spread malicious rumours around about *anyone*,' said Betty. 'It was you who automatically assumed that the gossip you heard about Robert came from me. And that was completely untrue.'

'The insinuations came from you.'

'I passed on to you what I'd heard, Catherine,' insisted Betty. 'I tried to warn you, to stop you from being hurt.'

'Well, you didn't succeed.'

'I'm hardly to blame for that.' Betty was upset. She got up from the sofa and went to look at a snapshot photograph of her and Catherine laughing together at a dinner dance they had both attended years before with their respective husbands. 'I find it so hard to believe that two people who used to be such good friends, who used to trust each other, and who used to care for each other, can drift apart because of such lies.'

'They weren't lies.'

Betty, shocked, turned round to find Catherine staring out of the window. As she did so, Catherine turned back to her. 'It was all true what you said, what everyone said. Robert *was* seeing someone. For all I know, he still is.'

Betty took a moment to take in what Catherine had just said, then went to her. 'Catherine . . .'

Catherine held up her hands to silence her. 'It doesn't matter now,' she said. 'I now take every day as it comes. As long as I don't know for certain what Robert is doing then I really don't care. What I really *do* care about – is if he's stopped loving me.'

Betty felt her inside fall apart. As she looked at her friend, standing there, those lovely emerald-green eyes so vulnerable, that had once been so full of hope, she wanted to throw her arms round her and hug her. But she knew if she did, it would seem to Catherine like pity, and that was the last thing she needed at a time like this. She waited a moment, then quite out of the blue asked, 'Catherine, come and work with us at the WVS?'

Catherine turned away.

'It would be so good for you. I saw Peggy a few weeks ago, and she thinks exactly the same.'

'Peggy has no right to discuss things like that with you.'

'Oh, for God's sake, Catherine!' snapped Betty, striding up to her. 'This war is not just about you and me and Robert and Peggy. It's about people who are dying every day of the week, people who are living from hand to mouth, with nowhere to sleep except in a cold and lifeless church hall or beneath the ruins of their own homes. Why d'you think I volunteered for this work? Not because I enjoy the sight of blood, not because I enjoy seeing people being pulled stone dead from buildings that have collapsed on them, but because we all have a role to play to keep this wretched country from falling apart.' Realising that she had perhaps gone too far, she stopped to pull herself together. 'The women I work with, Catherine,' she continued calmly, 'are no different from you and me. They have husbands, they have children, they have homes that they care for and want to protect at all costs. But they're also human beings who care for other human beings. The day we lose that, we don't deserve to exist any more.'

Catherine, arms folded, was staring down aimlessly at the floor, trying hard to avoid eye contact with Betty.

'*Please*, Catherine,' pleaded Betty, unconsciously touching the embroidered WVS badge on her uniform topcoat. 'I'm sure that Robert does still love you, but even if these stupid rumours *are* true, try to rise above it, try to remember that there are so many more important things in life than vicious tongues. You know, I haven't heard from my Brian now for months. For all I know he may be lying dead in the sand somewhere out in North Africa. But if I ever gave up hope, I could never do the job I'm doing now.'

Catherine finally raised her head and looked at her. 'I'm sorry, Betty,' she said. 'There are some things that you can't just roll under the carpet and forget. War or no war, I can't do what you ask me to do. My place is here, in my own home, with my own family.'

For one brief moment, Betty tried to stare her out. Then she accepted defeat with a shrug of her shoulders. 'Oh well,' she said, 'at least I tried. Goodbye, Catherine.'

Catherine lowered her eyes without answering.

Betty went to the door, but turned to look at her just one last time. 'I wonder whatever happened to duty,' she said.

The air-raid siren wailed out across Upper Holloway and, because it was the first daylight raid since before Christmas, everyone was taken off guard. Fortunately, Peggy and Frosty had just got back to the garage from the last journey of their morning shift in time to go straight to the staff air-raid shelter.

When they got there, all the usual gang had already taken up residence, together with a few unfamiliar faces from the trolley-bus depot on the other side of the road.

'I thought we'd finished with all this,' complained Peggy, as she took a seat on the bench between Frosty on one side and Elsie Parker on the other.

'Don't yer believe it,' replied Frosty, immediately lighting up a fag. 'They're comin' back ter finish wot they started.'

Even as he spoke, the place rattled as the first ack-ack gunfire opened up above. All eyes slowly turned towards the roof of the crowded shelter. After the tragic loss of life amongst bus crews all over London during the past few months of the Blitz, nobody was taking this renewed attack lightly. This was the first time Peggy had used the staff shelter since she had joined London Transport, and she could feel the anxiety and trepidation generating through her colleagues, so much so that when anyone spoke, they did so only in hushed tones during the brief lull in the deafening barrage outside.

'I really think I ought to be getting home,' said Peggy anxiously. 'I'm nervous about leaving my mother and grandmother alone in the middle of all this.'

'I fought yer said yer'd 'ad enuff er yer gram,' said Elsie.

'I have,' replied Peggy. 'But until her own house is repaired, I've got to put up with her as best I can. As it is, she and my mother are having to share the Morrison shelter.'

'Blimey!' said Frosty. 'I bet there'll be a few sparks there!'

'Well, if it ever gets too much fer yer,' said Elsie, 'there's always room at my place round the corner in Marlborough Road. It ain't exactly Buckin'am Palace, but at least it's clean and warm, and it's only a couple of minutes away.'

'Thank you, Elsie,' replied Peggy. 'I'll bear that in mind.'

A huge explosion nearby shook the shelter to its foundations. Everyone steeled themselves, and waited for the inevitable intensified barrage of gunfire that followed. All eyes were nervously transfixed on the ceiling. It was only when an eerie silence returned that Peggy suddenly caught a glimpse of Leo crouched on the floor amongst some of the other mechanics at the far end of the shelter. As their eyes met, he smiled and waved. She did likewise, but reluctantly. Elsie and Frosty saw what had happened, and exchanged sly grins.

A few minutes later, Charlie Pipes came rushing in. 'There's a big 'un come down just at the back of Central 'All!' he called.

Everyone looked up at him, shocked.

'Where exactly, Charlie?' called Sid Pierce, who was sharing his corner of the cold cement floor with Alf Grundy and the canteen girl Effie Sommers.

''Ard ter tell,' said Charlie, who was breathless from running. 'But somefin's burnin' up there all right. Yer can see from outside the garage.'

The others made a space for him to join them, but as they did so, Peggy suddenly sprang to her feet. 'I've got to go!' she said, rushing for the door. 'I've got to get to my mother!'

'No, Peggs!' yelled Elsie, as two of the men tried to hold her back.

'It's bleedin' murder out there, Peggs!' warned Charlie.

'Don't do it, Peggs!' begged Frosty, going to her. 'It's too risky!'

'I have to, Frosty!' replied Peggy, highly agitated. 'Whatever I think about my family, I'd never forgive myself if something happened to them.'

Frosty made a move towards the door. 'Then let me come wiv yer.'

'No!' Peggy insisted. 'I shall be all right, I promise!'

''Ere!' said Elsie, hurrying across to her. 'At least take my 'elmet!'

Peggy gratefully took Elsie's tin helmet, and quickly put it on. 'Thank you, Elsie!' she called, as she pushed past the others and rushed out the door.

Charlie was right: all hell seemed to have broken loose, for, once the ack-ack barrage had subsided for even a few moments, a fierce dogfight between RAF and German fighter planes was taking place high above the rooftops. The roar of dozens of enemy bombers was absolutely deafening, and it scared the wits out of Peggy. In one wild dash, however, she went straight from the shelter to the garage forecourt, where glass from the overhead fanlight tiles had

293

already shattered, and made her way out on to the main Holloway Road. In the distance the first thing she saw was the smoke from a huge fire spiralling up into the daylight sky. Again Charlie was right: it *was* coming from the Archway, there was no doubt about it. And so she started to run, faster than she had ever done before. It was uphill, and she had to stop every few yards to get her breath back. She had almost reached the junction itself when the emergency services seemed to appear from everywhere – sirens wailing, firebells clanging, and frantic people rushing as fast as they could to the fire that was now rising up from the ground like a mighty colossus. That, however, was as far as Peggy managed to get, for just as she was about to cross the main road to make her way home up the hill, a whistling sound suddenly came screeching down from the sky, but before the bomb had a chance to reach its target, Peggy found herself leaped on and dragged to the ground by someone whom she could not as yet see.

'Help me, God!' came her stifled yell.

'That's just wot 'e's doin'!'

Peggy barely had enough time to recognise Leo's voice before the bomb exploded with a devastating blast.

'Leo!' Peggy yelled out, immediately wrapping her arms around the back of her head for protection.

'Keep yer 'ead down, Peggs!' Leo yelled back, pressing her head down against the pavement. 'Down!

They lay there for several moments, listening to the terrifying aftereffects of the explosion, which had shattered glass all around them. And then, as always, came the eerie silence, until gradually the air again became fractured with frenzied activity.

When it was finally safe to get up, Leo helped Peggy to her feet. 'It sounds like it's over Kentish Town somewhere,' he said.

'Are you mad?' asked Peggy, who was angry more than grateful. 'What do you mean by following me? You could have been killed!'

'Why don't yer stop complainin' and just say fank you?' he replied. 'You was pretty mad yerself, comin' out in the middle of all this!'

'I've got to get home!' She started to rush off, but he grabbed hold of her arm. 'Let me go!' she shouted. But he silenced her protest by pulling her to him and pressing his own lips hard against hers. She tried to pull away from his kiss, and when she finally managed to do so, she raised her hand to slap his face. But he immediately deflected it, pulled her back to him, and kissed her again. 'Now you listen ter me,' he growled in her ear. 'You're *my* gel, d'yer understand? Wotever yer say or do, I'm not goin' ter let yer go – not now, not never.'

He allowed her to break away, but held on to her hands. 'Don't tell me you've changed your mind – again?' she replied, her face crumpled up, fighting back tears.

Leo pulled her straight back to him, and held her in a long, lingering kiss. This time she responded by wrapping her arms round him and hugging him tight. But the moment she broke loose, without saying another word, she left him, and rushed straight off.

Despite the mayhem all around him, Leo watched her go, battling her way up the hill against an oncoming tide of human panic, despair and desperation. Then he turned, and slowly made his way back to the garage – *down* the hill.

Chapter 15

During the first part of January the air raids on London were becoming relatively infrequent. This inevitably created a feeling amongst people that now that Jerry had been given a bloody nose by the plucky pilots of the Royal Air Force, the worst was now over. However, between the tenth and the thirteenth of the month, the Luftwaffe concentrated all its superior might on the coastal cities of Plymouth and Portsmouth, wreaking an enormous loss of life and devastation during three nights of intense bombing. Clearly, the worst was not yet over and, despite the news that British forces were having some success in their defence against the German military machine in North Africa, fears were renewed that it was now only a matter of time before Hitler ordered the invasion of the British Isles. However, if the battle on the home front was to be won, life had to go on as normally as was humanly possible. People had to go on eating, drinking, sleeping and, most important of all, they had to get back and forth to work in any way they knew how. Needless to say, the only way this could be achieved was through the enormous effort and courage of the London Transport bus and underground crews.

The traumas Peggy had experienced during her short time as a clippie on a petrol bus were nothing to what she was now having to endure doing the same job on the 'trolleys'. Smooth and silent they undoubtedly were, but operating the damn things was something she had dreaded ever since she had completed her few days' training two weeks before. For a start she found herself doing jobs that, in her opinion, should be the responsibility of the driver. It wasn't right, she told herself, that a woman should be expected to do such strenuous tasks as trying to juggle with the long, heavy bamboo poles that were used to hook the bus poles back on to the overhead electric wires. Then there were extraordinary devices with odd names to learn about, such as 'frogs', which were some kind of handles situated on 'traction standard poles' on the pavement at the side of the road, and which, when pulled down, enabled the driver to go into the 'turning loop' round the corner. What with that, and the constant anxiety of knowing that if the wretched bus was ever caught in a severe air raid there would be no way of getting the thing back to the depot in a hurry, the whole thing was a nightmare. And to make matters worse, her regular driver, a middle-aged man nicknamed 'Gummy' because he refused to wear false teeth, was deeply hostile to the idea of women working on the buses, so much so that Peggy was instructed by him not to use his nickname, but to address him as Cyril. Apart from the fact that she would only be doing the job for a few weeks at the most, her only comfort was that the route she had been put on was the number 611, which operated from Highgate Village to Moorgate in the City of London, and which passed her own front door on the hill. But being put on such a route proved to be more harrowing than she had expected, for she experienced her first glimpse of the widespread destruction that had been unleashed on the 'square mile' during the horrifying fire blitz attack that had taken place on the night of 29 December. Even though it was three weeks since the event, she was distressed to see city workers still walking around the streets dazed and stunned, and many sites smouldering from the bonfires that had been lit by demolition workers to dispose of the charred remains of office buildings.

Peggy's first brush with Gummy came one afternoon in mid-January when she was required to get off the bus at the junction of New North Road and Baring Street in Shoreditch so that she could pull down the frog handle on the traction standard pole which would enable the vehicle to clear the points and turn the corner. Once she had got down from the bus platform and reached the handle, she gave two knocks on the pole to let Gummy know that she was ready. Then, as she had been taught during training, she duly pulled the frog handle down, and Gummy moved the trolley to clear the points. However, once the bus had turned the corner, it did not stop long enough for Peggy to get back on, and with a look of horror, she watched the vehicle pick up speed towards the next stop. With clipping machine strapped around her shoulder, she ran as fast as her legs would carry her, and when she got there she found Gummy standing on the pavement waiting for her.

'You didn't stop!' she growled angrily, and out of breath.

'If gels can't move quicker than that,' he barked back, 'then they shouldn't be doin' the job!'

Peggy mentally noted what he had said, and from that moment on she was prepared for any nasty little trick he might play on her.

The number 611 trolley bus and its driver were not Peggy's only problem. At the end of her second week she found herself in a dilemma after a note arrived from Edwin Stevens to say that his son, Joe, would shortly be coming home on a weekend pass which he described as Joe's reward for 'a remarkable success on his officers' training course', and that nothing would delight Joe and the Stevens family more than if Peggy would care to take tea with them on the following Sunday afternoon.

Peggy's first inclination was to send a polite message back to Mr Stevens thanking him for his invitation, but declining with the excuse that she would be working on a split turn on that particular day. But when she came to think about it more carefully, she realised that it would be a very churlish and highhanded thing to do, for once Joe had completed his training, it was more than likely he would be sent off to active service, and she might never see him again. The only trouble was that during the past two weeks, she and Leo had started to become friendly again – not in the sense that they were walking out together, but that they were clearly too fond of each other to break off completely. And yet, in her heart of hearts, she knew only too well that she was fooling herself if she believed that that kiss Leo had given her on the day those bombs fell around the Archway, meant nothing to her. In fact it had meant a great deal to her; so much so that, consciously or unconsciously, she was prepared to forgive him for the way he had misled her. Despite the fact that she had agreed to give Leo the benefit of the doubt by letting him sort out his difficulties with Pam as soon as he possibly could, try as she may, she was still full of doubts, but she was at least willing to give their relationship another chance. Only time would tell.

As she left work at the end of the day, Pam was surprised to find Leo waiting for her outside the salon. It was already past blackout time and bitterly cold, for the first real heavy snow of the winter was now beginning to take hold, reaching a depth on the pavements of over half an inch in less than an hour. Pam's mates Josie and Babs came out at the same time, and the moment they saw who she was with they called, ' 'Allo, Leo,' in unison, then scuttled off in the dark, sniggering to themselves.

'Anyfin' wrong?' Pam asked warily.

'I'm not sure,' replied Leo mysteriously. 'I fawt we could

go round The Eaglet an' 'ave a drink.'

Pam hesitated. 'I did tell Mum I wouldn't be late fer tea,' she said. Then aware of his silence in the dark, she added, 'Come on – I'm game.'

She felt for his arm, and linked hers with it. She could feel his lack of enthusiasm, but as she felt the same way, she went along with it. As they struggled against a stiff wind, it took just a moment or so for their coats to be covered with the driving snow. Fortunately Pam was wearing an imitation fur-lined hood, and for added protection she pulled up the scarf she was wearing so that it covered the lower half of her face. The peak of Leo's flat cap was also pulled down as far as it would go, and he made sure that even though Pam was holding on to his arm, he kept both hands in his duffel coat pockets.

The same old regulars were crowding the public bar of The Eaglet, smoking their lungs out. At least the place was dry and warm. There were no seats or tables available so once Leo and Pam had fought their way to order their drinks, Leo found them a place to stand by the open fireplace.

'So wot's this all about?' Pam asked as soon as she had taken her first sip of port and ginger wine.

'Time fer a little chat,' he said, taking a gulp from his pint of bitter.

'Wot about?'

'Us,' replied Leo. 'We don't seem to meet up as much as we used ter.'

'That's not my fault, Leo,' Pam said quickly.

'I didn't say it was,' he replied just as quickly. There was a heck of a racket going on across the other side of the bar, so he had to lean close to her. 'D'yer still feel the same way about me, Pam?' he asked. 'I mean, I know we've talked about it a bit in the past, but then – in a way – we 'aven't, 'ave we?'

Pam stared down into the bright glow of the coal and wood fire, warming one hand as she did so. '*I'll do me best.* That's wot yer said.'

'I 'ave done me best,' he replied. 'But where do we go from 'ere?'

She looked back up at him. 'Where d'yer *want* it ter go, Leo?'

'That's wot I'd like *you* ter tell *me*,' he replied.

She was about to answer him when her eye suddenly caught a glimpse of someone propping up the bar with two other people. It was a young bloke in RAF blue, with dark hair and a corporal's flash on one arm. Pam tried very hard not to let Leo notice that she had become agitated. 'Would yer mind if we go inter the private?' she asked. 'I can 'ardly breave in 'ere.'

Leo nodded, and they slowly wound their way through the tightly packed crowd of customers, went briefly outside, then quickly re-entered the pub into the private bar. Even here, there were quite a few customers, but they did manage to find a quiet table in the corner.

For a moment or so they sat in silence. It was clear that both were trying to work out how they were to continue what they had started talking about.

Eventually it was Pam who took the plunge. 'I'm very fond er yer, Leo,' she said falteringly. 'I like – all the times – we've 'ad tergevver.'

Leo downed another gulp of his bitter. 'That's not wot I'm askin', Pam,' he said firmly. 'I'm askin' yer if yer fink we 'ave any future tergevver.'

'Yer mum says we 'ave.'

'I'm not askin' me mum. I'm askin' you.'

Pam took a sip of her drink. She tried to disguise the

fact that her hand was shaking. 'D'yer remember that first time we met?' she asked. 'You know – up the Calley market? I was at that junk stall tryin' ter buy a pet basket fer me cat. D'yer remember, you an' yer mum were there too? We met by accident. She was lookin' fer a present fer young Eddie's birfday.'

'Wos this all about, Pam?' asked Leo impatiently.

Pam hesitated and breathed deeply. 'It wasn't an accident, Leo,' she said. 'It was all arranged.'

Leo slowly put down his drink and stared at her.

'It all 'appened 'ere,' she continued, with difficulty, ' 'ere in this same bar. I was 'ere wiv me mum an' dad, and you was 'ere wiv yours. Yer mum saw me lookin' yer over. She never took 'er eyes off me all night. She could tell I fancied yer – an' I did.' She took another quick sip of her drink. 'When I went out ter the ladies, she followed me. She was so nice. She asked me who I was, where I come from. An' then she asked me about you – about wevver I liked yer. I said of course I did. Then she asked me if I'd like ter meet yer, and I said, no, I'd die of embarrassment in front of all yer pals. She said there was no need fer that 'cos she could fix it so we meet some uvver way. That's ow we met up the market.' She slowly shook her head. 'It was no accident, Leo.'

Leo found it hard to believe what she had just told him. 'Why?' he asked incredulously. 'Why should me mum try ter fix up a date fer you an' me?'

Pam shrugged her shoulders. 'Some people are just like that,' she replied. 'They can't 'elp themselves. I s'ppose it's their way of 'oldin' on ter someone they can't bear ter let go.'

Leo gradually felt angry. 'Fer chrissake, Pam!' he snapped. 'Why did yer let 'er do this? Why did yer just let 'er put yer up ter somefin' like this?'

'There *was* a reason,' said Pam.

Leo was so angry he ignored what she had said. ' 'Ow could yer let someone twist yer round their little finger?' he ranted. ' 'Ow could yer let me muvver treat you an' me as though we're nuffin' but a couple er mutts who can't run their own lives?'

'I said there *was* a reason, Leo,' she repeated adamantly. 'The reason was that I loved yer. At least – I fault I did.'

'Yer're a fake, Pam!' he yelled, getting up from his chair, and knocking it over as he did so. 'Yer're a one hundred per cent bleedin' fake!' He rested both hands on the table and leaned in on her. 'If yer 'ate so much wot she's done, why don't yer just tell 'er ter bugger off?'

'I can't, Leo,' she said, eyes lowered in anguish.

'Why not?'

Her eyes flicked up at him. 'Becos I'm scared.'

'Scared?' he bellowed. 'Scared er *my* muvver?'

Pam shook her head slowly. 'I can't tell yer,' she replied.

'No,' said Leo. 'Yer can't tell me 'cos yer just as bad as 'er! Let me tell yer somefin', Pam. All my life me muvver's done the runnin'. OK, so I used ter be scared of 'er. But not now. Not any more. An' d'yer know why? 'Cos fer the first time in me life, I've met someone I can trust – I mean *really* trust. Someone who's given me the confidence ter stand up fer meself, an' do the fings that *I* fink are right, an' not just becos me muvver says they are. I've got a reason fer livin' now, Pam. I've got someone ter live *for*, an' that's a chance I don't intend ter frow away.' He straightened up, and pointed a finger at her. 'Take my advice, Pam. Just fer once in yer life, try tellin' the troof. That way yer don't 'ave ter keep finkin' up new lies!' When he turned to go, he found everyone in the bar staring at him. 'So wot you lot lookin' at?' he snapped. With that, he pushed his way through the crowd of drinkers, and left in a rage.

Pam sat where she was for a moment. She felt physically and emotionally sick. But she gradually composed herself and stood up. Everyone was watching her and she could feel the sympathy they had for her. She slowly made her way through the customers and left. Outside, it had stopped snowing, but it was bitingly cold, and her breath was darting out from her mouth as condensation. She paused awhile to watch the muscular shape of Leo's figure disappearing into the dark. Then, once she had composed herself, she went back into the public bar again. Inside, she looked around until she saw the reason she had come back in. Gently pushing her way through the crowd of drinkers, through the choking smoke from their fags, she finally reached the bar counter.

When the RAF corporal suddenly noticed her, he turned away from his two drinking mates, and gave her a cocky grin. But that disappeared the moment Pam spoke.

'Yer bleedin' fool!' she growled.

Leo was so angry with his mum that, despite the snow under foot, he ran all the way home. This time she'd gone too far. It was one thing to encourage him to take up with someone that she approved of, it was quite another to arrange it all behind his back, to try to take over his life for her own personal reasons. But what reasons? Out of breath, he came to a sudden halt, his feet sliding in the fresh snow as he did so. Although it was freezing cold, his body was burning up with anger, so he gave himself a moment to calm down. Yes, what *were* his mum's reasons for behaving like a loony? he asked himself. Did she think that if he got hitched up to a girl of her choice, then she could keep tabs on him for ever? Why did she have this obsession with holding on to him? Why couldn't she just let go? He knew that if he stormed through that front door the way he was feeling right now, he'd probably say something both of them would regret, something that would never be forgotten. So he decided to wait a few minutes until he could think things over, think what to do, how to deal with this mad woman. He slowly trudged his way across the coal yard, which was now heavily covered with snow; even in the dark he could see that the empty coal carts were standing out as strange white shapes. He paused briefly to look up at the family's rooms above the office. The blackout blinds were down so he could only imagine what that interfering cow was doing at that moment – plotting, conniving, working out her next move that would put her in even more control over him and the rest of her family. He felt like shouting up at the window: 'Cow! Cow! Cow!' He wanted to – but no, something inside told him not to, told him to hold back from the brink, to think of his dad, of his brothers and – most of all – of himself. That was something he hadn't done in a long time – think of himself, think about what *he* wanted to do with his life. Now almost delirious with rage and confusion, he rushed around to the back of the building, where he found his way in the dark into the outside lavatory that the coalmen used during working hours. Once inside he bolted the door, and sat there in the dark, shivering with the cold. He dug deep into his duffel coat pocket, brought out his packet of Woodbines and matches, took out a fag, and lit it. He inhaled deeply; he needed it, he needed it so badly. He exhaled reluctantly. The match in his fingers was still burning and threw the sinister shadow of his own figure on to the back of the stark chipped plaster walls he was enclosed within. Inevitably his mind immediately became dominated by the image of his mum, and then what Pam had said about her: '*Some people are just like that . . . They can't 'elp themselves . . .*' The match he was holding suddenly burned down to his fingertips, so he quickly blew it out and dropped it on to the stone floor. Now he was in the dark again he had time to think of the advantages of what had happened. As far as he was concerned, he was a free man, free to do what he wanted, free to go with whomever he chose. And that meant Peggy. Pam was in the past, finished, forgotten. Peggs was the future, *his* future, and he would never let his mum come between them again. But first he had to show that he meant business. First he had to do what Peggs had told him to do – stand up to his mum and prove that he was his own person.

A sudden impulse brought him to his feet. He unbolted the door, rushed out into the yard, threw his newly lit fag down into the snow, and made straight for the front door, where he retrieved the key that was dangling inside the letter box on a piece of string.

The first person he saw at the top of the stairs was Horace. 'Ace!' he called. 'Where's Mum?'

Horace, who was still hobbling around on his bandaged foot, looked bewildered. 'In the kitchen,' he replied, terrified by his big brother's frantic appearance. He only just managed to get out of the way as Leo rushed past him.

Leo burst into the kitchen parlour as though the place was on fire. But to his astonishment, he found only his dad sitting there, halfway through a pint of brown ale, relaxed in his usual easy chair by the fire. 'Dad!' he gasped, taken completely by surprise.

' 'Allo, son!' replied Reg, his arm still in a sling, his foot resting up on a stool, but genuinely delighted to see the boy. ' 'Ere's a nice turn up fer the books, eh?'

Leo hardly had time to get his breath back when his mum appeared from the scullery, carrying two cups of tea. 'Ah!' she exclaimed, face lighting up. 'There yer are, son! In't it nice ter 'ave our dad 'ome again? They brought 'im back in an ambulance about an hour ago.' She put down the two cups of tea, went to Reg, and kissed him lightly on the forehead. 'The Quinceys are all back 'ome tergevver again,' she said in a sickly, loving voice. 'Now we've *really* got somefin' ter celebrate!'

Peggy didn't much care for her new base across the road in the trolley-bus depot. It wasn't that she didn't like the people she was working with, for most of them were good, honest, hard-working folk just like her own gang back at the number 14 garage. There was nothing wrong with the place itself either. In fact the facilities were a bit better than Kingsdown Road, probably because the place had been built later. But she much preferred the atmosphere where she had come from to where she was now. She blamed Gummy, her driver, for that: his prejudice against petrol-operated buses was relentless and very off-putting. But there were a couple of people that she did get on well with, including a lovely young Jewish girl called Miriam, who had showed Peggy the ropes on her first day. Miriam, who came from Stamford Hill and was the daughter of a man who owned a fleet of lorries, was married to a young dustman named Ted, who had been called up at the start of the war leaving her to look after their two-year-old baby daughter, who now had to be minded each day by Miriam's mother. Peggy liked her not just because her style of speaking was easier to understand than a lot of the other girls she worked alongside, but because she had always had problems with her father that were very similar to her own.

'Thinks he owns me,' she said when she and Peggy were chatting together in the lower deck passenger seats of one of two number 611 trolley buses waiting to move out from what was left of the badly bomb-damaged Moorgate terminus. 'He's done it ever since I was a kid at school,' she continued, smoking her Capstan cigarette. 'Even now he can't accept that I'm a grown-up woman with a child of my own.'

Peggy felt strangely encouraged to know that at least she wasn't the only middle-class person in the world who had a possessive parent. It also gave her the renewed confidence to pursue her goal of total independence. However, it did not prepare her for the turmoil that awaited her when she got home that evening.

'Given in her notice? Mrs Bailey?' Peggy couldn't believe what her mother had just told her. 'But that's ridiculous,' she said. 'Mrs B's been here for years.'

'That's what she said,' Catherine assured her. 'She says she's leaving at the end of the month and not a minute longer.'

'But why?' asked Peggy. 'She's always been perfectly happy here. What on earth's made her change her mind so suddenly?'

Catherine lowered her eyes.

But Peggy knew only too well what she was thinking, for when she turned to look across the sitting room, her grandmother was calmly playing a game of solo at the card table there. 'Is she here now?' she asked. 'Shall I go and have a word with her?'

Catherine sighed despondently. 'She's in the kitchen – but it won't do any good. Something has clearly upset her terribly,' she said, casting a disapproving look over her shoulder at her mother-in-law.

'I don't know what all the fuss is about,' complained Alice, without looking up from her cards. She knew she was being mischievous and was thoroughly enjoying it. 'Anyone can do the few things *she* ever does.'

'Well, I'm glad you think so, Mother,' returned Catherine

irritably. 'Everyone that's ever been to this house says what a good cook she is.'

'Anyone can cook,' sniffed the old lady.

'Well, I for one can't!' protested Catherine, slamming down her crochet. 'So I really don't know how we're going to cope.'

'Don't upset yourself, Mother,' said Peggy. 'I'm sure something can be worked out. Mrs B is not an unreasonable woman—'

'Ha!' grunted Alice.

'She is *not* an unreasonable woman,' continued Peggy. 'Once I've had a word with her I'm sure she'll change her mind.'

All Catherine could do was to sigh and shake her head.

Peggy kissed her gently on the forehead, took one brief glare at her grandmother, and left the room.

In the kitchen a thick pall of smoke was seeping out from around the oven door. Peggy started to cough as soon as she entered. 'Mrs B!' she called. 'Something's burning!'

'Good!' growled Lil Bailey. 'As far as I'm concerned, I couldn't care less if it burns to a cinder!'

Still coughing and spluttering, Peggy went straight to the oven, opened the door, and was hit by the smoke from a rapidly blackening roast chicken. She quickly turned off the oven, went to the kitchen door and opened it, then carefully slid her hand up behind the blackout blinds and opened the window. Whilst all this was going on, Mrs B was quietly concentrating on mixing some fresh breadcrumbs for the apple crumble she was making.

'Oh dear, Mrs B,' asked Peggy, going to her. 'What happened?'

'It's no use yer sayin' anyfin',' said Mrs B, refusing to

look her in the eye. 'Me mind's made up! I'm goin' an' that's all there is to it.'

'But at least tell me why,' pleaded Peggy.

Mrs B swung her an angry look 'Why?' she growled. ' 'Ow would *you* like ter be told that yer're not even capable of boilin' a kettle er water, that yer greens taste like dead grass, that yer spuds don't 'ave enuff salt, and that yer ought ter kill the chicken before yer cook it?'

Despite her sympathy with Mrs B, Peggy had to stifle a laugh. 'Why do you take any notice of her?' she asked. 'You know what Grandmother's like. She likes to get at people; it amuses her.'

'Well, it don't amuse me – and that's a fact!' she barked.

Peggy jumped at the ferocity of her answer. 'But you're one of the best cooks in the whole wide world,' she said. 'You know very well we all think so, and so do all of our friends.'

'It's not only about cookin',' Mrs Bailey said, calming down. 'It's wot she said about yer mum an' you.'

Peggy swung her a startled look. 'What do you mean?'

Mrs B wiped her hands on a dishcloth. 'She said as 'ow yer mum's always 'eld yer dad back from doin' better fings, 'ow 'e should've married someone who 'ad more guts.'

Peggy was horrified. 'Grandmother said that to *you*?' she asked incredulously.

'She did all right!' insisted Mrs B, stiffening up. 'An' a lot more besides!'

'But why?' Peggy asked. 'Why does she do such things?'

' 'Cos she's a mischief-maker, that's why,' snapped Mrs B, who had unwittingly picked up a carving knife from the table, and was waggling it angrily at Peggy. ' 'Cos she's got a nasty vicious tongue. 'Cos she can't rest unless she's makin' trouble fer people.'

Peggy sighed and shook her head in despair. 'But to

think that she should discuss these things with you – of all people. It's appalling!'

'Yer ain't 'eard the best of it,' said Mrs B. 'Like wot she said about you – *an'* yer new boyfriend.'

Peggy was now so taken aback that she slumped down into a kitchen chair.

Mrs B continued her angry diatribe. 'She said yer dad's goin' ter put paid ter that, an' that's fer sure. She said 'e'll never allow a daughter of 'is ter get mixed up wiv a scruffy gold-digger from down the 'ill.'

Peggy covered her face with her hands.

'She said a lot more besides,' continued Mrs B, who had decided to pull back from the brink. 'But that's all I'm goin' ter tell yer, 'cos yer mean too much ter me. I've known yer since yer was frowin' fings at me out er yer pram, an' I ain't goin' ter let some stuffy ol' cow 'urt someone who's worf a fousand times better than the likes of 'er!'

Peggy slowly got up from the seat, and went to her. 'I'm so sorry, Mrs B,' she said, throwing her arms around her comfortingly. 'You've always been such a good friend to this family. You don't deserve this kind of behaviour.' She pulled away, and looked at her. 'Promise me you won't do anything rash until I've sorted this out?'

Mrs B lowered her eyes and shrugged noncommittally.

'You mean a great deal to me too, Mrs B,' Peggy said, tender and reassuring. 'I don't know what this family would have done without you all these years.'

Mrs B sighed. 'All right – we'll see wot 'appens,' she replied.

Peggy gave her a grateful smile and another hug, then left the room.

In the hall outside, she felt quite ill. She had always known what a crafty tyrant her grandmother was, but this was intolerable. Why did she do such things? What did she hope to gain from stirring up so much trouble in the family, especially when she had only been staying in the house for a matter of days? Something had to be done, and it had to be done fast. There was no way she could continue to live under the same roof as a woman who was just born to disrupt. With this in mind, she took a deep breath and stormed straight back into the sitting room.

'Grandmother!' she bellowed, the moment she had opened the door. 'What have you been saying to Mrs Bailey?'

Alice looked up innocently from her cards. But to Peggy's surprise, it was her father who answered.

'What's this?' asked Thornton reprovingly.

Peggy hadn't realised her father had returned home. But she was determined not to stifle her anger because of him. 'I'm asking my grandmother,' she answered firmly, 'why she felt it necessary to discuss private family affairs with our cook?'

Alice exchanged a look with her son that suggested that she hadn't the faintest idea what the girl was talking about.

Peggy strode right across to her. 'Those comments about my mother,' she growled, 'and about my personal life are not only none of your business, but are also utterly despicable!'

'Don't talk to your grandmother like that!' ordered her father, immediately going across to his mother's aid.

Catherine, bewildered, looked in horror from Peggy to her mother-in-law, then back to Thornton.

'I shall say exactly what I *have* to say!' said Peggy. 'I ask you again, Grandmother, what is this all about?'

'Have you taken leave of your senses, child?' asked Alice, cowering.

'You told Mrs Bailey that in your opinion my mother is

not adequate for my father,' persisted Peggy, 'and that my father would never allow me to have a relationship with someone of my own choice.'

'Preposterous!' replied Alice, indignantly.

'Then why did Mrs Bailey say such a thing?'

'I have no idea,' replied Alice. 'But what I can tell you is that Mrs Bailey has resented my presence ever since I set foot inside this house.'

'That's a lie, and you know it!'

'Margaret!'

Peggy knew that her father's formal use of her name meant that she had him annoyed.

'Mother?' asked Catherine timidly. 'What are these comments you made about me?'

'Keep out of this, Catherine!' demanded Thornton.

'No, Robert,' replied Catherine, in a rare show of defiance. 'I have a right to know.'

'I told you what a malicious woman this cook of yours is,' insisted Alice, using her walking stick to ease herself up from her chair. 'God knows I warned you.'

'Mrs Bailey is *not* a malicious woman!' insisted Peggy, raising her voice louder than she had ever done before. 'She's a good, honest woman who has served this family well, and that includes *you*, Grandmother!'

'Well, if you're prepared to believe the word of a domestic rather than your own kith and kin,' Alice said, 'what more can I say?'

'You can say sorry,' snapped Peggy.

Alice stopped dead on the spot. '*Sorry?*' she asked in sheer disbelief.

'That's right, Grandmother,' returned Peggy. 'It's a word I've never heard you use throughout my entire lifetime. I wonder why, Grandmother? Is it because you're afraid of being proved wrong? Or is it because it would humble you too much, because you would be seen to be in danger of losing control?'

Alice's expression was like stone.

'Now you listen to me, miss,' said Thornton, trying to intervene.

'No, Father,' Peggy replied, going right up to Alice. 'I want Grandmother to listen to *me*. I want her to know that there's nothing in the whole wide world I'd love more than to have a grandmother whom I could confide in, whom I could call on to talk about the things that grandchildren want to know, things that they can't ask their own parents. I want a grandmother who knows how to love, not how to destroy.'

Alice made a move to stride off, but faltered when Peggy called after her.

'No wonder Grandfather feels the way he does about you.'

Alice, visibly shocked, made as gallant an exit as she possibly could.

Thornton waited just long enough for his mother to go, then went straight to Peggy. 'You will apologise to your grandmother.'

Peggy shook her head. 'She's the one who should apologise,' she replied defiantly. 'God knows she has enough to apologise for.'

'You will apologise to your grandmother,' repeated Thornton, with a look of cold steel, 'or you will get out of my house until you have learned to behave like a civilised human being.'

For a brief moment, Peggy stared him out. 'Whatever you say, Father,' she replied, with just the hint of a wry smile. Then she turned, and left the room.

Catherine made a move to go after her, but Thornton grabbed hold of her arm to prevent her from doing so. She gave him only a derisory glance, then shook herself loose, and followed Peggy.

Chapter 16

Edwin Stevens' house was imposing but singularly lacking in taste. Set amongst a cluster of well-to-do-looking properties in one of those areas behind Upper Street that prided themselves on being 'exclusive', its main claim to such a term was that it was in a 'terrace' and not a 'street'. Peggy suspected that that was the reason why Stevens had bought the place nearly twenty years before, for, being a solicitor, it was not only a good address, but convenient to both his now bomb-damaged offices near the Angel, and also his temporary offices in Liverpool Road. When Peggy arrived at the front door, the thing that impressed her most was the small front garden, which was festooned with overhanging plants and window boxes, which in the summer, she imagined, must look absolutely gorgeous. She did not, however, appreciate the pre-war attempts to give the front of the house a 'continental' look with its fake window shutters and additional glass-panelled porch, which the neighbours must have hated, Peggy imagined, for it stood out so embarrassingly from the other, far more dignified Georgian three-storey properties along the 'terrace'. However, despite the fact that there had been bomb blast even here, with many windows now boarded, it was obvious that most people in the neighbourhood had tried their level best to keep up appearances.

The Stevens' sitting room resembled a cosy country cottage with its floral chintz curtains and matching three-piece suite. What Peggy admired were the endless rows of shelves covering one whole wall from floor to ceiling, and containing a wonderful selection of books, some of the classics bound in leather, and other, more contemporary ones, which turned out to be first editions, so lovingly preserved over the years.

'Edwin does so love his books,' said Emma, his wife, a pretty, open-faced little woman who seemed to dote on everything her husband ever did. 'When we were first married, he used to read to me in bed every night. He has such a lovely speaking voice.' She turned to give him a loving smile. 'I think my particular favourite was *Mansfield Park*. Jane Austen wrote so well about us women.'

Stevens wasn't in the least embarrassed. He returned his wife's gracious smile with one of his own.

Taking tea with the Stevens family on Sunday afternoon was turning out to be quite an experience for Peggy. Not only was this the first time she had visited her former employer's home, but it was the first time she had seen his son, Joe, since he'd been called up. 'What about you, Joe?' she asked, balancing her cup and saucer precariously on her lap. 'Are you a bookworm too?'

'Good God, no!' replied Joe. 'I have enough trouble reading the newspapers.'

His two adolescent sisters, Jennifer and Lorraine, sniggered. They were sitting very formally and straight-backed side by side on a two-seater sofa, munching their mother's home-made teacakes. Joe was on one dining chair beside them, facing his father, who was on another. Peggy was sipping tea on the comfortable main sofa with Emma Stevens. She was much impressed and greatly surprised to see how Joe had changed in so short a time; he seemed to have lost a lot of weight, which made him look positively handsome in his naval cadet's uniform, and, unlike his father, he had developed a sense of fun which Peggy found very appealing.

Having purred with satisfaction at his wife's flattering remarks, Stevens was grinning like a Cheshire cat, watching carefully to see how his son and Peggy were responding to each other. 'I was so sorry your parents were unable to join us today,' he said. 'Such a pity they had a prior engagement.'

'Oh, yes indeed,' agreed Emma.

'I do so admire your father,' continued Stevens. 'He has such a fine reputation at the courts.'

Peggy merely smiled her acknowledgement of what was being said, and sipped her tea.

'I know he badly wanted to meet you, Joseph,' said Stevens, unperturbed, turning to his son. 'He was very impressed when I told him how well you're doing on your officers' training course.'

Joe nodded. He was too ill-at-ease to look at Peggy.

Once Stevens had taken account of Peggy's reaction, he smiled awkwardly, and sipped his tea.

Emma was the saviour of the moment. 'I hear Mr Willkie's over here,' she said, addressing her remark to Peggy. 'I do hope if he becomes President, he'll persuade the Americans to join us in this war.'

'I doubt it,' replied Joe, quickly answering for Peggy. 'Wendell Willkie is just like all the rest of them. All wind and no bite!'

'Oh, I think that's a bit unfair, son,' said Stevens. 'Mr Willkie's a Republican. His party is far more likely to understand what a menace Hitler is to the free world. Don't you agree, Peggy?'

Peggy looked up with a start as she was spoken to directly. 'I don't really follow politics myself, Mr Stevens,' she replied. 'But I would have thought that whether Mr Willkie or Mr Roosevelt wins the election, neither of them is going to have an easy time persuading the American people to go to war.'

'Peggy's right,' added Emma sympathetically. 'Watching

319

your children go off to war is very painful.' She looked across wistfully at Joe, who quickly lowered his eyes.

Peggy noticed this, and she felt a moment of concern for Emma Stevens. Despite the poor woman's pride in his achievements, there must surely be, if the war became much more intense, the dread of losing him. This thought was reinforced when Peggy noticed that the mantelpiece was absolutely crammed with framed photographs of the Stevens family taken during various happy moments over the years.

'Well,' said Stevens, putting his teacup down on to the small brown varnished table beside him, 'my only hope is that when it's all over, we shall get the old firm back on its feet again, *and*,' he added, with a pointed look over the top of his spectacles towards Peggy, 'with the team who know how to run it.'

'Hear! Hear!' agreed Emma joyfully.

'I have to admit the office hasn't been the same without you, my dear,' said Stevens to Peggy. 'Total chaos!'

'Oh, I can't believe that,' said Peggy. 'Irene has always been such a good organiser.'

Stevens, suddenly oddly withdrawn, sat back in his chair.

Peggy was puzzled and intrigued. 'Well, she is – isn't she?'

Stevens exchanged an uneasy glance with his wife. 'Irene is not quite the same person these days,' he replied.

Peggy looked briefly across to Joe, as if he could give her some kind of explanation. 'In what way?' she asked.

Joe shrugged noncommittally.

'It's difficult to put your finger on what *exactly*,' said Stevens awkwardly. 'It's just that I sometimes feel her mind is not always on the job.' He was suddenly aware of Peggy's concern. 'Oh, don't get me wrong. She's still very efficient, but there are times when she really is quite – sluggish.'

'Perhaps she has problems on her mind?' suggested

Emma adding, rather primly, 'A gentleman friend perhaps?'

'Irene?' blurted Stevens. 'A boyfriend? Good Lord no! She's well past that sort of thing.'

'Oh, come now, dear,' scolded his wife. 'Isn't that a little ungallant?'

'I'm told men can have affairs up to any age,' said Peggy, a touch cuttingly. 'So I don't see why women can't too. After all, Irene is only in her forties.'

After a glare from his wife, Stevens was suddenly embarrassed. 'Quite so, my dear,' he replied, flustered. 'Quite so.'

The clock struck the half-hour.

'Gracious!' said Emma, glad to break the awkward silence that had followed Stevens' remark. 'Half-past three already. How time flies.'

'Joseph, why don't you take Peggy for a little stroll around the neighbourhood?' Stevens suggested brightly, getting up from his chair. Then, turning to Peggy herself, he said, 'There are some very beautiful period houses in this part of Islington. I'm sure you'd find them most fascinating.'

Peggy shrugged. She knew exactly what Stevens was trying to do, but she was more than happy to be alone with Joe if it meant she could get away from the stifling atmosphere of this tea-party for a few minutes.

'It'll be dark soon,' said Joe to Peggy. 'But I'm game if you are.'

Stevens was right. There were plenty of beautiful houses in the area to look at. Peggy admired most of them, preferring the Georgian-style façades to the less attractive Victorian and Edwardian dwellings. But as she and Joe slowly strolled along the winding backstreets, she was curious to know who the people were that lived behind the lace curtains and the blackout blinds. Every corner they turned, they found themselves in a street or a road or a terrace that showed the difference between the well-to-do and those who quite clearly only barely managed to scrape a living. She also constantly gazed up at the rooftops, where some chimneys were billowing out palls of thick black smoke, whilst others remained poignantly unused. By the time they had reached the open expanse of City Road, it was beginning to get dark, and the further fall of snow that had settled overnight was now turning to ice. They eventually paused awhile at what was evidently a hastily erected low wooden fence with a handrail, which overlooked some bombed-out wharfs on the edge of what had been until recently a sheltered basin. As they stopped there, they gazed out on to a scene of the most terrible devastation.

'It's not true about me,' Joe said quite suddenly.

They turned to look at each other.

'I'm not doing at all well on my course. In fact, I'm dire!'

Peggy took this in for a moment, smiled, then joined him in a gentle laugh. His honesty prompted her to slide her arm through his. 'I'm pleased to hear it,' she replied, relieved.

'I don't know why they do it,' said Joe. 'Mother and Father, I mean. They're always making up things about me, trying to turn me into some kind of hero or something. It's crazy. I still don't know the difference between longitude and latitude!'

Peggy squeezed his arm with hers, and laughed.

'Mind you,' he continued, 'I've taken quite well to navy life. We went out to sea in a rowing boat the other day – not far, just half a mile or so from the beach. It was pretty rough. All the blokes were sick except me. But despite the freezing cold, I loved the fresh air. I felt so free! We couldn't stay out long, what with land mines on the beach and the threat of Jerry coming over at any minute.'

For one brief moment, Peggy leaned her head against his shoulder. 'As a matter of fact,' she said, 'I think you'll make a wonderful officer.'

'I have my doubts,' he replied. 'But even if I don't, I want to stay in the navy for a career.'

Peggy looked up at him in surprise.

'No,' he said, confirming what she was thinking, 'I don't want to go back to the firm.'

'I don't blame you,' she said. 'Neither do I.'

They lapsed into silence for a moment or so, both looking out at the endless heaps of rubble all around them. Quite nearby they could see two mongrel dogs fighting each other over some scrap of food one of them had dug out of the debris of what seemed once to have been a warehouse canteen. It became quite an ugly, savage scene, a real fight for survival, until quite suddenly one of the poor creatures conceded defeat, and hastily withdrew to search out something of his own from debris elsewhere.

'That's not the only thing I haven't told them,' said Joe.

Again Peggy turned to look at him.

'I've met someone,' he said.

Peggy took a moment to take it in.

'She's a girl at the base. She's in the WRNS. Her name's Susan.' He screwed up his face, concerned by what Peggy might think. 'I know it's stupid, but I've really fallen for her. She feels the same way about me too.'

Peggy stretched up and kissed him lightly on the cheek. 'Joe,' she said, 'I think it's wonderful. In fact I think it's the most wonderful news I've heard in a long time.'

Joe's eyes lit up. 'D'you think so?' he asked. 'D'you *really* think so?'

'Of course I do!' Peggy replied. 'Just look at you. You're a handsome devil, and any right-thinking girl would give her eyeteeth to be loved by you.'

'You never felt that way about me.'

She smiled warmly. 'Just shows you how mistaken one can be.'

He smiled back. 'So what about you?' he asked.

'Me?' she replied evasively. 'Who knows?'

'Are you going with anyone?'

Peggy looked away. 'I don't know, Joe,' she replied. 'Honest to God, I just don't know.'

As she spoke, the air-raid siren wailed out.

Marge Quincey had quite a job to get Reg into the air-raid shelter. The wheelchair that he'd arrived back home in had had to be returned to the hospital straight away, and it was still quite painful for him to hobble around on one crutch, mainly because one arm was in a sling. But once Marge had manoeuvred him safely down the stairs, it took just a little more effort to support him whilst he made his perilous way across the ice-covered coal yard, and finally those last few feet into their own personal brick and concrete shelter. By the time they got there, Horace and Eddie had already lit the paraffin stove, so the chill had been taken off the cold damp place. But the ack-ack barrage outside was once again in full swing, and in the distance they could hear the first clanging of fire engine bells.

'I 'ope Leo's all right,' said Marge, settling down in her worn-out easy chair opposite Reg. 'I don't like 'im comin' 'ome in the middle of all this.'

'Don't yer worry about Leo,' replied Reg. 'If 'e 'as any sense, 'e'll hold back at the garage till the All Clear.'

' 'E can't be too late,' continued Marge. 'Sunday night's 'is night fer goin' round ter see Pam.'

'Well, 'e's 'ardly likely ter do that under present circumstances – now is 'e?'

'Oh, yer don't know yer son,' replied Marge, carrying on with the cardigan she had started knitting for Leo the night before. ' 'E'd do anyfin' fer that gel. 'E won't let Jerry muck 'im up where Pam's concerned.'

Reg looked up from the football coupons he was studying for the following Saturday's games. 'So they're still goin' strong, are they?' he asked sceptically.

'Goin' strong?' blurted Marge. 'Course they're goin' strong! Pam's always tellin' me 'ow lucky she is ter 'ave a feller like Leo. She's mad about 'im – always 'as bin. She told me so when she was doin' my 'air the uvver day.'

Reg grunted wryly to himself, and returned to his football coupons.

'I bet Leo would sooner 'ave that gel up on the 'ill,' said young Eddie, who was sitting cross-legged, busily engaged in tormenting a large spider that was gradually spinning down towards him on its thread from the concrete ceiling. ''E's always goin' on about 'er.'

Marge stopped knitting, and glowered up at him. 'Shut up, Ed!' she snapped.

'It's true,' insisted Horace, who was stretched out alongside his brother, straining his eyes to read a comic in the flickering light from the paraffin lamp. 'This gel's on the trolleys now. Leo went fer a ride on it wiv 'er the uvver night.'

'All the way from 'Ighgate ter some uvver gate,' said Eddie.

'Moorgate, stupid!' growled Horace.

'I told yer ter shut up!' snapped Marge. 'Boaf er yer!' She angrily returned to her knitting. 'I wish ter God I'd 'ad the two of yer evacuated when the uvver kids went!'

Reg had a broad grin on his face. 'So fings don't sound all that good between 'im an' Pam,' he said mischievously. 'Wonder wot caused all that?'

'Now don't you start!' said Marge, putting him down.

Reg knew she was fuming, so he was determined not to let up. 'Must say, it's all very mysterious. Wouldn't mind meetin' this uvver gel meself.'

'Leo says she's smashin',' said Eddie.

' 'E fancies 'er like mad,' added Horace.

Marge refused to show that she was listening to one single word they were saying.

'I 'eard 'im talkin' ter George in the shop the uvver day,' persisted Horace. ' 'E said if it weren't fer 'er dad, fings'd be much better.'

Reg looked up from his newspaper again. ' 'Er dad?' he asked, curious.

'Real ol' bugger!' said Eddie, who had now succeeded in entrapping the spider on the palm of his hand.

'Oy! Oy!' scolded Reg. 'Wotch yer language, son!'

'Leo said 'er dad's 'orrible,' said Horace, 'that 'e won't let this gel out of 'is sight.'

'Follers 'er everywhere,' added Eddie.

'It was probably 'im that come up 'ere lookin' fer 'er,' said Horace.

'Wot was that?' asked Marge, suddenly turning on the boy.

'Wot?' asked Horace.

'Who come 'ere?'

'The man in the bowler 'at.'

Reg was carefully watching this exchange.

'Wot're yer talkin' about, yer bleedin' fool?' demanded an increasingly agitated Marge.

Horace suddenly got worried that he was saying too much. 'It was Ned,' he said nervously, sitting back in the bunk well out of his mum's reach. 'Ned – that coalman who works in the yard. He said this man in a bowler 'at come ter see yer one day. Said 'e'd come back an' see yer some uvver time.'

Marge put her knitting back into the cloth bag beside her. 'Wot did 'e look like – this man?'

'Dunno,' replied Horace falteringly.

'Tall, up 'ere,' said Eddie, pointing to the ceiling. 'An' 'e spoke like this thiiiiisssss . . .' He tried to imitate the man's deep posh voice.

Marge suddenly leaped up from her chair. 'I'm goin' back inside fer a minute.' She made for the door, stopped and turned. 'Don't any er yer start come lookin' fer me!'

Once outside, she took a deep breath. She felt quite ill, but the crisp cold air helped to cool the sweat that was running down her back. After she'd recovered, she quickly made her way back to the office building. It wasn't easy, for the snow was now solid ice, and her carpet slippers had difficulty in getting a grip on the slippery surface. She soon found the front door key, and the moment she had got inside and closed the door behind her, she turned on the light, climbed the stairs, and made her way straight to the bedroom on the top floor that Leo shared with his two young brothers.

With the ack-ack barrage building to a noisy crescendo outside, she went straight to the window and closed the blackout curtains. Once she could see the room in the light, it looked exactly as she had expected it to look – a real mess. The two young brothers' belongings were scattered all over the place and, by the looks of things, Leo wouldn't have had much room to keep anything of his own. The large bed which all three slept in was still unmade, and if Marge had checked more closely she would have found a film magazine that the two boys had been giggling over hidden under the bedclothes with a pin-up girl in a bathing costume on the front cover. She chose instead to go to the large brown varnished chest of drawers that Reg had bought in a jumble sale for a shilling a couple of years before the war. She soon discovered that the two top drawers were stuffed with Horace and Eddie's junk, mainly old tin boxes full of any useless gadgets they could lay their hands on, mixed up amongst their rolled-up underpants, vests, socks, short trousers, and dirty hankies which had never been brought out for washing.

But Marge was more interested in the bottom drawer, for she knew from past experience of trying to keep the room clean that that was Leo's drawer. For this, she had to drop to her knees and crouch. Inside, she found nothing of interest apart from his clean clothes, some pre-war football magazines, and an unopened packet of Woodbines. She closed the drawer again. There was nothing there that she was looking for. Now thoroughly irritated, she looked forlornly around the room to see if there was anywhere else worth investigating, and it was only when she was about to get back on to her feet again that she suddenly noticed the holdall that Leo used to take his football things in to Finsbury Park when he'd played there regularly every Sunday morning when he was a youngster and which was tucked underneath the bed. Without getting up, she crawled over to Leo's side of the bed, and brought out the holdall. It was already open, so she had no difficulty in searching it. Again – nothing of any particular interest. She returned the bag to where she had found it, but retrieved it immediately when she realised that she hadn't checked the side pocket.

This time her search was more successful.

Peggy's Sunday afternoon tea-party with the Stevens family had turned out to be far more enjoyable than she had expected. This was due almost entirely to the enchanting half-hour or so that she had spent with Joe strolling around the backstreets between City Road and Upper Street, and not to the misguided matchmaking efforts of his parents. It had been such a pleasant surprise to see how much Joe had come out of his shell, and in so little time. He had developed a sweetness that she would not have imagined possible in someone who had led such an inward-looking life. When he had told her about the girl he had taken up with, she had even, for one brief moment, felt the pangs of regret. It made her think of Leo, so different in every way from Joe, and whether she had the stamina and, more importantly, the love within her to develop a full relationship with him.

She didn't get back home until after the All Clear had sounded just after ten in the evening. Fortunately, apart from a ferocious ack-ack barrage early on, the air raid had turned out to be less worrying than she and the Stevens family had at first thought. Joe had wanted to accompany her back home himself, but she insisted that now that the roads were clear, the journey by bus would take no more than fifteen minutes at the most. When she reached the front gate of number 49A, she paused awhile to look up at the night sky, now mercifully clear of the agents of death and destruction. It was a strange interlude for her, for she had come to accept that she could no longer endure life under the same roof as her grandmother and her father. Tomorrow she would be gone. Tomorrow night she would look up at the sky from some other place – a different view, a different perspective on life as she had always known it. How would she cope with so big a wrench? Would she be *able* to cope? For, after all, this would be the bird leaving its nest for the first time, and it wasn't going to be easy. None the less, it had to be done, and the sooner she faced up to the challenge the sooner she could move on.

Inside the house, the first thing Peggy noticed was that there was a light filtering through from under the door of the sitting room. She wanted to investigate, but had no wish to confront either her father or her grandmother there.

So she made her way up the stairs as quietly as she could. But as she went, curiosity got the better of her. After all, what had she to fear from any of them, she asked herself? She turned round, and went back downstairs.

Catherine was all alone in the sitting room. She had her spectacles on and, by the light of a solitary table lamp, was working on the same crochet cushion cover that to Peggy had seemed like a lifetime in the making. As Peggy came into the room, Catherine looked up, took off her spectacles, and gave her an affectionate smile.

'I thought I heard you come in,' she said softly.

Peggy closed the door quietly, came in, and gave her mother a kiss on the cheek. 'Why aren't you in the shelter?' she asked.

'I left your grandmother there,' she replied, adding wryly, 'She has more to lose than I do.'

Peggy was concerned by her mother's bitter remark. 'You're the last person in the world *I* want to lose,' she said reassuringly. And as she looked at the poor woman's vulnerable face, she wondered how she could ever have brought herself to believe that she didn't care for her.

Catherine didn't answer. There was so much strain on her face, and her eyes were either red through too much needlework, or she had been crying. 'I've been thinking about what happened between you and your father. He didn't mean the things he said, you know.'

Peggy shrugged. 'I'm afraid he did,' she replied. 'But what difference does it make now? I've made up my mind.'

'You're still determined to leave?'

Peggy nodded.

Catherine sighed. 'How soon?'

'First thing tomorrow.'

Catherine's face crumpled up.

'It's all right, Mother, really it is,' said Peggy, putting a comforting arm around Catherine's shoulders. 'I shan't be far away. I'll see you just as much as ever.'

Catherine shook her head. She didn't believe a word Peggy had said.

'It couldn't go on the way it's been,' said Peggy. 'As much as I love you, I couldn't go on living under such a pretence for any longer. What Grandmother has achieved in the small amount of time she's been here has been little short of intolerable.'

'She'll only be here until the repairs are finished up at The Towers,' Catherine assured her.

Peggy shook her head. 'No, Mother,' she replied. 'I can't wait that long. Too much damage has been done already. If Father wants her to stay, that's his decision. But I won't be dictated to by either of them any more.'

'Oh God, Peggy,' said Catherine, close to tears. 'It's your twenty-first birthday on the twenty-eighth. Couldn't you at least wait until after then? I've been planning a surprise birthday party for you. I've invited some of your old school friends, and if you want, you could bring any of your new ones from the bus garage.'

Peggy smiled affectionately at her. 'I'm afraid I can't, Mother,' she said. 'I've had more surprises in my life than I can cope with.'

Catherine took a deep breath, and stood up. Peggy watched her go to the fireplace, where the cinders were still glowing in the dim light. After a moment, Peggy joined her there. 'You know, there was a time in my life,' said Catherine, 'when I thought I was the luckiest woman in the whole wide world. I had a husband, a daughter, and a home that anyone would be proud of.' Her face was now illuminated red by the glow from the fire, and the whole fireplace itself was reflected in her misty eyes. 'It's strange how everything can change so quickly. One moment a flower is in bloom, the next it droops and dies.' She turned, and looked straight into Peggy's eyes. 'I don't know why I carry on loving your father,' she said. 'Over the years he's brought me so much heartache.' She looked back into the fire again. 'I could have left him years ago. Maybe I should have. But every time I thought about doing so, I remembered the man I first saw, first loved. He was so worthwhile, so alien to the person he is now. I'm sure you wonder why I continue to cling on. I don't know. I really don't know. And the awful thing is . . .' She looked at Peggy again. '. . . if I had the chance all over again, I'd probably do exactly the same thing. Why, Peggy? Why?'

A short while later, Peggy was lying in her bed in the dark. It had been a day that she would not forget for a long time, and her mind was racing. But the one thing that hurt more than anything was to see her mother's face crumpled up in solitude and despair. Why *did* her mother go on loving her father? Why did *anyone* go on loving someone who could hurt them and cause them so much pain? It surely had to be one of life's imponderables.

Her eyes flickered and closed. Soon she would be drifting off into sleep, her last night in her own bed. It was an odd, strange feeling, lying there watching, listening, waiting, as though her entire life was drifting before her. But it had to be done. She had to leave this house, and she had to promise herself that she wouldn't be persuaded by anyone to change her mind. This was the moment, the right moment in time when the most important decision of her life had to be taken. There was no turning back. If she didn't take the chance now, there might never be another.

She turned over and eventually fell asleep. Tomorrow it would all be over.

Chapter 17

There was hardly enough room in Elsie Parker's flat in Marlborough Road to swing a cat. Although there were two bedrooms, the one that she'd given Peggy was only just big enough for a single bed, a small chest of drawers, and a tiny wardrobe. Fortunately Peggy had only brought a couple of suitcases with her when she left home that morning, so, for the time being at least, she could manage, but it was quite clear that this could only be a short-term arrangement, and no matter how much Elsie protested, she insisted on paying her ten shillings a week for her board and lodging.

Leaving home had been particularly traumatic for Peggy. It wasn't so much the house, for there were too many unhappy associations there, but parting from her mother, even though they would continue to meet regularly, was extremely distressing for both of them. Peggy was relieved that her grandmother had decided not to come down to breakfast that morning, for considering that she was the primary cause of Peggy's departure, an exchange between them would have proved very tense. Her father had left the house before she got up. He hadn't spoken a word to her since her outburst against his mother, and if the past was anything to go by, it was evident that he would not do so for a very long time.

'Now I want yer ter treat this as yer own 'ome,' said Elsie, as she readied herself to go to work. 'Yer're free ter come an' go as yer please, remember, and whenever I'm gettin' on yer nerves too much, I won't be at all offended if yer pack yerself off ter yer own room. OK?'

Peggy hugged her. 'You'll never get on my nerves, Elsie,' she replied. 'I think it's wonderful of you to let me stay here. I can't tell you how grateful I am.'

Peggy meant what she said. Elsie was a kind person, and had turned out to be a good friend. It made her cringe every time she remembered how much she had detested her when they'd first met in the staff canteen.

'Oh, by the way,' Elsie said, as she hurriedly buttoned up her uniform coat and put on her clippie's cap, 'I forgot ter mention the barfroom.'

'The bathroom?' asked Peggy, puzzled.

'We have ter share it wiv Ivy on the ground floor. She's a nice ol' gel, quite 'armless really, except when she takes Mussolini in ter 'ave a barf wiv 'er.'

'Mussolini?'

' 'Er moggie.'

'She takes a cat to have a bath with her?'

'Well, not *wiv* 'er,' giggled Elsie, 'but just ter keep 'er company.'

Peggy couldn't believe what Elsie had just told her. 'And his name's – *Mussolini*?' she chuckled.

'I know,' replied Elsie. 'It's a scream, in't it? An' I tell yer somefin'. That cat really looks like 'im too!'

They both laughed.

'Blimey, look at the time!' panicked Elsie suddenly, having looked at her watch. 'I'll be late fer me shift!' Quickly grabbing her shoulder bag she made a wild dash for the door. 'Make yerself a cuppa tea!' she hollered as she went. 'Don't worry about the coupons. I've still got plenty!'

Before Peggy had had a chance to say thank you, Elsie had gone.

'Bye-bye fer now!' her voice echoed as she hurried down the stairs.

'Bye!' returned Peggy.

Once she had heard the front door slam, Peggy suddenly felt terribly alone. As she sat down on a fairly basic hard-backed easy chair by the tiled-surround fireplace, she took a nervous look around Elsie's modest parlour room, and gradually it dawned on her that, for the first time in her life, she was going to have to start standing on her own two feet. The way she felt at the moment, it was an awesome prospect. All her life she'd been waited on hand and foot. Right from the time she had been born, her parents had employed not only a nanny, but also a cook and a maid-servant. She had been encouraged not to do a single thing that couldn't first be done by the domestics. If she wanted something, there was no need to get it for herself; all she had to do was to ask for it. Until Mrs Bailey took over long before the war, Peggy had never even been taught how to boil an egg. And as for washing and ironing her own clothes, she had never heard of such a thing. No, Peggy, like her mother and her grandmother before her, had been brought up to do absolutely nothing but sit back and take life as it came. Well, she asked herself, as she sat there pondering over what future lay ahead of her, *this* is the future so how do you intend to deal with it?

The first thing she did was to get up and put another piece of coal on the fire from a cardboard box Elsie kept at the side of the grate. She wanted to put on some more, but as fuel was very tightly rationed, Peggy didn't want to run down what very little stock Elsie had left. Then she went into the adjoining kitchenette, which like everything else in the flat was tiny, mainly because it was a part of the parlour room itself, divided only by a flimsy blockboard wall. After she'd washed the coal off her hands in the functional porcelain sink, she put some water in the kettle, and lit one of the two gas rings on top of the small-sized oven cooker.

Whilst she was waiting for the water to boil, she decided to find her way downstairs to the bathroom Elsie had told her about. It was situated on the next landing down, and could be identified quite easily by the somewhat basic scrawl on the chipped painted door which read quite simply 'LAV'. She went in. Again a small space which looked as though it too had been created from what must have once been a much larger landing. But it was clean enough, and the bath, although a bit ancient, was clearly quite functional, even though the room itself was unheated and very cold.

Before leaving, Peggy took a casual glance at herself in the hand-mirror on the tiled window-ledge. Her hair looked like hell and she knew it. But just at the point when she was about to buff it up a little with her fingers, she jumped with a terrified start as she suddenly saw the reflection of some hideous thing staring up at her from the closed top of the toilet seat behind her.

When she swung round to look, she couldn't believe her eyes. It was a cat, or at least something resembling a cat – black and white markings, fat, bloated, a jutting jaw-line, long whiskers and a face as round as a basin. Peggy swallowed hard. For a moment the two of them stared each other out, until the monster creature was first to utter, with a curling of his lips and a spirited hissing sound.

'Musso! Where are yer, yer bleedin' dago?'

The voice that rasped from the stairs outside immediately appeared at the open door. It belonged to a woman who could have been aged anywhere between seventy and ninety, and whose hair was cut severely, dyed a vivid black, and topped with a soldier's army cap worn at a rakish angle on the side of her head. 'There yer are!'

Peggy leaned back against the window-ledge, absolutely mesmerised by the apparition before her.

'Who are you?' demanded the apparition, the moment she saw Peggy cowering.

'I – I'm a friend of Elsie,' replied Peggy, falteringly. 'Elsie Parker from upstairs. I'm staying with her. Y-you must be – er – Ivy?'

'Yer ain't got no boyfriends up there, 'ave yer?' demanded Ivy, the apparition. 'I've told that gel I don't want no babies bein' born round 'ere. I need me sleep at nights. So does Mussolini 'ere. Don't yer, yer ol' windbag?' As she approached the cat and snatched him from the lavatory lid, Mussolini growled back. 'Don't you swear at me, mate!' Ivy scolded, shaking him. 'I'm bigger than you!'

Peggy watched the odd pair go. She couldn't quite believe what she had just seen.

The staff in the coal merchant's office were always grateful that Marge Quincey from upstairs rarely paid them a visit. She had been a pain in the neck right from the time that she and her family had moved in before the war, always complaining about things, such as the water supply was inadequate, or the outside lavatory was smelling so much that she had to keep her scullery window closed upstairs, or the coalmen were making far too much noise in the yard outside. So when they saw her walk through the front door so early in the day, their hearts sank.

'Which one is Ned?' she demanded.

'Ned?' asked Rita, the young receptionist. 'Who's that?'

'That's wot I'm askin' *you*!' growled Marge, eyes blazing. 'Coalman! Coalman!'

'You mean Ned Oaks?' This time it was Mr Foster, the manager, calling from the back office.

'Where is 'e now?' she demanded impatiently.

'Out on 'is round,' he replied tersely. 'Due back any minute!' He closed his office door on her.

Enraged, Marge stormed out of the office and into the yard. There were several coalmen just loading up their carts, and their horses were taking last meals of hay before moving off for the morning's rounds. 'Any of you lot seen Ned Oaks?' she bellowed.

'Who wants 'im?' called back one of the coalmen.

'*I* do!' yelled Marge angrily.

'Well, yer found 'im!'

Marge marched right up to the man, who was just getting down from his cart.

'Wot d'yer want?' sniffed the man gruffly.

'Who was this bloke come lookin' fer me the uvver day?' demanded Marge, practically eyeball to eyeball with the man. 'Tall, bowler 'at?'

' 'Aven't the foggiest.'

'Remember wot 'e looked like?'

The coalman shrugged his shoulders.

'This 'im?' she growled, suddenly producing a snapshot photograph of a family group from her apron pocket and holding it up for the man to see.

The man grabbed the snapshot and looked at it. 'Which one is 'et?' he asked.

'Open yer bleedin' eyes an' look!' she replied tersely.

'I don't 'ave me specs!' he growled back just as angrily. ' 'Ere – give us a butcher's.'

Marge turned to find one of the other coalman drivers coming towards her.

The second man snatched the snapshot from Ned and had a quick look at it. 'Yeah, that's 'im,' he said immediately. 'Bloke in the back. Just look at the size of 'im. Like a bleedin' giraffe!'

Without so much as a by-your-leave, Marge snatched the snapshot away from the man, and marched off back towards her front door with it.

'Fank you, madam,' the man called after her sarcastically. 'I'll do the same fer you some time!'

Peggy and Leo found their way on to Hampstead Heath via the North Wood entrance. They had taken the number 611 trolley bus to Highgate Village, and although the air was cold and crisp, they found the stroll down Hampstead Lane a real tonic after the greasy atmosphere back at the garage. When Leo first asked her to come out with him during her free time before the evening shift, he wasn't too sure that she'd accept, but when she did he was determined to try to put things right between them. But he waited until they had ambled past Kenwood House and climbed the steep slope leading up to a magnificent vantage point from where the whole of London was laid out before them, now doing its best to hide beneath a long film of still, white mist, a dazzling winter landscape which temporarily disguised the ravages of war. For several minutes they stood there, just staring out at the wilderness, from north to south, east to west, he with his hands in his pockets, she with her gloved hands tucked under both arms.

'My grandfather used to bring me up here when I was a child,' said Peggy. 'He could point out all the sights. He knew every one of them.' She strained her eyes to try to pick out a familiar landmark in the distance. 'Can you see?' she pointed suddenly. 'Big Ben!'

'Where?' asked Leo, trying to follow her eye-line.

'There!' she indicated. 'You can just see it if you follow the river. It looks so strange poking out of the mist like that . . . and there . . . d'you see, Leo . . . that's St Paul's! Isn't it beautiful? D'you know Miriam Jackson? She's that Jewish girl who works on the 611s with me, married to this boy called Ted – he's not Jewish, though; that's why she had so much trouble with her father . . . Well, she said that on that

Sunday night when the whole of London was on fire, she was on night shift in the City, and even though she's not a Christian, she thought St Paul's looked one of the most beautiful sights she'd ever seen in her life . . . surrounded by flames everywhere, the entire sky seemed to be on fire . . . there . . .' she was still pointing, 'can you see it?' Her enthusiasm was abruptly halted when she turned to find him staring at her. 'Leo!' she complained.

'Yer've got a red nose,' he said.

'So have you!' she replied playfully.

'Yeah,' he teased, 'but mine's booze!'

They laughed. Then silence. They were staring at each other again. Leo took one of his hands out of his duffel coat pocket and, without losing eye contact with her, gently stroked the tip of her nose. She allowed him to move slowly towards her. His face drew close to hers. But they were suddenly distracted by a Labrador dog who came sniffing at Leo's feet. They quickly parted to find an elderly couple struggling up the slope nearby.

'Gus!' called the man. The dog refused to hear. 'Gus!' he called again, this time more forcibly, and followed the call with a pathetic whistle. This time the dog obeyed, and went bouncing off back to them.

Peggy, embarrassed by the interruption, waited for them to disappear completely into the distance before she allowed Leo to come near her again. 'Leo,' she asked, 'is this a good idea?'

Suddenly put off by her question, he stopped dead.

'You still have someone else – remember?'

He sighed. 'Peggs, I've already told yer—'

'You can't just walk away from somebody.'

'Yer can when yer've bin set up,' he replied tersely. Irritated, he turned away and stared out at the view again. She gave him a moment, then went and stood at his side. 'Have you had it out with her yet?' she asked, putting her hands into her coat pocket to keep them warm. 'Your mother, I mean?'

' 'Ow many times do I 'ave ter tell yer?' he groaned. 'I'll tell 'er when the time's right.'

'And when will that be, Leo? Today, tomorrow, next week, next month . . . ?'

'Don't bully me, Peggs!' he snapped, turning on her.

Peggy resented this. 'Oh, I wouldn't dream of doing such a thing, Leo,' she replied, starting to wander off.

He quickly went after her, and pulled her round to face him. 'Look, Peggs,' he said. 'I've 'ad a lifetime er being sat on by me muvver. OK, so I could go down there right now an' tell 'er wot I fink of 'er, tell 'er that she's an interferin' ol' cow an' that there's nuffin' in this world that's goin' ter make me take on someone *she* wants. But d'yer know wot'd 'appen then? She'd crumple up, she'd cry, she'd sob 'er bleedin' 'eart out an' say wot an awful muvver she's bin, an' 'ow wotever she's done she's only done ter protect 'er kids.'

Peggy was puzzled, but she wanted to show that she understood his dilemma. 'So why are you so afraid to say these things to her, Leo?' she asked gently. 'Why can't you just tell her that you're a big boy now, and that she's just got to stop running your life?'

Leo hesitated before answering. 'Because,' he said, staring out at the view, 'because when I do, I want ter make quite sure that she never gets the chance ter do so again.'

Peggy sighed, turned, and started to walk off again.

Leo quickly followed her and brought her to a halt. 'I meant wot I said, Peggs,' he assured her fervently. 'Yer *are* me gel.'

She raised her eyes and replied, 'I hope so, Leo. But not yet. Not just yet.'

★ ★ ★

Robert Thornton completed his notes for the day, then locked them away in a filing cabinet at the back of his office. Three of the four cases brought before him in the magistrates' court during the course of the day had been fairly routine – two petty theft and one assault and battery were fairly open and shut, and had been dealt with swiftly – but the final case brought before his bench was more serious for it concerned the rape of a prostitute by a young soldier, and therefore had to be referred to both the Director of Public Prosecutions and also to the soldier's own military authorities for possible court martial. After a tiring day, Thornton was ready to leave the place and get home as soon as possible before the blackout.

Outside, it was already getting dark, and when he looked up at the sky he was none too happy that it was a clear evening with hardly any cloud cover to prevent Field Marshal Goering's bomber planes from continuing their regular onslaught. However, he felt slightly more reassured when he noticed the half-dozen or so barrage balloons tethered to their umbilical cords and scattered around the sky, so he felt confident enough to take his time making his way from the main entrance of the court to his taxi which was, as always, waiting for him at the kerbside. However, he had only taken a few steps when a loud rasping voice called to him: 'Oi – you!'

It brought Thornton to an abrupt halt, and he scowled at the middle-aged woman who was approaching him from the roadside. Fearing trouble, he tried to move out of her path.

'You the magistrate then?' asked Marge Quincey, blocking him. 'Your name Fornton?'

'What do you want?' asked Thornton brusquely.

At this point no one was taking much notice of the exchange, but Thornton made a mental note of where he could find the court's duty police constable if he needed some quick assistance.

'The name's Quincey!' she asked. '*Mrs* Quincey! I 'ear yer've bin tryin' ter pay me a visit.'

'I don't know what you're talking about, madam!' Thornton swung back, trying to brush past her.

'No,' replied Marge, holding him back with her hand. 'But I bet yer bleedin' daughter does!'

Thornton froze.

At that point, the very agitated duty constable rushed across. 'Are you having any trouble, Mr Thornton, sir?' he asked.

Thornton glared at Marge for a moment, then, without turning to the policeman, said, 'No, it's quite all right, Constable, thank you.'

The constable wasn't fully convinced, but after giving Marge a good look up and down, reluctantly withdrew back to the main entrance.

Marge grinned.

'What's this all about?' Thornton asked tersely.

'I was about ter ask yer the same question,' she replied provocatively. 'Yer came to me 'ouse. I wanna know why.'

After some hesitation he replied, 'I wanted to find out what sort of people my daughter was mixing with.'

Marge was furious. '*You* wanted ter know about *us*?' she barked. 'Who the bleedin' 'ell d'yer fink you are?'

Her raised voice caused Thornton to take a quick glance over his shoulder towards the constable, who was keeping a close watch for any sign of trouble. With this in mind, Thornton slowly led Marge Quincey away from the court towards his taxi. 'At least let's discuss this in a civilised way,' he said, lowering his voice. When he had taken her far enough away from the constable to be able to talk freely, he asked, 'First of all, you can tell me how you knew it was me who came to see you.'

'It ain't very 'ard ter put one an' one tergevver, yer know,' she said, digging into her coat pocket. 'Even I could add up at school.' She held up in front of his face a snapshot. 'That's you an' yer family, I presume?'

Thornton glared at the snapshot, and then back at her. 'Where did you get that from?'

Marge grinned at the power she was wielding. 'Could it be yer daughter gave it ter me son?' she asked smugly. 'I found it in 'is room. It weren't the first time I'd seen it. I come across it once before, when I was cleanin' up there. But I remembered it. I remembered it specially when they told me about this tall bloke wiv the bowler 'at who'd come callin' on me.'

Thornton ground his teeth together so much that he was in danger of cracking the fillings. He was inclined to hold on to the snapshot, but she quickly snatched it back from him.

'Yer feel the same way as I do about the two of 'em – don't yer?' she asked, now confident enough to lower her own voice. '*You* don't want yer hoity-toity little miss 'angin' round a snotty-nosed boy from down the 'ill any more than *I* do – do yer? Go on – admit it!'

Thornton found her utterly obnoxious. In his wildest dreams he could never have imagined that someone like this woman would match up identically to his worst possible fears. 'So what do you want to do about this?' he asked disdainfully.

Marge needed no hesitation to say what she had wanted to say. 'Put paid ter it!' she thundered. 'Put paid ter it right now before it goes any furver!'

Thornton took another anxious look over his shoulder to see if the duty constable was in view. 'It may not have occurred to you that, if your son and my daughter want to continue their relationship, there's little we can do to stop them.'

'Why not?' replied Marge, face taut. 'Yer a judge or somefin' in't yer? Yer're s'pposed ter know 'ow ter deal wiv people who carry on like this.'

'For your information, Mrs Quincey,' Thornton replied with a sigh, 'I am not a judge. And I can assure you that neither of these two young people has committed any offence.'

'Well, it's an offence ter me!' she snapped, raising her voice again. 'Where I come from we care about our kids!'

Thornton had to shake his head to make sure he had heard right. 'What on earth are you talking about?' he asked.

'I'll tell yer wot I'm talkin' about, Mister 'igh an' mighty judge!' replied Marge, wagging her finger at him. 'I'm talkin' about a good 'ard-workin' boy bein' used by a gel that's never 'ad ter want in life.'

Thornton stared at her in disbelief. 'Used?' he asked incomprehendingly.

'Yes – *used*!' she replied. 'Yer know bleedin' well wot I mean. Me boy may not 'ave much brain up 'ere,' she said, pointing one finger to her head, 'but 'e 'as plenty else ter offer – an' *she* knows it!'

Now Thornton knew she was mad. He turned and marched off to his taxi.

'Don't like ter 'ear the trufe, do yer, mate?' she hollered. 'Don't like ter admit wot yer own daughter's after 'im for!'

She suddenly found herself pounced on by the duty constable, who pinned her arms behind her back. 'That's all now, ma!' he said angrily, struggling with her.

'So if yer want ter come round an' call on me again, Mister judge,' she yelled abusively, 'yer know where ter find me. Only next time yer'd better come up wiv some ideas of yer own!'

Just as he was about to get into his taxi, Thornton stopped, turned, and took one last look at her. 'If I should have the misfortune of seeing you again, Mrs Quincey,' he said coldly. 'It will be inside and not outside the court.'

He got in, slammed the door, and the taxi drove off. He couldn't even bring himself to peer back through the rear window. What he had just witnessed had thoroughly repelled him.

The air raid had been going hammer and tongs for over four hours now. Catherine Thornton lay on her back in the Morrison shelter in the dining room, staring up aimlessly in the dark towards the cold concrete roof. She wasn't sure whether she preferred the deafening sound of gunfire or the relentless snoring of her mother-in-law, who was fast asleep at the side of her. She had come to loathe the night – every night – for it meant that she had to be cooped up in the claustrophobic space, knowing that if the house had a direct hit there was no way that such a crude device was going to prevent anyone from being killed outright.

Worst of all, she missed Peggy. The house wasn't the same without her; it was empty and devoid of love and care. Peggy had only been gone since the morning, and Catherine hadn't stopped worrying about her since she had left. She wondered whether she had got back safely to her new accommodation after her evening shift, whether her bed was comfortable, whether the linen was clean, and whether she was getting enough food to eat. She tried to imagine what Peggy's bedroom was like. Was it small or large? Did it have pretty wallpaper and somewhere nice to sit? Above all, this was her first night away from home, and Catherine agonised over what her girl was thinking. Unable to bear another minute in the Morrison shelter, she quietly raised the metal grille which closed the shelter in, and gently eased herself off the bed. By the light of her slim pencil torch, she just managed to slip into her carpet slippers, and leave the room.

In the hall, she could hear Thornton's breathing as he slept soundly in the space beneath the stairs. As she was wearing only her nightdress, Catherine felt quite cold, so she hurried upstairs as fast as she could, careful not to let the stairs creak too much as she went. She dressed quickly, making sure that she put on her warm rainproof galoshes and two thick woollen scarves, one for around her neck, and the other to cover her head. Then she tiptoed down the stairs again, collected her much stronger torch, and left the house.

For a few minutes, she paused on the doorstep outside, waiting for the last of the overhead raiders to clear the sky and the ack-ack barrage to subside. Then, as soon as she felt it was safe to move, she went down the front garden steps, and out on to the hill.

Although the sky was temporarily quiet again, there was clearly a great deal of activity in the distance, for she could hear the emergency services rushing back and forth from several directions. She decided to make her way in one of those directions. This took her down to Archway Junction and into the usually busy Junction Road, now completely deserted and as silent as the grave. The most frenzied of the activity seemed to be coming from the direction of Tufnell Park or, even further, Kentish Town, so she headed off that way at a brisk pace. Although she was perfectly aware that the sky was heavy with impending danger, she felt invigorated by the biting cold night air. It was the first time since she could remember ever having been out so late, especially on her own, and it gave her an extraordinary feeling of release. Even the crunching sound of her galoshes on the frozen hard snow as she walked gave her an awed fascination, for it somehow told her that she herself was making that sound, and she was doing it all by herself.

By the time she had reached Tufnell Park, the sound of people shouting, dogs barking, and generators powering up searchlights, seemed to be coming from along Fortess Road towards Kentish Town somewhere, so she quickly made tracks in that direction.

She eventually reached the source of the huge fire that she had been able to see burning all the way from Archway Junction. A complete row of three shops had had a direct hit, and were reduced to a pile of rubble. Next door was a block of Victorian flats, which was also burning fiercely, with grimy-faced firemen and women on the tops of precariously long and wobbly fire-cart ladders, struggling to contain the flames with jets of water from the nozzles of their hosepipes. When Catherine got there she was over-whelmed by what she could see, for everywhere around her men and women from the emergency services and also ordinary members of the public were doing their best to help, shouting out to the occupants of the flats who were stranded on the top floor, waiting to be rescued. Catherine watched all of this with a feeling of horror and awed fascination.

'Give us an 'and, gel!'

Catherine suddenly found an elderly woman in a woollen nightie, hairnet and carpet slippers, shoving a length of hosepipe at her.

'They're tryin' ter move it over ter that doorway!' called the old girl above the noise. 'We'll 'ave ter drag it over that wall that's come down!'

Before she knew what she was doing, Catherine found herself helping three other women volunteers and one teenage boy in pyjamas to lift the heavy flowing hosepipe into position.

'Oi – watch it!' yelled the old girl to one of the Home Guard helpers, who was perched high on top of the remains of what looked like an old piece of timber. 'That's my kitchen table yer're standin' on!'

A few minutes later, Catherine was swept along amidst a tide of people who had formed a chain to collect possessions that victims inside the block of flats were trying to retrieve before the building collapsed. In the space of a few minutes, she had collected and passed on everything from clothes and mattresses to suitcases full of precious family snapshots. At one time she even had a large chamber pot thrust into her hands, and that she got rid of as fast as she could. However, once the chain had served its purpose and had been broken up, Catherine was totally bewildered when she was suddenly handed a small baby wrapped in a thick woollen blanket, face barely visible, and bawling its head off. 'What shall I do with it?' she said, panicking.

'Give 'er to the St John's!' yelled a fireman from the top of the ladder. 'We're just gettin' 'er mum out!'

Frantic with worry, Catherine desperately looked around for an ambulance, or anyone who could take the poor small thing from her. Oh God, she thought to herself, why have you brought me to such a place?

'It's all right, my dear,' said a calming voice right behind her.

Catherine swung round to find a woman in a uniform of some kind, arms outstretched, waiting to take the baby from her. 'Oh!' she gasped with relief. 'Thank you!'

'Poor little mite,' said the middle-aged woman, whose accent was Kensington and certainly not Kentish Town. 'What a way to start a life.' Catherine watched whilst she covered the baby up snugly, and then kissed it lightly on its cheek. 'It's a good thing we're here, though, isn't it, little one?' she said to the small bundle she was holding. 'At

349

least *you've* got a chance to go on, haven't you?' She looked up, and smiled at Catherine. 'Thank you, my dear.'

Despite her anguish, Catherine just managed to return the smile. In the overwhelming glare of the floodlights that were suddenly switched on to search for survivors, she saw that the woman was wearing a uniform and hat that she recognised from somewhere else. It was grey and piped with green. The woman was a WVS volunteer.

Amidst the devastating sound of chaos and tragedy all around her, the only sound Catherine could really hear was the voice inside of her friend Betty Desmond: '*The women I work with, Catherine, are no different from you and me. They have husbands, they have children, they have homes that they care for and want to protect at all costs. But they're also human beings who care for other human beings. The day we lose that, we don't deserve to exist any more.*'

Chapter 18

Peggy woke to find a heavy weight on her chest and two large resentful eyes glaring at her. She leaped out of bed with a yell, scattering pillows and Mussolini. 'Get out of here, you brute!' she yelled at him, protecting herself with a pillow and one carpet slipper.

Elsie's worried voice called from outside the door. 'Peggs! Are yer all right?'

'I will be!' Peggy yelled back. 'When I've got this hairy monster out of my room.'

'Can I come in?'

'Yes!'

Elsie, fully dressed, appeared at the door and immediately threw one of her own carpet slippers at the indignant cat. 'Out, Musso!' she bellowed.

With a growl and a hiss, Mussolini fled for his life.

'Sorry about that,' said Elsie. 'I must 'ave left the flat door open when I went out ter get a paper.'

'Well, I hope it was worth it?'

'At a penny a time, no newspaper is worf it,' she grumbled. 'But I'm glad I did 'cos we've taken Tobruk!'

'I beg your pardon?' asked Peggy, who was yawning and stretching.

'Tobruk!' repeated Elsie, excited. 'Norf Africa. Our boys an' the Aussies 'ave captured this big place in the desert from Jerry. The papers are goin' mad about it. It's a t'rrific victory.'

'That's wonderful, Elsie,' said Peggy, who wasn't really

351

taking too much notice as she slipped into her dressing gown. 'Is it all right if I make myself a cup of tea?'

'Of course it is, silly! But yer'd better make two cups. Yer've got a visitor.'

Peggy did a double take. 'What? Who?'

Elsie grinned. 'Come an' see fer yerself.'

Peggy quickly followed her downstairs to the parlour where she was thrilled to see who was waiting for her there. 'Grandfather!' she yelled, overjoyed, immediately throwing herself into his arms. 'What a wonderful surprise! What are you doing here? How did you find me? Oh, I'm so pleased to see you!'

'I'm pleased to see you too, young rebel!' he replied, at the same time exchanging a grateful smile with Elsie.

'I'll leave you two to it!' said Elsie, disappearing back upstairs to her own room.

'But when did you get back from Harpenden?' Peggy asked. 'Have they finished The Towers yet? Are you coming back for good?'

'Hey!' he replied, flopping down on to the small sofa. 'One thing at a time. Let me take a look at you first.' He did so, giving her a quick look up and down. 'Well, I must say, you look marvellous. Seems like the bachelor girl life suits you.'

'I've only been here a few days,' she replied, sitting down beside him. 'I'll let you know when the war's over!' They smiled affectionately at each other. 'I've missed you, Grandfather.'

'I've missed you too, my dear,' he replied, adding, 'I'm so sad it had to come to this.'

Peggy shrugged. 'It was only a matter of time,' she replied. 'Father and Grandmother may not have realised it yet but between them they've given me just the push I needed.'

Herbert sighed, and lowered his eyes in despair.

'Have you been to see Grandmother?' asked Peggy carefully.

'Oh yes, I've seen her,' he replied, casually. 'She's talking about moving into a hotel.'

'A hotel!'

'Apparently she told your father that she feels guilty about forcing you out of your own home.'

'Ha!' grunted Peggy, getting up and going to poke the fire. 'She's a bit late for guilt. What about Mrs Bailey?'

'So far she's still there,' he replied. 'I suspect that's only because you persuaded her.'

'I couldn't leave Mother without help,' said Peggy. 'She wouldn't know how to cope.'

Herbert smiled. 'Well, I think that's about to change,' he said. 'Did you know she's volunteered for the WVS?'

Peggy did a doubletake. 'Mother?'

'I had a long talk with her this morning. She said she wanted to follow your example, do something useful for the war, do something for someone else for a change. I always suspected she had hidden depths.'

'But – what about Father?' asked Peggy, fired with curiosity. 'The idea of Mother doing something he disapproves of must have infuriated him.'

'Oddly enough it hasn't,' Herbert replied. 'Well, not that I can see. But he *was* in a very curious mood when I talked to him this morning.'

'In what way?'

'It's hard to tell. But he's certainly got things on his mind. At least he was far more affable than he's been for a long time.' He paused, clearly wanting to tell her something. 'Mind you, we had a lot to talk over. Mainly about you.'

'Me?' Peggy watched him anxiously as he got up from the sofa, and ambled nervously around the room without seeming to notice anything that he was looking at.

'Peggy,' he said, without turning to her, 'I want to give you some money. Just enough to tide you over until you get yourself . . .' he looked across at her, 'more settled.'

Expecting something more serious, Peggy breathed a sigh of relief. 'You don't have to, Grandfather,' she said. 'I promise you I can manage perfectly well on the wages I'm paid.'

Herbert smiled. 'I'm sure you can, my dear,' he replied. 'But I'd like to give you some. After all, you'll be getting most of my money after I'm gone.'

'Well, thankfully, I shall be an old woman myself before *that* happens.'

'Alas,' he said, almost casually, 'I fear you won't.'

Peggy felt a sudden chill. Going to him, she asked, 'What are you trying to tell me, Grandfather?'

He smiled at her. 'I have one or two problems, that's all. Nothing to worry about, but I want to have time to sort things out.'

As she looked closely into his ageing blue eyes, she felt her stomach go tense. He was ill, and she knew it. She'd known the moment she'd come into the room, for he seemed to be so lacking in energy, so lacking in concentration, as though his mind was perpetually occupied by other things. The thought that there was anything wrong with him made her shrivel up inside. She tried to dismiss any notion that he was in any danger, or that she might lose him. All she wanted to think about was that he had always been the one guiding light in her life, that without him ever being there, she would have been in despair. In her eyes, her grandfather was a god, the real father that she never had.

'Two hundred and fifty pounds.'

Peggy's eyes flicked as she returned from her brief inner

journey through their relationship. 'I'm sorry, Grandfather. What did you say?'

'I said I'm arranging for my bank to cash you two hundred and fifty pounds. I'll give you a cheque. You can collect the money any time you want.'

Peggy was about to object.

'Please don't,' he said quickly, gently placing one finger to her lips. 'One way or another, I've been quite frustrated throughout my life. But not now. Not at this moment. You see, what you're doing now, my dear, is what *I* should have done years ago. Taking difficult decisions is something we all have to do from time to time. But it takes courage, a special sort of courage. I've never had it, Peggy – but *you* have.' He moved closer. 'Let me do this for you, my dear – please. It'll be about the only positive thing I've ever done.'

A watery sun was clearly throwing quite a tantrum, because all morning it had been trapped behind an endless surge of racing grey clouds. It was early afternoon when it finally won the right to be seen, and when it did it managed to send a long ray of dazzling light on to the gently rippling waves of the River Thames, just below the Victoria Embankment.

Irene West chose her bench seat well. From where she was sitting, she had a wonderful view of the river from St Paul's Cathedral all the way along to Westminster Bridge, and on the opposite side facing her, the grandeur of the County Hall building, home of the London County Council, had shrugged off the effects of bomb blast by remaining firm and defiant. But it was still very cold, and Irene hoped that she would not have to wait long for her meeting. She was not to be disappointed, for even as Big Ben was sounding two o'clock, she could see the tall figure of Robert Thornton striding briskly towards her from the direction of Whitehall, his bowler hat clearly visible above the passing afternoon crowds.

The moment he arrived, Irene rose to greet him. 'I'm so sorry to have contacted you,' she said apologetically, 'but you said you wanted us to keep in touch.'

To her surprise, Thornton ignored what she was saying, too busy taking in the views. 'This is a wonderful spot,' he said, taking a deep breath of the fresh winter air above the river. 'So good for brushing away the cobwebs.' He indicated to her to sit, and once she had done so, he sat beside her.

She waited a moment before speaking. 'I hear they're back together again,' she said. 'Apparently a couple of weeks ago they had some kind of tiff. But it's all on again.'

Thornton did not reply. He continued to stare out towards the river, both hands resting on the top of his cane.

Irene was a little unnerved by his lack of response. 'The problem I have is that I can't hang around the bus garage too often because if they see me they'll wonder what I'm up to.'

'Did you know,' Thornton said quite suddenly, 'that in the old days this river was used almost entirely for commerce?'

Irene was confused. 'Er – no – I mean – yes. I think I did know that . . .'

'I think a river makes a city great, and not the other way round – wouldn't you agree?'

Irene found Thornton's behaviour disconcerting, especially as it appeared as though he was not addressing his remarks directly to her. 'Yes,' she replied. 'I suppose so.'

On the river itself, the horn from a coal-barge pierced the air as the long flat boat chugged its determined way up towards Westminster. Thornton rose from the bench and climbed some stone steps to watch it. Irene joined him.

'So they're back together again are they?' he asked.

'As far as I can tell.'

'Then perhaps we should just let them get on with it.'

Irene swung him a startled look.

He turned to look at her. 'Let's call it a day, shall we, Irene?' he asked.

She stared at him in disbelief. 'Y-you mean – you don't want me to . . . ?'

'I mean I want you to leave them alone,' he said calmly and rationally. 'I think it's time we got on with our own lives and left them to get on with theirs.'

Irene was too taken aback to reply.

'You know,' he said, 'there are some things I've done in my life that I'm very proud of. Unfortunately this is not one of them. I'm sorry I involved you in such a sordid business, Irene – I had no right to. I'm sorry also for what I've done. I don't know why I did it. I love my daughter. She means a great deal to me. I've never told her so, of course.' For one brief moment he took off his bowler hat and ran his fingers through his greying hair. Then he replaced the hat again, and looked at her. 'Will you forgive me?' he asked.

Irene felt that she was in a daze. 'Robert, I – I don't know what to say.'

'Say that you'll forget all about me. Say that you'll try to forget that I ever existed. Go and join your Land Army. Get away from Stevens, and law, and trying to be who you don't want to be. I promise you, I shall never trouble you again.' To her absolute astonishment, he leaned forward and kissed her lightly on the cheek. 'I hate this war,' he said. 'I hate everything about it. It turns people's heads.' He smiled at her.

The way she was feeling, it was the sweetest smile she had ever seen. It was also the first time she had ever seen him do such a thing.

'Goodbye, Irene,' he said.

'Goodbye, Robert,' she replied.

Then he turned, and strolled back in the direction he had come from. She watched him for what seemed like ages, the tall figure she had been so used to seeing, so used to dreading, gradually merging with the swirling crowd of passers-by and eventually disappearing from view.

Still stunned, she turned and made off. This time, however, it was in a different direction.

Reg Quincey and his two younger sons, Horace and Eddie, were rocking with laughter at the antics of Arthur 'Big-hearted' Askey and Richard 'Stinker' Murdoch, as they struggled to get Bertha, their nanny goat, out of their bath in the flat they all shared on the roof of Broadcasting House in London. Apparently Bertha had already eaten that week's copy of the Radio Times and was now stubbornly refusing to join the two radio stars and their domestic, Mrs Bagwash, down in their notorious Anderson shelter, which the famous duo had erected themselves with hilarious results. The situation was, of course, sheer madcap, but the laughs *Band Wagon* was bringing to millions of radio listeners throughout the country week after week during the Blitz, was certainly one of the shows that was helping the Quincey family to get through the long winter evenings, and by the time Big-hearted Arthur had finished the regular half-hour with his much-loved 'Busy, Busy Bee' song, the war had been long forgotten.

Unfortunately, however, the same could not be said of Marge Quincey. Even as the end title music was playing she turned off the wireless and rasped at the kids,

'Come on, you two! The bunks are made up. Down the shelter!'

Both boys groaned. 'Mum,' pleaded Eddie. 'Can't we stay in our room ternight? Do we 'ave ter go down the shelter?'

'Now!' she demanded.

'But there ain't no air raid on,' grumbled Horace.

One look from his mum told him that if he and his brother didn't move and move fast, then they risked a clip round the ear hole. In a flash they were up from the kitchen parlour table, where they'd been listening to the wireless, and out of the room.

'Ace is right, yer know,' said their dad once they'd gone. 'Wot's the point goin' out ter the shelter if there ain't no air raid? Why don't we all 'ave a good night's rest in our own beds?'

' 'Cos it's safer, that's why,' insisted Marge. 'Wot 'appens if the siren goes in the middle er the night? We'll only 'ave ter get up anyway. Even when there ain't no siren, most people go down the shelters just in case.'

Reg sighed and settled back to enjoy his glass of brown. As always, he had to accept that what his wife had said was right, but it still irritated him. It was also boring him out of his mind that his recovery from his injuries was taking its time, and he had to sit propped up in an easy chair with his foot on a stool all day and every day. 'Bet yer life yer won't find Leo goin' out ter the shelter ternight,' he said, taking another glance through his pools coupon.

Marge darted him a quick look whilst stitching a hole in one of Eddie's socks. 'An' wot's *that* s'pposed ter mean?' she asked suspiciously.

'Nuffin',' he replied, without returning her look. Then after a pause, he asked, 'Wot time's 'e due 'ome anyway?'

Marge looked up at the small alarm clock on the mantelpiece. 'Should be any minute,' she replied hopefully.

' 'E's tryin' ter work some overtime ter get some extra cash – just in case 'e gets 'is call-up papers.'

This time Reg did look up. 'Call-up papers?' he asked. 'I fought they give 'im deferred 'cos er me?'

'Yer're not on the danger list any more,' she reminded him.

He looked at her curiously. ' 'As 'e 'eard from 'em then?' he asked.

'Not directly,' she replied, concentrating on her sewing. 'But they *'ave* bin in touch.'

'Wot does *that* mean?'

'Some army bloke come round 'ere ter see 'im,' she said casually. 'Leo was at work so as yer was 'avin' a doze upstairs, *I* saw 'im.'

Reg looked at her suspiciously. 'And?' he asked.

'An' I told 'im yer was much better.' She gave one of her sickly smiles. ' 'E was a very nice bloke – a sergeant or somefin' – come from that army call-up place down near 'Olloway tube.'

Reg was staring at her. 'Yer told this bloke that I was much better?'

'Course, dear,' she replied. 'Well, yer are – ain't yer?'

'D'yer realise if they actually *know* that,' he said, getting riled, 'they'll take Leo off ter call-up quick as a flash?'

'I s'ppose they will.' She sighed. 'I must say, I 'adn't fought about that. Still,' she looked up from her sewing, 'we can't 'old on ter 'im fer ever, can we, dear? I know 'e's our boy, an' I'll miss 'im. But there's a war on, an' 'e's got ter do 'is bit like everyone else.'

Reg glared at her in disbelief. If looks could kill, Marge would have been stone dead.

So far so good. Peggy's final journey of the night was now on the home run, and once they had cleared the four busy overhead crossing wires immediately outside Old Street tube station, it would only be a matter of forty minutes or so before the 611 drew back into the Holloway trolley-bus depot. Fortunately, it had been a fairly routine run, except on the outward journey when two young building workers who had just rolled out of the pub in New North Road, blind drunk, had tried to get off the bus without paying, and another dicey moment when Gummy was travelling too fast and only just had enough time to pull to a stop when the remains of a bombed office wall suddenly collapsed on to the road on the approach to the Moorgate turnaround. In fact Peggy had once told Gummy about going too fast, so much so that on more than two or three occasions he hadn't bothered to acknowledge passengers who were trying to wave him down at a request stop. But, as usual, he had taken offence, and told her to 'get yerself a decent pair er knickers before yer try an' teach me my job!' Peggy hadn't the faintest idea what he meant, and went on with doing what she was paid for, hoping that her attachment to the trolleys, and her driver in particular, would soon be at an end. However, Gummy was not finished with her yet.

In City Road on the approach to the Old Street crossing, the 611 once again gathered speed. The few late-night passengers that were on board didn't really notice, for despite Peggy's reservations about the 'monster', it was always an exceptionally quiet and smooth ride. However, the moment it reached Old Street station on the other side of the road, both traction wires on the top of the bus suddenly jumped the overhead hanger wires, bringing the vehicle to an abrupt halt. Peggy immediately leaped off the bus platform, and as soon as she shone her torch on the offending wires, she knew exactly what had happened.

'Got a problem 'ave yer, miss?'

Peggy turned her torch beam on to Gummy's grinning face. 'I told you this would happen,' she protested. 'How many times have I told you, Cyril?'

'Why don't yer stop complainin' an' go an' get yer poles out?' he retorted, taking a dog-end from behind his ear.

'Well, are you going to help me?' she asked, agitated. 'It's not going to be easy doing this in the blackout.'

'Yer've got *yer* job,' he replied dismissively, 'an' I've got mine. So if yer don't want ter upset the customers, yer'd better get on wiv it!' With that, he turned his back on her and returned to the driver's cab.

Peggy cursed him under her breath, then immediately concentrated her attention on locating the bamboo pole in its holder beneath the vehicle. She breathed a sigh of relief to find it was there, for she had heard of some crews who had got out on the road only to find themselves in a similar predicament to her own, but with no bamboo pole on board. After sliding the pole out of its holder, she began the laborious and tiring job of lifting the long cumbersome pole to the upright position, and using its grappling hook to catch the topmost part of one of the renegade trolley arms. Her problem, however, was trying to hold the bamboo pole and the torch at the same time, and because of this, every attempt she made failed.

'Can I give yer a 'and, mate?'

To Peggy, the male passenger's voice at her side sounded like a gift from Heaven.

' 'Ere – give us the torch.'

'Oh, thank you so much,' Peggy said, handing him her torch.

Even with the man shining the torch beam on to the overhead wires, it was still a struggle to reconnect the trolley arms. But after several tries, she finally succeeded in getting the first one on line.

' 'Ow much longer, mate?' moaned some whining female passenger from the bus platform, who in the dark seemed to be smoking herself to death with impatience.

'Give the gel a chance!' the man yelled back. 'This ain't an easy job, yer know.' He lowered his voice. 'Take no notice of 'er,' he said to Peggy. 'She's gettin' late fer 'er customers!'

'I 'eard that!' growled the girl tetchily.

'Shouldn't listen ter uvver people's conversations!' Peggy's helper called back.

Peggy struggled on. 'If I can . . . just get . . . this . . . Blast!' She cursed as the second trolley arm slipped off the overhead wire.

'Take yer time, gel,' said her helper. 'There's no rush . . .'

As the man spoke, the air-raid siren sounded.

'Oh no!' gasped Peggy. 'Cyril!' she yelled. 'Can't you help?'

Once again, her helper came up trumps. Taking hold of the bamboo pole with her, they both gradually managed to guide the offending second trolley arm back on to the overhead wires.

'Gotcha!' came the helper's triumphant cry, accompanied by loud applause from the few bus passengers on board and a group of onlookers who had gathered to watch before rushing to take cover.

With the continued help of the male passenger, Peggy quickly replaced the bamboo pole back in its holder, and got back on to the bus platform.

'Thank you so much!' Peggy said to her helper. 'I don't know what I'd have done without you.'

'No trouble, mate!' he replied. 'No trouble at all. But if I was you I'd give yer driver a good kick up the arse!'

There was nothing in this world that Peggy would have liked to do more, but all she could do at that moment was to ring the driver's bell several times, knowing full well that it would infuriate him. When he refused to budge, she walked along the lower deck to the front, tapped with her knuckles on his window from the inside and, directing her torch beam directly on to the side of his face she called: 'Driver – you may go!'

Gummy turned and gave her a look of thunder, but as the first ack-ack gunfire echoed out from the distance, he reluctantly drove off.

The All Clear sounded just as the 611 was pulling into the forecourt at the Holloway Bus Garage. Most of the bus crews who had finished their night shift were now emerging from the shelters, and those who were not kipping down for the night in the emergency quarters were using bicycles, the late-night staff service, or any means at their disposal for getting back to their own homes.

The last person Peggy expected to see as she stepped off the bus platform was Leo. 'What are *you* doing here at this time of night?' she asked. 'You're not on late shift, are you?'

'I fought yer'd like me ter walk yer home,' he replied cheekily. 'I don't believe in young gels bein' out on their own in the blackout.'

They moved off together towards the conductor's check-in room. 'May I remind you that I'm a local girl now,' she said, as they went. 'Just round the corner in Marlborough Road, with Elsie. When Mussolini the cat isn't licking my face, I get a wonderful night's sleep there.'

'You wouldn't if *I* was wiv yer,' he said, grabbing her round the waist and squeezing her.

'Leo, stop it!' she said unconvincingly, as one of the mechanics came out from the adjoining workshop, and brushed past them.

'Ter tell yer the trufe, Peggs,' Leo said, bringing her to a halt, 'the real reason I wanted ter see yer was not just ter walk yer 'ome, it's 'cos I've got somefin' I want ter tell yer – you know, wot we talked about on 'Ampstead 'Eath the uvver day.'

Peggy sighed. 'Do we have to talk about it now, Leo?' she said wearily. 'I've just had one hell of a shift.'

'I'm leavin' 'ome.'

Peggy did a double take. 'What?'

'I've made up me mind,' he said. 'If you can do it, so can I. Alf Grundy says if I want I can move in any time wiv 'im an' 'is missus.'

'I don't believe it,' said Peggy. 'I *won't* believe it – until it happens.'

'Well, it's goin' to,' he replied confidently. 'So yer'd better start gettin' used ter it.' He found it hard to accept that she still doubted him. 'So – wot d'yer fink?' he said. 'Am I makin' the right move? Am I doin' wot yer want?'

'For God's sake, Leo,' she said, 'it's not what *I* want. It's *your* life. You've got to sum things up and make your own decisions. The more important thing is – what does *she* say?'

'Who?'

'Who d'you think?'

'Mum?' He hesitated. 'I 'aven't told 'er yet.'

Peggy shook her head, and started to move off. But Leo quickly held her back.

'I'm goin' ter, Peggs!' he assured her. 'Honest ter God I'm goin' ter. But I've got ter pick an' choose the right moment. Don't try an' make me run before I can walk. I've bin under 'er fumb fer years. When I get out, I want it to be fer good.'

She gradually warmed to him. 'I'm sorry, Leo,' she said guiltily. 'I sound as though I'm bullying you all the time, just like your mother. But it's one thing to *want* to do something, and quite another to actually *do* it.'

'I'm *goin'* ter do it, Peggs,' he said. 'Believe me. An' when I get me call-up again, the only person I'm coming back to is you.'

He led her into the shadows by the outside door, and kissed her gently. This time she responded fully.

'Well, well. Now 'ere's a touchin' little scene.'

They parted, to find Peggy's driver, Gummy, standing over them.

'This is none of your business, Cyril,' said Peggy.

'Wos the matter wiv yer?' Gummy said, puffing on his dog-end. 'Ain't yer never got nuffin' nice ter say ter yer driver?'

Peggy could feel Leo's tension, so she took hold of his arm and tried to lead him into the building.

'Do I know you, mate?' Gummy asked Leo.

Leo turned to face him. 'No, but I know you,' he replied.

'Yer from that lot across the road, in't yer? The 'Olloway chug-chug boys!'

Leo was taut. Peggy could see the anger rising in him, and was afraid he was about to hit Gummy.

'Well, let me tell yer somefin', my friend,' persisted Gummy. 'Yer wanna keep an eye on this gelfriend of yours. She's pretty dodgy in 'er job at the moment. Got our passengers in a right ol' stew ternight.'

'That's nonsense, Cyril, and you know it!' protested Peggy. 'If you hadn't driven that bus like a lunatic, we'd never have jumped those wires.'

'You just watch it, Miss mouf an' trousers!' blurted Gummy, flicking his dog-end to the ground. 'Just remember yer still on free munfs' probation. That trolley-bus licence yer're wearin' is temp'rary. One word from me an' yer've lost it!'

Peggy could restrain Leo no longer. 'Wos yer problem, mate?' he spluttered angrily.

'*My* problem?' Gummy asked. '*My* problem is bein' lumbered wiv amateurs like this who they put on my bus wivout any trainin', wivout any savvy er life on the buses. Before I could get this job, I 'ad ter do weeks er bleedin' trainin' out at Isleworf. But once *this* lot put on a pretty uniform they fink they know it all.'

'There's a war on, Cyril!' Peggy reminded him. 'It's no one's fault that women have to fill men's places when they're called up. There isn't time to do the training as it used to be done.'

'The likes er you wouldn't know 'ow ter do this job if yer spent the 'ole er yer lives on it! The only fing *you'd* be any good at,' he took a sly glance at Leo, 'is a good ol' bunk down!'

Leo waited no more. In a flash he lunged at Gummy, and landed a hard fist on his jaw.

'No, Leo . . . !'

It was too late. Gummy toppled back, missed his footing and ended up sprawled out on the cold stone ground. He slowly recovered, rubbed his jaw, and gave Leo and Peggy a look of thunder. 'OK, chug-chug boy,' he spluttered, a trickle of blood running down from the side of his mouth, 'if that's the way yer want it – that suits me fine!'

Peggy grabbed hold of Leo and led him off. But as they turned, they found themselves surrounded by a group of shocked and bewildered onlookers.

Chapter 19

Divisional Superintendent Peter Foster had always hated disciplinary proceedings. It was the one area of his work with London Transport that he dreaded, especially in war time when, to his mind, there were more important things to think about. Now in his early fifties, he had been with the company for just over thirty years and during that time he had dismissed about seven employees, albeit reluctantly in the majority of cases, but absolutely necessary in the case of two which involved theft in the staff locker rooms. He was also a family man, with four kids of his own, so he knew only too well the pain a loss of a job could mean to a breadwinner who had a wife and young mouths to feed. That's why he had not looked forward to this meeting in the area manager's office.

'Take my word fer it, sir,' said Gummy, who was sporting a swollen jaw, ''e come at me fer no reason at all. All I wanted was a quiet word about the shift wiv me conductress, an' this is wot I get.' He squirmed in agony as he felt his aching jaw.

Leo, sitting with Peggy opposite the superintendent's desk, smirked.

The superintendent noticed this. 'You're from Kingsdown, across the road,' he said, referring to some notes on his desk. 'Is that right, Quincey?'

'Yes, sir.'

'What were you doing over here?'

Peggy looked down at her lap as Leo replied, 'I came over ter speak ter Peggs 'ere.'

'What about?'

Leo hesitated. 'Personal, sir.'

'I see.' The superintendent flicked a quick look at Peggy. 'Was it urgent?'

Leo shrugged. 'Not really, sir.'

'Were you on duty at the time?'

Peggy answered for him. 'Neither of us was, sir,' she said. 'I'd just come back from evening shift.'

The superintendent nodded without reacting. Then he leaned back in his chair. 'So what was the fight all about?' he asked all three of them.

Gummy was quick to reply. 'An unprovoked attack, sir,' he insisted.

'Yes, Cyril,' said the superintendent. 'But there must have been a reason.'

'The *reason*, sir,' Gummy said, refusing to let the others get a word in, 'is that I'm not satisfied with this gel as me conductress.'

'Oh really?' asked the superintendent. 'Why is that?'

'She don't know nuffin', sir,' replied Gummy. 'Ask 'er ter do somefin' – anyfin' – an' all I get is lip.'

'That's not true, Cyril!' protested Peggy. 'You never *ask* me to do anything. You demand!'

'Thank you, Miss Thornton,' interrupted the superintendent. 'Let's keep this calm, shall we?'

Peggy and Leo exchanged a look of sheer hopelessness, recognising what a bad sign it was that the superintendent was calling Gummy by his first name, and that he was showing distinct signs of bias. Going through Peggy's mind was the thought that not only would this incident spell the end of her short career as a clippie, but that it would almost certainly mean the sack for Leo.

'I see you're still on three months' probation with us, Miss Thornton,' said the superintendent, glancing casually at his notes again. 'And that you're on temporary transfer from Kingsdown Road? Is that right?'

Here it comes, thought Peggy. 'Yes, sir,' she replied.

'D'you find it difficult working on the trolleys?'

'It hasn't been easy, sir.'

'Yer see!' interrupted Gummy. 'She admits it!'

'I'm not admitting anything!' she snapped. 'I'm as capable of doing the job as *anyone*!'

'Then why couldn't yer even hook those arms back on the wires last night – wivout gettin' one of the passengers ter 'elp yer?'

'Only because it was during the blackout!' she insisted. 'If I can't get help from my own driver, what else can I do?'

'Yer see!' ranted Gummy to the superintendent. 'See 'ow lippy she gets!'

The superintendent held up the palms of his hands to calm them all down. 'I have to say,' he said, 'that this is not the kind of behaviour we expect from our employees. Times are bad enough without the staff getting at each other's throats.'

Gummy grinned smugly. He took this as a very clear reprimand for both Peggy and Leo.

The superintendent turned directly to him. 'Thank you, Cyril,' he said. 'I don't think there's any need to detain you any longer. Why don't you get back to your wife and family?'

'Fank yer, sir,' said Gummy, getting up from his chair.

'Oh, by the way, how *are* your family?' asked the superintendent, just as Gummy was leaving.

Gummy's face lit up. 'Oh, they're well, sir, fank yer, fank yer very much indeed, sir.' He took one last smug look at Peggy and Leo, and left.

Once he had gone, Peggy and Leo waited for the worst.

'Do you smoke?' asked the superintendent, picking up a packet of Player's Weights from his desk.

Peggy and Leo looked up with a start. 'No, sir,' Peggy replied.

'How about you, Quincey?'

Leo looked confused. 'Er – yes, sir,' he said, taking a cigarette out of the packet the superintendent was holding out to him. 'Fank yer, sir.'

He and the superintendent lit up together.

'Been dying for this all morning,' said the superintendent. 'That's the effect poor old Gummy has on one.'

Peggy and Leo couldn't believe what they were hearing.

'You mustn't take him too seriously,' said the superintendent. 'But you can't afford to ignore him either.' He took a deep puff of his cigarette, and relaxed back in his chair. 'I've known him a long time. Unfortunately, he's always been a pain in the arse.'

Peggy and Leo hardly knew where to look.

'You don't have to be embarrassed,' continued the superintendent. 'Poor old Gummy has quite a reputation. This isn't the first time he's created about absolutely nothing at all.' He grinned to himself. 'Not that a punch on the jaw is quite nothing at all!'

Leo contained a smile.

The superintendent puffed on his cigarette and looked them both over. 'Are you two going together?' he asked. 'No, don't answer that. It's none of my business. I only ask because if you are, it's probably one of the reasons why it's getting up Gummy's nose.' He looked at Peggy. 'D'you think that's the case?' he asked.

Peggy shook her head. 'I think it's simply because he doesn't like me,' she replied.

'Because you talk posh – or because you're a woman in a man's job?'

'Both.'

The superintendent smiled. 'He's not alone, you know,'

he said. 'There are plenty of blokes around like him who think the same. Not only on the buses either.'

'We've only been brought in to help until the war's over,' said Peggy.

The superintendent smiled knowingly. 'Maybe,' he replied. 'And what about you, Leo?' he asked. 'Chip off the old block, eh?'

Leo was puzzled. 'Sir?'

'I knew your dad well – when he worked up here on the trolleys.'

Leo lowered his eyes.

'You don't have to feel guilty,' said the superintendent. 'Reg was a first-class mechanic – one of the best. Bit of a temper, though. Like father, like son, eh?'

Leo smiled half-heartedly.

'I never agreed when they – did what they did,' said the superintendent. 'When someone makes a mistake, they should be given a second chance. A person who makes one big mistake and doesn't get a second chance to put it right has to pay for it for the rest of his or her life. In my opinion, that's not fair – that's not fair at all. The same thing happened to me – years ago, when I was stupid enough to walk out on my wife for another woman. I made a mistake, and I've regretted it ever since. Poor old Reg. Yes ... I always felt sorry for him.' He looked up and found Peggy and Leo looking at him. 'Point is, where does this leave you two?'

'The one thing I have to say, Superintendent,' said Peggy, 'is that there's no way I can go on working with this man. Everything I do is wrong. Ever since I came across to trolley buses, I've dreaded going out on the road with him.'

'You don't have to any more,' replied the Superintendent. 'We have a new intake arriving within the next few days. I see no reason why you shouldn't get back to the number 14s after the weekend.'

Peggy glowed. 'You mean it?' she asked excitedly.

'Of course I mean it,' replied the superintendent, getting up from his desk. 'I was talking to Frosty the other day, and he's getting withdrawal symptoms not having you around!'

'Oh, thank you, sir!' said Peggy effusively. 'Thank you so much!'

'And as for you, young man,' he said, turning to Leo. 'I know it won't be long before you go off for your call-up, but until then do me a favour, and try to remember not to mix business with pleasure!'

'I will, sir,' replied Leo with a broad grin.

'*And*,' the superintendent added, 'keep your fists in your pockets – OK?'

Leo nodded.

Once they were outside, Peggy and Leo noticed Gummy waiting to see their reaction as they left the office. He was disappointed to see that they didn't look as though the world had fallen in on them. And he couldn't believe it when they both went across to him.

'No 'ard feelin's, mate?' said Leo, offering his hand.

Bewildered, Gummy took Leo's hand, and quivered visibly as it was shaken hard.

'Bye, Gummy – oh, sorry – Cyril,' said Peggy, grinning mischievously. 'Don't drive too fast now.'

With that, she and Leo walked off hand in hand together – leaving one very irritated trolley-bus driver to watch them go.

Catherine Thornton sat at dinner in silence with her husband and mother-in-law. Honouring her pledge to Peggy to stay on for the sake of her mother, Mrs Bailey had cooked them all a delicious meal of roast chicken, baked potatoes, green cabbage, parsnips, and carrots, followed by a light caramel custard. But since Peggy's departure, there had been a great tension in the household, which was what had resulted in Alice threatening to move into a hotel. So far, however, and much to Catherine's disappointment, the old lady's threat had not been carried out, and to make matters worse, Thornton had strongly objected to his wife taking up voluntary work for the WVS without consulting him. But it was Alice Thornton in particular who was most disturbed by the signs that Catherine was seeking her own kind of independence.

'Why are you doing housework when you employ a domestic?' she complained irritably, when Catherine collected the dishes at the end of the meal and started to wash them in the kitchen sink.

'Mrs Bailey only works until six o'clock, Mother,' Catherine replied, carrying on with what she was doing. 'We're very lucky to have anyone to work for us at all at a time like this.'

'Poppycock!' replied Alice. 'My neighbour Cynthia Buckhurst has three full-time domestics. She doesn't have to do a thing.'

'Then perhaps you should go and stay with her,' suggested Catherine. 'It would be so much cheaper than staying in a hotel.'

The old lady swung her son a look of outrage. Thornton ignored it, wiped his mouth on his napkin, got up from the table, and left the room. Alice immediately got up to follow him.

'Oh, by the way, Mother,' Catherine said, as the old lady was about to leave the room. 'I shall be on duty tonight, so you'll be able to use the Morrison shelter on your own.'

'Out again?' Alice asked haughtily. 'Is this going to be a regular habit?'

'I shall be making beds up for homeless people in the church hall,' replied Catherine, without turning to look back at her. 'We have a duty to look after them, especially the elderly.'

'I would have thought that duty starts at home,' sniffed the old lady.

Catherine turned briefly from the washing-up. 'Whatever gave you that idea?' she asked.

In the sitting room, Thornton made up the fire, then collected a cigar from his humidor on the mantelpiece.

'Are you going to do *nothing* about your wife?' demanded Alice as she entered the room.

Thornton looked back at her whilst lighting his cigar.

'You should be careful,' the old lady warned, as she sat down in her usual chair by the fire. 'That woman is getting out of hand.'

'I'm afraid I haven't the faintest idea what you're talking about, Mother,' replied Thornton, picking up the day's copy of *The Times* from his own chair, and sitting there.

'Did you know she's going out again tonight?'

'Really?'

'Well, don't you care?' The old lady's eyes were like saucers. 'Your own wife out all night on her own?'

'Catherine is a grown woman, Mother,' Thornton replied, nonchalantly sorting through the pages of his newspaper. 'I'm sure she's perfectly capable of taking care of herself.'

Alice looked at him in total bewilderment. She was convinced that her son had taken leave of his senses. In fact she thought the entire household had taken leave of its senses. First that domestic woman's impertinence, then Peggy leaving home, and now this. She tapped her fingers impatiently on the arm of her chair, glaring at her son, who was clearly more interested in reading a newspaper than discussing a very serious situation with his own mother. She aimlessly looked around the room. She had never liked the place; it not only had no taste but it also lacked style and dignity. She was bored, beginning to feel unwanted. Oh, what a mistake she'd made by coming here in the first place. She should have gone to Harpenden with Herbert, except that she couldn't bear that brother of his. For God's sake, how much longer were they going to take to repair The Towers, she asked herself? She felt safe and secure there. It was the only place where she could say and do what she thought without having to worry herself about what others think.

'You don't mind this job she's doing then?' she asked caustically.

Thornton peered over the top of his newspaper. 'I beg your pardon, Mother?' he said. 'What did you say?'

Alice took an angry deep breath. 'I said,' she repeated tetchily, 'you don't mind her doing this job that takes her out all night?'

Thornton collapsed the newspaper on to his lap. 'Mother,' he replied with an irritated sigh, 'I am Catherine's husband, not her gaoler. If she feels she wants to do something, has to do something, then it's no business of mine.'

'No business?' Alice sat bolt upright in her chair. 'Your own wife goes walking around London in the middle of the night, in the middle of an air raid, and you say it's no business of *yours*? My God, Robert! What's happened to you? You were never brought up to be like this. I never gave birth to a son who would one day lose complete control over his own family.'

'I don't want *control* over my family, Mother!' he snapped, getting up and slamming his newspaper down on to his chair. 'I want their love, I want their respect, I want their care. It's something I've never had, something I've never worked for. But I've got to start doing something about it now. I've got to make up for lost time.' He suddenly realised that she was staring at him in absolute horror and incomprehension. 'You don't know what this is all about, do you, Mother?' he asked. 'Well, you will. I've got an awful lot to learn, but one thing I know is that I've got to start building my life again in a different way, in *my* way, and not yours!' To her amazement, he went to her, stooped low and gently kissed her on her forehead. 'We're never too old to learn, my darling,' he said softly. '*Neither* of us.'

Alice watched him leave the room; she was stunned. Then for several moments she just sat back in her chair in a state of shock and disbelief. She didn't know what to do or what to think. All she could feel at this precise moment was that her son had gone stark raving mad. How was she going to deal with this, she asked herself? She wouldn't be able to stay in this house a moment longer, that was now quite certain. But where would she go, who could she turn to? Oh yes, she could move into a hotel until The Towers was finished, but that wouldn't solve the problem. For some reason or another, her son was deserting her; he didn't need her any more, he didn't need the advice of his own mother, a mother who had brought him up to believe that a family needed to be held together not by love and understanding, but by a strong will and the guidance of those who had the experience to *know*. But she couldn't do it alone. She was now too old to cope with insurrection in her family without someone to lean on. But who? She closed her eyes, and leaned her head back. As she sat there, she could smell the eau-de-Cologne she had dabbed behind her ears before she came down to dinner. It made her feel drowsy, lonely, rejected. But only because the man who had given it to her for a Christmas present was Herbert, the one person she knew she could always have turned to at times like this. But even he wasn't around any more.

Pam Warner knew she had to do something, but she didn't know what. Ever since the beginning of the previous week when she had told Leo about Marge Quincey's involvement in their relationship, she had hardly slept a wink. Over and over again she had recalled what she had done in The Eaglet that night, and every time she thought about it, she cringed. But what else could she do? She was trapped between two situations and the only way to sort it out was to tell the truth. And yet, the only thing she had achieved was to anger Leo so much that he wouldn't even talk to her now. How could she have been so stupid? Why couldn't she just tell Leo that she didn't love him and that if he wanted to go with someone else that was fine by her? No. It wasn't as easy as that. There were too many complications. One way and another, she needed him, and that meant, for the time being, she needed Marge Quincey too. So what to do? Who to turn to? She had an idea; it was risky, but it was worth a try. If she was ever going to get Leo to trust her again, if she was ever going to get him to help her, she would have to come clean with the person he really loved.

'Peggy Fornton?' asked one of the clippies at the Kingsdown Road garage when Pam enquired if Peggy was on duty. 'She's over on trolleys across the road. Dunno if she's on duty though.'

Pam didn't know what the hell she was doing; going to see Peggy was like playing with dynamite, except that it might clear the air a bit if Peggy could hear from Pam herself that there was definitely nothing going on between her and Leo any more.

Pam had never been to the trolley-bus depot before.

Whenever she had been to meet Leo, it had usually been when he had been doing maintenance work on a petrol bus in the Kingsdown Road forecourt. In either place, however, she had always felt very conspicuous, although she had to admit to herself that she had never actually done anything to deter the wolf whistles she invariably got when she waited inside for Leo. In many ways, Pam was a smart girl, far shrewder than most people thought, and certainly far removed from the dumb blonde most men took her for. It was just that she had plenty of physical attributes and knew how to use them. It was, however, these same attributes that had got her into such a mess, and after what had happened to her during these past few months, she knew that she only had herself to blame.

When she got to the trolley-bus depot, the first thing she discovered was that Peggy had just completed her transfer, and was off until after the weekend when she would be returning to the number 14s at Kingsdown Road. Pam breathed a sigh of relief to know that she had been given a chance to abandon her reckless idea. But just as she was about to leave the depot forecourt, someone called to her.

'What do you want?'

Pam turned with a start to find Peggy making towards her.

'I'm told you're looking for me?' said Peggy tersely, as she approached.

Pam was taken completely off guard. 'I – I—' she spluttered. 'My name's Pam Warner.'

'Thank you,' returned Peggy. 'I know who you are.'

'I was wonderin' if we could 'ave a chat.'

'What about?'

'About me an' Leo.'

'I have nothing to say to you.' Peggy turned away.

'*Please!*' begged Pam. 'Just a few minutes. At least give me the chance ter explain.'

'What's there to explain?' asked Peggy. 'You've had a relationship with Leo, and you don't want it to end.'

'That's not true,' said Pam.

Peggy stared at her. 'What did you say?'

'I said it's not true,' replied Pam. 'Leo an' me are finished. It's all over. But I still need 'im. I need 'is 'elp. If yer'll just let me explain I'll tell yer. But yer've got ter believe me. It's all over between me an' Leo. I swear ter God it is.'

Although it was already way past blackout time, there was very little cloud cover, which gave three-quarters of the moon a chance to cast some light down on to the coal yard in Hornsey Road. But it was an eerie sort of a light, and even the presence of a small moggy slinking past the back wall cast a shadow of such gigantic proportions that it looked like a giant creature from the jungle.

Inside the house, Marge Quincey, who had temporarily left the kids with Reg in the shelter, was taking the opportunity to have a few moments on her own. Despite her outwardly boundless energy, she always did her best to conceal the weariness that from time to time was in danger of engulfing her. Ever since she'd been a child she had had a restless mind; she had to move on without standing still; there was never ever any time to listen because to her way of thinking *she* always had the most interesting things to say. But her overactive mind had brought her endless problems, for it made her intolerant of anyone who questioned either her opinions or what *she* thought was for the best. Over the past few months this had become abundantly clear when she tried to arrange the direction of her eldest son's life. There had never been any doubt in her mind that what she was doing was in the boy's best interests; the thought that he would be getting himself mixed up with those who were not his own kind filled her with loathing and disdain. But despite all her efforts, things were not going as she had planned. Until now, she had not only failed in keeping Leo away from his 'madam on the hill', but there were now signs that 'little' Pam Warner was not being as co-operative as Marge had at first hoped. As she sat alone in the kitchen parlour, in the dark, sipping a cup of cocoa, and with only the red glow of the fire embers in the grate reflected in her eyes, it was this thought that was now plaguing her mind more than anything else. It was therefore quite a shock when someone suddenly turned on the light switch and practically blinded her.

'Wot're yer doin' in the dark?' asked Leo, who was standing in the open doorway.

'I'm tryin' ter get five minutes on me own!' growled Marge, shielding her eyes.

Leo turned off the light again. Then he sat in a chair opposite her in front of the grate.

'Wot yer doin' 'ome so early?' asked Marge. 'Pubs don't close fer anuvver hour.'

Leo ignored her catty remark. He had grown so used to them. 'Mum,' he said, in a quiet, restrained voice, 'why did yer set up me an' Pam?'

This was the last thing Marge expected, and it took her by surprise. 'Don't know wot yer're talkin' about,' she replied, trying not to expose her weakness.

'Oh, I fink yer do,' replied Leo. 'That time up the Calley Market. Yer fixed it fer Pam an' me ter meet at that junk stall. Don't bovver ter lie, 'cos she told me yer did.'

Marge did not respond right away. Her mind was too preoccupied with Pam, and how she would like to strike her stone dead. ' 'Ave I committed any crime?' she asked haughtily. 'As I recall, Pam Warner was the one who was wettin' her drawers ter meet yer. All I did was ter 'elp. I fought she was a nice gel. Just shows yer 'ow wrong yer can be.'

Leo hesitated, then got up. He collected his usual dog-end from behind his ear, and lit it. He strolled to the window, eased back the blackout blind and peered out into the yard below. The smell of kippers Marge had cooked for Reg's tea was still lingering throughout the room. 'It wasn't 'er, was it, Mum?' he asked, the glow from his dog-end like a beacon in the dark. 'It wasn't Pam who wanted it. It was you.'

'What *is* this?' retorted Marge, sipping her cocoa. 'A bleedin' cross-examination?'

'No, Mum,' he replied. 'It's me, tryin' ter work out why yer want ter get so involved in my life?'

' 'Ere we go again!' sighed Marge, irritated that she was being confronted. 'I don't know wot that little cow's bin sayin' ter yer, but it strikes me she's turned out ter be a real troublemaker.'

'Yer weren't sayin' that before, Mum,' Leo reminded her. 'Yer've always said wot a marvellous gel she is, an' 'ow lucky I am ter 'ave someone like 'er ter go out wiv.'

'Well, I've changed me mind, ain't I!' In a fit of rage, she got up from her seat and rushed across to turn on the light.

Leo immediately sealed the blackout blind.

'So wot d'yer expect *me* ter do about it?' sniffed Marge, thumping her empty cup down into its saucer. 'Go down on bended knees an' say 'ow sorry I am?'

Leo watched her agitation in despair. 'No, Mum,' he said quite calmly. 'Yer don't 'ave ter do nuffin' like that. Wot's 'appened is no one's fault 'cept mine. I should've known better. I should've seen wot was goin' on. I don't blame yer, an' I don't blame Pam. So –' he flicked his dog-end into the grate – 'I want ter make sure that I put fings right fer boaf er yer, fer all of us.' He paused. 'That's why I'm goin' ter move out.'

Marge froze. 'Move out?' she asked, staring him out. 'Wot're yer talkin' about?'

'I'm leavin' 'ome, Mum,' he replied. 'It's time I learned 'ow ter stand on me own two feet.'

'Yer're doin' no such fing!'

Marge's words, although delivered calmly and without force, cut right through Leo. 'It's the best way, Mum, believe me,' he said. 'I can't 'ave yer runnin' me life any more. It's just – wrong. I know I'm not twenty-one yet, an' I know yer can stop me if yer want. But if yer did, it'd be wrong, 'cos I'd find a way – *some* way – ter get away from yer.'

'Is that wot yer want, son?' she asked. 'Is that wot yer really want – ter get away from me? Well, yer won't 'ave ter wait long.'

He watched as she went to the dresser drawer and brought out a buff-coloured envelope.

' 'Ere,' she said, handing it to him. 'It was 'and delivered when yer was at work today. Yer won't 'ave ter worry now. Now yer can get away from me wivout feelin' too guilty.'

She calmly left the room, leaving him to read the letter which contained the revised date of his call-up.

At the Holloway depot, Peggy and Pam sat talking quietly together in the dark lower deck of an out-of-service trolley bus. Peggy hadn't wanted to talk to this girl, but she was intrigued to know why Pam wanted to see her. It was an odd thing, but even in the first few minutes that they had been sitting there, Peggy had discovered that she didn't dislike the girl nearly as much as she thought she was going to. Although they were different people from totally different backgrounds, Peggy found Pam immediately appealing, and understood only too well why any man would be attracted to her.

'I don't want ter marry Leo,' Pam said, her voice only barely audible. 'I never wanted ter marry 'im. Oh, I fancied 'im all right. I still do. But I never wanted ter spend the rest of me life wiv 'im.'

'Then why didn't you tell him so?' asked Peggy.

There was a moment's hesitation before Pam answered. 'I couldn't,' she replied. 'I needed 'im.'

'Needed him?'

Although Pam had a tiny voice, there was an underlying strength in it. 'I've already told yer 'ow Leo's mum got me an' 'im tergevver,' she said with difficulty. 'Well – it wasn't quite like that. Yer see, a few munfs before I met 'im – I did somefin' stupid. I got mixed up wiv someone who I didn't really like at all.' She hesitated again. 'D'yer mind if I smoke?' she asked.

'No,' replied Peggy impatiently.

Pam's hands were shaking as she searched out a packet of fags from her coat pocket, extracted a cigarette in the dark, and lit up. 'Leo don't know I do this,' she said, inhaling and exhaling. 'I only 'ave one every so often – ter calm me nerves.' She waited a moment, and then continued, 'This bloke – I met 'im at a servicemen's dance up the Town 'All. 'E's a corporal in the RAF – good-lookin' – *too* good-lookin' – that was the trouble. Anyway, we went out tergevver a coupla times, always on the binge, always pub 'oppin'. I don't know why I did it. I don't really like booze.' She drew on her fag nervously. 'The crux of it all was we slept tergevver, just one night, at this B and B place up Paddin'ton way. I din't find out till after that it was a well-known knockin' shop.' She hesitated again. 'Ter cut a long story short – I got meself a bun.' She could tell by Peggy's lack of response that she didn't know what she was talking about. 'Yer know – "bun in the oven" the blokes call it – in the family way.' In the dark, she could hear Peggy's sigh of despair. 'Yeah, I know,' said Pam. 'Stupid bleedin' fing ter do. But there it was – it 'appened, an' I was lumbered wiv it. Well – soon after I found out, I told this bloke. I was quite convinced that'd be the last I'd ever see of 'im. Men're all the same: first sign er trouble an' they're off. But – yer know what? It din't turn out like that. 'E said 'e 'ad no intention of dumpin' me, an' that 'e'd stick by me wotever 'appened.'

'And has he?' asked Peggy.

'Oh yeah,' Pam replied acidly. ' 'E's stuck by me all right. That's the trouble. Yer see, a coupla days later I found I didn't 'ave a bun after all. Must've made a mistake – panicked when I was late. But it was true.'

'But you must have been so relieved,' said Peggy. 'If you disliked this man so much, all you had to do was to walk away from him.'

'No,' replied Pam, with a deep sigh. 'It wasn't as easy as that.'

'Why not?'

Pam faltered before answering. 'Because I'd already got married to 'im,' she replied, with a deep frustrating sigh. 'That's why . . .'

Chapter 20

Peggy's first journey with Frosty back on the number 14 was like a breath of fresh air. For her, being free of Gummy and his dictatorial ways was like being released from prison, and she felt like a new person. Although she had only been on transfer for two or three weeks, when she arrived for her first split turn at the Kingsdown Road depot, she was greeted like a long-lost friend, especially by Frosty, who, the moment he saw her, threw his arms round her and hugged her as if she was his own daughter. The other clippies were also delighted to see her and when she went into the canteen the first thing Effie Sommers did was to pour her a free cup of tea. Even Alf Grundy and Sid Pierce came in to welcome her back, and when she checked in for her tickets and change, everyone told her how glad they were to see her. She felt a warm glow to know that after a shaky start to her clippie's career, she had actually been missed. However, after a weekend in which her thoughts had been dominated by her meeting with Pam Warner, her mind was now in a state of turmoil as to what to do next. Would she be right to keep so much from Leo, she kept asking herself? She now understood why Pam needed Leo so badly – not because she loved him, but because she needed him to help her get away from the man she had married. It was clearly a terrible situation, for not only had Pam kept the marriage from Leo, but also from her own parents, who would have died of shock if they'd known that their daughter had forged their consent for her to marry whilst still under age. Peggy had suddenly found herself torn between her loyalty to Leo and her promise to help Pam. But how could she do it? How could she possibly continue having her own relationship with Leo, she asked herself, whilst at the same time urging him not to desert Pam? It was an appalling dilemma for everyone concerned.

'Are you going to Queen's Gate?'

At the Piccadilly Circus stop, Peggy was snapped out of her momentary daydream by a well-dressed woman who was struggling on to the bus carrying two white poodles in her arms.

'Yes,' said Peggy, helping the woman and her dogs on to the platform. 'Top deck, please.' Peggy waited for her to climb the stairs, then followed her up.

'One adult and two dogs to Queen's Gate,' asked the woman, once she had settled.

'Penny ha'penny, please,' replied Peggy. 'No charge for the dogs.' She clipped one ticket and gave it to her. As she did so, however, one of the poodles bared her teeth and barked at Peggy.

'Stop that, Phoebe!' scolded the woman, handing over the fare to Peggy. 'I'm so sorry,' she said. 'She's a little highly strung.'

Peggy smiled, took the coins, and popped them into her leather pouch. When she looked more closely at the woman she realised that her long thin features and pointed nose closely resembled those of her two pets.

Peggy moved on. 'Any more fares up here, please?' she called, checking from side to side for any response from the few customers on the upper deck. 'Any more fares, please?' she repeated. As she turned to go back downstairs, she suddenly noticed a middle-aged man sitting in the back seat, hand raised to her. As it was now late in the afternoon and the light was gradually fading outside, she hadn't noticed him, and imagined that he must have jumped on to the bus just as it was leaving the previous stop. 'Where to, sir?' she asked, as she approached him.

'Hello,' said the man, who had a very pleasant, cultured voice, and wore a grey overcoat with a trilby hat, which was pulled so low down over his forehead that it almost covered what seemed to be soft, handsome features. 'I can't remember if this bus goes anywhere near Buckingham Palace,' he said.

'Not really,' replied Peggy. 'Best thing is to get off at Hyde Park Corner and walk down Constitution Hill. It's only two or three stops.'

'Thanks,' said the man. 'How much is that?'

'A penny, please, sir.'

The man took some coins from his overcoat pocket, and handed over the penny. 'I think you're doing a grand job,' he said as he watched Peggy clip him a ticket. 'Looks like we're going to have to rely on you girls more and more to get us through this war.'

'I think the boys are having the worst of it,' said Peggy, handing over his ticket. 'The least we can do is to hold the fort for them until they get home – providing Hitler hasn't invaded us by then, of course.'

The man gave her a reassuring smile. 'Don't worry,' he replied. 'The next time I see Mr Churchill, I'll tell him to make sure that he doesn't!'

A few minutes later, the man came down the stairs, and got off the bus. As he did so, a woman nearly collapsed with excitement as she recognised him. 'Oh my God!' she gasped.

'What's the matter?' asked Peggy as she gave the woman a helping hand to get on to the bus.

'Didn't you see who that was?' panted the woman breathlessly. 'It was Leslie Howard.'

Peggy looked vacant. 'Who?' she asked.

'*Petrified Forest*! *The Scarlet Pimpernel*! *Gone With the Wind*!' The woman was flushed with excitement. 'Don't you ever go to the pictures?'

Peggy stared at the woman and shook her head. 'No,' she replied. 'I'm afraid I don't.' As the bus pulled away from the bus stop, she peered out from the platform and watched her celebrated passenger making his way slowly off towards Constitution Hill. If he was so famous, she said to herself, then perhaps he really might get to speak to Mr Churchill.

Marge Quincey was waiting for Pam as she left Estelle's salon. It had been a long and difficult day for Pam, for not only had Mr Koenitz never stopped nagging her about practically everything she had done, but she had been worrying all day about her meeting with Peggy and whether she had been right to seek her help.

'I wanna word wiv you, Pam Warner!' growled Marge, before Pam had hardly got out the shop door. 'Foller me!'

Pam tensed herself as she meekly followed Marge and her torch beam in the dark, crossing over Seven Sisters Road to Sussex Way alongside the North London Drapery Stores. After a few minutes or so, they came to a stop in the dark near a brick-built public air-raid shelter which local residents had boycotted due to the recent adverse newspaper articles describing such places as 'death traps'.

'So wot's all this yer've bin tellin' me son?' she said angrily, making very little effort to keep her voice down.

'I – don't know wot yer mean, Mrs Quincey,' replied Pam nervously.

'You know wot I mean all right!' replied Marge. 'Since when wos *I* the one who set you two up? Who was the one who spent the 'ole evenin' in the pub leerin' at 'im, eh? Go on, tell me – *who*?'

'I din't tell Leo nuffin', Mrs Quincey,' said Pam, struggling to keep her voice low. 'Honest I didn't.'

'I don't believe yer! I don't believe anyfin' yer say. I fought we were s'pposed ter 'ave an arrangement. I fought I could trust yer.'

'Yer *can* trust me, Mrs Quincey!' insisted Pam. 'All I said ter Leo wos that if 'e don't want ter go wiv me no more, there ain't much I can do about it.'

'An' 'e's told yer that 'e don't want ter go wiv yer, 'as 'e?' asked Marge.

'More or less – yes.'

'Why? 'Cos yer've been playin' around – is that it?'

'Please, Mrs Quincey,' begged Pam, 'that's not fair.'

'It may not be fair, but that's 'ow it sounded when yer was doin' me 'air the uvver day!'

Pam was now in a real quandary. On one hand she wanted to tell Marge the truth – that in fact she didn't love Leo, but on the other, for the time being she had to hold on to him. 'Leo's got somebody else, Mrs Quincey,' she said. 'I can't just force meself on 'im.'

'Why not?' replied Marge, quite shamelessly. 'Yer 'ave done so far – wiv *my* 'elp.'

Pam suddenly felt her hackles rise. If she had her way she would tell this woman where to get off, to mind her own business and keep out of her life. But she knew she couldn't do it, because if she needed Leo, then to do that she also needed to keep on the right side of his mum.

'Wot d'yer know about this gel?'

Pam was surprised by Marge's question. 'Who?' she asked.

'Who d'yer fink?' Marge snapped. 'This madam from up the 'ill.'

Pam hesitated. 'Nuffin' really,' she replied warily. 'I know she's a clippie.'

' 'Er farver's a judge up the courts.'

'I din't know that.'

'Well, *I* do,' sniffed Marge disdainfully. ' 'Im an' me 'ave already 'ad a little chat.'

Pam was shocked. 'Yer – yer've actually met 'im?'

'That's neivver 'ere nor there,' replied Marge evasively. 'The point is, are yer serious about wantin' my son or aren't yer? I want an answer once an' fer all!'

Pam felt her heart pounding fast. The stench from an overflowing pigswill bin on the street corner nearby was making her feel sick, and if it hadn't been for the ice-cold drizzle that was beginning to fall, she would have probably brought it all up in the kerb right there and then. What could she tell this woman? How could she tell her that the moment she had got rid of the man who was holding her life to ransom, she would have no more need of either her *or* her son. 'Yer know 'ow I feel about Leo, Mrs Quincey,' she found herself replying guiltily.

Even with the drizzle settling on her headscarf, Marge felt a warm glow. 'Then s'ppose yer start doin' somefin' about it before it's too late,' she said.

'Too late?' asked Pam, puzzled.

Marge drew closer. 'The army's cancelled 'is deferment,' she said. ' 'E's got 'is call-up papers again.'

Pam gasped. 'Oh – that's terrible,' she said.

'It is an' it ain't.'

Marge was now so close that Pam was overpowered by the acrid smell of the pickled onions Marge had always been so fond of.

'Like any uvver muvver, I don't want my son ter go ter war,' said Marge, her voice now uncharacteristically reduced to a whisper, 'but it's time 'e grew up, an' if 'e 'as ter go in the army ter do it, then that's it.'

Pam couldn't believe what she was hearing. 'Yer can't

mean it, Mrs Quincey?' she asked.

'I *can* mean it, an' I do.'

'But – Leo could get killed,' she said, appalled by Marge's heartlessness.

For a brief moment there was silence from Marge, until she eventually replied, 'Leo won't get killed. 'E's too tough. 'E's a Quincey, an' I'm goin' ter be proud er 'im. But 'e's my son, an' I won't be robbed of 'im by someone who ain't 'is own kind.'

Pam's blood turned to ice. The air-raid siren wailed out across the pitch-black sky.

Ivy Biggs had boiled a kettle of water and filled her hot-water bottle. As she was getting a bit ancient now, she usually turned in quite early, but not before she'd taken her china jug round the corner to the Marlborough pub to buy her six pennyworth of draught stout. That jug was her prized possession for it had been about the only thing left to her by her dear old mum who had died of the palsy following an undiagnosed bout of septicaemia soon after Ivy had got married to her soldier boy. Ivy had never been a one for possessions so the fact that at the end of her mum's life this was all the poor woman was worth worried her not one little bit. What worried her more was losing her Harry, the soldier she'd met just before the outbreak of the First World War, and who, alongside so many of his mates, had been struck down at the Battle of Mons. These days, Ivy had little to cling to but memories, and it was memories of Harry that had kept her going all these years. That's why she was such a good downstairs neighbour to Elsie, for, like her and so many other women, Ivy had answered the call in her day to help the war effort – in her case by working in a munitions factory. However, that was a long time ago, and now there was another war, a war against ordinary people in the street, and whether there was an air raid on or not, that meant regularly taking her jug of stout and hot-water bottle down to the Anderson shelter in the back yard each night. Therefore, as the air-raid siren had sounded several hours before, she was all packed up and ready to go. 'Just orf then!' she yelled up the stairs.

Peggy immediately came out of the upstairs front parlour and appeared on the second-floor landing. 'Right you are, Mrs Biggs,' she called back. 'Sleep well!'

'Some 'opes!' returned the old girl, who was wearing her thick woollen checked dressing gown, hair in net and curlers, and Harry's cap stuck on top. 'It's so bleedin' cold down that Anderson it's enuff ter freeze the balls off a brass monkey!'

Peggy laughed. 'Good night!'

This time her call was answered by a distinctly irritable Mussolini, who was being forced to abandon his nice warm rug in front of the fire to follow his breadwinner down into the shelter.

Peggy waited until she had heard Ivy's back door open and close, and then went back into the parlour. As Elsie was on a week's transfer to Tottenham garage, Peggy was spending a lot of her spare time learning how to cook. Elsie, of course, had already been a great help, and during the short time she had been there, Peggy had learned how to fry some basic things like sausages and Spam fritters, and in the last day or so she had taken on the challenge of dried eggs which worked pretty well in cake mixtures, but when it came to omelettes they tasted like old boot leather. Tonight, she had cooked herself a beef mince and onion rissole accompanied by fried mushrooms, boiled potatoes and green cabbage with lots of white pepper, and once she'd actually finished eating it she couldn't help feeling that if dear old Mrs Bailey had been there, she would have been proud of her.

Although the air-raid siren had sounded some time before, so far there had been no sound of either oncoming raiders or anti-aircraft gunfire. Peggy therefore took this as a sign that with a bit of luck she would be able to get a good night's sleep in her own bedroom without having to join old Ivy in the Anderson shelter. Once she'd heard the nine o'clock news on the wireless, she even took the opportunity of washing out some of her smalls in the bathroom sink on the landing below, and hanging them up to dry on a washing line above the bath itself. Whilst she was doing this, there was much to occupy her mind, especially her meeting with Pam at the depot the previous evening, and what Leo's reaction was going to be when he heard about Pam's absurd marriage to a man she didn't love. After she'd built up the fire for the night in the hope that it might still be alight the following morning, she snuggled up on the sofa, and with her mind still churning over what she was going to do about Pam and Leo, her eyelids flickered, and she dozed off.

A few minutes later she was awoken by two rings on the front door bell. Collecting her torch, and wearing only her winceyette pyjamas and dressing gown, she made her way down the two flights of stairs to see who was there. Before opening the door, she switched off the passage light. When she opened the door her torch beam immediately picked out who it was that was waiting on the doorstep outside.

'Leo!'

'I'm sorry ter call on yer, Peggs,' he said with some urgency, 'but I need ter talk ter yer.'

Peggy quickly opened the door to let him in. Once she'd closed the door behind him, she switched off her torch, and turned on the light again. 'You shouldn't be out,' she said. 'The All Clear hasn't gone.'

'Can I come upstairs?' he asked.

Peggy hesitated. 'I – I don't know, Leo,' she replied falteringly. 'Elsie's away. It wouldn't be right to—'

'I've got me call-up papers,' he said, interrupting her. 'I'm leavin' next Monday week.'

Peggy froze. Then she turned and went upstairs. He followed her. Once inside the front room parlour, she closed the door behind them.

'When did you hear?' she asked.

'Came by 'and,' he replied lightly. 'Special treatment, eh? They must need me pretty bad.'

Peggy hugged him, but quickly pulled away when he tried to respond to her advance by kissing her. She crossed to the fire and warmed her hands there. He followed, and stood beside her, both of them staring into the fire.

'I shall miss you,' she said.

'Yeah – me too,' he replied. 'So wot 'appens now?'

'About what?'

'About us?' He turned to look at her. 'Will yer wait fer me?'

Peggy hesitated. 'I don't know, Leo,' she replied.

'Wot's that s'pposed ter mean?'

'It means that I really *don't* know,' she replied. 'There are so many complications, so many problems. It would be wrong of me to make a promise that I couldn't keep . . .'

'Sorry I asked,' he said, turning and making for the door.

'No, Leo!' she said, holding him back. 'Please don't get me wrong. I – love you. I don't know why, after all that's happened, but I do. But I wouldn't want you to go away expecting me to be here for you when you return when – when there are so many problems – with your family and mine. Come on,' she said, taking his arm. 'Come and sit down and let's talk about it.'

After some hesitation, he allowed her to lead him back to the sofa where they sat together, side by side, her arm snaked around his waist, her head leaning against his shoulder. For a few moments they just sat there staring thoughtfully into the fire. Then Leo finally broke the silence: 'I told 'er,' he said.

Puzzled, she turned to look at him.

'Mum,' he said. 'I 'ad it out wiv 'er. I told 'er I was goin' ter leave 'ome.'

'Leo!'

'Funny, in't it?' he said. 'It don't matter wot yer do, she's always one step ahead er yer. It was 'er who got in touch wiv the army. She told 'em Dad was much better, an' there was no need fer me ter be deferred any longer.'

Peggy was horrified. 'No . . .' she said.

Leo smiled. 'Oh yes, *my* mum,' he replied, acidly, 'is out ter get 'er own way – an' that's a fact!'

'It's – beyond me,' said Peggy. 'It's absolutely beyond me. How could she actually *want* her own son to be sent off into the army – and at a time like this?'

'She wants it,' replied Leo, without any hesitation, 'becos she'll do anyfin' she can ter keep me away from you.'

Peggy sank back into the sofa. What Leo had said had completely stunned her. She found it hard to believe that a woman who professed to love her family could stoop to such extreme measures to get her own way. As she sat there, she tried to imagine what kind of a woman this was. She had never met her, so she had no idea what she looked like. But she hoped that she didn't bear any likeness at all to Leo. Quite impetuously, she stretched out her hand, placed it behind his head, and turned him round to face her. Then she gradually drew him to her, and kissed him lightly on his lips. Unwilling to be rejected again, Leo did not respond, merely allowing her to make whatever advance

she wanted. As she parted from his lips, she eased him out
of his duffel coat. Then she got up, took the coat to the
other side of the room, and dropped it on to a chair. She
took one lingering look back at him, then turned off the
light. On her way back, she slipped out of her dressing
gown, and let it fall to the floor. By the light of the fire, she
stood briefly in front of him, and slowly undid the buttons
on her pyjama top. In response, he got up from the sofa,
and stood face to face with her. She took hold of both his
hands, and led them to her breasts. He felt them. They
were warm and firm. She sighed as he leaned down and
with his lips, gently caressed both nipples. When he
straightened up again, they kept looking into each other's
eyes whilst she removed his pullover, slid his braces from
his shoulders, then slowly undid the buttons of his shirt.
When that was done, she removed her pyjama top completely, and he did the same with his shirt. She then had to
wait whilst he sat down again, and unlaced his boots. He
stood up, and once again they faced each other.

'Are yer sure?' he asked, his voice a mere whisper.

For one brief moment, Peggy hesitated. Was this what
she *really* wanted, or was she allowing it to happen because
she was afraid that there would never be a chance like it
again? But as she looked into Leo's eyes, she knew that this
was the man she loved, this was the first man she had *ever*
loved, and she couldn't imagine loving anyone else as much
as she loved him. And now she would show him how she
felt. She would not let him go away without letting him
know just how *much* she loved him. 'I'm sure,' she replied,
softly, reassuringly. Then she gently kissed him.

Simultaneously, she slid down her pyjama bottoms and
he did the same with his trousers and underpants. Now
completely naked, he drew her close and their bodies
embraced for the first time. With their fingers, hands and

lips, they explored incessantly, first him and then her. Both were so aroused they could hardly contain themselves. After a while, he gently eased her down on her back on the sofa, then, after he had taken the necessary precautions, he lowered his entire body on to her. She curled her arms around his neck, and groaned as he slowly entered her, their two bodies now as one. When it was all over, she just wanted to lie there with him for ever, hoping that the time would never come when she would have to let him go.

Alice Thornton woke with a start. As she gradually brought her mind back into focus, she realised that she had had a nightmare about being pushed off a cliff by a huge crowd of people, all of whom had the faces of those she had known at one time or another throughout her life. It took her several minutes to pull herself round, and when she did she struggled to free herself from the metal grille cage of the Morrison shelter that had entombed her each night ever since she had sought refuge in her son's home. She cursed her daughter-in-law for not being there any more to help her, she cursed herself as she searched the room in the dark for her torch, and when she did, she cursed that too. Putting on her woollen dressing gown was also a frustrating charade, which only made her more and more irritable.

In the hall, she could hear her son's heavy breathing as he slept soundly in his usual place under the stairs. She felt like shouting to wake him up, but she thought better of it, and chose instead to go quietly upstairs. As she hadn't been able to find her walking stick in the dark, it was not easy negotiating each stair, and she had to grip the banisters hard to support herself. By the time she had reached the first-floor landing, she was finding it difficult to breathe. As she had decided to ignore whatever signs there were that an air raid was still going on outside, the first door she made for was her own room. However, just as she was about to enter, a sudden impulse caused her to change her mind, and using the beam from her torch, she moved on to her granddaughter's room.

As she had expected, Peggy's room was neat and tidy, with not a thing out of place. As the blackout blinds had not been drawn, the room was in total darkness, so she had to use her torch to move around carefully. The dressing table was completely bare, for Peggy had clearly taken her personal make-up box with her, and when Alice looked in one or two of the drawers, they too had been cleared. The beam from her torch darted from one wall to another, highlighting the empty spaces where small pictures had once hung. But her greatest shock came when she went to one of the built-in wardrobes and found that most of Peggy's dresses, reeking of mothballs, were still hanging there. Alice felt the material of one long evening dress which was made of a blue taffeta, but she thought it very common, and quickly tucked it back in. Then she found another one, this time a cream colour and made of pure silk, which Alice remembered had been a present from Peggy's father when she had reached her sixteenth birthday. But the dress that drew her closest attention was small enough to have fitted a child no older than ten. Alice took the dress out. She thought she could still smell faint traces of the sweet perfume the child had sneaked from her grandmother's bedroom, and which she had smothered all over the bosom of the dress. She sat on the edge of Peggy's bed, turned off her torch and, clasping the dress firmly in her hands, she could feel and hear the past coming back to life. '*Look at me, Grandmother! I'm a princess!*' The words echoed round and round Alice's head as in her mind's eye she could see the ten-year-old Peggy swirling around in her new dress in the grand sitting room up at The Towers. '*One day I'm going to get married and have hundreds and hundreds of children . . . !*' Alice could still hear the laughter from her afternoon bridge companions, who watched and applauded the child's effervescent performance. And then the image and the voice disappeared as quickly as they had come, although the laughter lingered on for a little longer.

When Alice had finally come out of her impromptu trip back into the past, something made her reach up with her fingertips to touch her eyes. They were moist. Why, she asked herself? What had so suddenly brought her to this state of frustrated nostalgia? And then it dawned on her. In another impulsive fit, she turned on her torch again, got up, and quickly returned the child's dress to the wardrobe. Then, as fast as her aching body would take her, she left the room.

In her own bedroom, next door, the blackout blinds were drawn, so she turned on the light, and went straight to her handbag which she had left on the bed. Quickly sorting through it, she found what she was looking for. It was a small calendar. The moment she checked through the days of January, she knew why she had suddenly been drawn to the past, to her own life, to the images of a granddaughter that she had treated with such cold indifference. Tomorrow was the twenty-eighth of January 1941. Tomorrow her granddaughter would be coming of age.

Peggy and Leo snuggled up together on the rug in front of the fire. They had both partially dressed, and had covered their shoulders with Leo's duffel coat, and Leo was just finishing off a dog-end. After their lovemaking, they were in reflective mood which they shared in a mutual silence. Peggy's mood, however, was tormented. Not only was she brooding with guilt about what she had just done, but her thoughts were flooded with wave after wave of anxiety about Pam Warner.

'So how is she?' she asked Leo quite suddenly, as though they had been discussing the subject all evening.

Leo, surprised, looked at her. 'Who?'

'Pam Warner.'

'Oh no,' he groaned, throwing off the duffel coat from his shoulders. 'We're not goin' fru all that again, are we?'

'You know, Leo,' Peggy replied, 'I don't think you should just dump her. In many ways I feel quite sorry for her.'

He looked at her in disbelief. Her face was a warm red glow from the fire's reflection. '*Sorry* fer 'er?' he spluttered. 'Fer Pam?'

'She can't have had an easy time with your mother.'

'Then she shouldn't've got involved wiv 'er in the first place. Yer know wot I fink? I fink they're boaf as bad as one anuvver.'

Peggy responded with silence for a moment. 'She must still be fond of you,' she said.

'Baloney!' Leo retorted, flicking the remains of his dog-end into the fire.

'You can't say that,' said Peggy. 'She's actually a very nice girl.'

Leo swung her a puzzled look. ''Ow would you know that?' he asked. 'Yer don't even know 'er.'

'No,' replied Peggy, quickly correcting herself, 'what I mean is, I've heard nice things about her – from Elsie and some of the others at the garage.'

'Elsie 'ates the sight of 'er,' said Leo. 'She's always called 'er a real little tart.'

'I don't think that's fair,' said Peggy. 'I'm sure Pam has feelings just like anyone else.'

' 'Ow come yer've got this concern fer Pam Warner all of

a sudden?' protested Leo sarcastically. 'Speshully when yer ain't even met 'er.'

'It's not concern,' replied Peggy evasively. 'It's just that I feel that if you've had a relationship with someone – like you have with Pam – then the least you can do is to stand by her when she gets into trouble.'

Leo was getting curious. 'Peggs, wot's this all about?'

Peggy hesitated before answering. 'Leo,' she asked, 'what would you say if you knew that Pam was seeing someone else?'

'I'd say bleedin' good luck ter 'er! Glad ter get 'er off me back!'

'And what would you say if that someone was – not a very nice person, that he was treating her badly, and that he had some kind of hold over her?'

Leo now sniffed a rat. 'Come on then,' he said, suspiciously. 'Out wiv it.'

Peggy threw off the duffel coat from her shoulders, and got up. Then she went across to turn on the lights. 'Pam's in trouble, Leo,' she said, turning back to look at him. 'She needs your help – and mine.'

Leo, still crouched on the rug, watched her in disbelief as she came back to him.

'That story she told you – about getting your mother to fix up a date with you – it's only partially true.'

'Where'd' yer get this from?' Leo asked. ''Ave yer – *met* Pam?'

'Yes, Leo,' Peggy replied. 'I *have* met her. She came to see me at the garage last night. We had a long talk about you – and things.'

Leo tried to get up, but she sat on the edge of the sofa and eased him down again. 'Before she met you – she'd already met someone else – a corporal in the RAF. She thought she was having his baby . . .' She was trying not to fumble her words, '. . . so she got married to him.'

There was a delayed reaction from Leo. 'Christ almighty!' he gasped, staring at her in disbelief.

'The thing is,' continued Peggy, 'she made a mistake about the baby, and it never happened. She thought this RAF bloke would just walk out on her.' She hesitated. 'Unfortunately, it hasn't turned out that way. He wants to hold on to her.'

'Why?'

'For all sorts of reasons,' replied Peggy. 'But mainly because he's blackmailing her.'

'Blackmailin'?'

'He's apparently threatened to tell her parents about them getting married if she doesn't steal some money from the place where she works. Pam says her father would kill her if he knew what she's been up to.'

'Stupid cow!' said Leo, who could hardly believe what Peggy had told him. ''Ow could she get 'erself mixed up wiv someone like that?'

'Ah!' retorted Peggy. 'That's not the half of it. If you ask me, there's more to this man than we think.'

'Wot d'yer mean?'

'I'm not sure – yet,' replied Peggy. 'I've just got a hunch about all this, that's all. But whatever happens, we've got to help Pam.'

Leo pulled up with a start. ''Elp 'er? After all she's bin up ter be'ind me back?'

Peggy had a brief moment of doubt. 'I thought you said you didn't love her?'

'I don't!' Leo added like a shot. 'But if I'd known wot was goin' on all this time, I wouldn't've 'ad all these problems wiv my muvver. In any case, Peggs, why d'yer wanna get involved? Pam's got 'erself into this mess, so just leave 'er ter get on wiv it.'

off

'I can't do that, Leo,' replied Peggy. 'I don't know why, but I feel sorry for Pam. She's the sort of girl that's vulnerable to this sort of thing.'

''Cos she's stupid.'

'No, Leo,' said Peggy, gently correcting him. 'Because she's human, just like the rest of us. She wants love, she *needs* love. And if I can believe what you say, that's something you've never been able to give her.'

Leo sighed, and ran his fingers through his hair with frustration. 'I don't see wot *I'm* expected ter do about it,' he complained irritably.

Peggy drew closer. 'She wants you to go on seeing her. If she can pretend that you're still walking out together, it's possible this creature will think twice about pushing her too far – at least until she can raise enough money to get rid of him.'

'Well 'e can 'ardly push 'er much furvver, can 'e?' retorted Leo. 'Let's face it, she's gone an' got 'erself 'itched to 'im!'

After a pause Peggy replied grimly, 'There's more to it than that, Leo. Pam's scared of him. This man has threatened to beat her up if he doesn't get what he wants. No matter what you feel about Pam, you can't allow this to happen. She needs protection, Leo – *your* protection. The way *I* can help is to speak to my father about it. I'm sure he'll give me hell and tell me to mind my own business, but he's in a good position to help me dig around and find out about this character.'

Leo sighed again and slowly shook his head in despair. 'I don't know, Peggs,' he said, 'I really don't. My gut instinct tells me ter keep out of it. I mean, as far as I'm concerned, Pam's the past. Why should I put meself out ter 'elp someone who's bin nuffin' but a pain in the neck ter me?'

Peggy put her arm around him, and gently kissed his

ear. 'Because I know the sort of person you are. I know that if anything should happen to Pam, you'd never forgive yourself.'

Chapter 21

Somehow, it didn't seem like a twenty-first birthday. For a start, Peggy was on a split turn, so she had to be at work at twelve midday, and because most of her family and friends from the hill had no idea where she had moved to, there were no birthday cards from them. It was, however, her own fault, for she had kept quiet about the event, mentioning only in passing to Elsie some days before that she would be relieved when she had finally 'come of age'. But, as she got up that Tuesday morning in the cold light of a January day, the one thing it did get her thinking about was the value of friends, and who in fact they actually were. Those from her days at boarding school had, not surprisingly, all drifted their own ways, and Jenny Pearson, the only person that she could really call a friend, had, at the start of the war, been dragged away by her parents to live in the comparative safety of a remote village in Wiltshire. And so it was strange to class as her friends people who, until now, had all her life seemed so remote and different to anyone she had ever previously known. But were this new breed of 'friends' really any different? Only time would tell.

None the less, she did miss her mother, especially on a day like this. No matter how weak she had always thought the poor woman to be, she *was* still Peggy's own flesh and blood, and despite everything, she knew how much her mother cared for her too. For the moment, however, she had far more important things to think about, such as making herself some tea and toast, cleaning up the flat before Elsie came back home the following day, and doing some shopping.

As she came downstairs Peggy noticed that the front door was open, for old Ivy was talking to someone at the front gate. It wasn't until she got outside that she realised who that person was.

'Mummy!' she cried, hurrying out to embrace her. 'What a wonderful surprise!'

'Happy birthday, darling!' returned Catherine, eyes immediately welling up with tears. 'I haven't brought you the key of the door,' she said wistfully, 'but I hope this will do instead.' She gave Peggy a large envelope, which was obviously a birthday card, and a small parcel no bigger than a matchbox.

'What is it?' asked Peggy eagerly, curiously.

'Don't ask questions,' replied Catherine, smiling and dabbing her eyes with her fingers at the same time. 'Put it in your pocket and open it when you're on your own.'

'Yer berfday, is it?' asked old Ivy. 'Why din't yer tell me?'

'Just another day, Mrs Biggs,' said Peggy coyly.

'I wos just tellin' yer mum 'ere,' she said, 'when *I* was twenty-one, I wos workin' up 'Ighbury in the munitions. An' d'yer know wot the gels up there give me? Two pairs er bloomers!' She roared with laughter. 'Real passion-killers they wos!'

Peggy laughed with her; so did Catherine, except that hers was more of a refined chuckle.

'Well, I'll leave yer to it,' said Ivy, turning at the gate. 'Oh, by the way, d'yer like bread puddin'?'

Peggy exchanged a puzzled glance with her mother. 'I don't know, Mrs Biggs,' she replied.

'Wot!' cried the old girl, astonished. 'My 'Arry's favourite. I fink the only reason 'e married me wos 'cos I make the best bread pud in 'Olloway! You shall 'ave one!'

she vowed, as she returned to the house. 'I'll leave it outside yer door.' She stopped and called back. 'But don't leave it there too long. Mussolini's got a sweet toof!' She went inside, and closed the door behind her.

Peggy and her mother laughed. 'Mussolini?' she asked, puzzled.

'The cat!'

Again they laughed.

'Let me look at you,' said Catherine, her fingers reaching out and tenderly touching Peggy's face. 'Twenty-one years old. I can hardly believe it . . .'

'Neither can I,' replied Peggy. 'Especially when I see how young you're looking.'

Catherine shook her head. 'Oh no,' she said. 'I can't tell you how much I've aged since you left.'

Peggy lowered her eyes guiltily.

'Don't worry,' said Catherine. 'It's not all woe. I took your advice – and Betty Desmond's.' She grinned. 'I'm now a fully fledged volunteer for the WVS.'

'Mother!' Peggy's eyes gleamed. 'That's wonderful! Come on in and you can tell me all about it over a nice cup of tea.' She made towards the front door.

'No, darling.'

Peggy turned to find that her mother hadn't followed her. 'Why?'

'It – wouldn't be right,' replied Catherine uneasily.

Peggy came back to her. 'You mean – because of Father?'

Catherine sighed. 'Because of a lot of things,' she replied. 'I feel so ashamed of the way you've been treated.'

'That's all in the past, Mother,' replied Peggy. 'We should look ahead – all of us.'

'I wish you'd come home.'

Her plea upset Peggy.

'No, I don't mean for good – as much as I would love it.

I mean, come home for dinner one night, or Sunday lunch – anything.' Then she added warily, 'You could bring your young man.'

'Mother!' Peggy threw her head back in a strained laugh. 'Can't you just see Father's face, with a mechanic from a bus garage sitting with him at the table!'

'You mustn't be so afraid,' said Catherine. 'If you have principles, then you must be brave enough to follow them through. Besides –' She hesitated – 'I think you may find Father a little more – amenable – these days. He's changed his mind about my going out at nights to work for the WVS. He actually even supports me.'

'Well, that's something, I suppose,' said Peggy, with no enthusiasm.

'He misses you, darling.'

'*Please*, Mother,' Peggy pleaded, turning her face away, embarrassed.

'I know you find it hard to believe, darling, but it's true – I know it is.'

'How can you say such a thing? You know as well as I do, Father has never had any time at all for me – unless of course I'm doing what *he* wants me to do.'

'You're wrong, Peggy,' replied Catherine. 'He misses you, he genuinely does. I can see it in his look every time your name is mentioned.'

'Well, all I can say is, he has a funny way of showing it.'

'So why not give him the chance to prove it?'

Peggy averted her gaze. Ever since she had left home she had tried to put her father out of her mind. Her entire body always tensed when she thought about him, saw that harsh obstinate face ordering her around, giving way not one single inch. She looked up to one end of the road and then to the other. It wasn't exactly the most salubrious of neighbourhoods, with its tall Edwardian houses all in need of repair, and the people who lived in them struggling along with their heavy loads of bagwash over their shoulders or hurrying off to whatever job they had that would pay for the roof over their heads and the food in their stomachs, but at least this was a community where people talked to each other, and sorted out the world's problems as well as their own. In other words, *this* was what a home was all about.

'I'll let you know, Mother,' was all Peggy could bring herself to say.

Leo was giving his dad a wash down in front of the kitchen parlour fire. It was a job neither of them liked very much because, despite his many weaknesses, Reg was a very proud man, and the fact that his own son had to do something so personal for him gave him quite a lot of anguish. It wasn't that Reg was squeamish or embarrassed about the boy seeing him without any clothes on, for Reg had done a couple of years in the army during the First World War, when he and his mates had been used to bathing rough together in the trenches up front. It was just that, because of the injuries from his accident, he felt frustrated that he couldn't do any of these menial tasks himself. But for Leo's part, it was no problem at all – he just felt sympathy for his father's disability.

'So wot yer goin' ter do about yer gel now?' asked Reg, whilst Leo was washing his dad's feet with a flannel and a tablet of Lifebuoy soap. 'Wiv yer call-up an' all that?'

'Not much I *can* do, is there?' replied Leo.

'Yer'll still go on seein' 'er, won't yer? When yer get back, I mean?'

'*If* I get back,' Leo replied with irony.

For a moment, Reg didn't pursue the matter any further. He just sat watching his son going about his chores, and thinking to himself how fond he was of the boy, and how, if

411

he had the chance to live his life all over again, he would stand up to his wife more and give Leo and his two young brothers a better deal. 'But yer still feel the same about 'er, do yer?' he persisted.

'Who?' asked Leo.

'Yer gel.'

'If yer mean do I still love 'er,' Leo replied, 'the answer's yes.'

'An' vice v.?'

'She loves me all right. No question!'

Reg beamed, but was then curious. 'So wot 'appens about Pam now?'

Again Leo hesitated. 'Look, Dad,' he said, voice low, 'if I tell yer somefin' – somefin' really secret, will yer swear ter God yer'll keep it ter yerself?'

'I can only give yer me word,' he shrugged, 'fer wot it's worf.'

Leo wrung out the flannel, wrapped the soap in it, wiped his hands on the towel, and went to the kitchen parlour door and put his ear against it. When he was satisfied that his mum was still listening to the wireless in there, he came back to his father, and sat as close as he could to him. Then, with his voice low, he told him about Pam Warner being married, and the predicament she was in, and how she was using him to stall this RAF corporal until she could get enough cash together to pay him off.

When Leo had finished telling him, Reg's response was predictable. 'Christ!' he gasped in shock and disbelief. 'I knew that gel was up ter somefin'. I knew that's why she come along ter see me when I was up that scaffold on Chrissmas Eve. She was just tryin' ter suss me out, ter find out wevver she could persuade me ter make fings right between the two of yer.'

'I've told Peggs I'm not goin' ter get mixed up in it,' said

Leo. 'Pam's got 'erself in this mess, an' she's goin' ter 'ave ter get 'erself out of it. Am I right, Dad?'

Reg thought about it for what seemed like ages to Leo. 'No, son,' he finally said firmly. 'As a matter of fact – yer're not.'

'But Pam ain't my gel,' said Leo. 'I ain't under no obligation to 'er.'

'Obligation, maybe not,' Reg said. 'But the mere fact that this bloke's doin' a fing like this ter *anyone* is somefin' yer shouldn't let 'appen ter yer own worst enemy.'

'But why?' protested Leo.

' 'Cos it's wrong, son, that's why.' With his one spare hand, Reg picked up the towel and with great difficulty, started to dry his own foot. Leo immediately took the towel from him, and did the job himself. 'Yer know wot they say: "There's honour among fieves." Well, I reckon blackmailers is worse than fieves. It's not only their 'ands that's dirty – it's their *minds* too. I tell yer, I 'ate the sods – I really 'ate 'em. Ter me they're the lowest form er animal life, 'cept that I 'ave more respect fer animals. At least animals don't set out ter get somefin' fer nuffin'. They work fer their keep.' He breathed an angry sigh. 'Yer've gotta nail this sod, Leo, an' nail 'im 'ard – before it goes any furver.'

Leo finished wiping Reg's foot. 'Yeah – but 'ow?' he asked.

Reg leaned back in his chair. 'I don't know,' he replied. 'But we'll fink er somefin'.'

Robert Thornton left the magistrates' court quite early. His last case finished shortly after lunch, and because some bomb-blast repair work had to be carried out to the windows and ceiling, the following two cases had been postponed until the next morning. During recent days,

Thornton had been getting quite irritated by the trivial cases coming before him. As a stipendiary police magistrate, he had always tried to project himself as something more important than just a minor judicial officer, someone who was to be feared but admired in equal measures. But for some reason or other, his enthusiasm for the job was beginning to wane; he found it increasingly difficult to get up in the mornings in order to listen to the endless tales of misguided souls, some downright blackguards, some simply naive, who had done foolish things that were not only an affront to their friends and loved ones, but a waste of the State's time and money, especially during wartime. The effect that this growing irritation was having on him, therefore, was to force him to look at his own role in these routine day-to-day dramas, and to question why someone like him, someone who had difficulty in running his own life, should be entitled to sit in judgment on others.

But there was also another reason why Thornton was relieved to get away from court early that day. Peggy. Today was her twenty-first birthday, a milestone in her life – and his. Today his only daughter could officially do what she liked without asking his permission first. It concerned him. It concerned him very much that he had no more say in the course her life should take. In some extraordinary way, he felt as though he had lost her, not only because she had already moved out of the house, but because for the first time since she had been born, he could no longer make decisions for her. However, despite everything, this was not a day he could ignore, would *want* to ignore. No matter what her age, Peggy was still his child, he was still her father, and after being confronted by that appalling Quincey woman outside his court, it was clear to him that Peggy still needed his advice and protection.

First, however, he needed to find something for her that

would mark this special day, something not necessarily expensive, but chosen with thought and understanding, something that would show her that whatever she may have thought of him in the past, he *did* care about her. He *had* to make some kind of a gesture. It wasn't going to be easy. Not for him. Not for a man like him. But it had to be done.

Peggy was on the home run. It hadn't been an easy split turn, for during the rush hour it had started to snow, which made the roads extremely treacherous to move about on, especially for a large vehicle like a bus. Fortunately, Frosty was an experienced driver, and nothing in the world would persuade him to drive any faster than the road conditions allowed, therefore the number 14's timetable was inevitably thrown into disarray. The only advantage, however, was that with heavy snow clouds now draped over the whole of London, the chances of an air raid that night were fairly remote, which was a relief to everyone, not least to a young girl who was just coming of age.

At Hornsey Rise the evening shift crew took over, leaving Peggy and Frosty to travel as passengers as far as the Nag's Head, where they had to wait outside the Marlborough cinema for any bus that would take them back to the depot up Holloway Road. As it turned out, it was a long and uncomfortable wait, for the fall of snow was gradually turning into a blizzard, and with an exposed bus stop with no shelter, their uniforms were soon covered with what rapidly turned into a layer of ice. Although it was now past blackout time and Peggy could hardly see anything in the pitch-dark, she knew that poor old Frosty's nose must have been bright red, for, as his name suggested, no one felt the cold more than he. But it was different for her. On this special day, she had felt a warm glow at the kindness shown

to her by not only Frosty, who had given her as a birthday
present a wine glass with '21' etched on it, together with a
huge birthday card from all his family, but also by her own
mother, whose wrapped-up birthday present the size of a
matchbox had turned out to be a beautiful star ruby ring
set in eighteen carat gold which Catherine herself had
inherited from her own grandmother. There was also a
birthday card signed by both her mother and father, and to
her surprise, if not astonishment, one from her grandmother with a shakily written message that read quite
simply 'Love from Minty'. This was the nickname Peggy
had given her grandmother when she was a child because
the old girl always seemed to be sucking mint humbugs.

After waiting in the snow and the dark and the freezing
cold for over ten minutes, Peggy and Frosty finally climbed
on board a number 611 trolley bus, where to Peggy's
surprise she found that the clippie whose torch beam was
shining on to her face belonged to her friend Miriam, who
greeted her with a rousing, 'Many happy returns, old lady!
Welcome aboard!'

'How did you know it was my birthday?' asked Peggy.

'Don't be silly!' replied Miriam. 'You don't think you're
going to keep a secret like that, do you?'

'Yer wouldn't have a double brandy an' a nice coal fire
on yer by any chance, would yer?' groaned Frosty, who sat
beside Peggy on the bench seat, frozen to the marrow.

'Funny you should mention that, Granddad,' teased
Miriam. 'Only trouble is, I've got no matches to light the
fire!'

Both girls laughed as poor old Frosty groaned again.

'I wouldn't like to be you on the hill tonight,' said Peggy.
'The road's like a sheet of ice. If your driver uses the brake,
you'll slide all the way down!'

'Don't worry,' replied Miriam, 'we're going into the

depot. Anyone who wants to go up Highgate Hill tonight is going to have to go on skis!'

It was only three stops to the Kingsdown Road depot, so the two girls had no more time to chat. But as Peggy and Frosty got off the bus Miriam called from the platform, 'See you later then, Peggy!'

Peggy stopped, surprised, and turned to look back. 'What did you say?'

Miriam quickly corrected herself. 'I mean – I'll pop over and see you sometime. Bye! Have a good birthday!'

Peggy watched the dark outline of the trolley disappear, momentarily curious about that farewell remark from Miriam. But she quickly dismissed it from her mind, and hurried to catch up Frosty, who was already struggling his way across the main road to the depot.

As they approached the depot, the blizzard was now swirling so hard against them that they had to bend their bodies into the wind to make any progress at all. Matters were inevitably worse because of the blackout; they could hardly see a hand in front of them. However, relief came when the snow was left behind as they reached the cover of the depot forecourt itself. Frosty was exhausted, panting like an animal on heat, so Peggy quickly helped to brush the snow off his cap and uniform, then walked with him towards the canteen. As they went, one of the maintenance engineers who was working on the chassis of one of the buses called, 'Wotcha, Frost! Where's yer reindeer, mate?'

Frosty was not amused, and carried on his way.

'I'll catch you up,' said Peggy, opening the canteen door for him. 'I'll just go and pay in first.'

Frosty was too cold to answer, but he waved before disappearing into the warmth of the canteen.

At the cashier's counter, Peggy thought it noticeable that there were very few other crews around. One girl that she had met just vaguely came in to pay, but after a smile and a nod, she paid in her shift's takings, did her paper work, and left. Peggy found it took her a while to complete her cash total sheet, for the tips of her fingers in her mittens were so cold she couldn't even feel them. 'Pretty quiet tonight,' she said to the girl cashier. 'All been caught in a snow drift, I expect.'

'Wouldn't be at all surprised,' replied the girl cagily.

Peggy thought the girl was a bit high-handed, but she ignored her, and made her way back out on to the forecourt. She too felt it was no time to go traipsing back to the flat until the blizzard had calmed down a bit, so she made her way to the canteen to have a cup of tea with Frosty. However, the moment she opened the door, she had quite a shock waiting for her.

'Happy birfday!'

A sea of faces greeted her, all applauding, cheering and immediately breaking into a rousing chorus of 'Twenty-One Today!'

When it was over, the first person to rush up to her was her flatmate, Elsie Parker, who hugged and hugged her. ''Appy birfday, Peggs darlin'!' she gushed.

Then Alf Grundy came across and shook her frozen hands. 'Who's got the key ter the door then?' he teased.

'Who's got the key to 'er door yer mean!' called Sid Pierce, to gales of laughter.

'Don't listen ter the dirty sods!' yelled Effie, from the counter. 'Many 'appy returns!' Then, overcome by the occasion, she burst into tears.

Peggy swung a look from one face to another. She was utterly bewildered. 'I – I – what's this all about?' she spluttered helplessly.

'It's yer birfday,' said Elsie, putting a comforting arm around Peggy's waist, and leading her to a block of several tables that had been placed together and which contained several plates of sandwiches, sausage rolls, a mixture of home-made and shop-bought cakes, digestive biscuits, a huge slab of Cadbury's milk chocolate, a bowl of tomatoes, another bowl containing apples and pears, and a wizened pineapple that looked as though it had been imported before the war. There were also some bottles of beer and glasses alongside cups and saucers for tea. 'See this chocolate,' said Elsie, voice low, looking around as though the police were at her elbow. 'Someone 'ere (who shall be nameless!) got it on the black market. So make sure yer 'ave a bit before this greedy lot get at it!'

Peggy was still in a daze. 'I – I can't believe it, Elsie,' she said. 'You mean – you've all done this – for *me*?'

'Twenty-first birfdays don't come round every day of the week, Peggs,' replied Elsie. 'It's the least we can do.'

'I shall expect my reward, of course,' blurted Sid Pierce.

'Oh yeah!' growled Effie, who had joined the group. 'We know about *your* rewards!'

'One little kiss ain't too much ter ask – surely?' Sid protested.

Peggy chuckled, and gave Sid a peck on the cheek.

'Oi, oi, Duchess!' complained Alf. 'My missus ain't around. Wot about me?'

There were roars of disapproval from everyone, including some of the other crews and canteen staff who were watching from the sidelines. Then, whilst Effie and Elsie started handing around glasses and plates, the blokes got cracking on opening the bottles of brown and bitter. 'We're not supposed ter serve alcohol on the premises,' said Effie, 'but as it's a speshul occasion . . .'

Needless to say there was a mad rush for the booze, including all the men who were sitting around and who should not be drinking before they went out on their evening shift. Peggy finally had a glass of brown thrust in to her hand, and she was still in such a state of shock that she actually took a sip of it, and nearly choked.

'Well, it's worf a try,' winked Elsie, grinning at her mate's discomfort. 'After all it *is* yer birfday.'

Oh yes, it's my birthday all right, Peggy thought to herself. The most extraordinary, the most wonderful birthday she had ever had in her entire life. How could she have imagined, even a year before, that she would be spending her twenty-first in the company of such people? This was the first time anyone had taken so much trouble over her. Being the centre of attention had never figured much in her home-life before, where even birthdays were restrained and low key. As she looked around the table, and watched everyone digging in to the spread they had prepared themselves in her honour, she wanted to cry. It was hard to believe that these rough and ready people were the same who had initially rejected her as being too hoity-toity, too aloof to be part of them. And yet, she *did* feel a part of them, for they had embraced her for who she was and not where she came from.

' 'Appy birfday – Duchess.'

The quiet voice whispering in her ear caused her to look up with a start. 'Leo!' she said breathlessly, and they hugged.

Everyone cheered and jeered loudly, and even more so when the hug turned into a very public kiss.

Elsie smiled wistfully. 'Some blokes 'ave all the luck,' she said to the back of Leo's head.

To everyone's surprise, the lights suddenly went out, but out of the pitch-darkness came a glow of light from the kitchen door as it was opened on the other side of the canteen. To the strains of everyone singing 'Happy Birthday to you', one of the canteen staff came out carrying an iced cake with a red bus decoration on top, together with the words 'Happy 21 Duchess', and a circle of coloured birthday candles to light the way. The moment it had reached the table, the whole place echoed to the sound of cheers, applause and calls for 'Speech! Speech!'

Peggy waited for the noise to die down in the hope that nobody actually *wanted* her to make a speech. But it didn't turn out that way, for as she looked around the canteen, everyone was waiting. She swung a pleading look towards Elsie, but all she got was a reassuring smile and a wink. So she took a deep breath and tried to say something. 'Making a speech,' she started, fumbling for words, 'was the last thing I expected to do when I walked in here just now.'

Gentle and sympathetic laughter rose from around her.

'The fact is,' she continued, 'I've spent the best part of my life listening to people who had absolutely nothing interesting to say, so I've always told myself that it's far better to stand back and let *them* make fools of themselves rather than me. However,' she sighed, 'since you all clearly *want* me to make a fool of myself, I'll do my best.'

More gentle laughter.

'This much I can tell you without a single blush – working with you lot has completely changed my whole outlook on life. You see, I was warned about you. I was warned that if I ever put my foot where it wasn't wanted, it would get trodden on very hard. Well, thanks to all of you, both my feet are still firmly on the ground, and they're coping pretty well, despite having to rush up and down those stairs on the bus each day!'

More gentle laughter.

'Mind you,' she continued, with a casual glance at Leo, who was smiling affectionately at her, 'I'm only too aware that allowing us girls to take over from the blokes is still, for some, not easy to accept. But in this war, this stupid, idiotic, tragic war, it wouldn't be right for us to sit back and let the menfolk take all the knocks. If there's a gap to be filled, we *have* to fill it. I mean, there's no alternative, is there? Either we fight – or we give in, it's as simple as that. Girls, women – we can fight too. We're the background, "the home front", as the politicians like to call us. Who knows, if this war goes on too long, you won't be able to do without us.'

' 'Ear! 'Ear!' yelled Elsie from the front of the crowd. Sid Pierce glowered at her.

'But I'm telling you,' Peggy continued, 'I could never have done this job if it hadn't been for all of you. You know, up on the hill where I come from, they call you lot "working class". Funny that, because it kind of suggests that you're the only people who do any work. And you're not, of course. Most people have to work, whether it's in an office, or in the Stock Exchange or on the buses here in Holloway. But one thing you do have,' she said, looking directly at Frosty, 'is warmth, kindness and a generous spirit that's kept me going ever since we got to know each other. If I live to be a hundred – and the way I feel sometimes I doubt that very much – I'll never forget how much these past few weeks have meant to me. You know,' she said, turning to Leo, 'when I first came here you called me "Duchess". I hated it. It meant somehow that you thought of me as someone who was too lah-de-dah and high and mighty to mix with the likes of you. But I don't feel like that any more. And d'you know why? Because the way you lot treat me, I feel more like a princess. Thank you all so much.'

The moment she stopped speaking, she was greeted with a moment of total silence. But as she stood there, feeling awkward, strained and embarrassed, Effie Sommers was heard sobbing gently. Then Alf Grundy started to clap, softly at first, until this was gradually picked up by everyone.

By the time they had finished, even Peggy felt as though she was going to burst into tears, until Leo put his arms around her, and hugged her.

'It's a good fing yer don't make speeches too often,' he said in her ear, as he kissed it. 'Old Churchill'd 'ave ter watch 'is step!'

Frosty stepped forward and, choked though he was, he started to sing, 'For She's a Jolly Good Fellow', which everyone immediately picked up and joined in. However, the whole thing gradually petered out as they saw Peggy's eyes riveted to someone who had entered the canteen and was watching her and Leo locked together in a fond embrace. In the silence that followed, everyone cleared a path for the tall, well-dressed man, clutching a bowler hat and cane in one hand, and a small parcel in the other, as he came across to join them.

'Happy birthday, my dear,' said Thornton. He moved close, and kissed her gently on the cheek.

Peggy was too taken aback to say anything more to him than just, 'Father . . .'

Everyone exchanged surprised glances, and even more so when Thornton addressed Leo. 'My name is Robert Thornton,' he said, formally, but with a twinkle in his eyes. 'I'm very pleased to make your acquaintance, young man.' He offered his hand for Leo to shake.

Leo was taken aback. He looked to Peggy, then back to Thornton, and then to Thornton's hand. 'Likewise,' he replied, wiping his own hand on his trousers before he shook Thornton's.

'Peggy's mother and I would be very happy if you'd care to come over with Peggy to dinner one night,' said Thornton. 'Could you manage it?'

Again Leo, awkward as hell, looked to Peggy for support. But she too had no idea what to say, and so the only way

Leo knew how to react was to shrug his shoulders.

'Well – talk it over between you,' suggested Thornton. 'You'd be most welcome.' He turned back to Peggy. 'Oh, by the way, darling,' he said, handing her the small parcel he was carrying, 'this is just a little something for your birthday. It's nothing very much. But it's the thought that counts – don't you agree?'

Peggy smiled awkwardly, nodded, and took the parcel. 'Thank you, Father,' was all she could say.

Thornton leaned forward, kissed her gently on the cheek again, allowed his look into her eyes to linger for a second more, then turned to observe the sea of curious faces watching him. 'Good night everyone,' he called. 'Nice to have met you.'

'Wot about a drink, mate?' called Frosty as Thornton was about to leave. 'Warm yer up a bit.'

'Thank you kindly,' replied Thornton with a huge, grateful smile. 'Have to get home, I'm afraid. My wife is waiting to have dinner. Good night.' With that, he left them, and walked briskly out of the canteen.

After her father had gone, for a moment Peggy and Leo stared at each other in sheer disbelief. Then she nervously tore open the parcel her father had given her. Inside was an expensive leather-bound book with the gold embossed legend 'DIARY 1941' printed on its rich blue cover. And on the facing page was Thornton's own hand-written inscription which read:

> For my daughter, Peggy.
> The end of a dismal past, but
> the start of a bright new future.
> Love, Father.

Chapter 22

Corporal Ron Todd didn't like to be kept waiting. Since the weekend there had been quite a lot of snow, which had settled and turned the roads into rivers of ice, making the journey up from Hendon to Finsbury Park on a motorbike a real hazard. To make matters worse, today the sun had finally come out, and although it had brought with it a modicum of warmth to the bleak winter streets, it had also started a slow thaw, which meant that the roads were now covered in a dirty perilous slush. However, as an RAF courier, Todd was an experienced biker, so he took every journey he made in his stride, but despite the fact that he was wrapped up well in regulation fleece-lined leathers and hood, he didn't take too kindly to being kept hanging around in the cold by a mindless blonde who couldn't tell the time on a clock if she went to school for a whole year – which she probably never had anyway. Still, when he thought back to the first time he'd seen her, it wasn't Pam Warner's mind that attracted him – oh no. It was that neat little rump that drove him mad, and those headlamps ... He sighed, and smoked his fag. Perched on one side of his bike seat, both feet on the pavement, goggles pulled up across his forehead, he took an impatient look at his watch, and scowled. This'll cost her, he promised himself. Every minute this dumb blonde kept him waiting, it would cost her. Eventually he saw her, just turning into the park gates, pushing her way through the slush towards where he was waiting opposite the football pitch, white topcoat and headscarf, white galoshes, and a milky white face that was flushed with the cold.

'Wot time d'yer call this then?' he growled as she drew close.

'I 'ave ter go ter work, yer know,' she returned cuttingly. 'This is s'pposed ter be me lunch hour.'

'So?' he demanded impatiently.

'So wot?' she asked.

' 'Ave yer forgotten why yer're 'ere? 'Ow much?'

Pam crossed her arms and stared him out. 'If yer're askin' if I've got any money for yer,' she answered defiantly, 'the answer's no.'

The corporal's face hardened. 'That's not very clever of yer,' he said, ice-cold eyes meeting hers. 'Is it?'

'Look, Todd,' said Pam, 'I've told yer before, a 'undred quid's a lot of money fer me. It's a lot of money fer anybody ter find.'

'Yer go ter work, don't yer?' he snapped. 'They 'ave a cash till I presume?'

Pam stared at him in horror. 'Are yer mad or somefin'?' she said. 'Yer expect me ter *steal* – from me own employer?'

'I don't care *who* yer steal from,' snarled the corporal, checking from side to side to make sure that no one could overhear their conversation. 'I want that money or . . .' He stretched out one finger and gently, but menacingly ran it down her cheek. 'I'd 'ate ter ruin that pretty little face . . .'

As he spoke, two elderly women appeared, out strolling with their dogs on leashes. He glared at them and turned away. They ignored his glare, and continued their walk, but not before one of the two dogs had raised a leg against the front wheel of the corporal's motorbike.

'Did yer 'ear wot I said?' asked the corporal, once the two intruders had gone.

'I want a divorce, Todd,' was Pam's firm reply. 'An' I see no reason why *I* should pay for it.'

The corporal drew as close as he could to her. 'Now you listen ter me,' he whispered menacingly. 'I've got a very nasty temper – never been able to control it. Yer see, if yer don't do wot I ask, I can't be responsible for *wot* I might do. Furthermore, yer mum an' dad won't be at all pleased ter 'ear that their darlin' little daughter's bin bunkin' down wiv a randy RAF type.'

Pam sighed, but remained determined. 'Why are you doin' this, Todd?' she asked. 'You don't love me, an' yer know I'm goin' wiv someone else.'

'Oh yes,' grinned the corporal. 'I was fergettin' about yer new boyfriend from up the bus depot.' He leaned forward and leered at her. 'Bet 'e's not as good at gettin' 'is leg over as me – is 'e, Pam?'

'Don't be so disgustin'!' she snapped. 'I love 'im, an' 'e loves me. We wanna get married.'

The corporal's face beamed mischievously. 'Wot – anuvver weddin', Pam? So soon? Yer sure know 'ow ter enjoy yerself, don't yer?'

'I want ter marry 'im!' she insisted.

'Well, yer can't!' he growled back. ' 'Cos yer've got ter get rid er me first, an' yer won't do that till yer've paid me off.'

'I can't do that,' she insisted. 'An' I won't.'

The corporal paused, and shrugged. ' 'Ave it your way, Pam,' he said dismissively, crossing his arms. 'But I tell yer this much: if I don't get that money by the weekend, not only will yer poor ol' mum an' dad know all about it, but you ain't gonna look a pretty sight when yer walk up that aisle.'

'I'll go ter the police,' said Pam grandly.

'Police?' asked the corporal, with a wide grin. 'Go to the bluebottles, will yer? Well, OK, you go right ahead. But wot yer gonna say ter them, Pam?'

'I'll tell 'em that yer're a liar an' a cheat, an' that yer tryin' ter blackmail *me*, that yer're tryin' ter get me ter steal money for yer.'

He roared with laughter. 'Proof, Pam! Your word against mine.' He stopped laughing abruptly, as though he had suddenly turned it off with a switch. 'Yer're goin' ter 'ave ter do better than that, I'm afraid,' he said, staring right through her.

'Corporal!'

He turned with a start, and was shocked to find a young RAF flight lieutenant standing right behind him. He immediately straightened up and stood to attention. 'Sir!'

'Are you on duty?' asked the officer in a clipped RAF brogue.

'Yes, sir!'

'Which unit?'

'Hendon, sir!'

'What are you doing up here?'

'On my way back, sir. Special delivery at RAF Wethersfield, sir. Just stopped off fer a short break.'

The officer looked from the corporal to Pam, then back to the corporal again. 'So I see,' he replied acidly. 'Well, I've been watching you for some time, and I'd say your break has been quite long enough. So I suggest you get back on your bike and get back to Hendon as fast as you can. In case you hadn't noticed, there's a war on!'

'Sir!'

The officer waited whilst the corporal pulled down his goggles, and climbed back on to his motorbike. Then he turned and quickly strode off.

Once he was quite sure that the officer was out of sight, the corporal gave him the two fingers. 'Prick!' he snapped.

'Naughty boy,' said Pam, who had watched the whole exchange with smug satisfaction.

'The weekend!' snarled the corporal, starting up the bike, which immediately popped noisily into life. 'An' don't ferget. I know where yer live!' With a burst of smoke from his exhaust, he put the clutch into gear, and the bike roared off.

Pam watched the bike slither its way through the wet slush, until it finally disappeared out through the park gates and into the main Seven Sisters Road. As it went, she hoped that the bleeding thing would give way beneath him, so that she would never have to lay eyes on that ugly face ever again . . .

Peggy hadn't seen her Great-uncle George since she was a youngster. In fact she remembered the time exactly, for it was when he made one of his rare visits up to London to visit his brother, Herbert, on Herbert's sixtieth birthday. She also remembered having liked Uncle George enormously, for he seemed to laugh at practically everything, which always greatly irritated Peggy's father and grandmother. As she got older, Peggy had always promised herself that she would go and visit Uncle George at his cottage in Hertfordshire, but somehow it always seemed such a long way to travel for just a few hours. However, the message she had received from her mother about Grandfather Thornton's illness greatly concerned her and, despite the fact that the weather was still cold and difficult under foot, on her day off she willingly agreed to travel to Harpenden with her mother to visit the old chap.

Uncle George's cottage was actually outside a small village in the heart of the country, and the only sure way of getting there was by taking the train from King's Cross to Harpenden, and then a local taxi. Peggy found the cottage itself to be absolutely charming, built in the late Victorian period, with a red-tiled roof, small leaded windows, and walls constructed of grey stone taken from a quarry in the West Country. By the time she and her mother arrived there, Uncle George had made up two beautiful log fires, one in the hall and another in the sitting room where, since being taken poorly, Herbert had spent most of his time.

'Doctor says he's had some kind of a spasm,' said George, who was two years younger than his brother, a wonderfully eccentric-looking man, who had very little white hair left on his head but a full bushy white moustache and beard. 'I found him lying flat on his face on the bedroom floor. Gave me a nasty turn, I can tell you, especially when I tried to get him back on his bed. Never mind. He's on the mend now.' For some strange reason he laughed at his own remark, but Peggy soon came to realise that this was caused by nervous anxiety rather than his traditional sense of fun.

When they went into the sitting room, Peggy and her mother were shocked by Herbert's appearance. He was sleeping soundly in a winged armchair in front of the fire, his head leaning on one side, his lap covered by a thick woollen blanket. But his face was quite distinctly yellow, his cheeks drawn in, and he seemed somehow to have shrivelled up in his dressing gown.

'Herbert!' George called softly. 'Wake up! You've got visitors.'

Peggy immediately dropped to her knees by her grandfather's side. As he slowly opened his eyes, her face was the first thing he saw, and it immediately brought a smile to his face. 'Hello, Grandfather,' she said softly. 'Now what have you been up to?'

'You . . . shouldn't have come,' he said, his throat parched dry. Then he noticed Catherine standing alongside Peggy. 'Thank you for coming – both of you.'

'I'll go and make a nice cup of tea,' said George. 'He

sounds as though he needs one.' He stopped at the door. 'I've made us a jam sponge cake.' He winked. 'But I'm not going to tell you where I got the ingredients!' He went out, laughing merrily to himself.

'Your brother's a wonderful man, Herbert,' said Catherine gently. 'The best type of confirmed bachelor!'

They all chuckled.

'I've brought you some of your favourite tobacco, Grandfather,' said Peggy, taking a small packet of Fine Blend from her coat pocket and placing it on the small table at Herbert's side, together with his pipe and ash tray. 'But I'm not sure the doctor would approve.'

Herbert grinned, and waved his hand dismissively.

Peggy exchanged a passing look of concern with her mother. The rapid deterioration in her grandfather's condition that had taken place since she last saw him appalled her. But his eyes, although now sunken back into their sockets, were as crystal clear and blue as ever, and there were still signs there of that rich defiance that endeared him so much to her.

'Robert asked me to send you his best wishes for a speedy recovery,' said Catherine. 'He has a day off next week, and he's going to try to come to see you. He said that if there was anything you needed, you were to be sure to let him know.'

Herbert smiled and nodded his thanks.

'And Mother – Alice . . .' Catherine found herself awkwardly fumbling for words. 'I'm sure she'll be coming up to see you too. She moved out. She's in a small private hotel in Swiss Cottage.'

Again Herbert nodded. 'Thank God for that!' he answered softly, wryly.

Peggy and her mother exchanged a suppressed chuckle.

'I'll go and help George with the tea,' said Catherine,

making for the door. 'Even bachelors need a woman's touch!'

After Catherine had left the room, Peggy moved in closer and leaned her head on the side of her grandfather's chair. 'I don't think this is a very good idea, you know,' she said tenderly. 'If you have to get ill, please have the goodness to do it somewhere nearer North London, so I can take care of you.'

Herbert looked down at her, reached out with his hand, and gently stroked her hair. 'I want you to take care of her.'

Peggy looked up with a puzzled expression.

'Your grandmother,' he said. 'She thinks she knows so much, but she doesn't. The Towers won't be enough for her. She'll need so much more.'

'I don't understand . . .' Peggy answered.

'The nights,' he continued. 'It will be the nights she'll dread most. That's the time when the thinking begins. Looking back is always the hardest thing to do. It's always too late to do anything about it. There are so many things she should have said, but could never find the time. Just tell her that – I know.' He put his hand under Peggy's chin, and gently eased it up so that he could look at her face. 'It's an awful lot to ask of you, I know,' he said. 'But you're the only one, the only person in the world who would understand.'

George came back into the room, carrying the tea things on a large tray. 'Time for tea!' he announced, all hale and hearty. 'No more dark secrets, if you please!' Catherine followed him in with the home-made jam sponge, and they put everything down on a round table with a plain yellow tablecloth in the centre of the room.

Herbert had lowered his hand from under Peggy's chin, and she gently tucked the hand back beneath his blanket. She looked up, to catch her mother's pained expression as she observed Herbert.

'So here we are, then!' announced George jovially. 'One big happy family. Who's for a nice cup of tea?'

He looked disconsolately at Peggy, and then at Catherine. Unfortunately, they weren't interested. Nor was Herbert, who was fast asleep.

The air-raid siren sounded just as Marge Quincey was on her way back from shopping in Seven Sisters Road. She had had a frustrating couple of hours, during which time she'd queued for practically everything from smoked haddock in Liptons, a four-ounce ration of Cheddar cheese and her week's two-and-a-half-pounds sugar ration for the entire family from Sainsbury's, to a pathetic shilling's worth of mutton from Hunter's. But her most maddening moment came after she'd queued for nearly twenty minutes again outside Liptons, when the word got round that they had just got in a new stock of loose tea, and she discovered only when she'd actually reached the counter that she did not have sufficient coupons to get more than two ounces. It had all been too much, and when the air-raid siren came she cursed the entire world for expecting people like her to cope with an injured husband and three helpless kids. The ack-ack gunfire started to explode in the air above her before she'd even had a chance to get halfway home. What's more, it was almost blackout time, and she was weighed down with shopping bags. Her only thought now was to get home as fast as she could and get the two youngest into the air-raid shelter before things got any worse.

'Get yer fings tergevver an' get out ter the shelter!' she barked at Horace and Eddie the moment she got home. 'Where's yer dad?'

'Gone!' yelled Horace, as he and Eddie abandoned the game of ludo they were playing at the kitchen parlour table, and rushed down the stairs.

'Wot d'yer mean – gone?' Marge yelled after them.

' 'E's gone out!' called young Eddie.

Marge panicked. 'Gone out?' she screamed. 'Where? Wot yer talkin' about?'

' 'Ow should we know *where*?' protested Horace.

Marge rushed after them, and caught up with them just as they were about to run outside to the shelter. 'Ace, wot's this all about? Yer dad can 'ardly walk, so 'ow can 'e go out?'

' 'E went in 'is wheelchair,' said Eddie.

Marge's eyes widened. 'Wheelchair? 'E ain't got no wheelchair.'

' 'E 'as,' insisted young Eddie. 'It come from the Red Cross.'

'Leo got it fer 'im,' said Horace. 'They brung it round while yer wos out.'

'Christ!' gasped Marge. ' 'Ow the 'ell did 'e get down the stairs?'

Horace shrugged. 'They left it down 'ere fer 'im. 'E come down the stairs on 'is bum!'

He and Eddie laughed, but were terrified when their mum suddenly threw back the front door and ran out into the yard, yelling frantically, 'Reg! Yer stupid sod! Where are yer . . . ?'

Reg Quincey felt quite chuffed with himself. If getting down those stairs on his rump back home had been no mean feat, then using a wheelchair for the first time and along pavements that were glistening with ice was little short of a bleeding miracle. But there he was, he'd made it, he'd got out of that place that he was stuck in night and day, and now he was drinking a pint of his favourite bitter in his favourite pub, The Eaglet. But the need to get away from home for an hour or two and the need for a drink were not his only reasons for attempting such a perilous journey.

'Pam Warner?' asked Bert Miller, one of the regulars in the saloon bar, and one of Reg's closest drinking partners. 'Nah, mate. Last time I saw 'er in 'ere she was takin' a tank wiv some RAF corporal. As I remember, they was 'avin' a rare ol' barney.'

'Any idea wot about?' asked Reg, taking it easy in his wheelchair surrounded by his usual gang of pint-lifters.

Bert nodded. He was a heftily built bruiser of a man, and when he spoke, the foam on the top of his beer quivered. 'Kept themselves ter themselves most er the time,' he said. 'But by the looks er fings, she was doin' 'er nut.'

'Wot about this bloke she wos wiv?' asked Reg. 'Who is 'e?'

'Search me,' replied Bert, who raised his glass to the ceiling and drank a toast as a loud bang from an ack-ack shell outside suddenly shook the bar from end to end.

' 'Is name's Todd,' said one of the blokes drinking at the counter just behind Reg.

Reg swung round in his wheelchair to see who was talking.

' 'E's a bike courier or somefin',' said the young navvy, who had come to the pub straight from a demolition site and whose work clothes were still covered in plaster and dust. 'Based up at 'Endon – seems ter spend most er 'is time down 'ere, though. I've got an idea 'e lives round 'ere somewhere.'

'Any idea where?' asked Reg.

'Ain't got a clue, mate.'

'Sonderburg Road.' This time the voice was old Ben Rickett's, who these days was the regular piano thumper in the bar. 'I saw 'im chattin' up my missus the week before Chrissmas. Cocky sod, by the looks er 'im. 'E went inter one er those 'ouses near the corner. Why? Wos up?'

'Nah,' replied Reg. 'Just wonderin', that's all.'

Ben shrugged and went off to do some more piano thumping.

Briefly alone with his thoughts, Reg took a quick glance around the bar. In all the times he had been propping up the counter there with his mates, it had never occurred to him how much of a second home the place was to him. More than that, the saloon bar was a network of prying eyes: no one could do or say anything that wasn't noticed by the blokes whose lives seemed to revolve around the booze and the company there. It was no place for a stranger to throw his weight around. But Reg knew only too well that it was also no job for a man with one gammy foot, a plastered arm, and a gash in the back of his head. In some ways Leo was right: if Pam Warner had got herself into this mess then it was up to her to get herself out of it. But it wasn't as simple as that. Reg knew all about being married to someone who you were stuck with for life, someone who had you pinned down to doing everything they wanted. Pam had got herself landed with someone like that too, but this bloke was also a crook and that made it a thousand times worse. Pam Warner! Silly little cow! How the hell did she manage to go and get herself hitched when she was under age, without her mum and dad's permission, and without telling anybody? Worse still, how was she going to get out of it? She was going to need a divorce, and divorces don't come cheap. Maybe it was cheaper to get this bloke the cash after all, then tell him to sod off and not come back. Trouble about that, though, was that he *would* come back. He'd come back time and time again. His sort always do.

'Wot say I give yer an 'and ter get back 'ome?'

Reg was suddenly roused from his thoughts by his

mate Bert, who was standing over him.

'It's gettin' a bit rough out there,' Bert said, nodding towards to the door.

Bert was right. By the sound of things it *was* getting rough outside, and getting even rougher, for the ack-ack boys were clearly pumping the sky with as many shells as they could get up there, determined to break up that relentless drone of enemy bomber planes that seemed to be dropping their loads on to as much of London as they could manage.

'Reg?'

Reg looked up at his old mate, who was showing concern for him. He also saw the crowded bar, thick with fag smoke that had discoloured the cream-painted walls, and everyone staring up at the ceiling as though they expected it to cave in at any minute. For some weird reason, this brought a smile to his face.

'Come on, Bert,' he said cheerily. 'Wos all the panic? 'Ow's about one fer the road?'

The air raid was now becoming more ferocious than it had at first promised, and shrapnel from ack-ack gunfire shells was tinkling down on to the pavements everywhere. Peggy and Leo were lucky to reach the safety of Holloway Road tube station just in time, but it was touch and go, and only achieved by running the two hundred yards or so all the way from the Savoy cinema where they had had to leave a showing of *Gone With the Wind*.

As expected, both platforms were already crammed with people sheltering from the air raid, most of them families who regularly spent their nights camped out anywhere they could in the bowels of the London Underground system with the breathless air putrid with the smell of urine and human waste. It was the first time Peggy had been down to such a place, and her immediate impression was a mixture of admiration and incredulity that so many people were willing to sacrifice their comfort and dignity in the desperate struggle for survival. For the best part of a quarter of an hour she and Leo searched for even a few feet of space in which just to sit or even squat. But not only were the platforms overflowing with recumbent figures trying to sleep, the rail track itself was too. Entire families had made up beds between the live rails, which had been turned off to allow the mass overnight hibernation. Everywhere she and Leo went, Peggy was deeply impressed by the sense of resignation, determination and astonishing cheerfulness that pervaded throughout. Someone along the platform had even brought a wind-up gramophone and people around were wearily joining in to a scratchy well-used record of Gracie Fields singing 'There's a Long, Long Trail A-winding'.

As most of the bleak corridors leading from the platforms were already occupied by some of the more hardy shelterers, Peggy and Leo ended up in the only available space left to them, on one of the iron steps of the soulless spiral staircase which was the alternative to the lifts used to take passengers from the booking hall down to the platforms. But a cruel ice-cold draught gushed up the staircase, and as they crouched there, Peggy had to snuggle up to Leo to keep warm.

'Is this what hell is really like, I wonder,' she asked.

'Nah,' he replied. ' 'Ell is up top. There yer ain't got no chance at all.'

'What about all those people who were killed at Trafalgar Square and the Bank tube stations?' she recalled. 'If we were to get a direct hit, would *we* have a chance?'

Leo had no answer. Like everyone else he knew only too well that, in theory, a tube station *was* the safest place to shelter, but in the event of a direct hit by a deep-penetrating high-explosive bomb, the results could be quite catastrophic. He drew her closer and leaned his cheek on the top of her head. On the stair below them, a young mother, cradling her baby in her arms, was gently rocking the child to sleep whilst her equally young husband covered all three of them with a large tartan blanket. And on the two stairs above, two elderly women and an elderly man had somehow managed to squeeze into the tightest space imaginable, and were taking comfort from a flask of hot cocoa.

'So what are we goin' ter do about yer ol' man, then?' said Leo, holding Peggy close. 'Bit of a turn-up fer the books, ain't it – askin' me ter dinner?'

'It's so strange,' Peggy said, her thoughts miles away. 'It's the first time in my life that he's ever shown any real warmth towards me. I just don't understand.'

'Must be feelin' guilty,' suggested Leo.

'Yes – but why? Why *now* – after all these years? Something's happened.'

An intense, deafening barrage of anti-aircraft gunfire on the surface above suddenly rocked the entire station from end to end, bringing dust fluttering down from the booking hall on to the heads of the beleaguered people sheltering nervously on the spiral staircase below. Nobody panicked, for this kind of frantic activity in the skies above was now an accepted part of the nightly ritual of an air raid. But it did scare the kids everywhere, who timidly cuddled up close to the protection of their mums and dads, and the noise woke small babies from their sleep, their dazed cries sending ripple-waves of bleary-eyed consternation along the platforms, and throughout the bleak tile-walled corridors.

Leo wrapped his arms protectively around Peggy, and she pressed herself into his chest as tightly as she could.

When the cacophony of deadly sounds finally subsided, they settled back against the cold curve of the wall. For several minutes they said nothing, allowing the natural sounds of human fear and suffering to take over from the struggle for supremacy raging in the skies above. When calm and peace returned, Peggy and Leo turned and looked at each other; there was so much love and yearning in their eyes. Leo leaned forward, and gently kissed her on the forehead. 'Don't worry,' he said softly. 'We'll get fru this. We'll get fru *everyfin*' – yer dad, me mum, the army – even Pam.'

Peggy did a double take. She was about to say something but he put his fingers against her lips to stop her.

'I'll do wot I can for 'er,' he said. 'But I can't promise.'

Peggy's eyes lit up. Then she leaned forward and kissed him firmly on the lips. Leo responded, and they remained like that for as long as they could.

Behind them the three old people hadn't even noticed what they were doing, and even if they did it would have made no difference. It was, after all, impossible to be shocked by anything when they and everyone else were so constantly in fear of losing their lives.

Marge Quincey was out of breath. She had run halfway down Hornsey Road, halfway down Tollington Road, and every minute she was out in the middle of all this mayhem she reckoned it could only be a matter of time before she was either hit by a piece of shrapnel or simply blown to pieces by a bomb. And so she had had enough and turned back. As if to reinforce her fears, a cluster of incendiary magnesium bombs landed with a thud no more than fifty yards or so from where she was running, and with the slush on the ground that had turned to ice again at the onset of dark, she was almost blinded by the overpowering white glare from both snow and magnesium.

She had almost reached home when a thought suddenly occurred to her. The pub. That's where he was. Why the hell hadn't she thought of that from the start? If Reg *had* to get away from home for an hour or two it was surely the most obvious place he would make for. Defying all common sense and her own personal safety, she turned round, and made tracks for The Eaglet as fast as her legs would carry her.

She reckoned it was a miracle that she'd managed to get to the pub in one piece, but when she did she immediately heard the familiar banter and laughter of the usual crowd – Reg's crowd – that propped up the bar counter each night come hell or high water. She burst through the doors into the saloon bar, and her suspicions were immediately confirmed. Completely oblivious of the chaos in the streets outside, Reg was in his wheelchair, playing a game of darts with his fellow boozers. It was a rowdy affair, and everyone was not only well-oiled, but they were clearly having the time of their lives. When they noticed who had entered the bar behind them, the game came to an abrupt halt, and all eyes turned to a ferocious-looking Marge Quincey.

'Yer stupid sod!' she said directly to Reg's back. Then she yelled at the others. 'Yer're all stupid bleedin' sods!'

With one hand, Reg slowly turned his wheelchair round to face her, his face calm and impassive.

' 'Ow did yer get 'ere?' Marge bawled at him. 'Ain't yer got no consideration for nobody but yerself?'

'I'm 'avin' a drink wiv me mates,' said Reg, without raising his voice, but with a look of steel.

'All er yer!' yelled Marge, widening her anger to the rest of the men in the bar, who were now looking on in absolute astonishment. 'Ain't yer got no 'omes ter go ter?'

A totally dead response from them all.

'Don't yer know wot's goin' on out there?'

With one hand, Reg manoeuvred his wheelchair slowly towards her. '*You* go 'ome, woman!' This time his voice was clipped, raised and as firm as a rock. 'I don't want ter be disturbed. I'm 'avin a drink wiv me friends. Do yer understand that, Marge? Do yer understand wot I'm sayin'?'

Marge looked at him as though he was stark raving mad. And his eyes were glaring at her so hard that for the first time in her life she was actually scared of him.

Reg wheeled a few steps closer. 'I'm not Leo, Marge,' he glowered. 'I'm not the kids, I'm not Pam Warner. But I tell yer this.' He leaned forward in his wheelchair. 'If yer ever come lookin' fer me again,' he warned, his finger pointing menacingly at her, 'I'll cut yer down ter size. D'yer get me meanin', Marge? Do yer?'

Marge's face was ashen white. Unable to believe what was happening to her, she looked helplessly from one face in the bar to another. But eyes lowered every time she met them. Then after one brief, uncomprehending last look back at Reg, she turned, and left the bar.

In the street outside, the skies were suddenly, strangely at peace. Marge, however, didn't even notice them. She was too dazed, too numb, as she slowly shuffled her way back home along the Hornsey Road.

Chapter 23

It was the early hours of the morning before Peggy and Leo were able to leave the shelter of Holloway tube station. When they emerged into what they hoped would be the sweet fresh air outside, they were horrified to discover how much damage had been done during those few short hours of the air raid. Several fires were blazing in different directions, and it seemed that, despite the protective tape that had been stuck on to every shop window along the main Holloway Road, the pavements were littered with shattered glass, broken roof tiles and chimneypots that had come crashing down, and the remains of the familiar Belisha beacons at many road crossings, whose orange warning lights had been turned off at the outbreak of the war. Utterly weary after a sleepless night on the spiral staircase, Peggy made her sluggish way home on foot, accompanied by Leo, who walked with her as far as the corner of Marlborough Road before turning back home himself.

Peggy practically fell into bed, and when she woke up with a jolt to find Elsie standing over her, she was afraid that she must have slept so late that it was time to get to work again. And yet when she focused, she realised that the light was on, and it was still dark outside.

'Elsie,' she panicked, 'what time is it?'

Elsie was in a very subdued mood. 'It's all right, Peggs,' she said softly, perching on the edge of Peggy's bed. 'It's only seven o'clock.'

Peggy rubbed her eyes. 'Why so early?' she asked, puzzled.

'Yer mum's waitin' fer yer downstairs,' said Elsie sombrely.

It wasn't hard for Peggy to guess that something had happened, for Elsie couldn't bring herself to say anything more. So she immediately got out of bed, put on her dressing gown, and rushed downstairs.

Her mother was waiting in the parlour. Her eyes were red; she had clearly been crying.

'What is it, Mother?' Peggy asked the moment she entered the room. 'What's happened?'

'Grandfather,' replied Catherine, her face racked with strain. 'We had a telephone call . . . He passed away a few hours ago.'

Peggy felt her whole inside fall apart. She went straight to her mother, and they hugged each other. 'What happened?' she asked quietly.

Catherine gently pulled away and composed herself. 'He just went to sleep –' she replied, dabbing her eyes with her handkerchief – 'exactly where we left him the other day. George found him there. He said the end must have come peacefully, because Grandfather had such a sweet smile on his face.'

'He always had a sweet smile on his face,' said Peggy, recalling that with a faint wry smile of her own. 'He was that sort of man.'

'They've taken him to the hospital,' said Catherine. 'There'll be a post mortem. It all happened so quickly. His doctor said he'd been suffering from some kind of stomach cancer. It must have gone too far.'

Peggy took a deep breath, and tried to be practical. 'What about Grandmother?' she asked. 'Has she been told?'

'No,' replied Catherine, shaking her head. 'We're very worried about her.'

'Why?'

'The hotel she's been staying at said she's checked out.'

Peggy was shocked. 'But why? Did the hotel say if she'd left a forwarding address?'

'Yes,' replied Catherine anxiously. 'They said she'd gone home – to The Towers.'

Highgate Hill was shrouded in an early morning mist. It must have seemed a strange phenomenon to those who had never visited the area, for less than two miles away at the bottom of the hill, the air was crystal clear, which is probably one of the reasons why in times past it had been known as The Hollow Way. However, despite the ethereal beauty of the thin layer of frosty mist which hung low and protectively over the tall narrow chimneypots of Highgate Village, there was relief that this corner of London at least had escaped the worst of the previous night's air raid, and as the sun gradually gathered strength, the mist slowly began to evaporate.

Peggy's journey on the trolley bus up to the village was a sad one. The last time she had visited The Towers was at Christmas, and memories kept flooding back of that chat with her grandfather in his beloved summerhouse out in the garden. She couldn't imagine what life was going to be like without him; somehow he had always been around even if she didn't see him very often. The bond they undoubtedly shared was going to be hard to sever. But then, she told herself, perhaps it would never be like that. After all, because someone dies why should it mean that a link is broken for ever? Surely a parting is temporary and only lasts until you meet your loved ones again? She was comforted by the thought that her grandfather would never be too far away, for there would always be a place in her heart for him. But what of Grandmother?

This question was uppermost in her mind as she got off

the bus and made her way as fast as she could down
Hampstead Lane. It wasn't easy, for the slush underfoot
had now turned black from the number of boots and shoes
that had tracked through it over the past days, and the
kerbs were piled high with dirty mounds of ice and snow
that had been swept there by residents from outside the
front of their houses. Ever since she was a child, Peggy's
first sight of The Towers, when she saw it from the road,
always sent a chill down her spine. She had never paused
long enough to try to understand why, except that, like
today, even with the scars of bomb-blast, the old building
simply emanated the influence of a truculent old lady. But
what now for Grandmother Thornton? How would she
cope now that she had been left alone to stand up to the
reality of life's constant hardships? What was it her
grandfather had said of her? '*She thinks she knows so much,
but she doesn't. The Towers won't be enough for her. She'll need
so much more.*'

Peggy paused at the tall ornamental iron front gates to
see how much work had been carried out on the old house
after the incendiary bomb had caused so much damage a
few weeks before. The whole place was a web of scaffolding,
and as the tall red chimneypots and their stacks had clearly
crashed down into the front garden, the entire roof was
covered with a vast waterproof tarpaulin. As far as Peggy
could see, all the windows in the front of the house had
been blown in, and they had now been boarded up. It was
a sorry sight, which convinced her immediately that
whatever the hotel had said about her grandmother having
gone back home, there was no way that the old lady could
take up residence yet in this type of shambles. It was also
clear that it would be some time before the place could
possibly be habitable again, for with the wartime shortage
of manpower, no building firm could possibly spare more

than a couple of workers on site for long periods at a time. She carefully picked her way through the rubble, and climbed the few broken stone steps leading up to the massive oak front door.

The door was closed but not locked, so she opened it and went in. It was a sorry sight, freezing cold, very little light, and hard to imagine the contrast to what it had been like on Christmas Day, just a few weeks before, when her grandmother presided over her dreary family bridge and sherry party like the spoiled matriarch she was. Most of the hall furniture had been retrieved and sent off for storage, but the beautiful tiled floor was a sea of mud, and Peggy found it difficult to move about. All that remained of the wonderful nineteenth-century crystal chandelier, a magnificent centre-piece converted from candle power to electricity, and which had been her grandmother's most prized household asset, was a long brass rod dangling from the ceiling, attached to a large branch on which had once rested a dozen exquisite hand-carved holders and glass shades. It was much the same in the sitting room, where the incendiary device had ended up after penetrating the roof and passing through all three floors. What had once been an elegant room was now nothing more than a charred wreck. Peggy felt quite ill looking at it all, knowing that this room was where she had spent so many boring Christmas parties with her family. Most distressing of all perhaps, was the baby grand piano, which was burned beyond recognition. Her mother's fingers gliding effortlessly across that beautiful ivory keyboard whilst her father sang 'Come into the garden, Maude' echoed through her mind like the sound from a ghostly apparition. Her emotions were now so torn between love and hate that she felt she had to get out of the place as quickly as she could.

The rest of the ground floor was in a similar condition,

so her thoughts turned to what the situation might be on the upper floors. She approached the grand staircase with some apprehension, but was surprised to find that, apart from the fact that the expensive red stair carpet was in ruins, the actual structure seemed to be quite sound, so she carefully made her way up to the first floor.

Her first instinct was to go straight to her grandmother's room, which was off to the left, but her heart was pining more to go into her grandfather's room. However, just as she was about to move, she heard a movement along the corridor, which might have come from her grandmother's room, but could have been one of the builders working on the side wall of the house outside. None the less, she decided to investigate. The door of her grandmother's room was slightly open, and when she peered in, the place appeared to be in darkness. But, lingering there a moment, Peggy found her eyes gradually getting used to the dark. She made out the figure of someone sitting on a chair in the middle of the room, a thin ray of light piercing through a crack in the boarded-up windows, and picking out the familiar lined features of an elderly woman.

'Grandmother?' she called softly. There was no response, so she approached quietly, and repeated, 'Grandmother. It's me – Peggy.'

The moment Alice Thornton turned slowly to look at her, her face disappeared into the dark again. 'Yes,' she said softly, croakily. 'I knew *you'd* be the first to come.'

'You shouldn't be here,' said Peggy, crouching down beside her. 'It's very cold, and it's not safe.'

'It's the only place I know. So why should I leave it?'

'You can come back when it's all been put back together again,' said Peggy, feeling for the collar of her grandmother's coat, and turning it up to cover the old lady's neck. 'There's no point in making yourself ill.'

There was no response from Alice.

Peggy paused a moment before saying anything else. She could feel the damp and the cold of the lifeless room, and the smell of charred furniture and sopping wet linen. 'I'm going to miss Grandfather so much,' she said. 'I know you will too.' She didn't believe for one minute that the old lady was going to feel any such thing, but she felt she had to say it out of a sense of duty.

There was a long silence before Alice answered. 'He should have left me years ago,' she finally said. 'If I'd had any sense, any real pride, I'd have encouraged him to do so.' She hesitated. 'Thank God he didn't.'

The old lady had no gloves on, and her hands were like blocks of ice. Peggy took hold of them and tried to rub them back into life.

'I am what I am, you know,' said Alice. 'I may have made a lot of bad decisions in my time, but I've made a lot of good ones too. Why should I have to be something that everyone expects me to be? I'm not a saint. I wouldn't want to be one.' She unselfconsciously pulled her hands away from Peggy's. 'There's no room for weakness in this life. I learned that a long time ago. A woman has to be strong. If she isn't, everyone takes advantage of her. She also has to be strong for her man, for her family.'

'Why?' asked Peggy.

'What do you mean – why?'

'Why does a woman have to be strong for a man?' Peggy asked. 'Why can't a man be strong for himself?'

'Herbert was never strong,' replied Alice. 'That's why he needed *me*.'

'I don't think that's true, Grandmother,' said Peggy. 'From what *I* knew of Grandfather, he was very strong.'

'He never showed it to me.'

'Perhaps you never gave him the chance.'

Alice was clearly stung by this. She suddenly eased herself up from her chair and, with the aid of her walking stick, went across to peer through the solitary crack in the window boards. Peggy got up from her crouching position, and went across to join her. In the shaft of bright light that was shining on her grandmother's face, it was the first time that Peggy had noticed how lined it was.

'Why couldn't you have let him be himself?' she asked. 'Why did you have to make him feel that everything he ever said was so – insignificant? He was the most lovable man I've ever known in my entire life. Strength isn't everything, Grandmother. Nor is power. I know I'm only a fraction of your age, and I know I have no right to be talking to you like this, but if there's one thing I *have* learned in the short time since I left home, it's that you only get back what you give.' There was a long silence. Peggy felt somehow cruel and guilty for what she had said, and so quite impetuously, she slipped her arm around her grandmother's waist and leaned her head on her shoulder. It was the first time she had ever done such a thing, and it clearly took Alice by surprise. 'The last time I saw him,' said Peggy softly, 'he was trying to tell me something. I've thought a lot about it, and I think what he was trying to say was that nobody is really who they think they are. Deep down inside there's always someone else trying to get out, someone far better than that person on the surface.' She paused, and turned to her. 'Grandfather gave me a message for you. He said, "Just tell her that – I know." I'm sure you know what he meant.'

Alice resisted the temptation to show Peggy either gratitude, offence or affection. But when Peggy gently turned her round to face her, for the first time in her life she saw tears streaming down the old lady's face.

* * *

It was still dark when Leo had finally got home. But to his surprise, his young brothers were fast asleep in bed instead of in the coal yard air-raid shelter, which they usually rarely left until long after the All Clear had sounded. After the shattering night he had just spent curled up with Peggy on the cold spiral staircase in Holloway Road tube station, he was too dazed with tiredness to start asking questions, so he quietly crept into the double bed he shared with Horace and Eddie, and immediately fell into a deep sleep.

He was awoken brusquely by the rasping voice of his mum calling from the bedroom door: 'If yer want yer breakfast, it's on the table!'

Leo sat up with a jolt as she slammed the door behind her, and even though he was so dazed that he didn't know if he was alive or dead, the moment he heard his mum thumping back down the stairs, he knew that something was wrong.

In the kitchen parlour, there was an atmosphere so thick you could have cut a slice through it. Reg was at one end of the table in his wheelchair, eating his scrambled dried eggs on toast, his wife at the other end, sipping a cup of tea and trying to pretend that he wasn't even there, and Horace and Eddie stuck in between them, munching dry bread and the warmed up remains of the saveloys Marge had bought for tea the previous evening, and, much to their mum's intense irritation, reading their comics, which were spread out on the table whilst they ate. Nobody spoke a word as Leo came in, took his place at the table facing his brothers, and watched whilst his mum poured him a cup of tea. He took the cup without comment; the scrambled dried egg on toast in front of him looked so unappetising it almost dared him to eat it. By chance, Leo met his dad's eyes. Reg grinned, and winked. Leo looked across at his mum. She was sipping her tea without looking at any of them. Leo swung another look at his dad, shrugged, took the dog-end from behind his ear, and lit it.

Marge looked up with an angry start. 'Can't yer wait till we've 'ad breakfast?' she growled, trying to wave Leo's fag smoke away with her hand.

'Sorry,' said Leo sheepishly. 'Fawt yer'd finished.'

Marge ignored him, and got up from the table. 'Come on, you two!' she snapped at Horace and Eddie. 'School!'

'It ain't school!' complained Eddie. 'It's only Miss Eddison.'

'Stop yer lip an' get yer fings tergevver!'

Whilst the two kids rushed out to collect their coats and schoolbooks, Marge picked up her cup and saucer, and stormed off into the scullery with it.

'Wos this all about?' whispered Leo to his dad once she'd gone.

Reg waved his hand dismissively. 'We 'ad a bit of a barney last night,' he replied. 'She come down The Eaglet looking fer me.'

'The Eaglet?' said Leo, doing a double take. ' 'Ow d'yer get down there?'

' 'Ow d'yer fink?' said Reg. 'In this fing, er course! That's wot yer got it fer me for, in't it?'

'Yer wheeled yerself all the way down ter The Eaglet – wiv one 'and? It's not possible!'

'Wevver it's possible or not, that's why me 'an 'er got stuck in ter each uvver. She went just one step too far. Trouble is, she meant well, but when I'm out drinkin' wiv me mates, no woman's goin' ter show me up in front of 'em.'

Leo was flabbergasted.

'Anyway,' said Reg, lowering his voice, 'I 'ad a reason fer goin' there.' He shut up at once as Marge came charging into the room, wearing her hat and coat.

'I'm takin' the kids round ter their teacher,' she snapped, with not so much as a glance at either Reg or Leo.

'Wot time will yer be back?' asked Reg, quietly mischievous.

'I 'ave no idea,' replied Marge haughtily. She swept out of the room.

Before turning to Leo again, Reg waited until he had heard her and the kids leave the place, and the front door slammed behind them. 'I've bin doin' a bit er diggin' around about Pam's corporal,' he said.

'Oh, yeah?' replied Leo, lodging his dog-end between his lips.

'Ol' Ben down The Eaglet reckons he's a real cocky sod.'

'Sounds like it!' replied Leo.

'But,' warned Reg, 'no rough stuff, son. We've got ter play this by the book.'

Leo pulled a face. 'Wot yer talkin' about?' he asked.

'I'm talkin' about nailin' this guy wivout you nailin' yerself too. If yer get involved in a scrap wiv 'im, *you* could come off worst – an' that's the last fing we want.'

Leo was puzzled. 'So – wot am I s'pposed ter do?'

Reg leaned forward in his wheelchair. 'Just fire a little warnin' shot,' he suggested. 'Let 'im fink that wotever 'e says about bein' married ter Pam, she's *your* gel.'

'But she ain't!'

'That's not the point,' replied Reg firmly. 'Don't yer see? That's why Pam's bin stickin' ter yer. It's not becos she wants yer, it's becos she wants 'im ter fink that *you* want *'er*, and wot's more yer'll do anyfin' ter 'old on ter 'er.'

Leo looked thoroughly confused. 'I know all that, Dad,' he said. 'But do yer honestly fink this bloke's goin' ter take any notice er me just becos 'e's bin told by Pam that I'm 'er feller an' that we wanna get married?'

'Maybe 'e will,' replied Reg, 'an' maybe 'e won't. But if

'e won't – then that's anuvver matter.'

Leo looked at him suspiciously. 'An' wot's *that* s'pposed ter mean?'

'It means, son,' replied Reg, 'that if yer wanna get Pam off yer back once an' fer all, then yer're goin' ter need a little friendly advice – from someone who knows better . . .'

There was a sombre mood at 49A Highgate Hill. On being informed of the death of Herbert Thornton, the entire family had gathered together and were, as always happens at such times, discussing their individual memories of a dearly departed man who had meant so much to all of them. In truth, of course, Herbert Thornton hadn't cared a damn for any of them, for he knew only too well that they were only out for what they could get. In the sitting room, Peggy's maternal grandmother, Nora Tyler, was sobbing quietly to herself, and sitting with her discreetly in a chair at her side, her fatuous husband, Arthur, could think of nothing more to say than a repetitious, 'Poor fellow, poor fellow,' every time Herbert's name was mentioned. Two of Peggy's cousins were there too: one of them, named Melanie, had her husband, Jack, with her, but as none of them had ever really known Herbert, their presence was more of a duty than anything else. Catherine, however, was wonderfully controlled in the face of so much sadness, and as she handed round cups of tea that Mrs Bailey had made them, she made a special point of pausing to have a comforting little chat with everyone. Although none of her relatives would have realised it, Peggy was the one who had taken Herbert's death the worst of all. Seeing her grandmother sitting alone in the dark in her bedroom up at The Towers had been a very sad experience, but she was glad that she had insisted that her grandmother come back home to Highgate Hill with her, because she knew that

that would be what her grandfather would have wanted her to do.

'How is she?' asked Catherine as Peggy came into the room.

Peggy shrugged. 'She's – numb,' was all she could reply.

'Poor Alice,' called the tearful Nora from the other side of the room. 'We shouldn't leave her alone. Can't we bring her down here for a while? At least it would be company for her.'

Peggy shook her head. She knew only too well that if her grandmother felt anything like her, the last company in the world she would want at a time like this would be her own relatives. 'I think not,' she replied. 'She's trying to have a little sleep.'

'I presume Herbert's going with the rest of the clan,' said Arthur, who had just made his youngest daughter, Susie, laugh by burning his lips when he'd taken a sip of hot tea. 'Highgate Cemetery?'

Both Catherine and Peggy found this type of talk tactless and distasteful so soon after Herbert's death.

'No, Father,' Catherine called back quietly, discreetly. 'He told Robert years ago that he wanted to be cremated. In fact his last request was that his funeral was to be completely private.'

'For family only?' asked Nora.

'No family, relations or friends at all,' replied Catherine.

There was a shocked gasp from both Nora and Arthur, and an exchange of surprised looks between the cousins.

'That seems a little – inconsiderate, doesn't it?' suggested Arthur. 'How can we be expected to grieve if we can't even go to his funeral?'

'Perhaps he didn't want you to grieve for him, Grand-father,' said Peggy pointedly.

Arthur had no answer to that, so after exchanging a

questioning look with his wife, he shut up.

'Where's Father?' Peggy asked her mother.

'He's in his study,' said Catherine. 'He wanted to be on his own for a while. Why don't you go and see if he wants a cup of tea, darling?'

Peggy exchanged a knowing smile with her mother. She knew what she was really saying to her.

Robert Thornton's study was a small room at the back of the house overlooking the rear garden. It was only just big enough to accommodate a flat leather-topped desk, a few bookshelves, a two-drawer filing cabinet, and a small combination safe which was set in the wall behind a framed sepia photograph of the Thornton family taken in the garden of The Towers in the 1920s. Ever since she was a child, Peggy, like everyone else, had been banned from even setting foot inside the place, for this inner sanctum of her father's was where he wrote notes for some of his more difficult court cases, and, in the past, it also gave him the chance to get away from Catherine's afternoon bridge parties. And so it was with some trepidation that Peggy tapped softly on his door.

'It's me, Father,' she called quietly. 'Can I come in, please?'

'Come in,' returned Robert.

The first thing that hit Peggy as she entered was the smell of cigar smoke. Her father had never been a fresh-air fiend, so by the oppressive atmosphere in the small space, he had clearly never thought about opening a window.

'Am I disturbing you?' she asked tentatively.

'Yes,' he replied. 'Probably a good thing.'

Peggy came in. The room was flooded with light from the midday sun, and she found the bleak winter's view of the back garden refreshing. Her father had swung round in his chair from the desk, and motioned her to sit down on the small leather-studded easy chair by the filing cabinet.

'I feel so sad,' she said, with a sigh.

'Yes,' he replied. 'You more than anyone would feel that.'

'And you?' she asked.

'Me?' He turned to look out into the garden, and the light now illuminated one side of his face. 'He was a good chap. More than I deserved.'

'He was very fond of you.'

He swung back to her. 'Thank you, my dear,' he replied with a wry smile. 'I wish that were true, but I fear it isn't. But then – why should he feel anything for me at all? I was hardly the best of sons. When I was young, most people knew me as a mother's darling. And I was. That's been the trouble throughout my life. I've had to live with it.'

Peggy lowered her eyes uneasily.

'Don't be embarrassed,' he said. 'When you get to my age there comes a time for an assessment of oneself.' He smiled inwardly, and shook his head. 'I've been the most awful husband, you know. And the most ghastly father.' He grinned at her. 'I was hoping you'd try to convince me otherwise!'

She chuckled.

He leaned back in his chair, deep in thought. 'I don't know why I've done the things I've done in my life,' he said. 'The relationship between parents and their children is never easy, but my relationship with you has always been based on my own determination to do what *I* thought was best for you.' He paused. 'Until quite recently, I never for one moment believed that there could possibly be any other way.' He suddenly noticed that he had the stub of a cigar still smouldering on his desk, so he quickly twisted it into the ash tray where he had meant to leave it. 'To have to feel in control,' he said, briefly stopping what he was doing, 'is an inadequacy in oneself.' He finished off the cigar stub, and looked up at Peggy. 'It's a feeling of wanting to do everything yourself, of not trusting the other person to do the right thing.' He got up from his chair, put his hands into his pockets, and stared poignantly up at the Thornton family photograph. 'It was like that with you,' he said. 'I never trusted *you* to do the right thing. That's why I opposed everything you've done over these past weeks – leaving a good job with sound prospects, "doing your bit" on the buses, mixing with people that are so alien to the way we live, and –' he looked down at her – 'becoming involved with someone like Leo Quincey.'

Peggy didn't know what to say. Her entire life had been dominated by this man, and now here he was trying to explain why he'd done it.

'I had you followed,' he said quite suddenly. 'Did you know that?'

'Followed?'

'I *had* to know. I had to protect you from what I considered to be a quagmire of uncertainty. I didn't want you to be with this boy who was totally unworthy to mix with a daughter of mine. I wanted to find something that I could use to keep him away from you, and you from him.'

Peggy stared at him in disbelief. 'But why, Father?' she asked. 'Why?'

Thornton sighed. 'Because I didn't want to lose you,' he said. 'Because you're the only child your mother and I have, and I didn't want to lose you to someone who came from a class of society that I have always considered – inferior.'

Peggy leaned her head back in the chair and closed her eyes. She was in despair.

'That's why I asked Irene to follow you.'

Peggy's eyes sprang open. 'Irene?' she asked, sitting bolt upright. 'Irene West – my friend – from the office? You asked *her* to follow – me?'

'Yes.' Thornton avoided her gaze.

'And she agreed?'

'She agreed – because I made her.'

Peggy could hardly believe what she was hearing. 'You mean you got her to *spy* on me?' she said, getting up from the chair.

Thornton couldn't bear to look her directly in the eye, so he went to the window and stared out into the garden. 'Irene and I,' he said, struggling to make one of the frankest confessions of his life, 'once had – a liaison.'

Shocked, Peggy clasped her hand to her mouth.

'It was short-lived, very short-lived,' he said with deep anguish, 'but I ended it because it made me realise what a fool I'd been, and how ashamed I was to do this to your mother.'

'But Irene –' said Peggy – 'how *could* she?' Suddenly everything seemed to fit into place: Irene turning up at the pub just before Christmas when she, Peggy, was in there with Leo, and Leo's certainty that he had remembered seeing Irene in the street outside his home. Was there no one who could be trusted any more? How much more could friendship be devalued?

'You mustn't blame her, my dear,' Thornton pleaded. 'Despite what you think, Irene is a very worthwhile person. And one thing I *have* learned from this experience is that neither I nor anyone else has the right to control other people's feelings against their will.' He turned and looked hard at her. 'And that, my dear,' he said incisively, 'includes Leo Quincey's mother.'

Peggy thought about this for a moment, then decided this was a good moment to talk to her father about Pam Warner. 'Father,' she said, 'I need your help. It's about a friend of mine who's in trouble. She's got herself mixed up with a man who persuaded her to sleep with him, got her pregnant, and then forced her into marrying him.'

Thornton turned an anxious look at her.

'The trouble is, it all sounds like a put-up job to me,' continued Peggy, 'because he's now not only threatened to tell her parents what she's done, but he's also threatened to beat her up unless she steals some money for him from the place where she works.'

Thornton listened intently. 'What's the name of this person?' he asked, with interest.

'Todd,' she replied. 'Ron Todd. He's a corporal in the RAF.'

'Is he now,' said Thornton, deep in thought.

Peggy was watching him closely. 'Why?' she asked. 'Does the name mean anything to you?'

'Possibly,' he replied, unwilling to say more.

'But you have heard the name?'

Thornton hesitated briefly. 'Oh yes.'

Her father's vague replies were only exciting Peggy's curiosity even further. 'Are you saying this man's been brought up before you in court at some time?'

'Not yet,' replied Thornton.

'Not yet?'

'Look Peggy,' said Thornton, whose expression could not disguise his concern. 'When I get to my office tomorrow, I shall make some enquiries about Corporal Todd and get back to you as soon as I can. But until then, I want you to promise me that you'll be careful in your dealings with this man. From what I do know about him, he's a very dangerous character.'

Chapter 24

The Luftwaffe's onslaught on Britain was now taking a turn for the worse, for air raids were coming intermittently during the day as well as at night. The intensity of the attacks seemed to be increasing all the time, and this was blamed on the Germans' fury that their great railway stations and goods yards in Berlin were now the target of fierce reprisal raids by the Royal Air Force. However, that, together with the success of the British and Australian troops in the North Africa campaign, was beginning to fuel fears that the Nazis were becoming desperate and that an invasion by their ground and air forces of the British Isles was now not only possible, but extremely likely.

' 'Ave yer 'eard the latest?' announced Frosty, as he joined Peggy, Leo and Elsie at their table in the canteen. 'We've got ter carry our gas masks around wiv us on every shift. If we don't they're goin ter 'aul us up before the Board.'

'Yer're kiddin'!' protested Elsie indignantly.

'I'm not, yer know!' Frosty assured her. 'I just 'eard it from our div super in the pool room. 'E says it's a sure sign the Board's expectin' Jerry ter launch a gas attack. They must've got a tip-off or somefin'.'

'It's terrifying!' said Peggy.

'I don't believe it,' insisted Elsie. 'Poison gas on London? They wouldn't dare! Anyway, I can't take me gas mask wiv me all over the place. I use the box ter keep me sandwiches in!'

They all laughed. But their expressions gradually became

serious as the implications of the ruling started to sink in.

'Good fing I'm gettin' out of it then,' said Leo, puffing on his usual dog-end. 'Looks like I'll be safer in the army than wiv you lot!'

Peggy nudged him hard, and they all jeered him. Then they went gloomily silent.

'I tell yer this much, though,' said Frosty, who was unconsciously twisting one thumb nervously around the other on the table in front of him. 'If there's one fing I 'ate worst of all, it's gas. Gives me the real creeps finkin' about it. I saw too much er it in the last war. If yer din't get yer mask on in time, yer bleedin' choked ter deff.'

Elsie shivered. 'Don't let's talk about it.'

'Fings're goin' from bad ter worse,' added Leo sombrely. 'That's fer sure.'

'Bein' so cheerful as keeps *you* goin'!' Elsie's reply was a direct quote from *ITMA*, the favourite comedy show currently on the wireless.

'Well, we'll just have to keep our heads,' said Peggy stoically. 'If we let things get us down just at the thought of it, we'll have no energy left to face up to – whatever we have to face up to.'

' 'Ear, 'ear!' agreed Frosty, thumping the table with the palm of his hand. 'Peggs 'ere's got the right idea. No use givin' in. If we 'ave ter wear the bleedin' gas masks, then that's that!'

Everyone murmured their agreement, but without feeling at all confident. Peggy looked around the crowded canteen; she was amazed how many female faces were now appearing amongst the crews. No matter what she had said to the others to try to raise morale, her own thoughts were very different. Things *were* getting worse, there was no doubt about it. She wondered how many of those boys she had seen gradually disappear from the canteen would return.

She unconsciously felt for Leo's hand beneath the table.

'Still,' said Frosty, suddenly cheered up, 'it ain't goin' ter put me off me kid's party on Sunday. My youngest married daughter's just announced she's in the family way, so we're goin' ter celebrate. Yer're all invited, so yer'd better not let me down.'

'A party, Frosty?' asked Leo cheekily. 'Do I detect the prospect of a good booze-up?'

'Yer detect a cuppa rosy an' a rock cake!' he bantered. 'But if yer play yer cards right, yer might just get yerself a pint or two!'

'Cheers!' said Leo.

'I'll be there!' promised Elsie.

'Wot about you, Peggs?' asked Frosty, eager for her reply. 'I've told me wife all about yer.'

Peggy was suddenly quite nervous. What if Frosty's family found her too posh and lah-de-dah? What if they didn't like her voice, her looks, her manner? What if they just didn't like her and rejected her? She couldn't bear the thought that if such a thing *were* to happen, her relationship with Frosty would never be the same again. She suddenly snapped out of her split second of doubt to find Frosty's beautiful pale blue eyes staring at her anxiously. And then she broke into a broad smile.

'Of course, Frosty!' she beamed. 'I'd love to come!'

A few minutes later she and Leo walked together across to the depot forecourt. Frosty was still in the drivers' check-in room, going over the itinerary for the shift he and Peggy were just about to go out on, which gave her and Leo a chance to have a few quiet words alone together.

'I saw Pam terday,' said Leo. 'I told 'er I'm goin' round ternight ter sort out this corporal of 'ers.'

Peggy came to an abrupt halt. 'Sort him out?' she asked nervously. 'What does that mean?'

Leo pulled on his dog-end. 'It means,' he replied evasively, 'that 'im an' me are goin' ter 'ave a little 'eart-ter-'eart chat, that's all.'

'Don't be foolish now, Leo!' pleaded Peggy. 'Getting into a fight with someone like him will only exacerbate matters. You have to be far more clever.'

Leo tensed. If anyone else told him he had to be clever he'd blow his top. First his dad and now Peggs. So what was being 'clever' supposed to mean? Was it someone who went to a classy school and knew how to read and write and talk proper? So what? Sometimes a fist could be far more effective in a dispute than a barrel-load of words. 'I'm not gettin' inter no fight,' Leo assured her, without becoming worked up. 'I just wanna give 'im a warnin', that's all.'

Peggy bit her lip anxiously. She knew she had stung him. 'I didn't mean what you thought I meant, Leo,' she said, trying to put things right. 'It's just that . . .' she looked around to make sure no one could hear her, 'I've been speaking to my father. If you're going to see this man, then I think I can tell you something about him that may give him quite a shock . . .'

Marge Quincey felt unwell. It was nothing serious, merely a reminder that she had not yet fully recovered from the gall bladder operation that she'd had some months before. It was the worry, the anxiety, she kept telling herself. She had tried to do so much for her family, and all she ever got from them in return was scorn and indifference. Her problem now was that she was finding it difficult to come to terms with the way Reg had treated her when she had gone looking for him in The Eaglet the night before, and how he had humiliated her in front of all his boozing mates. How could he have done such a thing to her, she kept asking herself, when all she had tried to do was to make sure he hadn't come to any harm in the air raid? Every time she thought about what she'd gone through it made her sick in her stomach. What kind of a husband was it that, after all these years of marriage, could make her feel as though she was nothing more than a scullery maid?

And then she got to thinking. Leo. He was the one to blame for all this. Ever since he'd got himself mixed up with that madam from up the hill he'd had a mind of his own and put all the wrong ideas into his dad's head. She was glad Leo was going away, glad to get rid of him. Good riddance! But she knew only too well that whenever she thought like that there was someone else inside her, telling her that that wasn't the way to think at all, someone else reminding her that Leo was her son, her own flesh and blood, and that if he went off to fight in the war, she might never see him again, and if that happened, how could she ever live with her conscience again? But what could she do about it? Thanks to her, she told herself, Leo's deferment had been cut short and now it was too late to stop the army taking him away, even though he'd have to go sooner or later. Alone in the scullery, sweeping the floor, she sat down, broom in hands, and reflected on all she had done, and how she could undo it. '*Silly cow!*' said her persistent other self inside. '*Yer could start by talkin' to yer 'usband!*' She tensed. Talk to *him*? Talk to Reg – after all he'd done to her? No! Never! No talk, no contact. That was the way – the *only* way – to show him how much he'd hurt her. Not a word. Not a single word would pass her lips. Then he'd know. Then he'd *have* to say sorry. Or would he?

Reg was on his own in the kitchen parlour. From his wheelchair at the window, he was watching two builders high above him, repairing the brickwork on the railway bridge wall, which had been damaged during the incendiary bomb attack a few weeks before. It made him feel wistful, even more desperate to get out of the house, get out of the rut he was in, and get back to work where he belonged. His recovery from the accident was slow, and he knew it. But it was slow mainly because he was impatient, which meant that he was not giving his injuries enough time to heal. And so, for the time being, he had to content himself with doing mundane jobs that his physical limitations would allow him. Which is why, for the umpteenth time, he was struggling with one hand to polish the pewter mug he had received as first prize in the darts competition round The Eaglet before the war.

Marge came in from the scullery. She was carrying a bucket of coal to make up the fire in the grate. Reg hardly noticed her, and carried on with his polishing. Marge made up the fire. Not a word passed between them. She got up again, and started to leave. But she stopped, and without turning, suddenly spoke: 'I'm sorry fer what I did,' she said. Then she turned slowly to look at Reg. 'I shouldn't've shown yer up like that in front er yer mates.'

Reg looked up in total disbelief. But his reply was uncompromising. 'No,' he said, 'yer shouldn't've.'

'I only did it 'cos I was worried,' she said, struggling with herself. ' 'Cos – I din't know where yer'd gone in the raid, on yer own, in the wheelchair.'

'I'm perfectly capable er takin' care er meself, Marge,' he said firmly but not unkindly. 'I've always tried ter tell yer that – 'aven't I?'

Marge was too taut to agree with him, so she turned and quickly made off.

He called after her. 'Marge . . .'

She ignored him. But just as she reached the door, that

'other half' of her spoke within: '*Silly cow!*' She stopped and turned.

'Why don't yer come an' sit down?' asked Reg with a warm inviting smile.

Marge considered this for a moment, then went back to him, collected a kitchen chair and sat down with him.

'We ain't done this in a long time –' said Reg – 'sat tergevver on our own, I mean. Always someone 'ere, never any time ter 'ave a little chinwag.'

Marge sat straight-backed, her hands in her lap, eyes lowered.

'I'm sorry too,' he said. 'I shouldn't've talked ter yer the way I did. But I was angry. Yer know wot an 'ot 'ead I am.' With Marge still choosing to remain unresponsive, he gently took hold of her hand, and held it with his own. 'Yer know our trouble, don't yer? We get too worked up over our kids. It's pointless really. They've got minds of their own. One day you an' me won't be around, so they'll 'ave ter go on an' get on wiv it.'

'Wot're yer tryin' ter say, Reg?' asked Marge, finally speaking. 'That we should ignore the kids, and let 'em do anyfin' they want?'

'No,' replied Reg reasonably. 'That's not wot I'm sayin'. I'm tryin' ter say that everyfin' they do ain't necessarily wrong. We shouldn't yell at Leo becos 'e wants ter go wiv someone who don't come from our side er the road. People are people – whatever they are, an' wherever they come from.'

'Oh – so that's wot this is all about,' said Marge curtly. 'Leo an' 'is madam from the 'ill?'

'No, Marge,' insisted Reg, holding her hands tight. 'This ain't about Leo. It's about *us*, about why we bovver ter bring kids inter this world if we can't learn ter trust 'em?' He leaned forward in his chair and looked her straight in

467

the eyes. 'We 'ave ter question why we do fings, Marge,' he said. 'We 'ave ter ask ourselves exactly what it is we don't like about someone who loves our son.'

'*Loves* 'im!'

'Yes, Marge – loves 'im.' She tried to pull her hand away but he held on to it. 'Wot is it *you* don't like about this gel, Marge? Is it becos she talks diff'rent ter you – even though yer've never 'eard 'er talk? Is it that yer don't like the way she looks – even though yer've never met 'er? Is it becos she comes from a family that 'as money an' we ain't?' Marge struggled harder to pull away. 'Or is it becos yer're scared of 'er?'

'Scared?' With one hard tug, she managed to release her hand. '*Me*, scared of '*er*?'

'Yes, Marge,' Reg said quietly but firmly. 'Yer're scared 'cos she's capable er givin' 'im somefin' that you an' me could never give 'im, respect – an' peace er mind.'

Marge's face screwed up, and she would have got up there and then if it hadn't been for that voice inside her once again telling her not to.

'You an' me ain't 'ad much education, Marge,' continued Reg. 'But we've got enuff brains ter know that fings can't go on the way they've bin goin'. The world's gone mad, Marge. People are at each uvver's froats fer no reason at all. Wot diff'rence does it make wevver we come from the top or the bottom er the bleedin' 'ill? We've all got 'ands an' legs an' feet, an' eyes an' ears an' Christ knows wot! The only diff'rence between us is the way we *look* at life. If Leo loves this gel – whoever she is – then good luck ter 'im. If 'e's makin' a big mistake, then that's somefin' 'e's goin' ter 'ave ter live wiv. But I tell yer this much, Marge – all the bullyin' an' all the yellin' in the ol' wide world ain't goin' ter 'old 'im back. Leo's a man now, an' the sooner yer accept the gel '*e* wants, the sooner yer'll get 'is love an' respect.'

Marge listened to all Reg had to say with eyes lowered. As soon as he had finished, however, her eyes flicked up, and for a brief moment, she just stared straight at him with a cold dead look. Then she calmly got up from her chair, made for the scullery door, and left.

Reg watched her go, then slumped back into his wheel-chair. He was in deep despair.

Pam hadn't seen her corporal since their meeting in Finsbury Park. Since then she hadn't known which way to turn. She not only knew that there was no way she was going to get the money he was blackmailing her for, but that even if through some miracle she were able to lay her hands on such a large amount, it would not be the last she would hear from him. Things were made worse when, after her meeting with Peggy, Leo had contacted her to say that he wanted her to take him along for a little chat with her corporal. Pam, immediately afraid that Leo intended to batter the life out of Todd, at first refused Leo's request, but once Peggy had talked to her again, she was persuaded that Leo would not use force, and would be the right person to talk sense into the corporal. Pam, however, was still not happy with the idea; Todd was no man's fool, and he was wily enough to match brawn with brain any day of the week. Nonetheless, she finally agreed to take Leo along to meet Todd at the place where he lived in Sonderburg Road.

The fog was a great help. No matter that it was thick and choking, at least it kept Jerry away, and that was a great relief to all the Londoners who were weary of their endless nights kipping down in cold damp air-raid shelters, or crowding like cattle on to the tube platforms. For one night at least, as long as the fog drifted low over the rooftops, the skies were safe.

Pam was grateful too – not only for the fog, but also for the relief of hearing Leo's voice as he approached her outside The Eaglet pub.

'Are yer sure 'e's off duty?' Leo asked, the moment he saw her.

'This is Friday night,' she said. ' 'E always manages to wangle a pass – Gord knows 'ow. But 'e goes 'ome first. 'E don't usually come down the pub till late.'

'Sonderburg Road,' said Leo. 'Is that right?'

'Yes,' replied Pam nervously. 'But are yer sure this is a good idea?'

'Let's go,' said Leo, brusquely taking her arm and leading her off.

The air along Seven Sisters Road, such as it was, was stifling and stank of burning coal fumes. Pam was able to protect herself adequately because, apart from her thick white coat, which could be easily seen in the murk, she was wearing a scarf around her neck which she had pulled over her mouth, and another scarf tied around her head. Leo, however, was not so well equipped, but, despite the choking fog he was striding straight into, he continued to pull deeply on the last remains of his dog-end.

By the time they got to Sonderburg Road the fog was dense, and there was no way that they could use their torches, for the glare from the beams as they walked absolutely dazzled them. 'This is Sonderburg Road,' announced Pam as they came to a halt.

'How can yer tell?' asked Leo sceptically.

'I've bin 'ere a few times,' replied Pam cagily.

'So I 'ear!'

Pam was not amused by his acid comment. ' 'E lives just across the road,' she said, as she prepared to leave him. 'I'll be five minutes.'

'No longer!' demanded Leo. 'I might get lost in the fog.'

Pam disappeared, but reappeared almost immediately. 'I'm nervous,' she said. 'Yer won't do anyfin' stupid, will yer?'

'I couldn't do anyfin' more stupid than wot yer've already done,' he replied tersely. 'Now get goin'!'

Pam disappeared into the fog. He waited, listening to her galoshes striding across the iced slush in the road. Then he heard her knocking on a front door, followed by a man's voice which was pitched so low he couldn't hear what either of them was saying. Then the door closed.

'Leo, are you there?'

Leo turned. He had been expecting to hear Peggy's voice, for they had arranged that she would follow him and Pam without Pam knowing. 'Over 'ere, Peggs,' he called quietly.

Peggy's torch beam dazzled him as she emerged from the fog. The moment she reached him, she turned it off, and they embraced. 'I hope we know what we're doing,' she said softly.

'We'd better,' he replied, lightly kissing her ear. 'This is yer idea, remember. I just 'ope yer've got yer facts right.'

She abruptly prevented more talk by pressing her lips against his. They stayed like that for as long as they could without coming up for breath, totally oblivious of the freezing cold fog that was completely enveloping them. 'It's such a strange feeling, isn't it?' she said, her voice quiet and flat as though they were in a small dark room. 'We could be anywhere. It's like being on an island miles away from anything and anybody. Just you – and me.'

'Sounds good ter me.'

She sighed. 'Oh God, Leo,' she said, 'I don't want you to go off to this rotten war. I want you to stay here where I can be with you all the time.'

'Scarlett O'Hara.'

'Huh?'

471

'Yer sound like Scarlett O'Hara in that pitture we only saw a bit of the uvver night!'

'Stop teasing me!' she protested.

To show that he didn't mean to, he kissed her again. They were surrounded by an almost ethereal silence, which indeed created an illusion of their being the only people left in the entire world. He wrapped his arms around her waist, and she leaned her head against his shoulder.

'I was talking to Father today,' she said, voice barely audible. 'He wanted to know all about you. I told him what an awful person you are.'

'Good fer you.'

'He didn't believe me. He said he still wants you to come to dinner at home. Mother said the same.'

'They must be mad,' said Leo, grinning to himself. 'Did yer tell 'em I don't know wevver ter use a spoon or a fork ter drink me soup?'

Peggy laughed. 'Not quite,' she said. 'But I'm sure he'd soon get used to your funny ways.' She looked up at him. 'I know I have.'

They were about to kiss again when they suddenly heard a door open and close across the other side of the road. Then voices, followed by footsteps on the iced slush.

'Scarper!' ordered Leo.

Peggy quickly disappeared back into the fog.

Pam's voice was the first Leo heard. 'Leo?'

'I'm 'ere.'

'Huh?' The voice in the fog took the corporal completely by surprise.

'Todd,' said Pam nervously, 'I want yer ter meet a friend er mine. This is Leo.'

'Wos all this then?' said the corporal, turning his torch on to Leo's face, which was totally deadpan. 'Who the 'ell are you?'

'Leo's my fiancé, Todd,' said Pam. ' 'E's the one I told yer about. We're goin' ter get married.'

There was a long pause from the corporal. Then he chuckled dismissively. 'So that's it,' he said, turning off his torch beam. 'Bin set up, 'ave I?'

'Somefin like that,' replied Leo, talking from the dark again.

'Well done, Pam!' said the corporal spikily. 'Couldn't've done better meself. Though I must say, I fink yer could've chosen a better night than this ter tell yer boyfriend 'e's wastin' 'is time.'

'Me an' Pam're goin' ter get married,' replied Leo flippantly. 'Din't she tell yer?'

The corporal roared with laughter. 'Our Pam's already got an 'usband,' he mocked. 'Din't she tell *you*?'

'That's just the point,' said Leo. 'She ain't.'

There was a silent reaction from the corporal. 'Say that again?' he asked.

'I said, Pam ain't got an 'usband. So she's goin' ter marry *me*.'

Only just visible in the fog, Pam was in shock. She thought Leo must be out of his mind.

'I don't know wot school yer went ter, garage boy,' said the corporal, 'but yer din't learn much, did yer? In case yer 'aven't 'eard, two people can't be married ter the same person at the same time—'

'Can I ask yer a question?' asked Leo, cutting straight through him. 'Can I ask yer where this famous wedding er yours took place?'

'That's *my* business!' snapped the corporal, getting irritated.

'It was in Todd's place across the road,' said a bewildered Pam.

'Oh, I see,' said Leo. 'In a private residence – right?'

The corporal remained silent.

Todd's lack of response was convincing Leo that he'd at least got the bloke interested. 'Can I also ask who performed the ceremony?' persisted Leo. 'I presume 'e was a registrar or somefin' like that?'

'It *was* a registrar,' said Pam emptily. ' 'E's a mate of Todd's.'

'Shut up!' snapped the corporal angrily.

'It was!' insisted Pam. 'Yer said it was!'

For the corporal the situation was becoming bizarre. What was he doing there in the middle of the fog, he asked himself, being questioned, being challenged by someone who, in his mind at least, hadn't a leg to stand on?

'The law says yer can't 'ave a weddin' in a private residence,' Leo persisted. 'It also says yer 'ave ter 'ave two registrars present, an' a certificate, an' a licence. An' it also says yer can't get married if yer're under age. Pam 'appens ter be under age.'

'She's over sixteen!' growled the corporal.

'But she's under eighteen, so she needs 'er parents' consent.'

'Yer know *nuffin'* about the law!' barked the corporal, raising his voice for the first time. 'If yer'd care ter listen ter the facts, yer'd know that she *got* 'er parents' permission. It's there in black an' white fer anyone ter see!'

'Then why did yer threaten ter go ter 'er mum an' dad, ter tell 'em about a wedding they gave their permission for, but weren't even invited to?'

'I don't 'ave ter listen ter this!' yelled the corporal, turning to go. 'Yer know *nuffin'* about the law – absolutely *nuffin'*!'

'No,' called a voice from the fog. 'But *I* do.'

The corporal stopped with a dead start. 'Who the bleedin' . . . ?'

'Peggy!' gasped Pam.

'As a matter of fact,' said Peggy, 'I know a great deal about the law, and if you have any sense, I suggest you'll listen to what I have to say.'

All four of them kept absolutely quiet and still as they heard what sounded like two young girls giggling their way down the road in the fog. It was an odd sound, for the crunching of their galoshes on the frozen slush was dull, flat and lifeless, and it seemed to take for ever for them to evaporate into the choking cloud that was engulfing them. In the tense silence that followed, each of the four remaining shadowy figures stood and shivered with the effects of the savagely cold fog.

'First of all, Corporal,' started Peggy, 'allow me to tell you the law as it stands. A child – yes a child, over the age of sixteen but under the age of eighteen – cannot enter into a marriage unless she has a) the written consent of *both* parents, b) a licence issued by a superintendent registrar, and c) the marriage may not be conducted in any unlicensed premises.'

'Who the 'ell d'yer fink you are?' protested Todd, showing the first signs of panic.

'It doesn't matter who I am, Corporal,' replied Peggy. 'But believe me I *do* know what I'm talking about. You know as well as I do that you had none of the things I just mentioned. The letter of consent from Pam's father was typed with a forged signature by you – *with* Pam's knowledge and help, I concede, but without the knowledge that any such consent requires *both* parents' signatures. You had no licence. You held an unlawful marriage in your own home in the presence of someone you say was a registrar, when it is perfectly obvious that he was nothing of the sort. And, in any case, even in a licensed office, a marriage must be conducted in the presence of *two* people – the registrar of marriages and the superintendent registrar. I don't intend to blind you with legalities, Corporal, because it's quite clear to me that you haven't the faintest idea of how the law works, but I can tell you that what this all boils down to is that there is no way at all that Pam is legally married to you.'

Pam gasped.

'On the other hand, I'm sure you're only too aware that blackmail is a criminal offence which carries a heavy penalty. The law doesn't take too kindly to it – as I'm sure you already know. After all, this is not the first time you've blackmailed someone, is it, Corporal?'

Todd remained absolutely silent.

'Wot d'yer mean?' asked the bewildered Pam.

'As it so happens, Pam,' replied Peggy, 'I asked my father to make a few enquiries about the corporal here. As you know, Father's a magistrate, and is well placed to have the records checked about men who go around seducing young girls, forcing them into illegal marriages, and then black-mailing them into stealing from the place where they are employed. It's one of the oldest games in criminal records,' she assured Pam. 'And our friend the corporal here is well known to the police for being one of the great experts in the field. Unfortunately, they've never been able to gather enough proof to charge him – until now.' She paused, waiting for a response. 'Do I make myself clear, Corporal?' she asked, tersely.

Todd did not reply. All that could be heard was the sound of his footsteps in the fog as he hurried back across the road to the house where he lodged.

'Sod!' yelled Pam as loud as she could, her voice bouncing back at her from the wall of thick fog in which they were all engulfed. 'I'll get yer fer this . . . !'

On the other side of the road, the front door of the house slammed.

'Oh Christ!' sighed Pam in frustration and close to tears. ''Ow could I 'ave bin so stupid?'

'Seemed ter me it come quite natural ter you, Pam,' suggested Leo flippantly.

'Leo!' scolded Peggy.

''E's right, Peggy,' said Pam. 'I used ter fink I was quite bright, but after this . . . ! Ter fink that I could let meself be taken in by that – worm! Ter fink that I believed 'im. I believed everyfin' 'e said. All those fings . . . all those nights I've bin lyin' awake dreadin' wot Mum 'n' Dad were goin' ter say when that sod told 'em I was goin' ter 'ave 'is baby, told 'em I 'ad ter get married to 'im.' More out of relief than anything else, she started to quietly sob. 'I've caused so much trouble ter so many people. Especially ter you, Leo. I never meant ter 'urt yer – honest I didn't! All this time I've used yer, all this time I've plotted behind yer back. I must've bin mad. I should never've done it. I shouldn't've got involved wiv yer mum. I deceived 'er just as much as I did you. Yer're right. I'm nuffin' but a silly stupid cow . . . !'

'Oy!' said Leo, throwing his arm around her as she burst into tears. 'Come off it, mate. Fings could've bin much worse. Mum might've got me married off ter yer before all this!'

All three laughed.

'An' you, Peggy,' said Pam, dabbing her eyes on the sleeve of her coat. 'I don't know 'ow ter fank yer.'

'You don't have to,' replied Peggy, placing her hand on Pam's arm and giving it a comforting squeeze. 'In fact, *I'm* the one who should be thanking *you*. At least I know now where I stand with this brute.'

Leo reached out for her in the murk, and put his arm round her.

'All I can say is,' said Peggy, 'thank God for my father. I

couldn't've taken on your corporal without his advice. Mind you, not all that legal stuff I threw at him might have been – shall we say – a hundred per cent accurate, but I think we can assume that, one way or another, the corporal has well and truly got the message.'

Chapter 25

Frosty's Anderson shelter in the back yard of his small terraced two up, two down house just off Camden Road was hardly the place to hold a party for nine people, but since the air raid had started in the middle of Sunday afternoon tea, everyone had to put up with it. No one really complained, except Frosty's youngest daughter, May, but as the party was being held in her honour because she had just revealed that she had become pregnant for the first time by her young husband, who was an able seaman in the navy and was away on active duty, most of the family gathered there spoiled her by giving her more space than anyone else. That meant six bums sharing two narrow armchairs, two perched on the edge of the top bunk, and May making the most of her 'condition' by spreading out liberally on the lower bunk.

Peggy and Leo didn't mind sharing the top bunk, for it gave them a fairly legitimate opportunity to sit together all close and personal without raising too many eyebrows down below. As for Elsie, well, she was having a whale of a time, for she found one side of her bum pressed up enticingly against that of Fred Barratt, husband of Frosty's eldest daughter, Louie, who was home on a weekend pass from the army, and whom Elsie found so sexy that she nearly died every time he even moved on the chair she was sharing with him and Louie. Louie's features were more like her dad's than her mum's or her young sister's, but it was a look that appealed to Peggy, who found her to be a warm, cosy person, which was very like her dad. Frosty's wife, Edie, was everyone's favourite mum, and if the air-raid siren hadn't sent Peggy down into the shelter, she would have been so full of Edie's home-made cakes that Leo would have had to carry her back home. However, the last thing that was on the minds of Frosty, Leo and Fred was tea, for they were now well into their third quart bottle of bitter and totally oblivious to the ack-ack gunfire which was ruining the traditional peace of an early Sunday evening in the skies above.

'So where do your mum and dad go to when there's an air raid?' asked Edie, who was a dumpy little woman with tight curls in her hair that had once been blonde but was now greying most serenely.

'Oh – they have a Morrison shelter in their dining room,' answered Peggy, perched on the edge of the top bunk with Leo. 'When I lived at home, I used to share it with Mother, but I must say, we both hated it. Father sleeps under the stairs.'

'Yer see,' said Frosty. 'Us poor ol' dads. We always 'ave ter ruff it!'

The women jeered him playfully. 'Well, this is the first time we've got *you* down the shelter since the Blitz started,' Edie reminded him. 'It's like tryin' ter get blood out of a stone ter get yer out er *your* bed.'

'Men're all the same,' said May grumpily. 'They all fink they're bein' so brave, not comin' down the shelter wiv their families. They'd sooner get blown ter pieces than leave their own beds.'

'Too true,' agreed Frosty. 'An' yer can see the reason why, can't yer? I'd sooner take me chances up top than freeze ter deff down in *this* 'ole!'

Edie's lovely perpetual smile stiffened. Like every other wife and mother she had had more than her share of the war. What with Frosty being gassed in the previous war, both her sons-in-law dragged off to call-up, and the prospect of spending God knows how many more months or years with her two daughters, stuck down a hole in the ground in the back yard, she was in constant fear of harm coming to any of her family. In particular, she dreaded the thought of Frosty going out on shift work and coming home late at night. Since the start of the Blitz, she had become a regular clock watcher, always keeping her eye on the time to see how much longer it would be before he got home. She knew only too well the danger he faced every time he was on a shift in the middle of an air raid. She couldn't bear the thought of anything happening to him. Frosty was her life, her reason for living. With their ruby wedding anniversary coming up this year, she didn't want him to take *any* chances, whether it was on the buses or at home.

'Don't let's talk about it,' she said, with an anxious, ominous glance up at the cold, soulless curve of the corrugated iron roof. 'It don't bear finkin' about.'

Peggy noticed how Edie's anxiety was catching; it had the effect of dulling the previous few moments of forced bravado from the men. She also noticed how Frosty immediately leaned across and covered Edie's hand with his own. The understanding look they exchanged told a story all on its own; they were devoted. The warmth and unspoken affection these people had for each other was showing Peggy a kind of family life that she had never before encountered.

'Anyway!' said Frosty, suddenly perking up. 'I've got a bit er news fer all er yer. I've decided ter retire.'

There was an immediate roar of surprise from them all.

'Oh, my goodness!' gasped Edie, eyes positively glowing.

'Yer're jokin!' said Leo. 'Yer're too young ter retire!'

'Oh no I'm not,' Frosty assured him. 'I'm comin' up ter sixty this year.'

'Sixty!' said Fred Barratt. 'Come off it, Dad. Yer don't 'ave ter retire at sixty.'

'I know I don't *'ave* ter,' said Frosty, exchanging a prolonged pointed look with Edie, 'but I *want* ter. I've done me bit. I fink I'm entitled ter 'ave a bit er time wiv me family.'

'Oh, my dear,' gasped Edie with intense relief, giving him a hug. 'It's wonderful news!'

'That's all very well,' grumbled May, 'but wot yer goin' ter do fer money? It don't grow on trees, yer know.'

'We shall be all right, don't you worry,' replied Frosty confidently. 'Yer mum an' I 'ave bin puttin' a bit away each week ever since I joined the buses when I come out the army. It's wot we call our little nest egg – not very much, but enuff fer us ter get by on.' He turned to Edie. 'Right, mate?'

Edie nodded enthusiastically. 'Right, mate!'

'Wot about a pension?' asked Leo, suddenly becoming all practical. 'Retirement age on the buses is sixty-five, in't it?'

'I've got ter go inter all that when I 'ave a word wiv the div super next week,' replied Frosty. 'I'm not goin' till the summer, but wotever 'appens, I've made up me mind.'

'Well, good on yer, Dad!' proclaimed Fred, raising his glass to Frosty. 'But I don't think they're goin' ter be very chuffed wiv yer up the depot, speshully wiv all the shortage of blokes around.'

'Plenty er gels ter take their place,' offered Leo, giving Peggy a wink.

'Yeah, I know,' groaned Fred. 'The way fings're goin' they'll soon be 'avin gels driving the bleedin' buses!'

'An' wot's wrong wiv that, may I ask?' piped up Louie,

swinging him an indignant look. 'Gels are driving ambulances an' all sorts er fings these days. An' anyway, if they're all like Peggs 'ere, it can only be a change fer the better!'

Everyone laughed, and automatically turned to look at Peggy.

Peggy laughed too, but her laughter was tinged with sadness – and regret. The thought of losing Frosty filled her with despair, especially after the bad experience she'd had with toothless old Gummy on the trolleys. As she sat there and watched Frosty and Edie snuggled up together like a pair of young doves, a glass of bitter in Frosty's hand, she found it hard to believe that although she had only known him for a few weeks, he had become like a second father to her. She hoped she would never lose contact with him, for he had become a friend to cherish. 'Well,' she said, a little self-consciously, 'all I can say, Frosty, is that I'm going to miss you. The trouble is, I doubt very much if they'll *ever* find anyone to replace someone like you. I know I for one have got an awful lot to be grateful to you for.' For one brief moment her eyes met his. 'It's not going to be the same going into Sid and Mabel's fish and chip shop in the fog again without you.'

Everyone laughed. But Peggy's remark was one Frosty would treasure.

'Poor Mum!' said Louie, once she'd sipped her shandy with a touch of gin in it. 'Just fink wot yer've got ter put up wiv now. Dad at 'ome wiv yer seven days a week! Yer'll go stark ravin' mad!'

More laughter all round.

'Don't yer believe it, Lou!' protested Edie. 'This is the most wonderful day of me life!'

To emphasise this, Fred started singing, 'My Old Dutch'.

The others joined in, and soon the occasion turned out

to be what it had started out as, a celebratory party with a rowdy sing-song, competing only with the frenzied cacophony of ack-ack gunfire, droning airplane engines, and distant bomb explosions. Peggy didn't know the words to any of the songs, but with Leo's help, she swayed to and fro to the music, and when, to her absolute astonishment, Louie and Fred got up to attempt a dance in the unbelievably restricted space, Leo grabbed her too, and she found them all rocking and swaying to the booziest version of 'Knees Up, Mother Brown' that had ever been attempted in a small hole in the ground of a tiny back yard.

The All Clear sounded soon after eleven o'clock at night. Peggy, Leo and Elsie took their leave of Frosty, Edie and their family, and made their way by foot to the Nag's Head where they had intended to wait for the night bus which would take the two girls back home to more or less their own doorstep. But at the last minute Peggy changed her mind, saying that she was so much on a high after the Anderson shelter party that she wanted time to think about the wonderful time she'd had. Leo said he'd walk home with her, but Elsie decided to take the bus, which was just arriving at the stop as they got there.

Oddly enough, the effects from the air raid seemed to be far less than they had sounded in the shelter. There was a glow from fires burning on the skyline behind them in the direction of the Angel, and the City beyond, but, apart from the very distant sounds of fire engines racing off at alarming speeds, the great wide Holloway Road seemed to be bathed in a rare and almost unnatural peace. During the past twenty-four hours, there had been a slight rise in temperature, which meant that at last the slush had begun to thaw. But even though it had become much easier under foot, Peggy and Leo took their time. They had no need to hurry. They had all the time in the world.

As they passed the imposing grandeur of the fawn-tiled Gaumont Cinema on the corner of Tufnell Park Road, Peggy paused awhile to look at the photographs and posters of the current film that was playing there. As the cinema, like all the streets around, was blacked out and in complete darkness, she had to use her torch to pick out the action-packed pictures of French Foreign Legionnaires fighting in the desert in a film called *Beau Geste*. Peggy and Leo only stayed there a moment or so, for a large slab of loose frozen snow suddenly slid off the side of the cinema roof and came crashing down within feet of the covered exterior of the foyer where they were standing.

They moved on, shuffling rather than walking, arms tucked around each other's waists, she with her head resting on his shoulder, he with his duffel coat pegged up at the collar. Peggy was in her seventh heaven. As they went, she could feel the warmth of his body and it gave her such an overwhelming sense of contentment within herself. She still found it hard to believe that she could have fallen in love with someone so soon after meeting him. It was such a short time ago and yet she already felt as though she had known him a lifetime. She couldn't understand how she could feel so comfortable in the company of this rough and ready boy who was so basic, so lacking in knowledge of the essential workings of life, and yet – and yet – he had taught her so much about the heart of life itself. But what *was* that heart, she asked herself? Was it the human spirit rising to the challenge of a terrifying conflict amongst insane people who could only speak with weapons and not words, or did the heart of life mean just simply a *different* way of life, where people from opposite sides of a road could discover that they weren't really so different after all?

It took them some time to reach Archway Junction, but

when they did they decided that they wanted this night to go on for as long as possible. They wanted to savour it, to hang on to it. Leo suggested they climb the steps up to the Archway Bridge.

'D'you know this is the first time I've ever been up here?' Peggy said, as she and Leo stood in the middle of the great road bridge on the narrow walkway spanning the strategic Archway Road which led to the North of England. 'It's ridiculous, isn't it? All my life I've lived within a stone's throw of this place, and yet I've never even thought about coming up here.'

'Fing is,' said Leo, who had his arm curled around her waist, 'yer've got ter *want* ter do somefin' enuff before yer do it. I used ter come up 'ere when I was a kid. I come 'undreds of times – never told Mum, though. She'd've knocked the daylights out of me.'

'Why?' Peggy asked, puzzled.

'I dunno,' he replied. ' 'Cos I did somefin' wivout 'er, I s'ppose.'

They remained where they were for quite some time, staring out in wonder at the crisp clear night, a total black wilderness where only the dying remains of the desperately fought fires were still obstinately dotting the skyline in the distance. Far below them, the silence was only very intermittently broken by the irritating whirr of lorry engines as they ploughed their way defiantly up the main arterial road, probably heading to far-flung destinations that were in urgent need of goods that would sustain them during these troubled times. For what seemed to be ages, no words were spoken between them. There was no need. They felt as one.

'I had a letter from Irene,' Peggy said, her thoughts miles away. 'You know – the woman I used to work with. She's joined the Land Army. By now she's probably spreading pig muck down on a farm somewhere. It was quite a sad little note really. She asked me to forgive her.'

'Wot for?' asked Leo, puzzled.

Peggy hesitated. 'Oh – nothing really,' she replied, her voice small and slight in the gentle breeze. 'She made a mistake once, and didn't know how to put it right. I wrote back and told her that we all make mistakes, but that in time we all learn by them. Actually I was very fond of Irene. I still am. One reckless moment doesn't make you a worse person.' She slowly turned towards him. 'But I shall remember *this* moment,' she said softly. 'I shall remember it because it's been so – unexpected.' She leaned forward, and kissed him lightly on the lips. 'Am I still your "gel"?' she asked.

He responded by completely enveloping her in his arms and pressing his body as close and as tight against hers as much as he possibly could. They could feel their own and the other's heart beating in rhythm, the blood in their veins flowing as one. Then he kissed her, full and deep. His hands slid slowly down her back until they were low enough to cause her a tingling sensation.

In the darkness of a late winter's night they stood there, two silent figures, totally alone, in the middle of a bridge, the cold dark breeze caressing them sensually. For those few magical moments, time was standing still, and would only move on when it was ready to do so.

Peggy had not felt so good in her entire life. The reason, of course, was that Leo Quincey was now such an important part of that life, for even though he would soon be leaving to start his call-up in the army, at least she had now convinced herself that she would be waiting for him when he returned. She had also taken to making an occasional visit back home to number 49A Highgate Hill, where her

parents were showing real signs of reforming their relationship after so many ups and downs over the years. If her
father hadn't exactly made a transformation, then he was
certainly making an effort to be the type of husband
Catherine had always longed for him to be, and the thing
that Peggy had noticed more than anything on her previous
visit was that they were actually talking together, engaging
in conversation about the day's events as though it was
something they had been doing all their lives. However,
there was no doubt in Peggy's mind that the loss of her
grandfather had deeply depressed his son, Robert, and the
fact that the old chap had insisted on not having a family
funeral left both Thornton and his mother, Alice, with a
feeling of total helplessness and inadequacy. It was clear
that things would never be the same again for Alice, and
although she had agreed to return to number 49A, she
made it clear that it would only be a temporary arrangement
and that she would be moving back to The Towers as soon
as the bomb damage repairs were complete.

With only days to go before Leo's departure, Peggy
started a week of early shifts, which meant that she had to
be on duty by five thirty in the morning and not finish until
one in the afternoon. It wasn't easy arriving for work in the
dark, and if there was one thing that she always dreaded, it
was having to collect fares on the top deck where the early
morning manual workers always insisted on smoking their
lungs out without opening a window. But before today's
ordeal she and Frosty were at least early enough to grab a
few words and a cup of tea at the Hornsey Rise terminus
outside catering stall before setting off.

'I must say, my missus took a real shine ter yer,' said
Frosty, who was so wrapped up against the cold that in the
only dim light that was available all that could be seen of
his face were his eyes, nose and mouth, for his peaked cap

was pulled down so low that it had completely covered his forehead. 'She said Leo was the luckiest young bloke in the world ter find a gel like you.'

'Oh, I think I'm pretty lucky too,' insisted Peggy. 'I just hope we can work out our lives as well as you and Edie.'

'Oh you will, don't you worry about that,' he replied, adding, 'As long as that muvver of 'is leaves 'im alone ter get on wiv 'is own life.'

Peggy sighed. 'Well, that's something we shall have to work out,' she said. 'Trouble is, although Leo won't talk to me much about her, I have a feeling that his mother hates me. I only wish I knew why.'

'Oh, I know why all right,' said Frosty. 'Marge Quincey's a proud woman, runs that family er 'ers wiv a rod er iron. She'll never give in ter anyfin' she don't understand.'

Peggy warmed both her hands around her cup of tea. 'If only we could meet, I'm sure we could find a way of getting on.'

'Gettin' on?' Frosty chuckled to himself. 'I'll tell yer somefin', me gel,' he said. 'Gettin' on wiv people is one er the 'ardest fings ter do in life. I *know*, 'cos I've met all sorts in me time. When yer meet some people they carry on like they expect yer ter say somefin' that's goin' ter offend. My Edie calls it an inferiority complex. But I reckon it's more than that. They feel they're bein' rejected or somefin', that yer're tryin' ter get the better of 'em. Marge is like that. Say one word out er place an' she's down yer froat in a flash. I've never understood it meself. It's 'ard, I know, but yer 'ave ter make an effort ter get on wiv people. After all, yer know wot they say: "Takes all sorts ter make a world." '

A few minutes later, the bus was on its way. As expected, before it had even left the stop, the top deck was thick with fag smoke, and when Peggy tried to open a window she was greeted with a chorus of 'Where d'you live, mate? In a bleedin' barn?' Undaunted, she opened three windows, knowing only too well that by the time she got down the stairs they would all be closed again.

At the Nag's Head there was a universal groan from all the passengers as the air-raid siren wailed out. It was particularly irksome for the All Clear from the previous air raid had only sounded an hour or so before and at that very moment people all over the place could be seen emerging from the public air-raid shelters. Undeterred as ever, Frosty ploughed on, and despite the ack-ack gunfire that broke out within minutes, they picked up a group of rowdy female office cleaners who were all on the way to their regular jobs in the West End. However, they turned out to be a cheerful bunch of girls, some young, some not so young, and they certainly helped to detract from the din going on outside as they exchanged bawdy tales about what they'd like to do with some of the soldier boys they fancied who made the daily trek back to their units from King's Cross station.

In Euston Road, the air raid seemed to be hotting up, and during a lengthy pause at the bus stop Peggy called to her passengers that they had the option of either getting off to take cover, or continue with the journey. Most people stayed put, although some got off and made a quick dash for cover in the nearest tube station. However, Frosty had only just managed to turn the bus around the corner into Tottenham Court Road when a London Transport inspector flagged them down to tell them that because of an unexploded bomb there was a diversion ahead.

'Oh blimey!' groaned Frosty, from his cab up front. 'Not again!'

This time, most of the passengers did get off, and when Peggy went up front to confer with Frosty behind the blackout curtain at the front window, she was told that he had instructions to take the bus off the main road at the first turning on the left, then find their way as best they could around the backstreets until they were able to rejoin the road as close as they could towards Charing Cross Road.

With all passengers gone bar two die-hard office cleaning girls and one elderly male passenger who was still defiantly smoking himself to death on the top deck, Frosty followed the directions given to him by the inspector, and slowly wound the bus around the narrow backstreets. It was not an easy thing to do, for not only was this unfamiliar territory for any bus driver, but all the streets were blacked out, making it extremely difficult to find the way without any form of street or bus lighting. Things got worse when a series of incendiary bombs lit up the sky from a nearby street, causing Frosty to put his foot down hard on the brakes because of the dazzling white glare. But within minutes, he was on his way again, crawling slowly, meticulously, with Peggy shining her standard-issue torch through the front side window in a desperate attempt to identify the name plates on each street corner.

'I fink we're goin' ter 'ave ter take cover soon, Peggs!' yelled Frosty, as a frenzied deafening barrage of shells suddenly started to crack up into the dark early morning sky. 'It's gettin' too 'ot up there!'

'Right!' Peggy called back, as Frosty pulled the bus to a halt. The two office cleaning girls immediately made a dash to get off, leaving Peggy rushing to the bottom of the stairs to yell out, 'Everybody off, please!'

No sooner had she spoken than a whistling sound came hurtling down from the sky. Both she and the elderly male passenger only had enough time to cover their heads with their hands when a deafening explosion and a blinding blue flash lifted the front of the bus straight into the air.

'Frosty . . . !' Peggy yelled frantically, as she and her only remaining passenger were catapulted up along the lower deck of the bus, then thrown back again to the conductor's platform.

It took the emergency services just a few minutes to reach the scene. When they got there, they found the bus up-ended, covered in large chunks of masonry, and with the driver's cabin embedded into the window of a first-floor office building. And as they finally dug their way through to the rear of the bus, it took them quite some time to remove the carnage of shattered glass and the mangled remains of the conductor's platform.

The Middlesex Hospital was the sort of hospital that Leo had never expected to visit, due mainly to the fact that it was situated in the heart of London's West End, which was very much beyond his own 'patch' in Holloway. But this was wartime, and if at one time there *had* been any feelings of class divide, things were very different today, for apart from the patients who were suffering from the everyday illnesses that beset human life, the wards were overflowing with emergency casualties who had been rushed in during the course of the ongoing air raids on the surrounding districts. And in the mortuary downstairs, hospital attendants were having a difficult time dealing with the number of bodies that had been brought in from the various church and public halls from where they had been taken after being dug out of the ruins of the endless devastated buildings.

The corridor outside the intensive care ward was also overflowing with people, for the previous night's air raid had been particularly ferocious, leaving a trail of fire and destruction right across London. Amongst the horde of weeping, desperate relatives and friends trying their best to comfort each other and hold on to even the slimmest vestige of hope, was Leo. He was there with Elsie, who was quite inconsolable with tears from several hours of shock and distress at the news of what had happened to Peggy. Unfortunately, Leo could offer no comfort for Elsie, for he himself was too numb, standing in the only available spare corner he could find, leaning against the bare white wall, an unlit dog-end stuck rigidly between his lips, hands in trouser pockets, his eyes not once tempted to stray from the bland lino-tiled floor. Elsie, however, was unable to keep still. Even though she had managed to find a place on one of the few bench seats, her eyes kept flicking up and down anxiously to the ward door, hoping for a sign, *any* sign, that a doctor or nurse or anyone was coming out to tell them that Peggy was going to survive this most horrifying struggle for survival. Eventually, it was too much for her, so she got up and joined Leo.

'She's goin' ter get fru, Leo,' she said, making a determined effort to control her tears. 'Peggs's got guts. Yer mark me words. She ain't goin' ter give in.'

Leo couldn't bring himself to look up. His entire body was totally immobile, like a cold stone statue.

His lack of response, together with the overpowering hospital smells along the corridor, made Elsie feel even worse. Unable to control herself, she broke down, and rushed straight off down the corridor into the ladies' toilet. As soon as she had disappeared, Thornton and his wife arrived, and quickly eased their way through the crowded corridor. The moment they reached the doors of the intensive care ward Thornton, like his wife, ashen-faced and distraught, immediately looked around for someone in authority to answer questions about his daughter. Disarrayed, his long dark overcoat damp with the early morning drizzle from the street outside, his eyes flicked all over the place until he finally caught a glimpse of Leo through the waiting relatives. He eased his way across to him.

'Is she still alive? he asked Leo falteringly.

Leo's eyes darted up to find himself face to face with the man whom he had only ever met once before, and who until only such a short while ago was prepared to wreck his own daughter's future. Without any energy left at all, he slowly took the unlit dog-end out of his lips. 'It's fifty-fifty,' he replied lifelessly.

Thornton immediately put a comforting arm around Catherine's waist as she broke down.

'What happened?' he asked, the signs of strain streaked across his anguished face.

'They was on diversion,' replied Leo, his voice little more than a croak. 'They got caught by this bomb – high-explosive they said – come down just be'ind 'em.'

'Oh God!' sobbed Catherine, hugging Thornton as tight as she could.

'Must've lifted the 'ole bus right up,' continued Leo. 'They found the back on the ground – an' the front stuck fru a window on the first floor er this buildin'.'

Thornton closed his eyes in horror. 'God in Heaven,' he said quietly. He took a moment to compose himself, then opened his eyes again. 'Where did they find Peggy?'

Leo swallowed hard before answering. 'The back er the bus'd bin blown right off.' He continued with difficulty. 'They 'ad ter dig 'er out. She was still alive when they found 'er – but only just. Frosty – the driver – 'e wasn't so lucky.'

'Oh, my darling,' sobbed Catherine into Thornton's chest. 'My poor darling Peggy . . .'

Thornton held her there for a moment, then gently eased her away to face him. 'Catherine, my dear,' he said comfortingly, 'I want to have a quiet word with Leo. Why don't you try to rustle up some tea for us from that trolley outside.'

Catherine took a deep breath, nodded her head, rubbed the tears bravely from her eyes with the knuckle of one finger, and went off.

For several moments, Thornton watched her go. Then he turned to Leo. 'This is such a cowardly war,' he said, his breath quivering with anger and despair. 'At least soldiers at the front are legitimate targets – but *this* . . . !' He looked all around him at the figures of weeping men as well as women, some of them clutching bewildered children who had been grabbed from their beds in the middle of the night, still half-asleep, and others, like Leo, staring aimlessly at blank walls as though they were completely unable to understand what life – *this* life – was all about. 'You are very close to me,' Thornton said, talking away from Leo. Then he turned to look at him again. 'Did you know that?'

Leo was still too numb to react.

'I know it may sound strange,' continued Thornton, 'especially when I don't even know you. But the fact is, Peggy has learned how to come to terms with her life. And that's a huge step forward for anyone to take. But best of all, she's learned how to deal with *me*.' He smiled faintly, wryly, to himself. 'That's no mean task, I can assure you. It's important to survive, but it can't happen without a struggle. Peggy's had to do that quite a lot, you know. A lot of people have had to – including me. I've had to struggle against myself, against my own intuitions, against my own feelings that everything I stand for – is the only way. But it isn't. When I stand outside my house sometimes, and gaze down the hill to what I have always thought of as alien land, I often tell myself that there is no way that a daughter of mine, my own flesh and blood, could possibly find a worthwhile life with someone like you – with someone from down there.' For one brief moment, deep in thought, he covered his mouth with the palm of his hand. Then he lowered it. 'I was wrong,' he said almost to himself. 'We can pretend that we're different, you and me, but one day my family – and yours – are going to have to learn that whether you come from the top of the hill or the bottom, there really is so very little distance between.' He paused briefly. 'I love my daughter, Leo,' he said falteringly, trying hard to suppress the emotion he felt. 'Peggy's going to survive this. And when she does, it's my fervent wish that you'll be there waiting for her.'

On the other side of the corridor, an attendant raised the blackout curtains at the window. Immediately light flooded in from the first signs of daybreak.

There was a sudden flurry of activity as a nurse appeared at the ward doors and called quietly, 'Anyone here for Margaret Thornton?'

Leo immediately sprang to life. But the moment he made for the door, he remembered that Peggy's father had the right to see her first. So he stood back to let him pass. Thornton took a few steps towards him, unable to control the tears welling in his eyes, smiled, and shook his head.

'Tell her I love her,' he said.

The ward itself, which was really a large room and in semi-darkness, was a maze of wires, small flashing lights, tubes, cardiac equipment and oxygen cylinders. Although it was quite clear that the number of beds in there was well beyond the capacity for such a specialised unit, there were surgeons, doctors and nursing staff monitoring every single patient who had been brought in from the carnage of the night's air raid, and who were all struggling for their lives.

Leo came in quietly, to be told by the nurse that he could spend no more than a minute or two with the patient.

At first glance he couldn't tell which bed Peggy was in, for every patient there seemed to be so swathed in plaster and bandages that it was almost impossible to know where she was. But when the nurse pointed to a bed in the corner of the room, he approached it with fear and apprehension. Peggy was lying there, a stone-like figure, her features almost obscured by the heavy bandages that covered her head, cheeks, forehead and chin, leaving only her closed eyes and mouth fully visible. He was relieved that he couldn't see the lower half of her body, for it was shrouded in what seemed like a mountainous protective cage, and there was a drip tube protruding from her nose, and an intravenous needle taped to a vein in the back of her left hand. He felt quite sick, not from the sight of blood, which during his own short lifetime he had seen many a time during scraps out in the street or in the pub, but because of the feeling of total helplessness, the desperation of seeing someone he had grown to love so much reduced to such a state of reliance on others. He cowered at the thought that even one single thread of that beautiful red hair might have been dishevelled, and the blood rose in his veins as he felt the frustration of not being able to pick her up in his arms and hug her tight.

'She's goin' ter live, ain't she?' he blurted out to a doctor who suddenly appeared with a small thin torch to check the pupils of Peggy's eyes.

The elderly doctor ignored Leo's question and, using the tip of one finger, gently raised Peggy's eyelids one by one, and only replied when he had completed his examination. 'I'm sorry,' he said softly, with a sigh. 'I can't tell you very much at the moment, but – it's not looking good. I'm afraid she has very little resistance left. She's just – hanging on a thread.'

Leo stared mesmerised at the man as though he was

mad. When he was alone again, he turned and looked down at Peggy, who was clearly not stirring. Then he leaned as close as he could, and talked softly into her ear.

'Who d'yer fink *you* are then?' he jibed, voice racked with emotion. 'I've told yer before, Duchess – yer ain't no bleedin' Scarlett O'Hara. This ain't the pittures. This is *real*!' His own comments were upsetting him, and tears were beginning to well up in his eyes. ' 'Angin' on by a fread. Bleedin' nonsense! Now you listen ter me, Peggy Fornton. I've told yer before – yer're my gel, an' don't you ferget it! Yer said yer'd wait fer me. Yer said a lot of fings, so if yer want me ter believe yer, yer'd better get yerself out er this bleedin' bed as soon as yer like!' He was now cracking up, so he leaned towards her, and gently kissed her lips. With tears running down his face he whispered, 'Don't you dare die, yer silly cow! Don't you dare die on me . . .'

He was so overcome that he didn't notice the commotion taking place at the ward door.

'Please!' called the very stern voice of a nurse behind him. 'Only one visitor at a time . . .'

Leo turned and looked up.

Standing there was his mum, Marge Quincey, face dark and impassive, her eyes glistening with the reflection of the small flashing lights that were buzzing from the specialised equipment all around her. Dazed, unsmiling and with a totally impassive expression, she looked first at her son's face, now crunched up and streaked with tears, and then to Peggy's. Defying the nurse's attempts to lead her back towards the door, she moved closer, and kissed the boy comfortingly on his forehead. Then she turned abruptly, and left as quickly as she had come.

Chapter 26

The summer of 1950 was turning out to be extremely hot. In Seven Sisters Road, some women – some of the younger ones it should be said – had taken to wearing rather daring clothes such as revealing blouses and short skirts, and one or two of them had even been seen wearing shorts and high-heeled shoes to go shopping, much to the disdain of the older generation, but very much approved of by the male population – of *all* ages. Up in the bus depot canteen, Elsie Parker had told some of her grinning mates, such as Sid Pierce and Alf Grundy that if her landlady, old Ivy, was still alive, she would have deeply disapproved of the way women were being seen in public dressed so provocatively. But Elsie had to admit that now that women had become so much more liberated since the end of the war, at least they could pick and choose what they wanted to wear, even if everything was still in short supply and difficult to find.

The summer also brought out the best in people. After a long, harsh winter, they felt they had the energy to get out of the house and soak up as much sun as they could, which meant that now that most of the parks had been relieved of their many wartime restrictions, they were quite literally crowded with sun-worshippers, lazing idly in the midday heat, many of them stripped down to their bathing costumes, women in big hats, men in shirts and braces and handkerchiefs tied over their heads. Although the post-war years were turning out to be far more austere and tough than everyone had expected, there was such a feeling of freedom in the air, when people could just lie back and stare up into a crystal-clear blue sky, safe in the knowledge that the sky was no longer something to be feared.

Leo's hot Sunday summer afternoon, however, was not quite so relaxed, for he now had two kids to contend with. At four, Ben, the eldest, had a mind of his own, just like his dad, and was just as bad-tempered. When their mum looked at them both together from time to time, she often chuckled to herself at the similarity between them – same fixed, determined jawline, same terrible habit of wiping their noses on the backs of their hands, and the same obstinacy. The younger, Anna, who was only a few months old and was still being breast-fed, was, thought Leo, the living image of the pictures he had seen of the child's mum when she was still in her pram at that age. Ben hadn't been with his dad to Highgate Cemetery before, but as he had been told in advance that there were plenty of places where he could hide and play, Ben had been up since dawn, harassing his dad to hurry up and get ready.

Highgate Cemetery was vast. When Leo was a kid himself, he and his mate Kenny Pocket used to come up here and collect as many conkers as possible that had fallen off the trees. Playing conkers when they got home was the only game that Leo had ever really excelled in, but when he and Kenny played with some of the other kids, it usually ended up in a rough and tumble scrap when he and Kenny were accused of providing the best conkers for themselves. It was probably those memories that endeared the place to him. As he watched young Ben having the time of his life, darting in and out of the gravestones, he looked around and wondered how many people were buried there. Hundreds? Thousands? It seemed an awesome thought to him. Inevitably, however, it was the peace and tranquillity that drew him so often to the place on a Sunday afternoon.

Somehow he always felt safe in the company of so many of those from a former life, and was sure they wouldn't object to his boy using their headstones for a game of hide-and-seek.

Once Leo and his wife had got off the trolley bus with the kids, passed through the cemetery entrance gates, and gradually wound their way towards where they were making for, Leo felt as though they had walked for miles. At the age of twenty-eight, he was feeling very out of condition these days, mainly because his job as market manager for a fruit and vegetable firm up at Spitalfields Market in the East End was quite taxing, for he had to be up at five every morning and sometimes didn't get back home until eight in the evening. But married life and a decent wage made him feel good, for being the breadwinner in the family gave him a feeling of responsibility, which he had never had when he lived at home. *Home?* A few rooms above a coal merchant's yard, and a bedroom that he had to share with two young brothers? For a brief moment it brought a smile to his face. But it slowly faded when he remembered that his two brothers were now both conscripts in the army, and although they were not in any real danger because there was no war on – after all he'd had to go through during the D-Day landings – he would never lose his protective feelings towards them. But at least his mum and dad had now got some time on their own together. It did his heart good to see his dad as happy as a sandboy, earning a good wage as a foreman for a firm of building contractors who, because of the urgent need for new homes, had, since the end of the war, been able to recruit hordes of demobbed ex-servicemen.

And his mum – still as prickly as ever, but no longer the scourge she used to be. It would be a long time before he would forget that amazing incident when she turned up at

Peggy's bedside, and kissed him on the forehead. Over the years, he had often thought about that moment, and had come to the conclusion that it was the only way his mum knew how to say sorry.

As 'the little woman', as he called his wife, had strolled off ahead with Anna in the pram, by the time Leo and Ben had caught up she was already at the graveside.

'What took you?' asked Peggy, teasing him.

'Old age,' replied Leo. 'An' five years of married life!' he joked.

'Ah – you mean five years of my good cooking,' she also joked. Like Leo, Peggy had filled out a little, but only because she had had two children. But neither of them had put on any real weight, and if anything, the extra flesh suited them. Married life seemed to suit them both too, especially Peggy, for she had acquired a wonderful maturing radiance, which, despite all the drudgery of having to stay at home to look after her kids, gave her the compensation of contentment.

'Come on, Ben,' she said. 'You can put the first two flowers on – one for you and one for Anna.'

Ben was given two white dahlias that Peggy had taken from a bunch of mixed flowers that she had bought. Then she crouched down beside the grave, and whilst Leo stood behind her watching, Ben carefully laid his and his little sister's flowers on the dry rough earth.

' 'Allo, mate,' said Leo nostalgically to Frosty's headstone. 'We all miss yer.'

'Who was he?' asked Ben, who had picked up his mum's more cultured tones rather than his dad's Holloway twang.

'He was a very nice man, Ben,' replied Peggy. 'He was your granddad.'

Ben, puzzled, scratched his head. 'But I've got a granddad,' he said, fidgeting. 'I've got *two* granddads!'

'Well, fink yerself lucky,' added Leo. 'Most people only 'ave two granddads. *You've* got three.'

'But where is he?' persisted Ben, looking down so close to the earth on top of the grave that his face was almost touching it. 'I can't see him.'

'You may not be able ter see 'im,' said Leo, 'but 'e can see you.'

A few minutes later, Leo took over the pram from Peggy, and with Ben running on ahead, he slowly started to make his way back to the gates. He knew this was how Peggy preferred it. Every time he and she had come here together without the kids, she had always wanted to be left alone at the graveside.

'Hello, Frosty,' she said, whilst she arranged her flowers in a vase alongside the others that Edie and her family had clearly only just left. She was now used to talking to him. After all, that is what they always used to do together during those breaks on shift, him with his fag and she with her cup of tea. She found it hard to believe that he'd been gone for over nine years now. Even though they had only known each other for such a short time, somehow she felt strongly that he had never really left her. Visiting his grave always revived the past for her. It was like living through it all over again.

'Guess what?' she said. 'My father's retired. Can you believe it? I never thought it would happen, but Mother kept on at him. She said they ought to be left with a few years to enjoy themselves. They're doing that all right. They're going on another foreign holiday together. To Paris! A second honeymoon, I hope! Oh – and guess what? Leo and I are moving into The Towers next week. My grandmother's finally gone into a residential home in Hove. She said she wanted us to have the place because it was Grandfather's wish. I didn't really want to live in such a big place, but it'll be marvellous for the children, and anyway, it'll be a great improvement on our two-bedroom flat in Kentish Town. It's so cold there in the winter, and stifling in the summer.' She paused a moment to reflect. 'I thought you'd like to know that.'

She got up and filled the vase with water from a standpipe tap nearby. When she returned, she rearranged the flowers, and returned them to their original position. For a moment or so, she remained where she was, crouched there, a burning hot afternoon sun blazing down on to her white-brimmed straw hat, the shoulders of her thin white cotton dress, and her bared arms. Her few moments of silent reverie were cracked only by the distant shrieks of laughter from Ben.

'We were a good team, weren't we, Frosty?' she said. 'It didn't last very long, but you know something? You were the tops. You always were, and you always will be. And I'll tell you something else. As soon as the children are old enough to be looked after, I'm going back to the buses. Your Edie said she'd keep an eye on them and help out any way she can. My mother said the same – and guess what – so did Leo's mum.' She chuckled to herself. 'You wouldn't know her now, Frosty,' she said. 'Leo's mum, I mean. She and his dad came to tea last week. She held the baby – yes! She held little Anna in her arms until she went to sleep. She even said what a beautiful child she was – just like me! Can you believe that? Leo's mum of all people!' She smiled to herself, and paused. 'I do so miss you, Frosty,' she said. 'I miss you because you were the best driver London Transport has ever had. I miss you every time I see those red double-deckers taking the road from one shift to another. But most of all, I miss you – because you're my friend.' She got up, and stood looking down at the grave. 'Do you remember what you once said to me, Frosty? You said that getting on with people is one of the hardest things to do in life. Well, I'll tell you something. It wasn't at all hard to get on with *you*.'

She paused for one last silent moment, then turned and rejoined Leo and the kids. As she made her way along the winding narrow path, she resisted the temptation to turn and look back. She imagined that Frosty wouldn't have approved of that. After all, wherever she went, one way or another he was always going to be with her.

Now you can buy any of these other bestselling books from your bookshop or *direct from the publisher*.

FREE P&P AND UK DELIVERY
(Overseas and Ireland £3.50 per book)

My Sister's Child	Lyn Andrews	£5.99
Liverpool Lies	Anne Baker	£5.99
The Whispering Years	Harry Bowling	£5.99
Ragamuffin Angel	Rita Bradshaw	£5.99
The Stationmaster's Daughter	Maggie Craig	£5.99
Our Kid	Billy Hopkins	£6.99
Dream a Little Dream	Joan Jonker	£5.99
For Love and Glory	Janet MacLeod Trotter	£5.99
In for a Penny	Lynda Page	£5.99
Goodnight Amy	Victor Pemberton	£5.99
My Dark-Eyed Girl	Wendy Robertson	£5.99
For the Love of a Soldier	June Tate	£5.99
Sorrows and Smiles	Dee Williams	£5.99

TO ORDER SIMPLY CALL THIS NUMBER

01235 400 414

or e-mail <u>orders@bookpoint.co.uk</u>

Prices and availability subject to change without notice.